KEEPER OF THE RINGS

AWARD-WINNING AUTHOR

NANCY J. COHEN

OGP
ORANGE
GROVE
PRESS

Chapter One

"If we don't start soon, I'm going to faint. Dear deity, what if I trip over this thing when we're called to the dais?"

Leena adjusted her royal blue robe with trembling fingers. Unaccustomed to its length, she grimaced at the sight of her satin slippers peeking out beneath the hem. She couldn't believe she'd earned the privilege of wearing the sacramental vestment.

Karole patted her shoulder. "You'll do fine. You always appear so well poised."

Leena met her friend's gaze. "Today is different. My father is in the congregation, and I don't want to embarrass him. And where's my brother? It's unlike Bendyk to be late."

"He could be seated with your father in the Inner Sanctum. They're not allowed back here." Karole swept her arm in a broad gesture encompassing the Robing Salon. Their fellow initiates stood around fidgeting like lower school graduates.

"You're right." Leena placed the ceremonial headdress over her head of blond hair.

Soon she and her newfound friends would become official members of the aide corps that served the Synod, the ruling body of priests on Xan. They awaited a signal from Dikran, the Arch Nome, who would begin the annual Renewal service. At its completion, Leena would assume her honored role as a Caucus delegate.

Her pulse raced with excitement. Ever since she was a child, she'd wanted to learn more about the Apostles who had established the religion of Sabal on her world. Her father, a high-ranking Candor, had inspired her interest in archeology by his study of ancient religious texts.

Growing up beside a crumbling ruin had sparked her imagination as she thought about life in days of old. Where had the Apostles originated? They'd established the magnificent reign of Lothar, their god, and then vanished. Why did they leave, and where had they gone?

Craving knowledge of her forebears, Leena realized the Synod held the key to wisdom. The ecclesiastical leaders were privy to secrets known to no one else. Joining the Caucus was the swiftest route to enlightenment.

A solemn bearded figure marched into the room. Planting himself firmly in the center, he peered around at the young initiates, waiting until everyone fell silent.

"It is time," Zeroun intoned.

"Holy waters." Leena's knees quaked. "I can't believe we've made it this far. May Lothar guide us."

"You're supposed to be near the front." Karole prodded her. "Get in line."

Leena wiped her sweaty palms against her flowing robe. Not even her graduation from archeological college had made her this nervous. Was it because Malcolm was in the congregation?

Her wealthy neighbor had been after her hand in marriage for several years now. Lately Leena had been inclined to accept, mainly for the security he could offer. She felt mildly affectionate toward him, but something made her hesitate.

Lining up behind the others, she tilted her chin in the air and marched forward with Zeroun in the lead. Leena had been in the cathedral-like Inner Sanctum many times during the past six weeks of training, but it hadn't prepared her for the sea of faces that greeted them in the cavernous hall.

She took a seat along with the nineteen other initiates in the front row that had been reserved for them. The members of the Synod filed in, claiming their spaces on the dais.

Arch Nome Dikran sat on a throne-like chair, wearing his

gold robe with the dignity that befit his eighty years. A towering headdress covered his head, and it was much more resplendent than the simple ones Leena and her friends wore.

She may not care for formal dress, but because her father held a high position, she was accustomed to elaborate affairs.

As she settled the robe about her legs, she wished for the comfort of the breeches and short-sleeved shirts she wore on her archeological digs. There was no pretense when you scoured a site for ancient treasures.

Malcolm didn't approve of her career. He would expect his wife to stay at home and manage his household. Leena had plenty of experience in managing her father's property, having done so ever since her mother's death five years ago. That tragic accident had given her brother his true calling.

Good Lord, where was Bendyk? She craned her neck, searching for her brother's familiar face, but she didn't spot his blond head anywhere in the crowd. Returning her attention forward, she mentally checked off the dignitaries on the dais.

Sirvat, the most prominent woman on the Synod, looked stiffly proper in her white robe tied with the gold sash of office. Magar sat beside her, his eyes twinkling beneath a crop of white hair. Karayan, a family friend, caught Leena's eye and smiled. Flushing, she looked down at her blue robe, eagerly anticipating the moment when she would be given the gold cord signifying her as an ordained servant of Lothar.

She shifted impatiently, watching Dikran rise and approach the podium. His shuffling gait proclaimed his age, but his dark eyes were sharp as they pierced the crowd like orbs of glowing embers. The service began with a hymn praising Lothar for his beneficence.

"We come here today before the face of our deity, the miraculous Lothar," Dikran spoke into a microphone. "Together in worship, we sanctify our existence and praise Lothar, ruler of Xan. Who is like unto you, O Holy One, majestic and awesome in splendor? Who can compare to your generosity? Let the name Lothar be hallowed unto the world for all time. Let his name be glorified and exalted although he is beyond praise, because he is so mighty and powerful."

The congregation raised their voices in a hymn, and Leena's song joined them. The familiar melody brought her the same calm serenity as it had throughout her life at similar services. Renewal was a time to recall one's past deeds, one's joys and triumphs, one's tragedies and sorrows, and to look ahead to the new year with reborn hope.

"May the coming year bring us peace, joy, and exaltation." Dikran raised his arms toward the vaulted ceiling. "May you bless us, O Lothar, with plentiful rains so our crops may grow bountiful and our fields be fertile. May our rivers flow and our lakes remain unblemished.

"We count on you, O Holy One, to maintain our land and to provide us with your blessing that keeps us from ill health. May our redemptive labors make us happy and our struggle for purity not fail. Let us toil at our work to the best of our ability. Blessed is the vision of holiness that exalts us from on high."

Leena joined in a series of responsive readings. Her heart opened to Lothar and his generosity to her people. Truly they were blessed to have such a wonderful god looking out for them. He provided them with fertile soil with which to grow adequate foodstuffs. Xan was a rich, bountiful world. The lakes and rivers teemed with fish. The land blossomed with fruit, and the air was pure and clear. Truly, what more could anyone want?

Zeroun got up and exchanged places with Dikran. Minister of Religion, Zeroun's presence was powerful, the hunch of his shoulders indicative of his forcefulness.

"Praised be Lothar who unifies all creation." His gaze pierced the congregation as though he would read their souls. "May the Holy One fill our minds with knowledge and our hearts with wisdom, and praise those who labor to bring harmony to our world. Let the next year be a fruitful one for us. Be gracious, O Lothar, and treat us generously. Be our teacher and guide." He raised his hands toward heaven.

As the choir began to sing, melodious music filled the clerestory. Leena's heart soared with faith and love for Lothar. *Please help me clear my father's name*, she prayed. *I know the answers are here in your Holy Temple. I vow that I will find them before the next Renewal.*

The communion of those around her filled her with comfort and peace as she followed the service.

"Let us bend in humility before Lothar." Zeroun bowed low, his headdress dipping. "Let us give praise unto the one who established our land."

"May the Holy One be gracious and bring us peace," the congregation intoned in unison.

"As the new year begins, so is hope reborn," said Zeroun. "Lothar has been resting after the toil of the harvest, but now is the time for Renewal. We must blow the sacred horn to awaken our god from his rest so the life cycle may begin anew. Behold the vessel for summoning Lothar."

Karayan, Minister of Justice, and Eznik, Minister of Labor, rose and approached a set of immense carved wooden doors at the rear of the Grand Altar. Uttering incantations, they reached out to draw the doors apart in front of the awed congregation.

Leena held her breath. The sound of the horn was more than a symbol for ushering in the new year. It summoned Lothar, and when he awoke, he reset the climatic cycles of Xan for another year. Without his beneficence, her world would revert to the wild, untamed fury of the past. No one ever wanted that to happen. It would mean the end to civilization as they knew it. Renewal was the pinnacle of all the seasonal holidays.

"Show us the horn," Dikran shouted as he faced the rear.

Karayan and Eznik drew the doors apart, and a collective gasp went up from the congregation.

Emptiness yawned from within the richly lit interior.

"Dear deity," Leena whispered. Where was the sacred horn?

Dikran had a stunned look on his face, while the other members of the Synod wore horror-stricken expressions. Dikran cast a quick glance at Zeroun before indicating the doors should be shut.

As he stepped forward to the podium, he signaled the choir. A trumpet always played after the horn to reflect the holy voice. Now the trumpet player began a haunting melody that reverberated throughout Leena's soul. When he finished, the congregation remained mute.

Dikran, his expression stony, spoke into the microphone. "Our opening of the holy chamber this year was symbolic. The sacred horn, after so many years of continuous use, has required a cleansing in sacramental water. We have blown the trumpet in its stead. It is Lothar's will that this be done. Hear us, Holy One, and awaken from your rest."

He raised his hands toward the congregation. "Bless our people and grant them freedom from sickness and sorrow. Let us love our neighbor as ourselves, walk humbly with our god, and convert our thoughts into faith and our words into good deeds. And so we say, Mahala."

He beamed pontifically. "And now, it gives me great pleasure to call upon our initiates. These young people have dedicated their lives to serving the Synod. By their faith, they serve Lothar and thus you, the people. Treat them with the respect due their station. You may step upon the dais." He gestured to the trainees with an imperious wave.

Holy waters, it's time. Leena trembled as she made her way to the elevated platform. On the dais, she faced the congregation in line with her fellow initiates. One by one, Zeroun called them by name. He gave each candidate a lit candle and a gold sash signifying their station. Holding their candles, they repeated the words they had rehearsed.

"We pledge ourselves to serve the members of the Synod in good faith, with loyalty, dedication and compassion, and in so doing we pledge ourselves to you, O blessed Lothar. Praised be the power that brings us peace and prosperity. Praise Lothar, who sanctifies us all. Mahala."

They blew out their candles to denote the end of the Renewal ceremony. The congregation remained in place while Dikran, the Synod members, and the new Caucus filed from the sanctuary to head for the reception hall.

A huge feast had been prepared, for Renewal was a happy, joyous occasion. Lothar was awakening. He would provide for them for another whole year, a year free from ill health, a year blessed with bountiful fruit and produce of the land.

Leena's heart soared with joy as she followed her robed companions through the nave toward an archway at the rear.

Someone planted a hand on her shoulder in the reception hall. He whirled her around and planted a firm kiss on her lips.

"I'm proud of you." Malcolm flashed her a grin that showed his white, even teeth.

Leena scanned his handsome features. His brown eyes reflected warmth and something more when he looked at her.

"Thank you," she murmured, pleased by his sincerity. "Have you seen Father?"

"He's over by the refreshment table. Can I get you a drink?"

"Yes, I'd like that."

She glanced around for Karole, wanting to introduce her friend to Malcolm, but couldn't locate her in the crowd. People stood about in clusters, drinks in hand, chatting and laughing. Friends and relatives had come from miles away for this special occasion.

Most people attended religious services in their hometowns or at the regional worship centers, but guests of the elite were invited to participate in services at the Holy Temple, and such invitations were highly coveted.

Leena wondered where Dikran had gone. She wanted to put in a good word with the Arch Nome for her father. But Dikran was nowhere in sight, and neither were the top members of the Synod. Where had they gone?

Dikran should be here to give his blessing to the bread so they could eat. But it was Jirair, Minister of Agriculture, who offered the prayer. A moment of doubt overwhelmed her as she recalled the stunned looks on Dikran's and the others' faces when they noticed the horn's absence.

Had it really been intentional that the horn not be here for Renewal, or was this a surprise to the Synod that Dikran had hastily covered up? They were certainly experts at cover-ups, as she well knew.

Malcolm interrupted her thoughts by returning with a cup of fruit punch.

"Thanks." She gulped the drink down, her throat dry.

"What's the matter? You look worried."

She lowered her voice. "The sacred horn… do you really think it's being cleaned? This seems an odd time to be doing a chore like that. We need the horn blown for Lothar to reset the cycles."

Malcolm raised an eyebrow. "Are you calling Dikran a liar?"

Leena's heart skipped, because it *was* Dikran's veracity she questioned. Fortunately, she was saved from a response by her father's arrival.

"Congratulations, my dear." Cranby embraced Leena in a huge bear hug. He was a large man, and his crimson robe of office made him even more imposing.

"Thank you, Father." Sliding back, she gazed at him with loving affection.

Gray sprinkled his blond hair, receding from a high forehead. Years of grief over the loss of his wife had dulled a set of blue eyes similar to her own. Clearly a pressing matter weighed heavily on his mind as he regarded her with an anxious expression.

"Have you heard from your brother?"

"He's not here? I tried to contact him earlier, but communications to Amat were out. I can't imagine what might have happened. He should have arrived by now." Her stomach churned. It was unlike Bendyk to be so late.

Malcolm raised his hand. "I'll go make inquiries. Amat is located in Seacrest Bay?" At Leena's nod, he hastened away.

"Malcolm is a fine young man," Cranby said, eyeing her carefully.

Leena lowered her lashes. "I'm still not sure about him, Father."

His look grew stern. "You've achieved a great deal for a woman of twenty-five years, daughter. Now it's time to think about your future."

"I've just been admitted into the Caucus. My immediate future is here." Her heart sank, knowing where this conversation was leading, but she tried to head him off regardless.

"Do you hope to be promoted to Docent, as do many of your peers?" Cranby pursed his lips. "I hadn't known you to be so religiously inclined."

Leena guarded her expression. Her father didn't know the true reason she'd joined the Caucus, and it was best he remain ignorant. Otherwise, he'd warn her against her course of action.

She didn't mean to stir up trouble but meant to uncover the truth about her religion's origins to quell the doubts in her heart. Leena wasn't the only one questioning their faith. The Truthsayers protested rule by the Synod. They demanded reforms, claiming Lothar was a false god created by the priests. The spate of recent weather disasters gave solidity to their words and shook the credibility of their religion.

The Synod proclaimed Lothar was angry at the people and punished them for their doubts, but Lothar was normally a god of compassion and mercy. There had to be some other reason for the climate changes on Xan, something only the Synod knew. That was another item of information she hoped to discover.

Her father shook his finger at her. "Mark my words, not another Beltane will pass with Malcolm and you unpledged. I shall speak to his father myself. It is still within my authority to troth you a husband, miss, and so I shall."

"I don't want a husband right now. I have too much to do in my new role."

"Nonsense, that's just an excuse. You dilly-dally too long, and this indecisiveness is unbecoming in a lady. You'll lose the young man if you don't snare him now."

"I'm not ready."

"You'll never be ready at your pace." He glowered at her. "No more arguments. The matter is settled."

Leena bit back a retort as the Minister of Justice bore down on them.

"Cranby, my old friend." Karayan slapped a hand on Cranby's shoulder, then vigorously shook both his hands as was the custom. "How good to see you again, and what a thrill to celebrate your lovely daughter's success." His pale grey eyes swung to Leena, expressing approval.

"I'm looking forward to serving the Synod." She smiled warmly. Karayan had always supported her father, even during his censure.

Karayan gave a slight bow. "You honor your family by your service." He tilted his head at Cranby. "I understand your son Bendyk is earning a name for himself as a missionary. We have word that requests are pouring in from the villages for his counsel. If he keeps going at this pace, I see him being appointed soon as a Docent." Karayan glanced around. "Where is the young man? I thought he was supposed to join us today."

"Bendyk never got in. I called Amat earlier but couldn't get through." Leena adjusted her headdress, which had begun to tilt. The heavy piece made her temples ache. When could she get away to change into more comfortable clothes? Probably not until this reception was over.

Karayan's eyes widened. "Did you say Bendyk was in Amat? We've just received word that there's been a terrible disaster at Seacrest Bay. A tsunami struck last night. There have been massive casualties, and a rescue effort is underway. I'm uncertain of the details."

"Dear Lord. Bendyk was supposed to leave last night. I hope he made it out."

Karayan laid a hand on her arm. "The Synod has called an emergency meeting to deal with the tragedy. Come with me."

She gave her father a brief kiss and hurried after Karayan.

Muttering a quick prayer that her brother would be found safe and unharmed, she followed Karayan through the maze-like corridors of the Palisades complex.

Chapter Two

The night before, Bendyk had attended the town council meeting in Amat. He'd planned to leave early to make the Renewal ceremony at the Palisades, but as dusk rapidly approached, it didn't seem his departure would occur anytime soon.

Wellis, the village priest, had requested a private audience with him. Now, as he sat across from the older man in the living room of his oceanfront bungalow, Bendyk fingered the medallion hanging from his neck.

"I fail to understand your meaning when you say people are straying from the Faith," he said. "The turnout at the service this morning was phenomenal."

Wellis wagged his finger. "That's because the villeins are putting on a pretense of piety for your benefit. They're afraid you'll report their indiscretions to the Docent."

Bendyk tightened his lips. No doubt Wellis felt he knew his flock better than any representative from the central authority. But the priest had sent for help, realizing the situation there could get out of control. After all, on whose head would the wrath of Lothar fall if he failed? Yet the blasphemous talk circulating through town wasn't evident during Bendyk's inspection. He wasn't surprised, considering how fearful the villeins were about retribution.

Wellis had hoped his arrival might inspire a renewal of faith. In truth, the service Bendyk had conducted this morning had been exemplary. Perhaps his visit had done some good after all.

He faced the priest across a table laden with fresh fruit and nuts. "Don't forget it's tithing time. The tax collector is here, even in the midst of Renewal celebrations. That's enough cause for heightened tension."

Wellis gave him a weary smile. "Not in this case. We've been fortunate to have the same agent each year. She counts in our favor and exacts a toll on ten percent less than the amount actually produced."

"You mean, this agent reports an inaccurate count? Why, that's a criminal offense."

Wellis leaned back in his chair, while a warm salty breeze swept in through open windows. His bungalow, a short distance from the ocean, stood on stilts like the rest of the houses by the shore. Further inland, other dwellings rose along a gentle slope that footed the Jerrise mountain range.

"It appeases people," Wellis said with a shrug. "I hear grumblings about laws that don't take into account the needs of individual districts. My people enjoy a simple life. They live off the bounty of the sea, plus their industries of rope-making and small boat building. No one earns enough revenue to warrant an investigation."

"That's not true. The Docents are responsible for making adjustments. If they rule unfairly, you can appeal to the Candor."

"The Candors are concerned mainly with their own wealth. Things have gotten out of hand."

Bendyk shot to his feet. "My father is a Candor. He's always judged people fairly and considered their needs."

"Cranby is an exception." Wellis regarded him with shrewd eyes. "Do you deny that dissatisfaction with the Synod's power is growing? Aren't your services widely in demand in an attempt by local priests, like myself, to stem this tide of disloyalty?"

"It is the work of Truthsayers. They want to undermine our Faith and establish anarchy in its place."

Footsteps sloshed outside, and Wellis held up a hand to silence his guest. "Hush, here comes the village council. I have summoned them to hear your advice. Go easy, young man. Your fiery tongue does you well in sermons but not in debate."

At his signal, Bendyk hastened to open the door. Five older men and one woman, the village leaders, shuffled in. To his surprise, a young lady accompanied them. Possessing a willowy frame, she moved with the grace of a forest *lyier*.

Bendyk's gaze swept from her pretty face to her short black hair that dipped inward toward her chin. The thrust of her jaw hinted at a stubborn streak, and her unorthodox style of dress confirmed it. Shocked, Bendyk peered at the skintight breeches she wore and the dark green sweater with its revealing neckline.

"I hope I meet with your approval," she said in a sarcastic tone as he continued his blatant stare.

Startled, Bendyk's glance lifted to meet hers. Her blazing amber eyes glared back at him.

"I'm Bendyk Worthington-Jax, representative of the Saballic Order of Missioners." He offered her a slight bow.

The young woman stretched out a hand. "I'm Swill Braddock."

They exchanged a firm handshake. Her palm was small, fitting into his larger hand like a ball into a catcher's mitt. He liked the weight and warmth of her.

"Swill?" He shot her a questioning glance.

"You got a problem with that?" Her brows furrowed in anger.

Clearly this woman took any remark as a challenge. Bendyk was amused. He'd never met anyone as bold and brazen as she before.

"What are you doing here? Surely you're not on the town council," he remarked. She didn't fit in with the other robed members whose dignified bearings and conservative dress bespoke of traditional attitudes.

"I'm the tax agent. It's time for the tithing count."

"You're the one? I hear your counts are favorable to the villeins."

She cocked her head. "Perhaps."

His eyes fired righteously. "Dishonesty is a sin."

"It all depends on who's in the know." Smiling sweetly, she

brushed past him and joined the others, who were already seated around Wellis's oval table.

"Come Bendyk, sit down," said Wellis.

"Why are your feet all wet?" He gestured toward the trail of water the visitors had left from the door to the table.

"The tide is washing in," spoke one white-haired gentleman. "It's higher than normal tonight."

"Aye," said another. "I don't remember it coming up this far in recent years."

"Never mind." Wellis indicated Bendyk. "Our guest has to leave for the Palisades soon, so let's begin our discussion. We asked for Brother Bendyk to serve our village because we've heard rumblings of discontent lately. He's noticed no such problem. Of course, the villeins are afraid of incurring retribution should they loosen their tongues in his presence."

The councilwoman leaned forward. "Ever since the hurricane that devastated the Rockmount Islands and the tornado on the Ruas Plains, people have been questioning Lothar's intent. Why would our Lord bring such disaster to his people? He's always been gracious and merciful. Why does he deal us these catastrophic blows at this time?"

Bendyk hunched forward in his seat. "It is because of the Truthsayer movement. Those malcontents who would protest rule by the Synod mean to leave chaos in its place. Our laws were put here for a reason, and we must abide by them to please Lothar. Health care, education, and housing are provided for everyone. I don't understand what the Truthsayers want instead."

"They want freedom to control their destiny," spoke Swill in a low tone.

All eyes swiveled in her direction, and Bendyk became aware of the seductive pull of her presence. She sat across the table from him, but every nerve in his body stood at attention when she directed her gaze at him. Those eyes, round as dew drops, could draw a man into their depths, and Bendyk found himself eager for her next word.

"People don't like having no choice over where they can live. If someone wants to move from one village to another, he has to submit an application. Populations are strictly regulated. It's unfair, and people are tired of having a central authority making these decisions for them."

"There is a reason for every law." Bendyk tapped his finger on the table. "A town's population is limited so it doesn't overgrow the needs of its citizens. The cities of old were rife with problems, such as poverty, crime, and lack of sanitation. Lothar placed limits on a town's populace for that very reason. In smaller villages, it doesn't matter as much. People care about their neighbors. In the larger cities, however, no one has any concern for what's going on next door. The ruling is a wise one."

"If you say so."

He stared at her. "What do you know of the Truthsayers, anyway? What right do you have to report a false count on the tithe? I should turn you in for your dishonesty."

"Be my guest." She lifted her chin, her gaze defiant. "The people I serve are happy because I let them keep more of their own produce. Why give it to a central authority that doesn't concern itself with their needs?"

"You speak blasphemy." Bendyk slammed his fist on the table. A strange banging echo caught his attention, only it wasn't an echo. It was a rhythmic thump-thump that sounded from somewhere below the house.

"What's that?" the councilwoman asked.

Wellis's face darkened. "It must be the empty oil drums banging together beneath the foundation. That means the water has risen to the level of the steps outside. That's not good. We'd better take a look to see what's happening."

Bendyk rose and hastened to the outer porch, needing to get away from Swill's influence. What an unusual name. But then it went along with her strange manner of dress, short cropped hair, and abrupt manner. He didn't know what to make of her. Clearly she was a rebellious sort, yet he found her oddly attractive.

He sensed her presence when she came outside and could almost feel her hot breath on his neck. Ignoring her, he glanced out to sea.

His heart leapt in alarm.

Dusk had fallen, and the town's lights lit the heavens with a soft golden glow. On the horizon, he could discern where the sea met the darkened sky. But it was the water by the shore that disturbed him. It had receded, exposing the seabed. Several beachgoers who'd been observing the sunset rushed out to delightedly pluck wet seashells from the exposed sand.

"What in the world?" Bendyk had never seen a phenomenon like this and didn't know what to make of it.

Behind him, Wellis sucked in a breath. "Dear Lord. A big sea is coming. We must flee!"

Swill's eyes widened. "Do we have time to reach our riders?"

"We can try." The priest signaled to the town's council members to join them.

Water sloshed about their legs as they rushed toward their vehicles only to find them jammed together by the latest wave. With cries of dismay, the group turned as one, ran across the yard of the nearest house, and charged inland away from the rising water.

Bendyk's heart raced as he fled toward higher ground. A dull rumble sounded, like a distant train. It grew into a monstrous roar. He glanced over his shoulder and nearly stumbled at the sight that greeted him.

An incoming wall of water rushed toward the village center. It must have been easily over six feet high.

Seconds later, the wave crashed into town with brutal force. Brilliant blue-white sparks marked the impact as the wave shorted out electrical circuits. Loud explosions accompanied the destruction of buildings.

A brief greenish arc flashed through the sky. Bendyk's jaw dropped. That meant the wave had reached the power plant at the south end of the bay. Sure enough, the entire area plunged into darkness. But it wasn't so dark that Bendyk couldn't make out the terrifying wall of water surging in his direction.

Loud booms announced the sound of walls being crushed and buildings being demolished as the wave progressed. Swill screamed as the tower of water descended upon them.

The wave lifted Bendyk and swept him inland. He submerged, and his pants leg caught on a piece of debris. Holding his breath, he tugged with a desperate edge until he broke free.

He kicked to the surface and gasped for breath. Fallen beams, broken furniture, and heavy appliances rushed past, bumping into him and threatening to drag him under again.

He heaved himself onto a wood plank that floated past as a terrible sucking noise reached his ears. His heart pounded. The water would be returning to its home, taking everything with it out to sea.

People fought the current along with the swirling debris. Some rode on the tops of their houses; others clung to treetops. Some people swam, but everyone screamed in terror.

A body swept past, and Bendyk's gut lurched in sudden recognition. Letting go of the plank, he swam with the current, grabbing Swill by the shoulder and flipping her over to raise her face out of the water. It was difficult to support her while they were both swept along, but he managed to keep both their heads up. She had a gash on her temple, but she was breathing, and that was all that counted.

As the water ebbed back to shore, his feet touched solid ground. Bracing his legs against the remains of a stone wall, he prevented them both from being pulled out to sea. He spotted one of the town leaders wedged with an arm trapped under a fallen tree. Of the other council members, he saw none.

Collapsed cottages, downed wires, concrete rubble, and smashed vehicles collected near the shore. After the sea subsided, people lucky enough to have survived began to stir and call out. Frantic parents searched for their children. Children wept for their missing parents. Husbands and wives sought absent spouses, and the first rescue efforts began.

Not one residence remained standing. The center of town yawned as an empty, dark hollow. In the ocean, heads bobbed in the heaving water as people struggled to stay afloat.

Bendyk laid Swill on the ground and examined her wound. As he touched her skin, her eyelids fluttered open, and she gave a soft moan.

"Don't move," he told her, annoyed with himself for noticing how her sodden clothes clung to her body. He knelt at her side, ignoring the discomfort of his own wet shirt and trousers. "You've been injured. How bad does your head hurt?"

She stared at him, her amber eyes wide. "I'm dizzy. What happened to the others?"

"The tsunami demolished everything. I saw only one member of the council. I don't know if anyone else survived who was in that meeting. I don't understand." He shook his head. "This region hasn't had waves like this in hundreds of years. It must be a sign of Lothar's wrath. Wellis admitted the people were harboring doubts. This must be Lothar's retribution."

Sighing, he surveyed the sorry scene about him as people wailed for missing relatives and their destroyed homes.

"Perhaps as a result of this tragedy, the villeins will confess their sins and give themselves to the Lord," he said.

Swill brushed his hand off and sat. "Is that all you can think about? Your stupid religion? People need our help."

A cool breeze raised the hairs on his arms. "We'll get chilled in these wet clothes. We can't help anyone in this condition. We should find shelter."

Swill attempted to rise but stumbled and would have fallen if not for his intervention. She swatted him away. "I can manage by myself, thank you."

"I think not." He gripped her around the waist. Rather than protesting, she leaned against him.

Bendyk considered how long it would take for word to reach

the outside world about what had happened there. For now, he had no way to contact Leena. She'd be worried when news of the tsunami reached her.

But even if he could find a means of transportation, he'd choose to stay. The survivors might wish to express their gratitude to Lothar, and Bendyk knew he should be the one to lead them in prayer. Holding onto Swill's slim waistline, he hoped he could convince her to join them.

Chapter Three

Kolb and Voshkie were engaged in a heated argument when Leena entered the meeting chamber of the Synod.

"We need to assemble an emergency response team," Kolb insisted.

As Minister of Health, the lean, thin-faced gentleman was responsible for the worldwide network of trained healers. While Lothar's lozenge, which everyone swallowed each year at the festival of Mistic, would prevent disease, injuries still required the care of skilled personnel.

"The expense would not justify such an alarming action." Voshkie, in charge of commerce, constantly railed against people's demands for a broader choice of consumer goods.

In the short time she'd been there, Leena had assessed the attitudes of most Synod members, and Voshkie's dislike of materialism was well known. The black-haired woman led an austere life, setting an example for those who wished to emulate her.

In contrast, Sirvat, in charge of the Treasury and the other prominent woman on the Synod, dressed with more flair. She wore her thin red hair under a variety of hats, while she favored the robes of office for her manner of dress. Since her reed-like figure did nothing for her womanliness, this style suited her. Her unsmiling mouth and the permanent frown on her face bespoke of her frustration as a spinster of fifty-two years.

Sirvat's green eyes, pale as a frozen sea, flickered briefly in Leena's direction. Seats were arranged around a central table in concentric circles. The members of the Synod had the first tier of seats, directly against the table. Behind them sat the aide corps. Leena found a seat next to Karole and took her place as unobtrusively as possible.

"I trust you are discussing the tsunami at Amat," said Karayan, settling his robes as he claimed a chair. "Missionary Bendyk was last known to be at that location. Has anyone heard from him?"

"We're still working to reestablish contact," Magar, the Minister of State, explained. "In any event, that's not why we are gathered here."

Karayan nodded. "Ah, yes. We have a much more pressing issue to discuss."

With those words, all eyes turned toward Dikran, who occupied the head of the table. The Arch Nome nodded for the door to be shut then spent a few moments in silence. He peered at each one of them, including the new members of the Caucus.

"We have a grave matter before us." Despite his age, Dikran's voice retained its forcefulness. "The sacred horn is missing."

The Caucus gasped in unison. Leena surmised the Synod members already knew, judging from the looks they exchanged.

"During the service," Dikran continued, "I said it had been taken for cleansing. Sooner or later, questions will be raised. We must find the horn before the truth gets out, or panic will ensue."

Zeroun's dark brows drew together. "How has this happened?"

"No one except the Synod has access to the sacred closet," Dikran replied, referring to the small chamber in which the horn was kept. "That can mean only one thing as far as I'm concerned." He paused, eyeing each one of his ministers. "One of *you* has stolen the horn."

Cries of outrage sounded throughout the room. Leena glanced with fright at Karole. By all that was holy! One of the Synod had taken the horn? But why?

Her doubts rushed back, and she stared at Dikran, her mouth hanging open, waiting to hear what he would say next.

"This is absurd." Karayan jabbed a finger in the air. "You are accusing one of us of being a thief?"

"I see no alternative," Dikran replied. "Besides myself, only the twelve of you have access to the Inner Sanctum. We must recover the horn as soon as possible unless, of course, one of *you* wishes to return it immediately."

Dear deity, Leena thought. What would happen if it was not found? Truly the trumpet was insufficient to awaken Lothar. He needed the special frequency of the sacred horn. Without his divine intervention, their climactic cycles would fail to reset.

Rains would not arrive during growing season, meaning their crops would wither. And what of the lozenge? Lothar provided it every year at Mistic. If they didn't partake of his bounty, sickness could devastate the land.

"We are now in the final cycle of the year," Dikran reminded them. "If we do not find the horn within the next three months, more natural catastrophes of even greater magnitude will occur. If the thief does not wish his or her identity to be known, place the holy relic in the sacred closet when no one is there. Further questions will not be asked. But if the horn isn't recovered by this time tomorrow, we will launch a thorough investigation, and every piece of information that was ever known about you will be revealed."

Silence descended upon the room like a mausoleum while Leena's mind reeled with possibilities. Lothar timed his renewal to begin in Fearn, the winter season. Without the horn to awaken him, surely disaster would befall their people. But was this all that worried Dikran?

The Arch Nome dismissed the gathering with instructions that they should reconvene in the same place at the same time the following day if the horn had not been returned. Meanwhile, the Caucus was to assume their duties immediately.

To Leena's disappointment, she had been assigned to

Zeroun, Minister of Religion. She had hoped she would be with Karayan since he was her father's friend, but the artifacts she had been studying were the property of the religious order. It was logical she should be assigned to the Department of Religion.

She trailed Zeroun to his offices in another section of the Palisades. Each department had its own wing. Civilians performed the clerical functions. By being in the religious hierarchy, Leena became a personal aide to Zeroun. With the privileges accorded to her status, she could attend his private meetings, sit in on Synod councils, and carry out his direct orders.

He sat behind his desk chair while he indicated for her to take a seat opposite. His close-set ebony eyes pierced her like an avenging angel. Dark thick-slashed eyebrows converged into a frown as he assessed her and reviewed her duties.

His thin compressed lips and hawk-like nose completed the image of a man who would let nothing stand in his way. Even the puffs of black hair rising behind his ears and flanking his receding hairline proclaimed his staunch aggressiveness. Disciplining his body as well as his soul, Zeroun maintained an athletic figure, an accomplishment for a man of sixty-four years.

Leena trembled in her seat as she listened. She wanted to ask him what he had done with the artifact he had confiscated from her but was afraid to mention it for fear of being disciplined. Zeroun was vehement in his faith, and he allowed for no dissension. Those who talked against the faith were even known to have disappeared, if not being outright banished to the pagan Black Lands.

Of his role in her father's censure, she was unclear. Cranby had never talked much about the incident, but she knew it had greatly disturbed him. Rather than face banishment, as would have been the punishment for one of his station, he had chosen to renounce his words and submit to a year of penance as was his due. Knowing her own background was less than exemplary, Leena scurried to obey Zeroun's commands.

It was a relief to retire to the dormitory-like quarters she shared with the other female initiates at the end of the day. They ate their evening meal in the dining commons and then were free for the rest of the evening. Everyone was eager to discuss recent events, and so the time passed quickly.

Leena's father came by and gave her the good news that Bendyk had contacted him and was safe. He'd made plans to take the first transport out from Amat and would be arriving at the Palisades within the next forty-eight hours. In the meantime, Bendyk was busy helping with rescue efforts in the village.

Leena tried to discuss the matter of the missing horn with her father, feeling she could confide in him if no one else, but Cranby didn't seem to want to hear her news. He waved his hand, brushing off her report as though it were nothing more significant than a schoolgirl's tale.

"I would advise you to keep your ears open and your mouth closed. If you do as you are told," Cranby said, his gaze skittering away, "your efforts will be rewarded."

Karayan was more sympathetic to Leena's concerns, listening to her fears and admitting his own when she encountered him in the corridor the next morning.

"It's a grave matter," he agreed about the missing horn. His solid features brought her a measure of comfort as he gazed at her with a warm expression. "Dikran checked this morning, and the horn is still absent. I'm going to recommend that you be allowed to investigate."

"Me?" Leena gaped at him, open-mouthed.

He laid a hand on her shoulder and smiled. "You're the only one among us who is educated in archaeology. With your dedication and zeal, you're the perfect choice to lead an investigation. The new members of the Caucus can aid you."

Leena stared at him. A stickler for propriety, Karayan always presented a well-groomed appearance, from his carefully-styled brown hair to his manicured fingernails to his personally-tailored frock coats and trousers.

As Minister of Justice, he supervised the higher courts led by the Candors with the same enthusiasm that he exhibited for his favorite hobby of art collecting. Leena was impressed by his air of quiet confidence. She had visited his estate and knew he managed his affairs with the same meticulous detail as his own appearance.

At fifty-eight years, Karayan was one of the youngest members of the Synod, and also one of the most energetic. Leena glanced down, and her eye caught on the large gold pinkie ring on his left finger.

"I'll do my best to follow any instructions you give me," she said, aware of her father's admonition.

Dear deity, how can I be in charge of finding the horn? Dikran and the others won't agree. I have no status here at all. I'm just a simple aide. Why would they choose me?

In her opinion, Karayan should be in charge of the investigation. But when the Synod and the Caucus met later, Dikran had other ideas.

"The thief is one of us. Whoever leads this investigation must be an unbiased third party who can check into our backgrounds. We need a person of extreme integrity."

Karayan rose and brushed off his robe. "I agree. This requires a two-pronged effort. We should appoint a representative who will remain at the Palisades to investigate our members, but we also require someone to search for the missing horn. It is my recommendation that Leena Worthington-Jax be put in charge of this expanded investigation. Her life's work has been to study the relics of our past."

All eyes turned in her direction, and Leena felt like sinking through the floor.

Karayan continued. "Her brother Bendyk is a missionary with an exemplary track record. Why not select him to work with his sister? He can be the one to check into our backgrounds while Leena pursues the missing horn."

The Synod voted, and Leena and Bendyk were chosen to work together. They'd each get a letter authorizing them to seek whatever help or counsel they'd need.

Stunned by the responsibility assigned her, Leena strode down the hallway after the meeting adjourned. She was barely aware of her surroundings when she heard her name mentioned from beyond a partially closed door.

She flattened herself against the wall to eavesdrop.

"How can you allow Leena to take charge of such an important matter?" Zeroun demanded. "She's a danger to our faith. We only invited her to join the Caucus so we could keep an eye on her."

Leena gasped. Was this true? Did they believe her to be disloyal?

"She has the background to verify the horn's authenticity," replied a muffled male voice. "As an expert on the carvings left by the Apostles, she's familiar with the symbols etched onto the horn's surface. No one else has the required expertise."

"I suppose you're right. The Truthsayers may try to prevent her from recovering the horn. They'd like nothing more than to destroy our credibility. It would serve their purpose if the holy relic was never found."

"Perhaps they stole it in the first place."

"Maybe Leena is one of them. She asks too many questions. Let's keep a sharp watch on her."

A rustling noise indicated the speakers were about to depart. Leena slipped inside the next open doorway, waiting until she heard their footsteps pass.

Trembling at what she'd overheard, she considered the repercussions. Zeroun didn't trust her, yet she came under his authority as a member of the Caucus.

Not anymore, she reminded herself. He was subject to her scrutiny same as the others.

His words about the Truthsayers gave her pause. Maybe they *were* involved in the theft. They claimed Lothar was a false god the priests had created to bolster their power. Without the horn being blown, Lothar would not reset the climactic cycles. Disaster would ensue. She envisioned a society torn by anarchy.

Her world must not come to that. She had to find the horn, but the awesome responsibility made her quiver with dread.

"Bendyk, come quick," she whispered. She needed her brother for support, because who else could she confide in?

****

Hours later, Bendyk finally arrived. After he exchanged greetings with their father and Karayan, and filled them in on the latest news, he retired with Leena to a private corner of the dining commons.

Dark circles showed under his eyes, which held deep sadness. "Many people were lost in the tsunami. I did what I could to help, but there is still so much more to be done. Power has yet to be restored, and rubble removed. At least communications have been restored."

"I'm just glad you're here." Leena basked in the warmth of his presence before informing him of their assignment.

He stiffened. "What? The sacred horn is missing?"

"Hush! Lower your voice."

"What do you mean, I have to check into the backgrounds of the Synod members? Why me?"

Leena gave a harsh laugh. "That's what I've been asking myself. You're not attached to the Synod. You can pursue this with an objective mind."

His blond eyebrows furrowed. "I'll have to examine their individual records, verify background checks, and delve into financial accounts. I can't do it alone." He tilted his head to peer at her. "When I was in Amat, I encountered a local tax agent, a woman named Swill Braddock. She's supposed to be a whiz at finances. Maybe I could request her as my assistant."

Leena noticed the gleam in his eyes. If she didn't know better, she'd think her brother looked forward to seeing this woman again.

"And you met her how?"

"She helped out after the disaster. She knows how to get a job done, although she's very sympathetic toward the plight of commoners. I hope she'll agree. Did I mention she can be opinionated?"

Leena grinned, eager to meet this paragon. "We have a meeting with the Synod to discuss strategy. You can mention adding her to our team at that time."

During their next gathering, the Minister of State addressed Leena after a round of subdued greetings.

"You'll need protection," the seventy-year-old, silver-haired gentleman told her. "The Truthsayers may try to stop you from recovering the horn, or your search could take you into dangerous territory. Our representatives may not always be available to render aid. I know a man who's perfect for the job if he'll agree."

Magar supervised relations among the different districts. His twinkly blue eyes and ready smile engaged her trust. Responsible for entertaining visiting dignitaries, he made his preference clear for fine wines and dining by his portly figure and rolling gait. A casual dresser, Magar favored comfort over formality. He presented quite the contrast to Karayan, who always dressed in the height of style.

Leena wondered who Magar meant to accompany her on the perilous journey. She wasn't aware of anyone who could defend her in the manner he suggested. Her people were a peaceful race. Few had fighting skills or experience in dealing with hostile situations.

"Who is this man?" she asked. It would be easier to go with someone she knew.

"His name is Taurin Rey Niris. He's perfect for the job."

"Where can we find him?" Karayan cut in, a frown creasing his brow.

Leena was grateful for his concern. It was the closest thing to having her father there. She wished Cranby would attend these meetings, but she'd seen his diffident manner around the members of the Synod and despised his cowardice. He humbled himself before them, and it only served to humiliate her family.

She wondered again why she and Bendyk had been chosen to find the horn. Nettles of doubt pricked her spine. Were there forces at work here that she didn't understand?

"I'll provide that information later." Magar's voice hardened. "Leena, have you thought about where to begin your investigation?"

She understood that Magar didn't want the others inquiring too deeply into the background of this man named Taurin. Who was the fellow? Where did he come from? Where would she have to go to ask for his assistance?

Sirvat spoke up. "If the horn has been stolen, it's very likely passed through Grotus's hands."

Leena's eyes widened. Grotus was a renowned dealer of stolen artifacts. Suspected to employ a worldwide network of smugglers, he'd evaded prosecution much to the annoyance of the authorities. If someone had stolen the horn for money, it would very likely go to Grotus first. He seemed as good a place as any to start.

She shrugged. "Very well, I will seek out the help of this Taurin Rey Niris, and then we'll travel together to see Grotus." She'd need the man's protection if what she had heard was true, that Grotus lived on an isolated island fortified with defenses.

She had no idea how she would get herself admitted to see him, let alone why he would share information with her. But she could worry about that later. First, she'd better see if this Taurin fellow was willing to help her. She agreed that it could be dangerous for her to travel alone. The Truthsayers posed an ever present threat, and who knew what other peril would find her?

As she and her brother said their goodbyes—he on his way to contact Swill, and Leena en route to find Taurin—her brother regarded her solemnly.

"I am less than thrilled about you traveling the globe with a stranger." He stroked his jaw while eyeing her.

"We don't know if he'll agree to help. If he refuses, I'll call you, and we'll revise our plans." She lifted her eyebrows. "And you'll have to let me know if this tax agent agrees to work with us. It would be useful to have a financial expert on our side."

Bendyk nodded. "Have you thought about a motive?"

"Maybe one of the Synod needs money. You'll find out when you check their records. Otherwise, I could ask Father if he has any ideas." After so many years in the service of Sabal, her father might possess knowledge of priestly secrets that could prove useful.

"I don't think we should tell him what we're doing," Bendyk advised. "The fewer people who know about our mission, the better. Promise me you'll call as soon as you make contact with Taurin Rey Niris."

"Of course. I'll let you know what happens."

"If he agrees to your proposal, you must not travel together in sin."

Her breath hitched. "What do you mean?"

"Have you no notion of the harm that would befall your reputation if it became known you traveled alone with a stranger?"

Leena laughed and tapped his arm. "We're not so strict in our society."

His face pinched. "This is not Beltane, when coupling is encouraged and trial marriages take place. If you embrace such freedom outside our customs, you'll be jeopardizing your future plans."

"Oh," she said, catching his drift. "You mean Malcolm? He won't know anything about it."

"What if he finds out? Do you think he would take it lightly that you traveled around the country with an unattached male?"

"He'll understand when he hears my reasons. At any rate, he's not supposed to know anything about our assignments."

Bendyk glowered at her. "Let's hope your suitor doesn't learn about it from anyone else. Call me the minute you and Rey Niris reach an agreement."

"*If* we reach an agreement."

His expression turned sly. "Don't worry about the proprieties. I'll see to it that your behavior is exemplary."

Her brother could be a pompous ass sometimes, Leena thought. Nonetheless, his words filled her with misgivings. Just what did he have up his sleeve?

Chapter Four

Leena drove her sleek red rider along a rural road flanked by rolling green fields and wooded hillsides. Ospreys swooped and soared over a broad stretch of brown stubble, the remains of a recent grain harvest. Their graceful bodies were stark white against the muted earth tones.

The Blenheim region was one of the most fertile in Celia, the province that housed the Palisades in its central hub. This area supplied a bounty of fresh produce, milk, and cheeses savored around the globe. Magar's estate was close by, his family being one of the largest landholders in the area. Leena hadn't realized Taurin resided in the same locale and was surprised Magar neglected to mention it.

Glancing at the paper with his written directions on the seat beside her, she noted that the turn-off to Taurin's place should be coming up ahead. Sure enough, it was just around the next bend. She followed an oak-lined private road that ended in a circular driveway. After stopping her rider with a squeal of brakes, she shifted gears and turned off the ignition.

An attractive, tidy house faced her. Beyond it stretched rows of cultivated fields. Was Taurin a farmer, and if so, what crops did he raise? Her curiosity climbed a notch as she examined his home.

A trimmed yard spread out in front like a brown-tinged carpet, the grass obviously too dry. Bordering the foundation of the house was a rounded evergreen hedge. A short flight of steps led up to a wraparound porch on which sat a couple of cushioned lounge chairs, a small table, and various potted plants.

The one-story dwelling, painted pastel blue with white shutters edged in a scallop design, gave an impression of neatness and simplicity. This appealed to Leena the way a home-cooked meal would appeal to a frequent traveler.

The quiet exterior of the house greeted her as she emerged from her vehicle. Unseasonably warm autumn air struck her like a blast from a furnace. Glad her gown was made of a lightweight silk, she climbed the few steps to the portico.

No one responded to her loud knocking.

Buggers, Taurin must have gone out. The driveway held no other vehicles besides her own.

Taking an appreciative sniff of the rich, earthy scent coming from the freshly-plowed fields, she was startled at a sweet fragrance that drifted into her nostrils. Following her nose, she trailed around to the rear of the house to stare at row after row of brilliantly-colored flowers.

Taurin Rey Niris grew flowers? She pictured him as a rural farmhand and couldn't conceive how he'd protect her from danger.

This hadn't been a good summer for farmers with the lengthy hot, dry weather, but Taurin seemed to have done well. Was the difficult climate a result of Lothar's wrath at his people's unfaithfulness, as the Arch Nome proclaimed, or could it be another sign that something was terribly wrong on her world?

Squinting in the bright sunlight, she decided to return to the house before her shoes became encrusted with dirt. The shady porch beckoned to her, so she climbed the steps and approached a back door.

A glimpse in a window showed her that the gold circlet covering her head had become tilted. She straightened it along with the attached blue veil that matched her elegant gown. She wore her hair loose, preferring a freer style in defiance of propriety, which demanded that unwed females fix their hair in a modest upsweep.

Beyond her reflection, Leena's gaze fell on a pile of books

visible through the window. She could just make out the titles. Her curiosity piqued at noting they were archeological texts.

Disregarding her sense of caution, she pressed her nose against the pane to get a closer view. She surveyed a broad tile counter holding woven baskets with yellow onions, polished red pommes, potatoes, and green stiglers. The baskets were arranged in rows like the flower beds outside. Not a dirty dish was in sight. Was Taurin so tidy, or did he have a housekeeper? Even his kitchen utensils hung with an eye to precision.

Then again, what made her think he lived alone? She'd gotten that impression from Magar, but maybe she had been mistaken. After all, what kind of man would live in isolation, raising flowers and studying archeology?

She strolled to another window to search for more clues as to the man's puzzling nature. A cozy living room held a stone fireplace, couches you could sink into and—wait, what were those drawings? It appeared as though Taurin was working on something. An easel stood in a corner.

So now she had a flower farmer with aspirations of becoming an artist. She narrowed her eyes. Those figures on his sketch struck a familiar chord.

She stepped to the side, and her ankle banged against a solid object that crashed to the ground. Dear deity, she hadn't seen the flower pot. Bending her knees, she gathered the broken pieces from among the spilled dirt then heaped them in a pile. She straightened, flushing with guilt. Now Taurin would know for certain someone had been snooping around.

Brushing off her hands, she headed toward her rider, deciding she'd return later. In the meantime, she was thirsty and could use a snack. On her way through town, she'd noticed a pub. It would be a good place to get a drink while gathering information.

****

The dimly-lit interior of the pub was a welcome respite from the unusual heat of the late-afternoon sun. Leena stood just inside the doorway so her eyes could adjust. Straight ahead was a polished mahogany bar with gleaming brass trim. Glasses hung on racks overhead, and behind the bar were bottles and kegs in differing sizes.

The tantalizing smell of sautéed onions drifted into her nose from a dining room off to the right. A few of the tables were occupied. A young couple claimed one corner. They were fancily dressed as though they were visitors like herself. A family with three noisy children occupied another table. Roughly-dressed farmhands hunkered down at the far end, drinking ale and speaking in loud tones.

Leena strode to the bar to place her order. "I'll have a glass of claret, please. May I see a menu?"

The bartender, a burly fellow with a shock of red hair, complied.

Leena smiled sweetly at him. "I'm looking for a man named Taurin Rey Niris. Would you know where I can find him? I have an urgent matter we need to discuss."

The bartender examined her more closely. His eyes widened when he noted her telltale gold circlet. He nodded at a dark corner.

"Rey Niris sits in that booth over there. Be careful how you approach him, Your Honor."

Leena stifled a smile. Obviously he didn't know the proper form of address for a Caucus member. "Why should I be cautious?"

"Just heed my words." The bartender's face closed. He turned away to pour her glass of red wine.

Leena accepted the drink along with a menu. She took the items and strode toward the shadowed nook.

With his back to the wall, Taurin's face was barely visible in the gloom. He was swathed totally in black, including a covering that wrapped around his head. The cloth shaded his eyes so she couldn't read his expression, but she sensed an air of tension about him. His broad shoulders hunched forward, as though he was ready to spring up at a moment's notice. She could imagine his gaze surveying the entrance, searching for the first hint of a threat. But what threat could there possibly be in this peaceful village?

If he turned out to be the man she sought, how would she convince him to assist her? He appeared much more formidable than she'd expected. Nearing his table, she muttered a quick prayer to Lothar for guidance.

****

Taurin noticed her the moment she stepped through the door. Backlit from the sunlight streaming in the entrance, the woman appeared a vision of loveliness. If Taurin were a religious man, he would have heard the music of angels accompanying her presence.

A mass of golden hair floated about her head like waves of spun silk, framing a face with features as fine as porcelain. He couldn't see the color of her eyes, only that they were large and round as she peered about the room. Her body, slender and curvaceous, was encased in an exquisitely-styled gown that was cinched at the waist and flared out in a skirt that drifted about her ankles with each graceful movement.

What was a woman of her obvious wealth doing here?

He watched while she exchanged words with the proprietor. Holding a glass of red wine, she approached in his direction. As she got closer, he realized she wore the gold circlet and blue veil that signified a Caucus disciple. Her eyes matched the royal blue of her gown, and he could only stare in awe as she stopped in front of him.

"Good and welfare, brother. I'm looking for a man named Taurin Rey Niris. Are you the one I seek?"

Her voice, sweet and musical, rang in his ears like a spirit calling him to worship. She inspired idolatry, he thought, gazing into her eyes.

He couldn't let her know how strongly she affected him. "What is it you want?" he asked in a wary tone.

"I have a proposition to make."

"Who are you?"

"My name is Leena Worthington-Jax."

"You're in the religious order."

"So I am. Look, are you Rey Niris or not?"

At his curt nod, she placed her glass on the table and took a seat. Taurin shrank further back into the shadows so she couldn't read his face.

"I have no interest in anything you have to offer. Who sent you here?"

"Just listen, will you? I need your help, but we should talk in private." Her hands trembled as she took a sip of wine.

Was she afraid of him, or did she fear his refusal to help her? Taurin couldn't possibly imagine what she wanted or who had encouraged her to approach him. Necessity had forced him to keep a low profile since his arrival, and he'd succeeded in keeping mostly to himself except for occasional excursions into town. Why, then, was she here? What did she want? And who had put her on his trail?

Curiosity overwhelmed his better judgment. "There's a room upstairs. I'll ask the owner if we can use it."

****

Leena followed him toward the bar and was gratified when the owner agreed. Taurin stood aside so she could pass and precede him up the steps. She brushed against his arm, the contact eliciting a shiver. The man presented such a dark, imposing figure. She could barely make out his face under the covering that swathed his head.

Upstairs, they entered a private dining room that reeked of

stale liquor. Taurin had ordered a drink brought up from the bartender, and they waited in tense silence until it was served. Bright lamp lighting gave her a glimpse of his steel gray eyes and the shock of black hair that curled onto his forehead.

A forbidden thrill warmed her blood, but she pushed it aside to focus on her mission. His aquiline nose and firm jawline proclaimed him to be a man of character. Hopefully his sense of honor would prevail, and he'd agree to help her.

They took seats opposite from each other at a small round table. Taurin gulped down a few swallows of his ale.

"What I'm about to tell you must not leave this room," she began. "You will not reveal a word of it to anyone. Swear it upon your sacred honor."

He quirked an eyebrow. "You've aroused my curiosity. I swear that whatever words we exchange here will go no further."

"Someone has stolen the sacred horn, and it has not been blown at this year's Renewal ceremony. We are facing disaster if it is not recovered soon. I have been assigned the task of retrieving the horn, and I need your assistance."

His gaze darkened. "Absolutely not."

"Magar told me to ask for you."

"He did, did he?" Taurin didn't sound pleased.

"My quest is dangerous. The Truthsayers could be involved, and they might try to stop me. Magar said you're the only one who could provide protection."

"What else did he say?" With a jerky motion, Taurin brought his glass to his lips and finished his drink.

"Very little," Leena admitted.

Taurin scraped his chair back and stood. "I won't be involved in the affairs of your kind."

"What do you mean? Everyone will be affected if the horn isn't blown, even you. Your crops will wither and die, and your farmland will languish. If you assist me, you'll prevent that from happening."

"Sorry, you'll have to find someone else. I'm not your man."

She opened her mouth to make an angry retort, but a loud commotion erupted downstairs. Raised male voices yelled over a couple of heavy thuds. The sound of glass breaking reached her ears.

Without so much as a backward glance in her direction, Taurin thundered down the stairs into the dining room, where workmen were engaged in a brawl.

Leena gasped as Taurin threw himself into the fray. In a flurry of well-placed kicks and punches, he subdued the combatants within minutes. They lay sprawled around the room, staring at him in fear and wonder.

"Fighting will not be tolerated," he announced in a commanding tone. "You'll make reparations to the owner of this establishment. Is that understood?"

The men nodded their agreement, their expressions making it clear they feared a reprisal should they refuse. His fists clenched, Taurin hovered over one cowering miscreant, as though wishing the fellow would lash out at him so he could react in violence once again. A shudder racked his body as he straightened. Without another word, he stalked toward the door and departed.

"Wait!" Leena rushed outside, but when she emerged into the sunlight, he wasn't anywhere in sight. She glanced at the riders parked along the curb. One was just pulling out, and as she tried to identify the driver, the vehicle roared away.

Buggers, that had to be Taurin. Now she'd have to make a repeat trip to his farm. Her lips pressed tight, she strode toward her rider, hoping he'd go directly home.

The violence she'd seen unleashed in the pub made her heart race and dread pit her stomach. It was truly a sign that people had strayed from the Faith. Hardly anyone ever fought on Xan, even when intoxicated. It wasn't their way of life and defied Lothar's teachings. Change was in the wind, and it didn't bode well for her world.

Taurin had jumped into the fight without so much as a

second thought. That demonstration of his skills proved he could serve as her protector. The man was no gentle flower farmer. Dressed in black with tension emanating from every pore, he appeared more like a warrior of storybook fame than a simple farmhand. His choice of occupations and hobbies intrigued her. The different sides of his personality didn't mesh, making her wonder at his origins.

His farm occupied a corner of Magar's huge estate. Was he a tenant farmer, offering part of his produce to Magar as rental payment? Or was he a freeholder, owning the land himself? She couldn't conceive of their relationship and resolved to question Magar about it at the first opportunity.

Her stomach grumbled, and her glance strayed to the timekeeper. No wonder! It was six o'clock, and she'd forgotten to order from the menu at the pub.

She detoured by a local market to purchase a loaf of crusty bread, a hunk of cheese, and some bottles of cider.

After putting her purchases into the back seat of her rider, she slid in front and turned on the ignition. A warning light glowed red on the dashboard, but Leena ignored it as she had on her way into the village. She'd take care of it tomorrow; today her business was too pressing.

She approached Taurin's house, intending to plead her case again and leave. His windows were open, letting in a fresh breeze. With the sun's descent, the air began to cool. Soon it would be dark. If the man agreed to help her, she'd return tomorrow to further their discussion.

She gathered her bundle of groceries and marched toward his front door. The door swung wide at her summons.

Taurin scowled at her. "What do you want? I thought I made it clear that I would not help you."

He'd removed the cloth swathed around his head, revealing his thick black hair. His angry gray eyes slammed into hers with a fierceness that took her breath away.

"I brought some food. May I come in?" She used her

sweetest, most beguiling tone of voice, but it didn't budge the man. He stared at her impassively.

"Go away," he said, about to shut the door in her face.

Leena wedged her foot inside. "We haven't finished our discussion."

"Yes, we have." The hunch of his shoulders told her he would resort to force to remove her if necessary.

"I told you Magar sent me," she inserted hastily, hoping the name of his neighbor or landlord, whichever it was, would influence him.

Taurin hesitated, and Leena snatched the opening. She pointed to the easel propped in a corner. "I see we have similar interests. I'm an archeologist. My background and experience are why I'm the one assigned to find the sacred horn."

"An archeologist?" He studied her with renewed interest. "Perhaps you should come in." His voice softened ever so slightly. He stood aside while she brushed past, bundles in hand.

Leena's breath came short at his nearness and the menacing aura he presented. But her mission was too important for her to be awestruck around him. She needed his help, and she'd get it any way she could.

She aimed for his kitchen, where she plunked down her packages and unpacked the contents. "I've brought bread, cheese, and cider. Would you like some, or have you already eaten?"

"I haven't had the chance yet. Your repast is welcome."

"You could get me some plates and a knife. I'll cut this cheese into wedges."

He complied, observing her as she busied herself with nervous fingers. The man totally unsettled her. She felt like an intruder in his home, and he undoubtedly resented her presence.

When she'd completed her preparations, she whirled around, her gown swishing at her ankles. She smiled bravely and offered Taurin a plate of bread and cheese.

Without uttering a word of thanks, he took it from her, helped himself to a mug of cider, and sat at the polished wood table. She took a seat opposite and examined at him openly. His irises were a dark shade of smoky gray. Something greenish flickered inside them whenever a shadow crossed his face. Fascinated by the dancing lights in his eyes, she didn't realize she was staring until his gaze darkened. His glance roamed from her circlet to her wavy hair to her breasts and then lifted.

"Does your mate know you have come on this errand?" he asked with an implacable expression.

Leena arched her eyebrows. "I have no mate."

"You're a member of the religious order, meaning you follow strict directives. Your loose hair denotes your married status, although you don't wear a ring." He indicated her left hand.

"Oh, you're wondering why I wear my hair this way? I prefer the style." She gave a defiant grin then sobered. "My presence here in no way threatens my reputation. Bendyk, my brother, knows I have come. So do the members of the Synod."

Magar wouldn't have sent her if he didn't trust the fellow. She squirmed in her seat, half-fascinated by Taurin and half-wary. She took a bite of bread, wondering if he disapproved of her quest. She couldn't read his face to determine his opinion. The bread melted on her tongue, and she savored it before swallowing.

"Tell me about the missing horn." He popped a chunk of cheese into his mouth and chewed.

"Very well. The horn could only have been taken by someone with access to the Inner Sanctum. That points to one of the Synod members. My brother Bendyk is looking into their backgrounds for any hint of financial strain. Meanwhile, you and I need to contact Grotus, a dealer in stolen artifacts, to see if the horn has come his way. If he has it, we'll offer a ransom."

She leveled her gaze on him. "I am prepared to give you a substantial sum for assisting me."

****

Taurin couldn't allow this fragile female to meet with Grotus alone. He had heard of the man, and Grotus was not the sort Leena should encounter by herself, assuming she could procure an audience with him. But still, he remained reluctant to get drawn into her problems.

He took a large draught from his mug of cider. "I have not agreed to help you. I have my farmlands to tend," he said, denying the flame of desire that sprang up at the wistful look in her sapphire eyes.

"Your crops are not thriving. If the horn isn't blown, how will they survive? This drought will worsen. Do you not wish to see Lothar awaken from his rest, so he can bless our land with nourishing rain?"

"Lothar be damned." Taurin knew her god wasn't responsible for the climactic cycles, at least not in a direct sense. He didn't understand what was happening on her world, but it wasn't his job to find out either. He just wanted to live in peace. He had been through too much horror in the past to seek violence again. This farm served as his haven, and he had no wish to leave it.

"I'll take my chances like everyone else." His firm tone challenged her to refute him.

Leena's fingers tightened around her mug. "Don't you care that people are going to get sick and die if Lothar's lozenge isn't available in the month of Mistic? People are already facing sickness and hunger, not to mention the unnatural weather disasters causing havoc around the world."

She leaned forward. "My brother Bendyk was just in Amat on Seacrest Bay. It was hit by a tsunami. Scores of people died, and many others were injured or lost their homes. Do you want this to continue? You're being given a chance to help. I can't do it alone." Moisture tipped her lashes. "I trust Magar sent me to the right person."

Taurin didn't answer. Magar knew his talents very well. Indeed, he was the only person in their entire region who could protect this woman from trouble, but by involving him, Magar put them both at risk.

Damn, what was he to do? Taurin stood and paced the kitchen, dashing a hand through his unruly hair. So she was an archeologist, was she? Maybe she could help him interpret the secrets he'd kept hidden all these years.

Leena's gaze radiated sympathy. "Look, I'm sure I can get the Synod to send someone to tend your farm if that's your main concern."

True, Taurin wouldn't want to see all the work he'd put into the place go to waste. He'd toiled long and hard to make this piece of land prosper, and the flowers he grew were important to a significant someone in his life. He didn't want to disappoint that person by not being able to make his monthly shipments.

"Let me show you something. Wait here." He disappeared through the doorway into the living area then returned a moment later holding his sketch from the easel. "I've made a study of these symbols. Since you're an archeologist, maybe you can interpret them for me."

She rose for a closer inspection. "These are similar to the inscriptions that mark the ancient ruins around the globe. No one has been able to decipher them. I suspect they're messages left us by the ancient Apostles. I'd like to learn where those beings originated and why they left." She gave him a pointed glare. "So will you help me in my quest or not?"

"All right," he muttered, "but I would like someone to work the fields in my stead."

"I'll make arrangements. I need to return to the Palisades to pack." She regarded him with a determined gleam. "How long of a journey is it to Grotus? Do you know anything about him?"

"Not much," he replied, unwilling to reveal what little he did know.

"I'll ask Sirvat for details. She's the one who suggested his name to me. Sirvat is in charge of the Treasury," Leena explained. "Anyway, I'd better leave now. I'd like to head back before it gets too dark."

****

Leena wondered how far they would have to travel to reach Grotus and hoped it wouldn't be a long trip. Certainly her brother Bendyk's concerns were justified. Taurin hadn't made a move to open the door for her. He stood on his porch while she walked to her rider. How could she go on such a perilous journey with someone so disinterested in her welfare?

Yet it was worth any peril if she could recover the horn.

She keyed the ignition, but nothing happened. The engine didn't turn over, nor did the headlights come on.

Oh, no. She pounded the steering wheel in frustration. The recharger must be dead, and all the stations would be closed. Now what?

Biting her lower lip, she supposed she could call Bendyk. It would be an hour and a half drive in the dark for him to come and get her. She hadn't noticed any hostelry nearby either.

Taurin sauntered over and peered through the open window. "Having a problem?"

"My charge is drained." Leena felt foolish. She'd never ignored a warning indicator before, and now look what had happened. Once emptied, the circuit chamber needed hours to renew.

"The nearest station is closed. You'll have to wait until morning to get it fixed." Taurin stared implacably at her as though unwilling to burden himself with her difficulty.

With an annoyed frown, Leena stepped from the rider. "I'll call my brother. He'll come to pick me up."

But when she messaged him, Bendyk didn't respond. Maybe he'd left to seek the help of the Swill woman. It appeared she was stuck here.

She turned to view her host with trepidation.

Chapter Five

Bendyk remembered Swill saying she'd be going home from Amat to spend her earned leave time with her family. The town of Kameron-by-the-Knoll was located in one of the most desolate, uncomfortable settings he'd ever set foot in. Having arrived by special air transport, he'd hired a ground vehicle to take him to her address, which Sirvat had supplied. As a tax agent, Swill's job came under the Treasury Department.

The town was at the heart of a dustbowl, where dried weeds tumbled through the streets on a breath of hot wind. Digging for scaly grubs was the main industry, according to the rental agent. The grubs, considered a food delicacy in certain parts of the world, commanded a high price. However, the cost of living in such a place discouraged all but the most solitary souls from pursuing the trade.

Swill's parents owned a squat tan house in a sparse development that ran up a hillside. Cactuses and hardy weeds provided the only greenery in sight, while the sun blazed overhead. Hopefully this sojourn wouldn't take long. The pilot had orders to wait for him at the airfield.

He rang the doorbell and listened for a response. Shuffling footsteps sounded from inside the house, and then the door was thrust open.

"Yo! Who be you, young 'un?"

"Good and welfare, brother." Bendyk took a step back.

The smell of spirits hit his nose, and from the bloodshot eyes of the stout man facing him, Bendyk would say he'd been drinking. The man's plaid shirt hung loose over a pair of baggy pants, and his work shoes were encrusted with dirt. He reeked of liquor and sweat, making Bendyk force himself to smile politely.

"I'm Bendyk Worthington-Jax, servant in the Sabalic order of Missioners." He fingered the medallion dangling at his chest. Because he worked among the people, he could wear clothes of his choosing. The medallion signified his station.

"So?" Clearly unimpressed, the fellow scratched his balding head.

"I'd like to see Swill if she's home."

"Swill? You're here to see my daughter?" The man's face broadened into a grin, exposing yellowed teeth.

Krimas, Bendyk cursed under his breath. This was Swill's father? No wonder she had such a tough attitude.

"Come in, good sir. I'm Royce Braddock." He led the way into a living room holding faded secondhand furnishings. "Swill, get in here! You have a visitor."

Swill appeared in the hallway and stood stock-still at the sight of Bendyk. His gaze swept over the rust-colored top that barely bound her thrusting breasts and her white shorts that halted mid-thigh. Inadvertently his glance slid down her shapely legs.

Another woman with a worn, tired face and wearing a soiled apron entered the room. She barely diverted his attention, but apparently Braddock had already noted the appreciative look in his eyes.

"Gemma, this young man is here for Swill," he told the woman who Bendyk assumed was his wife.

Swill's mother rushed forward to shake both of Bendyk's hands in greeting. "I'm so glad she's found someone."

Bendyk's face warmed in embarrassment. "I'm not... I mean, I need her to come with me."

"Of course, but first you'll have to tell us how you two met. Royce? Now you won't have to worry no more about Swill finding a man. She's gone and gotten herself a beaut."

Braddock gave a loud belch. "About time it is, too. Let's go mix up some drinks to celebrate while the lovebirds greet each other."

"Pa," Swill said, "I think Bendyk may be here on business."

"Nonsense, he's got eyes for you, girl. You've got a good thing here." Braddock winked. "Give him a proper greeting now."

He staggered after his wife into another room, leaving them alone.

Swill faced him with her hands on her hips. "Are you here to arrest me?"

"Arrest you?" Bendyk stared at her in astonishment. "Whatever for?"

"For misrepresenting the tithing count. That is why you're here, isn't it? You reported me to your superiors, and they sent you to bring me in?"

Bendyk saw the flicker of fear in her eyes quickly hidden by a mask of defiance. "I'm here to bring you back with me to the Palisades. I need your help on a special project."

Doubt crossed her expression. "What? You need *my* help?"

"Yes, that's correct." Stepping forward, he took her hands in his. The contact sent delicious tingles up his arms. "I can't share the details now, but your interviewing skills and financial acumen are exceptional. I'm conducting an investigation and could use your talents."

She withdrew her hands and moved back, a wary look in her eyes. "What's in it for me?"

"An increase in pay and the knowledge that you're doing people a service. That is important to you, isn't it?"

Her chin tilted upward. "Everyone needs a break. I do what I can to help."

"So I've noticed." He couldn't help his sarcastic tone, aware she didn't play by the rules. Unlike her, he believed discipline strengthened the spirit. He wondered at the state of her soul when she mocked their laws.

"This isn't about anything religious, is it?" she asked. "Because if it is—"

"We'll talk about it later. You'll have to trust me for now."

"Trust you? Ha! I'd just as soon throw myself into a kougar pit."

"Dammit, agree with me for once, would you?" He didn't have time to argue. Why couldn't she conduct a single conversation without being antagonistic?

Her lips compressed. "I don't like to be told what to do. I've had enough from my Pa in that regard. Sorry, find yourself another lackey."

"If you don't cooperate, I'll inform Sirvat about your conspiracy regarding the tithing count. The villagers will be punished. You wouldn't want innocent families to come to harm because of your misdeeds, would you?"

"Fine, I'll do it, but you *will* regret this."

He raised an eyebrow. "Is that so? I'll look forward to your retribution." His voice hardened. "Get your things. I'll give you fifteen minutes to be ready."

She howled with frustration as he turned toward the door, intending to wait outside for her to join him. What was it about this woman that irritated and yet intrigued him? His blood boiled from their encounter, but other body parts stirred as well. Be careful, he warned himself. Look to your soul, or she'll steal it like she did Lothar's tribute.

He exited the house, resolving to offer a special prayer asking their deity for forgiveness. His thoughts of Swill were far from pious, which indicated a sinful weakness of his spirit.

****

Leena looked so downcast after switching off her comm unit that Taurin couldn't help feeling sorry for her. If only her eyes weren't so large and such a unique shade of azure. Her presence energized his nerves and heightened his senses in a way he hadn't felt for a long time.

She wears a circlet, he reminded himself. *She's pledged to serve Lothar.*

"What does your brother do?" he asked, wondering if her sibling was also a member of the Caucus.

"Bendyk is a missionary. He's devoted to the principles of our religion. He must have left to seek help from that woman he met in Amat."

"Too bad. Now you're stranded here." Taurin stepped forward until their bodies nearly touched. Her vanilla scent pervaded his nose, tempting him to do something wicked.

"I can drive you home," he offered against his better judgement. "Leave your rider key here, and I'll take your vehicle to the station in the morning."

"I'm sorry to be such a burden, but I appreciate your help." After retrieving her cloak from the rider and handing him the keys, she followed him to his vehicle.

Taurin held the passenger door open for her, his loins stirring as she slid inside, folding one long leg after the other.

He forced away the unwanted surge of desire that held him in its powerful grip and pulled a dark cloth from his pocket to swathe about his head. He couldn't risk the woman seeing his eyes at night.

In the driver's seat, he started the ignition then set off, rushing along the winding country roads to make the trip as brief as possible. The black-painted rider had a low-slung design that made it hug the road like a tightrope walker.

Beside him, Leena clutched her seat. "Can't you slow down?" she asked, her voice strained.

Taurin noted her pallor. Without commenting, he eased back on the accelerator.

"I'll get a ride out here in the morning," she told him. "It's best if we don't delay our journey. Will that give you enough time to get ready?"

He nodded, displeased at the idea of visiting Grotus. He had a feeling Captain Sterckle might have sold his bibliotomes to the unscrupulous artifacts dealer. Sterckle could even have told Grotus about him. Was the danger involved worth the possible rewards?

He sought only two things in life—peace for his troubled soul and knowledge of his origins. The first he'd already achieved, but Leena could help him obtain the second.

He was well aware of the danger her presence posed. Her delicate beauty and unattached status offered a temptation he could barely resist, but she was off limits to a man like him. Leena's station forbade her from associating socially with a mere farmer, and she must never discover his true background.

Magar had sworn him to secrecy in exchange for giving him the small plot of land he called his own. He was obligated, upon his honor and for his safety, to remain silent. But that wouldn't prevent him from learning what the symbols carved into Xan's ancient ruins meant. If Leena didn't know, perhaps they could find out together. Those inscriptions were linked to his heritage. By deciphering them, he might discover his destiny.

Yes, the time had come for him to emerge from his secure cocoon. Magar was sending him on this errand, which meant the situation was critical. The personal danger to him was minimal compared to the global threat. And yet, as they sped along the darkened rural roads, he had the feeling they'd merely touched the tip of an iceberg.

An even greater peril loomed, one that none of them could fathom in its immensity. The signs were there in the missing horn, the Truthsayer movement, and the weather changes. Xan was plunging inexorably toward catastrophe. Would he and Leena be able to stop the forces of evil from overwhelming her world?

Where Taurin came from, they'd already won. He had sworn he wouldn't let the same thing happen here.

****

Bendyk and Swill arrived back at the Palisades late that night. In the morning they held a strategy council with Leena, who took an instant liking to Swill, noting the rebellious gleam in the girl's eye. Leena smiled warmly and grasped both her hands in welcome.

"I'm so glad you've agreed to help my brother," she said. Bendyk had told her Swill was twenty-one, four years younger than herself, and two years younger than her baby brother.

The young woman wore a wraparound skirt and sweater, more conservative garb than Leena would have expected from Bendyk's earlier comments. Swill gave her an appraising onceover, as though Leena wasn't what she'd expected either. Leena wore her long hair loose in defiance of the custom, and she lacked the righteous airs her brother possessed.

"I didn't agree to anything," Swill confessed, slipping her hands free. "Your brother blackmailed me into coming here."

Leena cast a startled glance at Bendyk. "Oh? Would you care to elaborate?"

"It's a private matter between Swill and me. We'll do fine together," he stated with a grin.

Swill muttered an expletive, then addressed Leena. "Sorry. I forgot we're in a holy place."

"Don't worry about it." Leena studied the fine contours of the girl's face and the upward tilt of her chin, which indicated strength of character. Her blunt haircut and unadorned clothes showed that comfort and practicality mattered more to her than societal standards. Certainly, Swill must offend her brother's sense of propriety.

Leena glanced at Bendyk. His gaze hadn't lifted from Swill ever since they'd stepped into the room. She wondered at his obvious interest. What had occurred to make Swill so hostile toward him?

Their father wished she and Bendyk would both settle down. Bendyk was younger and had time to seek a mate. But Leena had often wondered how he would find a woman who'd appease his sense of morality. She'd always thought the daughter of a Candor, someone like herself, might attract him, but it appeared instead that this rebellious young woman had captured his attention.

"What do you find so amusing?" Bendyk demanded.

Leena waved a hand. "Never mind. Let's discuss how we're

going to stay in touch with each other. I've asked Sirvat to join us so she can give instructions on locating Grotus, and Karayan said he would stop by also. Have you eaten yet?"

"Aye," Bendyk said. "We had breakfast delivered to our apartments earlier this morning. So tell us about this Taurin fellow. What kind of impression did he give you?"

"He's an odd sort, but I think he might be the right man for the job."

Before she could say another word, Karayan strode into the room. He greeted each one of them in turn, including Swill after Bendyk introduced her.

"Good and welfare, children. Have I interrupted your planning session?"

"I've asked Leena to tell us about Taurin Rey Niris," Bendyk told his father's friend.

Leena nodded. "The man has agreed to help me, but he needs someone to tend his farm while we are gone."

Karayan peered at her. "His farm? Where does he live?"

"He raises flowers down at Lexington Page."

"Isn't that the same region where Magar has his estate?"

"Yes, it is. If you recall, Magar is the one who suggested I approach Taurin."

Karayan's brow furrowed. "What else did you learn about this fellow?"

"He lives by himself. He has an interest in ancient ruins. I saw some sketches of the carvings I've been studying, but I'm not really sure why he's interested in the subject. My mention of being an archeologist seemed to sway him in favor of accepting my proposal."

"Did he say where he came from?" Karayan asked.

"No, he's told me nothing about his background. The man is a skilled fighter. He broke up a brawl in the town pub. He may be the right choice for a protector, but it will be difficult traveling with him. He's not much of a talker and reveals little about himself."

"I don't know if I am pleased by your words or not. Your safety is our prime concern. How do we know we can trust this man?"

"The Minister of State would not have sent me to someone unworthy. I trust Magar's judgement."

"What is your destination?" Bendyk cut in.

"Sirvat needs to give me that information," Leena answered. "I hear footsteps outside. Maybe that's her coming now. Swill, could you please open the door?"

Sirvat, wisps of red hair peeking from beneath a wool fascinator hat, walked in amid a swish of white robes. "Karayan," she snapped. "What are you doing here?"

"I was just looking after these young people's welfare," he stated amiably, flicking a speck of imaginary dust from his tailored frock coat. Aside from religious ceremonies, he preferred his own style of dress to ecclesiastical garb.

In contrast, Sirvat liked to flaunt her station with pristine robes. Her one concession to vanity was the hats she wore, which also served to cover up her thinning hair.

"Our conversation must be private." Sirvat gave him a meaningful glance.

"In that case, I was just leaving." Karayan offered her a mocking bow, then turned toward Leena and Bendyk. "Message me if you need any assistance, children. I am always available to help you."

"Good and welfare," Bendyk called as Karayan left.

"This is your brother?" Sirvat asked Leena.

She introduced him and Swill, realizing Sirvat hadn't had the chance to meet them earlier.

"Where do you plan to start your investigation?" Sirvat said to Bendyk.

"I was thinking we should look into Treasury funds," he said in a mild tone.

Sirvat stiffened. "My department can undergo any kind of scrutiny. You'll find our record-keeping is exemplary." Her gaze narrowed at Swill. "Haven't I seen you somewhere before?"

A smile curved the corners of Swill's mouth. "I work in your department, Your Honor. I'm one of the tax agents."

"Ah, I thought you looked familiar."

Leena cut into their conversation, hoping to get the information she required. "Taurin Rey Niris has agreed to accompany me on my journey. What can you tell me about Grotus? Where can I find him, and what makes you think he might have the horn?"

"I have no idea if he has the artifact," Sirvat admitted, "but I believe he's the best person to ask. If anyone stole it for money, it would have crossed through Grotus's hands by now. And if not, perhaps his agents possess useful information. You can always suggest a trade," she said, a sly look coming over her face.

"What do you mean?" Leena asked.

"If Grotus has not heard the horn is missing, you'll have valuable information to offer him. In return, there are things he might know that you could find of interest."

"Such as?"

Sirvat shrugged. "That'll be for you to find out."

Leena peered at her suspiciously. Sirvat appeared to know more than she was willing to tell. It would be interesting to see what Bendyk's investigation uncovered. "Where do I have to go?" she said, curiosity taking hold.

Sirvat reached into a pocket in her voluminous robe and drew out a piece of parchment. She moved to a table and unfolded the document, which turned out to be a world map.

"We can provide air transport for you to Port Donner, located here." Sirvat pointed to a spot on the coastline of a subtropical region halfway around the world. "From there, you'll have to find a means to cross the Tortis Sea to the Black Lands."

Leena gasped. Those who defied the Faith were banished to the Black Lands, and since they didn't worship Lothar, the region lacked his protection. She had never dreamed that her quest would take her into such a wilderness.

"There is commerce between Port Donner and Garu, the

southernmost village in the Black Lands," Sirvat went on. "Transport should be available between those two points. You may have greater difficulty traversing the land mass. Its terrain varies from rugged, snow-capped mountains in the central portion to hot and humid coastal lowlands. Rivers and streams flow down the mountain slopes. The largest river, called the Kile, has a broad swampy delta. Steep mountain ridges, grassy plateaus, and deep forested valleys cover much of the interior."

Leena swallowed hard. Missionaries had gone into the area to convert the native tribes, as well as to counsel the dissidents, but their reception had been hostile. Indeed, some of them had never been heard from again.

"We believe Grotus resides on an island in this archipelago." Sirvat indicated a series of dots in the Pavian Ocean, located off the northern coast of the Black Lands. "No one knows his exact location. You'll have to find some means to reach this place, assuming you're able to pinpoint it. Grotus must have his own means of transportation, because we're unable to track his movements. Be careful when you make inquiries. Anyone attempting to search for Grotus's hideaway has vanished."

"Vanished!" Bendyk exclaimed. "What do you mean?"

"He guards his privacy as a *langmuir* does its den. It is impossible to get close to him. As you know, there have been widespread thefts of artifacts from holy sites around the world. Unscrupulous collectors would pay anything to get their hands on these valuable objects. We suspect the smugglers are linked to a network operated by Grotus, but no one has been able to trace them. Your journey will be dangerous. Even if you manage to reach the ringleader's island, he might have you killed upon arrival."

Her cool jade gaze focused on Leena. "Take your circlet along to convince Grotus of your identity, but keep it hidden during your voyage. If the Truthsayers get wind of your mission, they're apt to try to stop you. It would be best if you travel incognito."

"But how would the Truthsayers know what she's doing?" Bendyk said. "Only the members of the Synod and the Caucus, along with Swill and I, know of her assignment."

"One of us stole the horn, remember?" Sirvat's eyes blazed. "I don't trust anyone in this place."

Brother and sister exchanged glances. Leena was fast learning she had no one to turn to except her own brother. How sad that her world's leaders couldn't even be trusted. For that matter, how did Sirvat know so much about Grotus? Her detailed descriptions were odd unless she'd had the smuggler investigated by her Treasury department.

Sirvat brushed a stray hair off her stern face. "After you've seen Grotus, message me immediately. I'll do what I can to aid you on the return journey. Dikran said you should report back to the Palisades when you have completed your task."

Their chances for success seemed slim, and Leena's spirits sank. "What if we fail to obtain the horn? Grotus may know nothing about the theft."

"True, but once he learns it's on the market, he may pursue the horn himself. You can keep an eye on him and follow his trail."

Chapter Six

Once Leena and Bendyk were alone, she smiled at her brother. "I like Swill. She seems to have a sensible head on her shoulders. She'll give you good advice."

Bendyk grimaced. "Yes, if she talks to me. In your presence, she acts polite, but when we're alone, she barely speaks."

"Did you insult her with your religious dictates?"

He stiffened. "I merely commented on the moral standards applicable to our society."

Leena snorted. "No wonder she dislikes you. Be more tolerable, and she might soften."

Bendyk put a hand on her shoulder. His eyes, the same deep blue as hers, held a serious expression. "I'm worried about you. Your journey is dangerous, and you travel with a stranger. I should be the one going on this mission. I am used to traveling and meeting all types of people."

"But only I can verify the horn's authenticity," Leena replied. "What if someone produces a counterfeit and tries to ransom it back to the Synod? The horn is inscribed with the same carvings I have been studying. It's an amazing piece. There is nothing else like it on our…"

Halting abruptly, Leena bit her tongue. She had almost said there was nothing else like it on their world. What had she been thinking to nearly blurt out such a thing to her brother?

It was the same type of observation, made about the ring she'd found in the ruins on her last dig, that had gotten her into such deep trouble with Zeroun. No one was allowed to question the teachings of Lothar, or to speculate about where the Apostles had originated. To even propose that they might have come from another world was to doubt their divinity.

She'd tried to interpret the inscription on the ring's thin band. It was the same sequence of symbols she'd seen on the walls of ancient ruins and on the horn, but she didn't have any more success than in the past. Taurin's sketch displayed the same markings, she remembered, vowing to learn more about him at the earliest opportunity.

"What type of clothes should I take on this trip?" she pondered aloud. "Perhaps I should take my archeological outfits. We might run into savages in that untamed land."

Bendyk stared at her in horror. "Wearing breeches goes against your womanly nature, Sister. You'll take your gowns lest this Taurin fellow thinks you're a loose woman."

Her brother may be right, Leena thought, but she'd still pack a couple of more practical items into her valise just in case. Perhaps some of her tools as well.

****

Several hours later, Leena was packed and ready to depart. Dikran, the Arch Nome, summoned her for a final audience.

"I want you to report directly to me upon your return," the older man said.

"Yes, your eminence." Leena was dismayed by the distressed look on Dikran's face. He must be terribly shaken by recent events, especially since he couldn't trust anyone among his senior counselors. Aging had stolen his strength and the ability to command his people with the rigid authority that was required. Zeroun might do better in his stead, but she feared that under his dominance, oppression would rule the land.

There was no easy solution, except for her to find the horn and bring the situation to rights. The dissension and uprisings were for people like her brother to eradicate. Her job remained within the archeological realm, and for the first time a sense of excitement filled her veins. This would be the ultimate adventure, and the recovery of the horn, her greatest find. She must succeed!

She bid farewell to Dikran and hastened through a series of elegantly-appointed chambers toward the exit. Bendyk waited for her in a rider outside, her luggage already secured in his trunk.

"I'm looking forward to meeting your escort," he said. "If the man doesn't measure up, I won't allow you to go with him."

"Nonsense," Leena scoffed. "Who else will protect me? I've witnessed with my own eyes his prowess as a fighter. His violent nature might not thrill me, but Magar chose him for this mission. Where is Swill?"

"She has already begun her audit of Treasury records. I'll meet her later this afternoon to compare notes. Meanwhile, I've enlisted the aid of the Caucus in running background checks on each Synod member. I will supervise those efforts myself."

"One of them is a thief, who won't want his villainy to be discovered. There could be danger for you at the Palisades, even though it may be less evident than the road I travel."

"Understood." A frown creased his forehead. "It disturbs me that I won't be able to contact you."

She laid a hand on his arm. "I promise I'll message you at the earliest opportunity."

The drive took an hour and a half. Leena enjoyed the breeze that blew in from the open rider windows. Bendyk's vehicle was a sedate, forest-green sedan. Like Voshkie, Minister of Commerce, her brother didn't believe in overt displays of his status. Modesty was his byword, and he had glanced with disapproval at the two large suitcases she'd brought along.

"You told me to pack my gowns," she'd reminded him.

"Yes, but you've brought enough for months of travel."

Leena shrugged. "Who knows how long we'll be gone?" Inwardly she quivered at his words. For all she knew, they could be true, and she dreaded spending so much time in Taurin's taciturn company.

Apparently, Taurin was expecting them. As soon as their vehicle pulled into his driveway, he flung open the front door.

"You must be Bendyk," he told her blond-haired brother, shaking both his hands in greeting. Taurin's muscular build was barely concealed beneath a belted black longshirt and a pair of hip-hugging trousers. "I took your sister's rider in for servicing this morning and got a lift home. It would help if you could pick it up after the work is done, since Leena and I will be gone."

"I'll take care of it," Bendyk agreed.

As Taurin handed him the receipt from the station, Leena cast a surreptitious glance at the tall, darkly handsome man. She was pleased to find his head uncovered by the cloth he favored. Recalling that he'd only worn it in the tavern and the darkened interior of his rider, she wondered at its purpose. Unencumbered, Taurin's striking features commanded her attention.

"I'm going on this journey with your sister because I hope to learn the answers to questions similar to hers," Taurin explained to Bendyk. "I know little about your god or this missing horn but will do my part in helping to find the holy object."

Bendyk pounced on his words. "What do you mean, you know little of *our* god? Do you not worship Lothar?"

A half-smile twisted Taurin's countenance. "I have my own beliefs, or lack of them. What I believe is irrelevant to our mission."

Bendyk's hair glinted gold in the sunlight. "Your opinions certainly do have relevance. I won't allow you to travel with my sister in sin. There's only one option. I will see you both wed before I go."

"What?" Leena and Taurin both said in unison.

"Normally a trial marriage may only take place during Beltane, but exceptions can be made. I have the authority to make such a decision. I repeat, Sister, you will not travel with this man in sin. I will marry you, and when you complete your mission, the vows can be annulled. They need be in name only, but it will legalize your companionship."

Taurin's face darkened with fury, and the sense of menace emanating from him was like a thundercloud blotting out the sun. "This is absurd. Let's get on with our business. We must leave immediately."

"We have a flight to catch in forty-five minutes," Leena reminded her brother. "We cannot waste time."

Bendyk's hand clasped her arm. "I insist on this, Leena, or I'll tell Father what you're doing."

"So what? I don't care if it spoils my chances of marrying Malcolm."

Taurin tilted his head. "Malcolm? Who is that?"

"A man she will be wed to come next Auden," Bendyk stated. "Malcolm will understand the circumstances once your role in recovering the horn is explained, but he would never forgive you if he learned you traveled with a stranger under immoral conditions."

Leena's heart twisted with indecision. At the moment, she didn't care what Malcolm thought about her, but she had been considering accepting his proposal. She'd messaged him and her Father to let them know she'd be away on ecclesiastical business without going into any details. Malcolm had wanted to see her to discuss a date for their formal betrothal, but she'd put him off.

Facing him upon her return would be easier if she didn't have to rationalize her situation. She and Taurin had no idea what arrangements they would have to make in traveling together. It would be convenient if she could say he was her husband, although the notion made her tremble.

She raised her eyes to meet his dark expression. "It would bring me a measure of comfort," she told him quietly. "My brother is empowered to conduct the ceremony. We shall be wed in name only, and you will have no further obligations when our task is finished."

She swallowed hard, afraid he would reject her offer, but the man stared at her with an odd light in his peculiar gray eyes.

"All right," he said. "I agree. But like all good wives, you must obey my commands thereafter."

A beatific smile lit Bendyk's face. "That's a fair agreement. I am not happy about this deception, but I won't have it said that I let my sister travel with a strange man in sin. This is the best solution. Where do you come from?" he asked Taurin, as though realizing he knew little about the man about to become his sister's husband.

Taurin's gaze skittered away. "I'm from Iman."

Leena knew of the remote region even though she'd never traveled there. That might explain Taurin's abrupt manner.

Bendyk performed the marriage ceremony in Taurin's living room. When it was over, her brother glanced around with interest. "I see you've been studying the ancient inscriptions like my sister."

Sketches lay everywhere, ink drawings of symbols from ancient ruins. Books on the subject were scattered about the room. Otherwise, the house was kept in a meticulous fashion.

"I have my own reasons for my research," Taurin commented without elaborating.

He had only one valise. Bendyk put it alongside Leena's luggage in the trunk of his vehicle. He would drive them to the airfield and then return to the Palisades to pursue his own investigation.

Leena sat in front beside him, afraid to be near Taurin, who'd climbed into the backseat without a word. At the last minute, Taurin had decided he didn't need anyone to tend his farm in his absence, and Leena realized he didn't want anyone snooping around the place.

"I'll have to ask Magar about their relationship," Bendyk had whispered into her ear on their way out. "This property seems to occupy a corner of Magar's estate, but it isn't fenced off like it would be if Taurin owned the land. Maybe I'll find out more when I check into Magar's background. I can also send inquiries to Iman about Taurin's origins."

"Don't worry about me, Bendyk. I'll be fine."

"May your words reach Lothar's ears. I will pray for you."

She hoped her brother was praying for them when their flight took off from the airfield thirty minutes later.

****

Taurin sat stiffly in a seat beside Leena. They were alone in the aircraft cabin, the vessel having been commissioned for their private use. The crew remained up front, behind a cockpit door.

He noted a self-service refreshment center located toward the rear and a rack filled with magazines. None of them appealed to him. As Leena sagged back on her cushion and closed her eyes, he stared out the window at passing clouds.

How had he fallen into this predicament? Leena's attitude seemed impious compared to her brother's serious intensity, yet here they were as man and wife. His heart thudded at her proximity. She looked too lovely by far, with her blond hair streaming over her shoulders and the ruby-red gown hugging her curves. Her vanilla scent reached his nose, and his body responded.

How had he let himself become responsible for her? She was dedicated to the service of Lothar, and he, an unholy soul, had been put in charge of her protection. He could barely contain the lust that percolated beneath his surface in her presence. How would he protect her from his own desire? Demon's blood!

He had never been so surprised as when her brother had made his proposal. Too stunned to argue, he had merely let the trial marriage take place. Usually, Beltane lasted for a month, but some trial marriages continued for years.

He didn't expect their farce to go on for long. Annulments were common after the handfast ended, and doubtless his bride would apply as soon as their mission finished. In the meantime, he'd have to keep his secrets close. His young wife would be repulsed if she learned the truth about him.

Raking a hand through his hair, he shifted his position. The flight was supposed to take eleven hours, with a refueling stop along the way. Without a moving picture to entertain them, it would be a long journey indeed.

****

Deep in the bowels of the Palisades, a revered member of the Synod discussed their mission using a scrambled messenger system.

"They are heading for Port Donner," the Synod member told the person who'd answered the line. "Leena and Rey Niris seek an audience with Grotus. They must not return. Do you understand?"

A chuckle sounded at the other end. "Of course. It is best if the horn is not recovered."

"Never mind the horn. Leena knows too much. Make sure they're intercepted when you pick up their trail."

"Your will shall be done, Your Honor. Hail to the cause!"

The Synod leader terminated the communication, smiling grimly. Once these orders were carried out, the threat from Leena would be eliminated. The leader would keep an eye on her brother, and if he posed a problem, he'd be disposed of as well. Their plans had been set into motion, and no one would be allowed to interfere.

Glory will be mine! Soon all of Xan will bow before me. Lothar's time is nearly over, and my reign is about to begin.

****

"Tell me more about the missing horn," Taurin said to Leena after she'd awakened from a brief nap.

Leena glanced at him, her nerves taut. The unexpected wedding ceremony had taken its toll, especially after Bendyk had said he would enter the marriage into the ecclesiastical books to make it legal. She trembled at the thought of being with this taciturn man in the days and nights to follow.

"You already know the horn's function," she replied. "It's

needed to awaken Lothar. I had a chance to examine it once. The horn is made from a strange material that has a creamy, almost translucent color. Have you ever been to the Holy Temple during Renewal?"

"No, I haven't. What do you know of the symbols carved into the relic?"

"They represent a repetitive sequence. I haven't been able to decipher what it means. There are many things I don't understand about our past that I would like to learn. The horn is made of a substance unknown anywhere else on Xan. And so is the ring I found on my last excavation."

As soon as the words left her mouth, she realized she'd made a mistake. Hopefully he wouldn't catch her on it. But Taurin was sharp.

"What ring?" he asked, glowering at her.

"I'd recovered a small, circular object on my last dig. The ring was made from the same pearly substance as the horn. I reported it to my superior, who in turn told Zeroun. He impounded the ring, saying it was important for security that we keep this discovery under wraps."

"So you never heard anything more about it?"

"No, but I did receive an invitation to join the Caucus. I realized Zeroun wanted to ensure my silence, but why? What was the significance of that artifact? Where had it originated? Did it relate to the Apostles? Why did they establish the rule of Lothar and then leave us alone?"

"No one has those answers." Taurin's gaze darkened as though the subject troubled him, too.

She shook her head in confusion. "I wish I knew what was going on. We might be able to understand the weather disasters that are plaguing us now. I don't believe they're due to Lothar's wrath. Something isn't right."

Should she inform him about her father's deviation from the Faith? Probably not, she decided. It wouldn't be in her best interest to reveal too much at one time.

"How did you get interested in archeology?" he asked with a quick glance her way.

She shrugged. "I've always been fascinated by Xan's history. We lived near a ruin where I grew up, and I explored the site. I love the excitement of uncovering secrets from the past. What gave you an interest in the ruins, Taurin? Why do you have sketches of those symbols around your house?"

His expression shuttered. "It's merely a hobby. Look, here comes one of the crew."

Leena lifted her gaze, but no one emerged from the cockpit. Mere moments later, however, the door opened and out strode the co-pilot to offer refreshments and see to their comfort.

How did Taurin know the man would be coming?

She accepted a fruit drink and a snack and waited until the crew member returned to his duty before turning back to Taurin.

"Tell me, what made you decide to raise flowers for a living?"

He munched on a handful of nuts. "I owed a baker who had done me a great service, and I wished to repay him. I remembered the candied flowers he used on his sweet breads. The blooms were extremely expensive, so I decided to raise edible flowers myself. I send him a complimentary shipment every month, and the others I sell on the free market." A proud look entered his eyes. "It's quite a lucrative business. There aren't many other flower farmers who grow this crop."

"I would think not," Leena agreed. "And do you pay Magar with produce as well?"

"Magar?"

"I noticed that your property abuts his estate, and I was wondering if you rented from him."

"No, I own my piece of land."

Leena fell silent, realizing he didn't wish to talk about his relationship to Magar. Still, it puzzled her. There was something going on between the two of them, but this wasn't the appropriate time to make further inquiries. Besides, Bendyk was working the other end. He might find out more about Magar's secrets.

"You have no woman," she blurted out.

Taurin coughed and grabbed a gulp of water. "Does that bother you?"

"It must be a lonely life, tending the farm and living at your cottage without companionship."

"I've sought peace and harmony my entire life, and I'd finally found it. At least I did, until you showed up."

Chapter Seven

Taurin sat rigidly in his seat as Leena's fatigue overwhelmed her. Her head drifted onto his shoulder. Honeyed tresses trailed across his chest, their fragrance as sweet as the blossoms in his garden. With trembling fingers, he touched a lock, relishing the silken feel of her hair as it rippled through his fingers. She breathed softly, her breasts rising and falling with each respiration.

He pressed his lips together as she repositioned herself. Her slender hands folded one on top of the other in her lap, and he quelled the surge of desire that rose within him. How would he tolerate being in such close contact with her in the weeks ahead?

His gaze drifted down the length of her gown. She was perfection, not only in body, but also in spirit. She was devoted to her god and loyal to her people. Intelligent as well as beautiful, she'd make a fabulous mate for a man. If only he could hope for a union with someone like her. But it was impossible. She was too good for him, too pure, never mind their difference in stations in life. She would be horrified if she learned his true background.

The description of the horn intrigued him. The substance sounded similar to the entwined rings he wore as a band around his right arm, hidden under his clothes where no one could see it. When separated, the three rings served as a baby's toy. They had been left with him when he was abandoned by his parents, and the gang leader who'd taken him in had let Taurin keep them. Spinning the rings had been one of his favorite pastimes as a child on Yllon. The musical notes had delighted him, and there had been few joys on that violent world.

It wasn't until he was older that he'd learned how they fitted together into a wide bracelet. Viewed as a single band, the symbols carved into the material became evident. Taurin realized those symbols were significant when he saw them engraved onto books hidden in the repository on Yllon. Those same carvings had shown up on Xan, and it was one of the reasons why he'd settled here. He'd hoped to learn more about his heritage and how the two worlds, total opposites in nature, were linked.

He'd spoken of peace, but now that peace was threatened. The harmony throughout Xan was on shaky ground. Dark forces marched across the land, and Taurin feared their evil. He'd grown up with it and had cast it away, and now it was inexorably creeping in his direction again, drawing him into the darkness.

****

Leena's senses sharpened as she awakened. With sudden clarity of thought, she realized her head was leaning on Taurin's shoulder. It was a remarkably comfortable position, but a too familiar one. Despite her being able to call him husband, she wished to avoid personal contact between them. His slightest touch unnerved her, and she didn't care for him to notice.

Clearing her throat, she straightened and smoothed down her dress. Her motions seemed to discomfort Taurin, who'd been sitting with a rigid posture. Abruptly he got up and strode toward the rear of the aircraft, where the restrooms were located.

Leena ran a hand over her face. The man was so dark and imposing, yet she felt more alive in his presence. He'd only left her for a few moments, and already she felt bereft of his company. It was with relief that she watched him return and settle into his seat.

Edging herself away from him, she smiled shyly. "Will we be landing soon?"

"We have an hour left before the layover," he replied, busying himself with reading material in the interim.

They ate a light meal before landing, spent a couple of hours on the ground while the plane refueled, and then resumed their flight. The rest of the trip passed easily as Leena told him what she knew of each Synod member.

They finally arrived at Port Donner on the afternoon following their departure.

Outside, Taurin gathered their luggage and surveyed the scene. The small airfield was not frequented often, and theirs was the only plane in sight. According to what the pilot had told them, outcasts from society were brought here and then taken across the Tortis Sea to the Black Lands, where they spent the rest of their lives in exile. No one else ventured far from here except for some merchant ships, which made regular runs to Garu for trade and mail.

"I'll find us a ship," Taurin told Leena after a driver transported them to the wharf. "Perhaps we can sail around the eastern tip of the Black Lands to the archipelago."

Leena nodded, excited by the idea. It would be much better if they didn't have to cross the width of the Black Lands. Her eager gaze scanned the bustling waterfront scene. Masts and spars from sailing vessels reached toward the sky like outstretched fingers. Mountains of goods were piled high on the dock. A surging crowd of sailors, tradesmen, and fishing crews toiled laboriously, oblivious to the heat and humidity that caused perspiration to trickle down her face.

She longed for a cooling ocean breeze, but dark clouds lumbered overhead. A heavy stillness filled the air, which stank of fish. Distant rumbles of thunder sounded, and she feared it would rain before they found transport.

"Wait here with our luggage while I make inquiries," Taurin ordered.

****

Taurin strode along the pier, stopping at each ship until he found a captain willing to accept passengers. Captain Riez picked at his rotting teeth while contemplating Taurin's request.

72

"The facilities ain't much," Riez told him, "but you can jine us if you're able to pay."

"How much?" Taurin asked with a wry twist to his lips.

"Fifty chekels each, and I only got one cabin."

"What do you mean, *one* cabin? We require two staterooms."

"I thought you said you was married."

"Well… er… yes, but the lady requires extra space for her dressing room."

"One cabin; take it or leave it." Riez spat into the water.

"We'll take it," Taurin said hastily. "Is there someone who can help us with our luggage?"

The captain gave a short, raucous laugh. "Sorry, brother. We ain't sailin' for another two days. You'll have to put up in town if you want to ship out with us."

"Two days! You didn't say that before."

"You're not going to find anyone else to take you. I'll need a cash deposit."

Taurin saw the avarice glinting in the captain's jaundiced eye and realized he wouldn't get a better deal. He pulled a ten-chekel note from the wad in his pocket and handed it over. "Here you go. Is there anything else I should know?"

"Our grub ain't the best, so if you want to bring any of your own chow aboard, you may want to visit the village market 'ere you board."

"Thanks for the advice." Taurin tilted his head in acknowledgement, turned on his heel, and left.

****

Leena amused herself while waiting for Taurin's return by watching the frenzy of activity on the wharf. Huge cranes off-loaded bins labeled with the popular Chocola Company's logo from several vessels. Brawny workmen loaded bags of mail, crates of canned goods, and bales of fabric onto container ships along with machinery parts and medical supplies.

As the laborers caught sight of her standing by in her finery, they gave her lecherous stares that made her pray for Taurin's quick return.

At his approach, her heart sank. His face wore a darkened scowl. By all that was holy, now what was wrong?

"I booked us a passage, but the ship doesn't sail for two days. We'll have to find accommodations in town until then."

Leena's brows arched. "Where do you expect to find a hostelry here?" The town was nothing more than a cluster of taverns, warehouses, and small businesses catering to the marine trade.

"We'll ask in one of the taverns," Taurin suggested. "I'll take my case and this one of yours. Can you manage the other?"

"Of course." She'd carried heavier loads on her archeological expeditions.

Glancing with dismay at her pristine gown and low-heeled pumps, she yearned for her work clothes. With a resigned sigh, she lifted her valise and accompanied Taurin across the cracked and uneven pavement, careful to watch her footing.

He halted in front of a tavern, its open doorway allowing the raucous din from inside to penetrate the street. The scent of liquor wafted into her nostrils, mingling with the stench of garbage from a bin at the corner. She wrinkled her nose in distaste.

"What are you doing?" she asked, curious when Taurin pulled from his pocket the familiar black cloth that matched his trousers.

"It may be dark inside. Wait out here until I assess the situation." He swathed the cloth around his head so that his eyes were shadowed.

Leena squinted in the bright afternoon sunlight that was rapidly becoming obliterated by the clouds. A salty gust blew into port, heralding rain.

"Why do you cover your head like that?" She couldn't read his expression under the hooded cloth.

"I choose this garb for my… security. It's necessary when

the light is dim enough to cast shadows or when I'm in a dark environment."

"But why?" she persisted, wondering what possible effect the darkness might have upon him.

He ignored her question and strode into the tavern. It wasn't long before Leena heard a commotion ensue from within. A few moments later he sauntered outside, his clothing rumpled and disorderly.

"You may enter. I've rented us a room upstairs."

"In *there*?" Leena cried, horrified. The place appeared to be a den of impropriety, and she dreaded entering the foul-smelling interior. He must have noticed her hesitation because his voice softened with his next words.

"I will see to your safety," he said reassuringly. "Pretend you are my dutiful wife and follow me directly to our room."

Our room? Leena swallowed hard as she obeyed, picking up her bag and trailing after him with her head bowed.

Were they to share a room here and a cabin on the ship as well? In truth, they were man and wife, but in name only. Surely Taurin didn't expect her to perform her wifely duties, did he? Her brother had made it quite clear this marriage would be annulled after their mission was over. Taurin couldn't be thinking in that vein. He must have rented the only accommodation available, or else he was simply seeing to her safety.

And for that I'm grateful, she told herself, entering the smoky, dimly-lit interior that reeked of liquor. Men in rough garb stared at her as she passed by, her head lowered. She'd never felt more glad for Taurin's presence than at this moment. His shoulders seemed broader than she remembered, his body taller. Dressed as he was, all in black, he appeared as menacing as a demon. A loud clap of thunder sounded from outside, as though Nature agreed with her. Surely none of these men would dare offend Taurin when his very being emanated danger.

Feeling less than brave herself, she followed him up a flight of stone steps and into a cramped, musty bedchamber. Dear deity, were they to spend the night in here together?

Her gaze swept the wide bed with its tattered coverlet and alighted on a dented bureau and a small table with a couple of chairs. Off to the side was a door to the lavatory. Electrical appliances were noticeably lacking.

"Where are the lights?"

"I don't think this area has electricity." Taurin set their suitcases in a corner. "We'll have to use that oil lamp on the table and the candles on the bureau. Those will suffice."

No electricity? This situation is rapidly deteriorating.

She swallowed a sense of dread. "Where are we going to sleep?"

"That bed looks comfortable enough to me."

"But, you can't expect me to… you and I can't…" Leena sputtered, unable to complete her sentence.

"If you would rather sleep in the chair tonight, madam, be my guest, but I for one intend to get a good night's rest. I've ordered a meal to be served in our room. Thereafter, I intend to scout the town to learn what I can of our destination. We may need more supplies."

"What about the ship that is supposed to take us there?" Leena strolled inside the room. "Did you ask about sailing around the tip of the island to reach Grotus's place?"

"Unfortunately, I couldn't find a ship's master willing to charter us a boat, nor does anyone go elsewhere other than Garu on the Black Lands. I was lucky enough to find us the cabin space I did."

Leena hadn't been impressed by the condition of the ships in port so she didn't press him for a description. "How long will it take to cross the Tortis Sea?"

Taurin shrugged. "Could be three or four days, depending on the weather."

"That long?" Leena stared at him. She'd thought it would be an easy crossing.

"Look, you either take the breaks or you go back to your sanctuary at the Palisades and let me handle this."

Leena drew herself upright. "I've been in worse places on digs. Perhaps I should change out of this gown and into my work clothes. That might convince you that I don't need your protection."

"Oh, no?" Although she couldn't see his shadowed face, she could imagine him quirking his eyebrows. "Would you care to venture downstairs by yourself and see what happens?"

Leena shuddered. "I didn't ask to be put in this position. You're being unfair."

"Am I?" He sauntered closer, and she could almost feel the powerful warmth from his body as he neared. "Do you expect your faith in Lothar to get you through the days ahead?"

"Of course I do. Don't you?"

"I believe in myself, Leena Worthington-Jax. No one else will look out for me. I would advise you not to rely on any supernatural entity to come to your assistance."

"How dare you mock Lothar. He's watching over us to see to our safety."

"You are wrong," Taurin said. "It is I who sees to our safety."

She moistened her lips, noting how his gaze followed her movements. Would he honor their agreement and keep his distance from her this night?

Taurin turned away to stare out a window as the first splattering of rain hit the panes. The room darkened, and he hastened to light an oil lamp. A soft glow filled the room, casting shadows into the far corners.

He gestured toward the bed. "Why don't you sit down? You're hovering about like a nervous mother hen."

Leena's blood boiled. How could she endure an evening alone with this man? He didn't even trust her enough to uncover his head before her. Nonetheless, she did as he suggested, testing the edge of the bed against her weight. The mattress sagged.

"What do you believe in, Taurin? Are you a heretic?"

"I told you, I believe in myself." He sank into one of the chairs while the fury of the storm raged outside. Flashes of lightning and cracks of thunder rent the air, but inside their room, a momentary sense of security pervaded the atmosphere. "I grew up in a violent society," he mentioned.

"Oh? I thought you came from Iman."

"Where I lived, we had to scrounge for survival. Existence was brutal. We learned to trust no one except ourselves."

"What a cynical attitude. Without faith, your life holds no meaning. No wonder you live alone."

"On the contrary, I believe life must be lived in the here and now, and it's what you make of it. I choose to live the way I do." He rose abruptly. "Now if you'll excuse me, I'll check on the delivery of our meal." He stalked out, closing the door none too gently behind himself.

Leena sat on the bed, her hands folded, contemplating their conversation. Taurin didn't believe in Lothar, but could he possibly be aligned with the Truthsayers? He hadn't said anything about going against the Synod or their structure of government. He appeared to want to live his own life in peace, regardless of his or anyone else's beliefs.

She should be able to trust him as long as he did his job of protecting her. And that was why he'd come along, wasn't it? Still it troubled her that he didn't believe in the Faith.

How could anyone not bend their knee before Lothar, who provided them with such blessings as a fruitful land and a temperate climate? And what about Lothar's lozenge? Did Taurin partake of it, even though he didn't acknowledge the source?

Troubled, she went to her luggage to see if her tools were intact. They might have need of them, because who knew what dangers faced them at the Black Lands?

This trip was folly. How would they ever cross that wild territory? Would they be able to locate Grotus's island even if they made it to the other side? How would they get there, and would Grotus agree to see them?

She rubbed her throbbing temples. They had too many obstacles to overcome.

Lothar, please help us! Please let us succeed in our mission.

Taurin returned shortly thereafter, followed by the proprietor, who set them a decent table and delivered their meal. After he left, Taurin and Leena sat facing each other. Taurin's head was still covered with the cloth, but she could see his stormy gray eyes.

"We must pray," she chided as he reached for a piece of bread.

"I'm hungry." Taurin tore a chunk off the crusty loaf.

"Wait, we must thank Lothar for his bounty."

He gave her a burning gaze that warmed her blood and heated her skin. Then he hastily stuffed the bread into his mouth.

Tears sprang into her eyes at his blasphemy. "You have insulted Lothar! Now we shall be punished."

"Don't be absurd. You'd better eat or the food will get cold."

Leena closed her eyes and prayed for their absolution. "Please forgive him," she begged Lothar. "He has strayed from the faith that I know is in his heart. He must believe in you because he raises your beautiful creations for a living," she said, meaning his flowers. Surely, he acknowledged the importance of the elements. "It is you who provides the sun and the warmth, and the moisture for us, O Lothar. We thank you for your bread and sustenance and your generosity in the past. Please stay with us on this journey, and forgive this man for his digression."

Dear deity, she sounded just like Bendyk. She didn't want to turn into a moral activist like him. Opening her eyes, she was dismayed to see Taurin chomping away, obviously enjoying the meal without any regard for her feelings.

Eating in silence, she avoided looking Taurin directly in the eye. Upon completion of the meal, her hand inadvertently brushed his when they straightened the table. A delightful tingling sensation assailed her fingertips, and she snatched her hand away.

"I'm heading out to scout the premises," Taurin said gruffly. "Don't leave this room."

The storm had ended, but a faint pattering of rain still hit the roof. She had no desire to go anywhere and longed to make herself comfortable in the soft bed.

"Be careful." She figured the characters around here would just as soon beat and rob him than let them pay their own way.

"Don't worry, no one will come near me unless I approach them first."

His tone of voice was so menacing that Leena shuddered. Yet after he left she couldn't make herself feel glad about his absence. She busied herself rearranging the items in her suitcases until fatigue overwhelmed her. She took off her gown and spent a few moments washing up before donning one of her simple nightdresses. It was made of a thin maille fabric and came to just below her knee. The short-sleeve top was comfortable and allowed her ease of movement in her sleep.

She crawled into bed, neither caring that the mattress was too soft and lumpy nor that the sheets appeared somewhat soiled. It was a haven for the night, and she sank into blissful repose with barely another thought.

****

Hours later, Taurin entered the room. The oil level in the lamp was low, and he could scarcely make out the shapely form lying in the bed. Careful to be quiet, he stripped off his clothes down to his briefs and slid between the sheets. His bones were chilled, but his throat still burned from the liquor he'd consumed downstairs.

He hadn't been able to resist Leena's allure earlier. Again, he'd been reminded of her similarity to his image of an angel—not that he believed in them. Her golden blond hair floated about her shoulders like strands of gossamer silk. The color of her gown accentuated the startling blue of her eyes.

A sudden urge to take her into his arms and kiss her senseless had nearly overwhelmed him. Hastily he'd stuffed his mouth with bread to suppress his unwanted desire.

He'd gained valuable information in the bar, but all that he'd learned fled from his mind as the warmth from Leena's body penetrated his senses. His loins surged with an answering heat, and he tensed with the need for release.

Tossing and turning, he tried to find a comfortable position, but Leena's soft breathing and tantalizing vanilla scent continued to torment him.

In a frenzy of desire, he leapt from the bed and paced the room until his muscles relaxed to the point where he could settle down. But as he approached the bed, his gaze fell on her bared shoulder, which peeked out from beneath the blanket she'd thrown back. His glance slid along the edge of her thin shift. Demon's blood, he'd never sleep tonight.

Chapter Eight

When Leena awoke the next morning, her gaze lit upon Taurin sleeping in the chair. Poor dear, she thought. He looked so different in repose. His face was relaxed and his manly jaw was surrounded by early morning stubble. Dark eyelashes fanned his cheeks like black bristles arranged in a half moon shape. His hair, tousled from his restless movements, lay in an unkempt manner across his forehead.

Besides removing his head cloth, he'd removed his clothes and lounged merely in a short, snug pair of briefs.

Leena swallowed as she stared at his strong body, mesmerized by the sight. The man fascinated her, and she longed to touch him, to explore his hard muscles and rugged angles. Chastising herself, she decided she'd better stop gawking and get dressed. But as soon as she stepped from the bed, his eyes popped open and he straightened, instantly alert.

Leena halted, her face heating as she stood in front of him in her thin ivory-colored shift. "I was just going to get dressed."

Taurin gave her a slow, lazy smile. "By all means, go ahead." His hooded gaze made her body tremble.

"Do you have to look at me so…?" Leena faltered, unable to finish her sentence. The blaze of desire she saw in Taurin's eyes shook her to the core.

He's aware of me as a woman. By all that is holy, what do I do now?

Taurin watched her with an unfathomable gleam in his smoky eyes. Aware of his perusal, Leena yanked the first gown she could reach from her valise and rushed into the lavatory.

How could she go on like this, sharing a room with the man when every glance, every movement he made caused her to tremble like a foolish schoolgirl?

That would be all right if they could observe the proprieties, but it was impossible to do so under current circumstances. *I will just have to make the best of it*, she decided, pulling the bright yellow gown over her head.

She brushed out her hair until fine waves spilled over her shoulders. It suddenly seemed important to present herself in a most feminine way, unlike with Malcolm whom she always wanted to shock by wearing breeches. Leena had no desire to earn Taurin's disapproval. Indeed, she thrilled to that special look in his eyes when he gazed at her.

Giving herself a final admonition to behave with decorum, she reentered their sleeping chamber.

"By Lothar, what are you doing?" She gaped at Taurin.

"I am exercising. It should be obvious." He performed sit-ups on the floor. His muscles rippled with each movement. A sheen of sweat covered his body.

Leena's mouth went dry. "You can't do that here."

"Why not, wife? I always exercise in the morning. Get used to it."

"But… but we have to say our morning prayer."

"You say the prayer. I'm working out."

Too shocked to make a retort, Leena turned towards the eastern side of the building, facing the rising sun. She prayed to Lothar for a peaceful day, ending her worship with a silent meditation. When she'd finished, she spared a glance at Taurin, who was now running in place. His bare feet thudded on the floor. Thanks be to Lothar, he had put on a pair of black trousers.

"Do you not partake of any of the ritual prayers?" Her brows furrowed at the notion that she'd wed a heathen.

"I told you, I don't pray to anyone."

"But how can you not believe in our god? Lothar provides us with the lozenge that prevents sickness and moderates our climate. Why do you not offer him thanks for his graciousness?"

Taurin stopped his efforts, his face taking on a thunderous expression. "Look, you have your beliefs, and I have mine. Don't intrude on my life."

Leena stiffened. "I beg your pardon. Have you forgotten that we are wed?"

"In name only, and as soon as this journey is ended, I intend to have our vows annulled."

He turned away and grabbed a clean shirt from his open suitcase. Then he marched into the lavatory and slammed the door. Leena sank miserably onto the edge of the bed. How would they ever get along when their personal philosophies were miles apart?

She'd never thought about what it meant to respect someone else's right to his own beliefs, because nearly everyone Leena knew worshiped Lothar. It had always been that way through recorded history, at least as she'd been taught.

Without Lothar's rules of order, chaos would reign. Her god's commandments held their society together. The Truthsayers proposed to establish a separate government, but she didn't see how they could detach governing the land from Lothar's laws.

These are matters Bendyk deals with every day. I commend him for his work. Truly, I'd rather be spending my time at an excavation site. At least one dealt with concrete topics in the field of archeology.

When Taurin came out of the restroom, she asked him if he'd learned anything interesting during his tour last night.

He nodded, drops of water glistening on his damp hair.

"We'll need a guide to cross the Black Lands. The best route is through one of the valleys. We'll have to see who's available when we get to Garu."

****

Taurin resolved to keep to himself the other things he'd learned last night. They'd find out more when they got to the Black Lands. If his suspicions were confirmed, he'd have Leena pass the information along to her brother.

In the meantime, they had a day to kill before their ship left on the morrow. He'd obtained a few extra supplies, and early the next morning they could visit the market to shop for groceries. But for now they were free.

"Did you bring nothing but those gowns?" He swept his hand in a broad gesture.

Leena gave him a startled look. "I brought along the outfits I wear on my archeological digs, breeches and short-sleeved tops."

"We have a free day today, so I thought we could spend it at Hathers Beach. The place is south of here within easy walking distance."

He'd had rare opportunities to spend time at the shore. Such a frivolous activity was unheard of on his world, and here he'd been too busy establishing his farm to engage in leisure pursuits. Sitting on a beach and gazing out to sea seemed to be the ultimate relaxation.

He'd looked forward to sharing the experience with Leena, but after their conversation this morning, he had his doubts it would be so pleasurable. If she kept expounding on her faith like her brother, he'd be tempted to clamp a hand over her mouth and toss her into the waves. He'd just have to steer the conversation in another direction.

He studied her fair, unblemished skin. "You'll be too hot in your gown. We'll buy you something new to wear at the marine shop, including a hat to shade your face."

Later on the beach, Taurin watched Leena as she tested her feet in the water. She wore a short tan tunic, which they'd found in the marine shop. He'd suggested she buy a couple of extras for their journey. Tunics were less cumbersome than her long gowns and would make traveling easier. He stared at her long, shapely legs as she faced the water, soaking her feet in the sun-kissed surf.

His chest bare, he enjoyed the warmth from the sun's rays that penetrated his skin. It was nothing compared to what he felt as he watched Leena. Every movement she made bespoke of grace and fine breeding. His loins stirred, and he yearned to take her into his arms, lower her onto the soft sand, and taste the outlines of her body with his lips.

No doubt she's thinking of her god, he thought ruefully. Xan was a beautiful world, and those who lived here were truly blessed. Perhaps there was a Creator who had designed the perfections of life. Certainly the flowers he grew indicated a higher intelligence at work. The brilliant colors, concentric circles of the petals and uniqueness of the varieties couldn't have developed from random evolution, could they? Is that what he believed in—that all things came from the fortunes of Nature? Or was there something more?

He'd seen how Lothar brought comfort to those who believed in him. He couldn't explain where the lozenges came from, except that they materialized in a sacred receptacle at each regional worship center during Mistic. The people attributed this miracle to Lothar. Nor did he know who controlled the weather satellites stationed in orbit around the planet, which he'd seen during his approach. Was it the hand of god or the hand of man at work?

One thing was for sure—only Dikran and the members of his Synod knew the answers.

Leena knelt down and splashed water on her face. Taurin observed her, wishing he could believe as she did. It would make life easier to feel you were not alone. His journey through life had been a difficult one. He'd earned his peace and harmony, thanks to his determination and hard work. But perhaps some deity was guiding his destiny. Unfortunately, Leena couldn't be part of it after their assignment was done.

His yearning for something he couldn't have saddened him. To shake off his morose mood, he decided to go for a swim. Exercise would get his mind off his dark thoughts. After stripping off his pants, he strode toward the water in his swim trunks. A moment later, he plunged into the ocean, his strong strokes taking him past Leena toward deeper waters. It felt good to plow through the waves. The vigorous exertion energized him.

Finally, he emerged from the water and waded onto shore. Leena sat on their beach blanket, a wide-brimmed hat shading her face. As he toweled himself off, her admiring eyes drank their fill of him. Her gaze roamed from his hairy chest downward to where his wet shorts clung to his hips. As though her mouth had suddenly gone dry, she grabbed for one of the water bottles they'd brought along and gulped down several swallows.

Taurin plunked himself down beside her. "Your arms are getting burned. I'll put some lotion on you." He couldn't help wanting to touch her and used the first excuse he could find.

"I can manage." Leena reached for the tube.

"Let me do it." Taurin snatched it up first and squeezed a line of creamy substance onto his fingertips.

****

Leena closed her eyes as his touch on her hot skin sent spirals of delight along her nerves. His smooth hands trailed up and down her arm, rubbing in the lotion. Even when she was sure the sunscreen must be fully applied, he continued to caress her skin. Both his hands moved to her shoulders as he gave her a light massage.

"You're too tense," he murmured, his low voice seducing her into a curious languor.

He kneaded deep into her muscles, and her body relaxed into a pliant state, like putty being molded. His practiced fingers knew just where to apply pressure or to lighten the touch. A small cry of pleasure escaped her lips when he tickled the back of her neck. Never had she imagined that a man's hands could feel so wonderful.

She opened her eyes and half turned so she could gaze into his face. The desire that blazed in his eyes made her breath come short. Her mouth parted, and before she knew what was happening, she was being swept into his arms, his mouth descending upon hers with crushing force.

Her mind reeled with the incredible sensations he created within her. His kiss had a desperate edge to it as he slanted his mouth over hers again and again. Then he was pushing her back onto the blanket, covering her body with his, his kisses becoming more urgent.

Taurin moaned her name, and her heart thudded faster. The weight of his body pressed her down, and the mere strength of him rendered her senseless with wanting. She snaked her arms around him until her hands splayed on his bare back. His muscles rippled beneath her fingers. Leena had never craved a man's touch before, but now she longed for him to move his hands across her body, touching her in all the places that burned with fire.

Taurin's mouth moved with the desperation of a man consumed by thirst. When his tongue plunged inside her mouth, she jerked beneath him, startled by the unexpected action. After she grew accustomed to his exploration, she hesitantly reached out with her own tongue. The swirl of sensations drove her to a frenzy she didn't understand.

Suddenly she felt a release, and when she realized his weight had lifted from her body, she opened her eyes, knowing her disappointment would be evident.

"Forgive me. I never meant for this to happen." He hovered above her, his eyes dark with remorse.

"Please don't apologize," she replied, glancing away. "It's my fault, too."

Taurin stood and brushed the sand from his body. "It won't happen again. I wouldn't want to earn your brother's disapproval upon our return to the Palisades."

Leena could imagine Bendyk's reaction. She flushed with embarrassment at her wanton behavior. Nonetheless, her glance slid to Taurin's riot of ebony hair, piercing gray eyes, and powerful physique. It was difficult for her to resist his overpowering masculinity. Truly their journey was fraught with danger, her interest in this man being the foremost threat.

As they packed their belongings, Taurin kept his distance

from her. Nor did he touch her again as they went into town to catch a quick meal at a café hidden away on a side street. Only when they were back in their room did he address the subject that caused such tension between them.

"I cannot sleep beside you," he confessed, "or I'll be tempted to take you into my arms. I'd better stay in the chair again tonight."

Leena quivered at his words. He desired her, and yet there were too many gulfs between them to yield to passion, even if she were willing. Sadly, she nodded her agreement and then changed the topic of conversation. After a while, he went out, leaving her alone. Feeling bereft of his presence, she fell into a troubled sleep.

The next morning when she awoke, the smell of liquor lingered in the room. *He must have been drinking*, she thought. *Did I cause him to do that?*

He faced her with a stony expression. "I've hired a porter. He'll bring our cases to the pier. Meanwhile, I ordered breakfast to be prepared for us in the parlor."

"I must perform my morning prayers. Do you care to join me?" Her voice held a note of hope, even though she knew he would refuse her offer.

"No, I'll meet you downstairs." Without a backward glance, he stomped out.

After breakfast, Leena followed Taurin to the market for provisions and then to the ship he'd hired to take them to the Black Lands. The wharf bustled with workers, the scene being similar to the one that had greeted them the day they arrived.

Leena's mouth gaped when she saw the ship named the *Predator*. A two-masted sailing vessel, her hull was painted stark black. The masts were square-rigged, and the bowsprit stood out like an *elgar*'s horns. The rigging rose high above, with the sails secured for mooring.

A man with a shuffling gait came out to greet them as they stepped onto the deck. His unshaven face held a permanent scowl.

"I am Captain Riez. Welcome aboard. Haddok will show you to yer quarters." He gestured to a thin fellow with a gray beard and tattered clothes.

The man hunched over the deck pounding some kind of material between the planks. At his master's signal, he dropped his tools and hastened over.

"Show our passengers to their cabin." Riez smiled broadly, showing his crooked yellow teeth like a crocodile might before devouring its victim.

The crewman indicated an entry that led below. Wrinkling her nose in distaste, Leena followed him, with Taurin bringing up the rear. They climbed down a set of steps and entered a narrow dank passageway with a low ceiling. A door stood on each side, with another door at the far end. Haddok opened the door on the left, indicating a space so small that Leena thought her closet at home must be bigger. A stench of rot permeated the air, and she drew back, affronted.

"This is unacceptable. I can't be confined in there for the entire voyage."

Haddok spit into a corner. "It's my understandin' there ain't no other ship to take you where you want to go, lady."

Taurin brushed past her. "Don't mind my wife. We'll manage."

Leena forced herself to step inside. A couple of bunk beds rested against the wall. On the opposite side was a sink. A small partition concealed a private toilet. A built-in chest on the bulkhead wall was the only other item of furniture.

"This is it? Are there no other cabins available?" She stalked outside and yanked on the door opposite. It was locked and so was the one farther down the passage.

Captain Riez showed up, his face darkening. "If you wish to jine us on this voyage, you will follow orders."

"We are guests," Taurin told him, "not crew members."

Something in his voice must have warned the captain, because he gave Taurin an oily smile. "Of course, brother. We hopes you and the lass will enjoy yourselves. Chow is served at five o'clock this evenin'. To reach the mess deck, go up the steps and toward the waist of the ship. On the other side is a companionway that'll take you there."

****

At the evening repast, Leena and Taurin met the other crew members, as well as two passengers, who had joined them at the last minute.

Taurin turned to Captain Riez. "I thought you only had one cabin available," he said in an accusatory tone.

Captain Riez sat at the head of the warped wooden table, his hand on a mug of ale. His dark eyes gleamed with avarice. "Your fellow passengers were in desperate straits. They're clergy—how could I refuse them?"

The captain had introduced the pair as Brother Aron and Sister Bertrice. Leena examined the pair who each wore the medallion identifying their membership in the Order of Missioners. The gold medals bore the antler-like design representing the branches of life that Lothar sustained. The crew members, who shared the table with their passengers, wore similar pendants made from simpler materials, showing they followed the Faith.

Brother Aron led them in evening prayers. He was swarthy-skinned and dark-haired, with high cheekbones. The woman beside him had platinum hair, hazel eyes, and a long nose that gave her face a stern expression. A pair could never look more incongruous, Leena thought. From the richness of their garments, she assumed they'd paid Captain Riez well for their berths.

"What brings you to the Black Lands?" she asked them out of curiosity.

"We plan to make contact with the native tribes," Sister Bertrice answered in an amiable voice. "There remain many unconverted heathens among them."

"Won't it be dangerous for you to go there? The exiles may bear a grudge against the Ministry of Religion."

"Lothar will guide us," said Brother Aron. He slurped a spoonful of brownish glop that the cook called stew.

Leena ate very little, coveting the cheese and bread she and Taurin had stashed in their cabin. She'd eat later, since those items were much more appealing than this repast.

She kept her gaze averted from the crew. They were an uncouth lot, scruffy and ill-dressed, with one exception. A new man had replaced an injured sailor just before the ship set sail. He wore clean clothes and had neatly combed hair along with an alert expression.

Taurin surveyed the others while he devoured his meal. He sat tense beside her, surreptitiously studying their table mates. Any one of their companions could be a Truthsayer or a paid spy for the thief who'd stolen the horn. They couldn't trust anyone except each other.

"I've heard the best way across the Black Lands is through the central valley," he said to the captain. "We'll need to reach the northern coast. Have you any advice on how to get there or who we should hire as a guide?"

"My advice is to avoid the highlands," Captain Riez said, chewing on a soggy breadstick. "The tribes in those mountains don't like outsiders. You go in there and you won't come out."

"What about the lowland areas?" Leena asked, remembering Sirvat's instructions. "Is it possible to go around the island on the outskirts?"

Riez shook his head. "Too swampy. You'd be crazy to cross through it, but the valley following the river is yer best bet."

Taurin leaned back in his chair, a casual look on his face. "I also heard the Chocola Company has an interest on the island." His steely gaze met Captain Riez's rheumy eyes, which skittered away at the contact.

"That so?" the captain muttered.

"I saw a lot of crates labeled with their company's name on

the wharf." Taurin hunched forward. "From what I've learned, the beans are grown at plantations scattered across the island. The product must pass across the Tortis Sea by ship. Then they'll need a processing center. There are very few flights out of Port Donner. Where do those crates go?"

"They travel by rail, if you must know. And, yes, the Chocola Company does own plantations in the Black Lands. But it won't do you any good to stick your nose into that business."

His tone held a warning that Leena didn't miss. Chocola plantations in the Black Lands? Who worked there—the exiled dissenters? Who oversaw the operation and made sure it ran smoothly? And how could the Chocola Company have gotten permission from the Ministry of Religion to use the land for this purpose? Or did it come under the Ministry of the Interior?

If they could investigate, Leena would pass along any information they gleaned to her brother. Somebody was fattening his pockets with the proceeds, and the trail might lead all the way to the Synod.

She voiced her opinion later as she and Taurin strolled along the upper deck.

"Yes, we should pursue the matter," he agreed, his head swathed once again in his cloth.

Night had fallen, and myriads of stars gleamed overhead. Never had Leena seen so many in the night sky. Even though her hometown didn't produce much of a glow, the effect dampened their view of the heavens. Now, at sea, she gazed with awe at the twinkling dots of light.

"Have you ever wondered what those stars represent?" she asked Taurin, pointing upward. She couldn't read his expression, but his face tilted toward the darkened sky like hers. "Do other worlds circle them, and do they harbor life? Has Lothar's presence visited them, or is ours the only planet blessed by his bounty?"

Taurin's posture tensed. "Would you be shocked if you learned there was life elsewhere?"

"I don't think so. That ring I found in the ruins, and the horn, are both made from the same type of material. It's like nothing I've ever seen on Xan. Either the Apostles constructed these things using a process unknown to us, or they obtained the raw materials from somewhere else. Perhaps up there."

She rolled her eyes toward the heavens. "They came out of nowhere, established the order of Sabal, and then left. Where did they go? Back to where they'd come from? And if so, do you think they're watching over us from the expanse?"

His mouth curved downward. "Let's hope not, because they wouldn't like what they see."

"You're right. People are losing faith, and it bodes ill for our world."

She rested a hand on the rail just as Taurin's head jerked up. With a cry of alarm, he grabbed her by the shoulders and shoved her to the deck, throwing his heavy body atop hers. Something crashed by with a deafening roar and splashed into the sea.

"What was that?" Leena cried, her heart thumping.

"Someone tried to knock us overboard. Here, let me help you up." He assisted her to stand then scanned the rigging on the foremast.

Leena followed the direction of his gaze and discerned a figure making a hasty descent along the ratlines.

"Stay here," he ordered.

He charged after the shadowy figure, but the person scuttled below before Taurin could reach him. Likely they'd been betrayed by a traitorous Synod member. Now they'd really have to watch their backs.

Leena approached him. "Did you see who it was?"

"No, he was too fast. Let's return to our cabin."

Back in the confines of their quarters, Taurin climbed to the top bunk and stretched himself out. Leena sat below on the lower bunk, her head ducked.

"I'd say our best bet is the new crew member." Taurin's voice, low and rumbling, came from above.

Leena's nerves reacted to the richness of his tone and his close proximity. Alone in the cabin with him, she became aware of every breath he took and every movement he made. His presence made it difficult for her to formulate her thoughts, but for the sake of their mission, she made the effort.

"Didn't Captain Riez say the regular crewman had an accident before sailing? It was awfully convenient that this man was available."

"I'll ask him a few questions tomorrow," Taurin determined. "It's likely he'll make another attempt. If I'm not with you, stay in this cabin with the door locked. Understand?"

Leena was about to sputter a protest, but she acknowledged his concern. "As you wish."

A long silence ensued. She could tell Taurin was awake by his restless movements and the erratic sound of his breathing. Did he lie there worrying about the success of their mission?

They had so many obstacles yet to overcome, but at least they wouldn't have to face them alone.

Chapter Nine

The next morning while they were walking on deck, Leena noticed the crew seemed edgy. Her stomach, queasy ever since they'd set sail, rebelled as increasingly tumultuous waves rocked the vessel. Wondering if a storm was brewing, she decided to ask Captain Riez while Taurin questioned the new crew member.

Ignoring Taurin's orders for her to remain in their cabin, she located the captain who was downing a quick meal in the mess hall. She breezed in through the open hatchway, her yellow gown billowing about her ankles.

"Good and welfare, Captain. I was just on deck and noticed the crew going about their duties in grim silence. The sea is rough this morning, and the sky has a peculiar pinkish tinge. Is anything amiss?"

The captain, unshaven and wearing clothes that hadn't seen soap in a fortnight, grimaced at her.

"We're entering Fool's Quadrant. The passage isn't always safe."

"Not safe?" Leena's voice cracked. "What do you mean?"

"The water can thicken."

"I don't understand. How can water thicken?"

Riez scratched his ample belly. "It has something to do with the growth of microbes. The sea turns to the consistency of glue. Eventually the water liquefies again, but it ain't good to be stuck here in the meantime."

"Why not?" Leena asked, fearful of the answer.

Stuffing a forkful of mashed tubers into his mouth, the captain gave a furtive glance at the cook, who stood by listening to their exchange. "The flying lungefish, Sister. They'll swarm a man." His voice lowered. "I've never seen one, but I've heard tell they have suckers on their tentacles. The things secrete an enzyme that can dissolve a man's flesh."

"We wouldn't be here if we wasn't steered off course last night," the cook blurted.

Startled, Leena glanced in his direction. The portly fellow wore a stained apron that sported several hairs from his graying head.

"I means what I says, lady. That new crew member, Sprawls, he was on duty. The fool didn't know his charts too well, did he?"

The captain grimaced. "Now it's too late to circle around Fool's Quadrant. We'll have to go through. I just hope we make it without any trouble."

Leena hastened away, eager to find Taurin to share her news. She wondered if he had found that fellow Sprawls and was even now questioning the man.

A sense of unease enveloped her as she strode across the deck. A strong breeze whipped strands of hair about her head. Salt spray stung her face as the planked flooring rose and dipped in tune to the high swells. She gripped a section of railing to steady herself.

Shouts and curses rang down from somewhere above. She twisted her neck to gaze upward, and her jaw dropped as she detected Taurin's lean body silhouetted against the sails.

****

Taurin chased the crew member, who had fled upon his approach. It seemed the man hoped to lose Taurin by scrambling into the rigging, but Taurin had no regard for his own safety. He'd started after him immediately. Since he wasn't able to shimmy up the mast like the crewman, he climbed the shroud, using the ratlines as a ladder.

The main mast towered above the deck, supporting four

levels of sails, and the crewman had already attained the topsail. Taurin reached up, grasped the lowest deadeye, and hauled himself atop the rail. He stretched as far as he could into one of the middle shrouds, grabbing a ratline to ease his climb. He needed to pull with his arms as well as boost himself with his legs. Line by line he advanced.

Glancing down, he saw the deck of the ship grow smaller and smaller. Leena's bright yellow dress stood in contrast to the rolling green sea. He felt as though he were climbing into the clouds. His muscles ached from the exertion. His heart pounded, but he didn't stop for even a moment. He neared the crewman, who'd paused to rest at the trestle tree just below the top gallant spar.

Taurin kept climbing, ratline by ratline, cursing as his hands grew slippery and his senses reeled. He halted with the rigging inches from his face, waiting for his breathing to slow.

"You come any closer, and I'll throw you off," Sprawls yelled. He had one arm wrapped around the mast.

"You tried to knock us overboard, didn't you?" Taurin shouted back. A sudden wind blew up and whipped his hair into his face.

"Aye, that I did. And I'll see to it that you and yer woman don't reach the Black Lands. I've got me orders."

"Orders from whom?"

Taurin lurched upward, hand over hand, vowing to get closer still. As he reached the crewman's perch, he noticed a gleam of metal in the man's hand just before Sprawls attacked. Taurin kicked at the man's arm with his foot. The knife arched up and away.

With a howl of rage, the man launched himself at Taurin. They grappled at each other while the lines flapped around them.

"Who sent you?" Taurin said after he'd gotten a grip on the man's throat.

"That ain't no concern of yours." The words came out as a choking gasp.

"I think it is." Taurin squeezed harder, and the man's face turned a dark shade of red. The crewman twisted his frame, loosening Taurin's grasp and breaking free.

"Once I get rid of you, I'll take care of the lady. Neither one of you will leave this ship alive."

The uppercut to his jaw caught Taurin unawares. He reeled from the force of the blow. His grip on the line was the only thing that saved him from slipping off and falling into the sea.

Sprawls took advantage, pummeling Taurin about the head. Taurin ducked a blow and lashed out, striking his adversary in the ribcage. An urge filled him to throttle the fellow until he was dead.

Before he could succumb to his bloodlust, the ship dipped. With a scream of terror, the crewman lost his grasp and plummeted to the depths below.

Clutching the mast, Taurin swayed in place, his muscles trembling. Sweat dripped into his eyes, blinding him. He waited until the wind cooled his brow before contemplating the hazardous journey down.

As the ship rocked against the strengthening waves, he clung to the rigging and began his descent. The tilting horizon made him dizzy, but he forced himself to place one foot below the other. Sails filled and smacked against him, at times nearly smothering his breath. Finally, he reached the mainyard and climbed down the remaining distance to the wooden deck.

His rubbery knees collapsed once he felt a solid surface beneath his feet.

Leena rushed over to him. "By the grace of Lothar, are you all right? I've never been so scared in my life."

Taurin glanced at her. "Are you saying you care about me?"

"Of course I do." She grabbed his elbow and helped him to stand.

"I'm all right." He shook her off and rubbed his aching arms. "It's been too long since I've practiced rope-climbing."

"Listen to this. I heard that Sprawls, the new crew member, steered us off course last night."

He nodded. "Sprawls admitted his orders were to keep us from reaching the Black Lands."

She bowed her golden head. "Only the Synod members knew we were going on this mission. You know what that means."

"Aye, someone betrayed us. We'll have to be doubly cautious from now on. Either the traitor sent his own assassin after us, or he tipped off the Truthsayers about our purpose and Sprawls was one of them."

She gave him an assessing glance. "We're safe for now. Let's go below. Your hands need treatment, and you should rest."

Taurin let her fuss over him in their cabin. She brought him a drink and salve for his raw palms. He didn't feel the need to lie down but was too glad for her ministrations to refuse. He'd never had a woman care for him before.

Having been raised by one of the dominant gangs on Yllon, he'd had no real parents. Baker Mylock and his wife were the only ones who'd ever shown him kindness.

Leena smoothed his cheek with her hand, and Taurin let a deep sigh escape his lips. Her touch was like an angel's kiss. Last night, as he lay on his back in the bunk above her, he could barely control his need. The scent of her perfume and the rustle of her gown as she changed positions drove him mad.

But the sweet torture she brought him now was even worse. He yearned to smooth his hands over her exquisite body, to run his fingers through her golden waves of hair. His body burned for the beautiful woman caressing him with such innocence. Her expression, full of concern for his welfare, moved him deeply. Gazing into her eyes, he thought he'd never seen anything so pure in his entire life.

"Leena," he murmured.

"Yes?" She stood on tiptoes to reach him at eye level.

He reached out a hand to cup the back of her head. Her hair felt like spun silk, and his resolve evaporated. He'd been able to push away from her at Hathers Beach, knowing it wasn't right for him to steal kisses regardless of their legal relationship. But now he drew her toward him until his mouth hovered inches above hers.

"I want you."

Leena's eyes widened. Her body trembled, but instead of pulling away from him as he'd expected, she parted her lips and tilted her face upward. "Kiss me, Taurin. I want to be closer to you."

With a cry of exultation, he smashed his mouth onto hers.

****

Leena thought she'd never experienced anything more heavenly than the press of his mouth on hers. His kiss was deep and passionate. She'd been so afraid for him on deck that she had to be closer to him to reassure herself of his safety.

Standing on tiptoes, she thought kissing him was more rapturous than anything she'd imagined. Malcolm's feathery touches were mere polite formalities in comparison. When Taurin kissed her, she felt consumed by a hunger too intense for words, and she never wanted him to stop.

His arm wrapped around her shoulder in a protective embrace. Closing her eyes, she gave in to the ecstasy of the moment, relishing the feel of his mouth on hers as his lips moved frantically, expressing his need. He desired her! The wonder of it took her breath away. But it shouldn't be his arms around her, it should be Malcolm's.

Guilt ate at her consciousness, giving her pause, so that when his hands roamed toward her breasts she jerked away, stricken with remorse.

Taurin's eyes darkened to slate-gray. "What's wrong? Am I going too fast for you?"

He heaved himself into a sitting position and then jumped down so he stood facing her directly. "I want to touch you, Leena. Kissing you isn't enough. I want to have all of you."

Her heart thudded wildly in her chest. By the Faith, how handsome he looked, with his dark swirl of hair curling onto his forehead and his piercing gaze. "I'm not yours," she reminded him. "Our marriage is in name only."

She might wish it were otherwise, but too many obstacles precluded their being together. Not that she was considering such a possibility! Malcolm still waited for her, and although he wouldn't necessarily expect her to be a virgin, he might rescind his offer if he learned the circumstances of her journey. He certainly wouldn't be pleased if he suspected she and Taurin had coupled during their sojourn abroad.

"It would dishonor us if we consummated our union without an emotional commitment," she added. Her voice came out stiffer than intended but she felt an explanation was necessary.

Taurin's mouth thinned. "Of course. Your brother wouldn't approve, would he?"

She inhaled at his scornful tone. Before she could utter a reply, he'd spun and stormed from the cabin.

"Taurin, wait." Too late; he was already gone.

Perhaps it would be best to leave him alone. In retrospect, she shouldn't have let him kiss her again. She'd responded with shameless abandon, but she couldn't help it if her limbs weakened and her breasts ached for his touch whenever he was near. The only solution was to maintain a safe distance from him. Once their mission was over, she'd resume her station in life, and that didn't include socializing with men like Taurin.

The ship's motion quieted a short while later, and she went on deck to see what was happening. She found Taurin, along with some of the crew members, staring out to sea.

Her breath hitched. "What's going on?"

When she glanced at the water, her blood ran cold. It had thickened to the consistency of gelatin and entrapped the ship in its viscosity.

"We're stuck," Taurin replied in a flat tone.

Captain Riez, who was conferring with his men, called out

to her. "Ye'd better go below, lady. You don't want to be caught here if the flying lungefish attack."

Before she could heed his words, a giant sucking noise erupted off the port bow. The sky filled with scores of fluttering wings. Dozens of flying bodies hurtled at a lone crew member standing on the forecastle deck. They engulfed him so completely that she lost sight of him. She could hear his screams, however.

His blood-curdling shrieks were quickly silenced. When the swarm flew away, a murky puddle remained on the deck, all that was left of him.

Leena covered her mouth in horror. The creatures soared into the sky and then veered downward in a spiraling turn, heading back toward the ship.

"Take cover!" Taurin shoved her toward the companionway.

She screamed as they charged past, aiming for another crew member who howled in terror. The captain shouted orders as the crew scurried to obey him.

Leena stepped backward in an effort to flee and forgot the open hatchway in the center of the ship's waist. For an instant, she teetered on the edge. Panic blossomed as she flailed her arms and was unable to catch her balance. She fell, toppling into empty space. Something cracked her skull. White-hot pain exploded in her head and then all went dark.

****

Taurin's breath caught in his throat as Leena vanished. He charged forward, his fingers fumbling for a grip on the ladder that led down into the cargo hold.

When his feet touched the bottom, he probed the darkness until he felt her soft form, limp on the floor. His heart hammered as he felt for her pulse. A weak, erratic beat brought him a measure of relief, but she needed treatment.

After a moment his eyes adjusted to the dark, and he could see as clearly as though it were daytime. With a grim smile, he noted that if she could see him now, she'd be frightened by the glowing luminescence of his eyes. It was the reason why he swathed his head in cloth—so no one could see that he wore the demon's sign. A gash on the side of Leena's head showed him what had rendered her unconscious.

Carefully, he scooped her into his arms and climbed the ladder onto the waist of the ship. The siege from the flying creatures continued as he hustled into the passenger quarters and entered their cabin. Gently, he placed her on her bunk. As he did so, her eyelids fluttered open, and she moaned with pain.

"Don't move. It's my turn to care for you now," Taurin told her. He found a spare cloth and moistened it with cool water. Then he carefully cleansed her wound. His hand wandered to stroke her cheek. "I'm sorry if I got carried away earlier."

"No, don't apologize. It was my fault. I shouldn't have let you… I mean, I could have stopped—"

Taurin put a finger to her lips. "Hush. It's not necessary to explain. We both enjoyed it, but it shouldn't have happened. Let's leave it at that."

He cursed inwardly at the hurt look in her eyes. He had never wanted to possess a woman as much as he wanted her, but it was impossible. Why waste his time with someone he couldn't have? Even if she agreed, she was too good for him, and the life she was meant to lead was far different than his.

Pretending to freshen the cloth, he walked to the sink so she wouldn't see the longing in his face. Honest intimacy with a woman was something he could never have. It would frighten her if she knew his true nature.

He returned to her side, ministering to her wound until she pushed his hand away. Screams and cries sounded from above.

Her frightened gaze snagged his attention. "What if those creatures get all of the crew members? We'll be left alone."

Taurin couldn't think of anyone else he'd rather be stranded with, but he didn't believe that would happen. "The water should be liquefying soon, then we can get underway again. If you'll be all right here by yourself, I'll go and take a look."

Leena grabbed for him. "Don't go. It isn't safe out there."

Her concern warmed his heart. "I'll be all right. Wait here. I won't be long."

By the time he returned, Leena lay on her bunk with her eyes closed. She must have fallen asleep. When she awoke, the ship was moving again.

She tried to sit up, but Taurin stopped her. "You've been injured. You need to rest."

With a heavy grunt, he heaved himself onto his bunk and lay down. Tomorrow they would reach the Black Lands, and then they would see where their assignment led. The attack from the flying creatures might seem mild compared to the dangers ahead.

****

The approach to the Black Lands was a delight from Leena's viewpoint. At first a shadowy shape on the horizon, the island grew larger as the *Predator* sailed toward land. Soon verdant green slopes and mountainous peaks became visible. She leaned against the rail, a breeze tossing her hair about her head as Captain Riez maneuvered the ship into a wide harbor.

The wharf area was a morass of squalor, but the forested mountains rising behind promised a land of lush beauty. As the ship approached the dock, a frenzy of activity energized the pier. Vendors, traders, and stevedores prepared for the new arrival.

Once the mooring lines were secured, Captain Riez assigned a porter to assist the passengers with their luggage. As soon as they stepped upon the pier, they were left to fend for themselves.

The missionaries stood beside Leena and Taurin, bewildered looks on their faces as they observed the bustle going on around them.

"I understand you're heading into the interior. Perhaps we can share a guide," Brother Aron suggested. The richness of his cloak made him the object of envious stares.

"What's your destination?" Taurin's hand shaded his face. The tropical sun blazed overhead, momentarily blinding him.

"We intend to contact the native tribes and teach them the ways of Lothar. I have a map of sorts that we can follow." The missionary withdrew a document from a pocket in his long-skirted garment and showed it to Taurin.

Leena addressed Sister Bertrice. "Aren't you afraid to approach the primitive tribes? Some of them might never have seen an outsider before. They could be hostile."

Sister Bertrice smiled benignly. "Lothar will protect us."

Taurin and Brother Aron hurried off on their errand to find a guide. While Leena waited for their return, she watched workers on the dock distribute the ship's stores. Brawny men loaded bags of mail, containers of food, medical supplies, and sundry goods onto trucks belching foul-smelling fumes.

None of the smaller vehicles appeared to be motorized. The only private conveyances were simple carriages or carts drawn by *enixes*—strong, proud beasts known for their easy domesticity.

Trucks carrying sealed crates stamped with the Chocola Company's name rumbled onto the wharf. An operator drove out a large crane and began hoisting the containers into the cargo hold of the *Predator*.

Sister Bertrice nodded at the crane. "I understand that motorized equipment is vigorously guarded on the island. Those in exile might build boats, you know."

Leena glanced at her in surprise. "The waters are patrolled. Even if some of the inhabitants did make it off the island, they'd be caught."

Those who were sent here rarely received a reprieve. Their fate was to live out the rest of their lives on this large island, their only company being fellow dissidents or primitive natives from the interior.

"Do most of the…" She almost said *prisoners* but guarded her tongue. "Do most of the people who come here reside in the lowlands?"

"They live along the coast and at the foothills of the mountains." Sister Bertrice patted the bun at the nape of her neck as though to ascertain her hair was still properly bound. Her hairstyle gave her face a severe look, and her eyes when she studied Leena held no hint of friendliness.

Leena had little time to ponder Sister Bertrice's puzzling demeanor because Taurin and Brother Aron returned, accompanied by a white-haired gentleman whose pompous swagger was undercut by his faded, worn clothes. If exiles did not receive packages from home, they were dependent on charity. For the first time, Leena wondered at the harsh penance prescribed by the religious order for those who disagreed with their tenets.

Lothar's grace and compassion were absent from this place. Although the island was lush with greenery and boasted a pleasant climate, its watery boundaries were the same as prison walls for the people entrapped here. Modern technology was lacking, no doubt because people might convert sophisticated items of machinery for their own use. It was a harsh existence, she acknowledged, staring at the ramshackle wooden buildings that faced the pier.

Realizing this fate might have been her father's had he been exiled here, she felt a rush of gratitude toward Karayan for speaking on his behalf. A year of penance, no matter how unpleasant, was much preferable to a lifetime in this lonely place. Renewing her vow to see her father totally exonerated, she studied the new arrival.

"Ives will be our guide," said Taurin, introducing the man. "He says our best route is to follow the lowlands to the east and then cut across the island through the main river valley."

Leena gazed at him in dismay. "It'll take days without any motorized transport."

Taurin pursed his lips, clearly displeased by the prospect. "We have no choice. Ives will take us to a place where we can stay for the night. We'll get an early start tomorrow morning so we can cover a longer distance."

Ives helped them load their luggage onto his cart, a large conveyance drawn by four spirited *enixes*, who snorted and pranced as they waited for their passengers to board. A wooden bench seat lined the inside perimeter. Leena and Taurin took seats together. Sister Bertrice and Brother Aron sat opposite them.

Ives climbed onto a raised platform in front, gripped the reins, and uttered a cry that spurred the beasts forward. They galloped through town, raising a dusty cloud in their wake. Shortly thereafter, they veered down a trail alongside a marsh that stank of sulfur and rotting vegetation.

Leena held onto the seat with one hand and her hat with the other. She was glad Taurin had insisted she wear the forest green tunic he'd bought for her in Port Donner. Sleeveless with a scooped neckline, its shorter length would keep her cool in the heat.

Their cart tilted from side-to-side and shook as they rushed along the bumpy trail. A salt-laden breeze refreshed her face as they sped forward.

After an hour of driving, they stopped to share a drink from a jug of water provided by their guide and to eat a snack of fresh *karanas*, a soft yellowish fruit that peeled easily and filled her stomach.

The cart lurched ahead as they resumed their journey and turned inland toward the foothills. Scrub brush grew in profusion along the hillsides, but there weren't many tall trees. If she'd thought being on land would be easier than on a ship, she'd been mistaken. Her stomach roiled as the cart bounced beneath them.

"What will we do once we reach the other side of the island?" she shouted at Taurin, her voice carried by the wind.

His black hair tossed about his face, but she caught the instant warmth of his eyes as he responded, an enigmatic smile on his face. "Don't worry, I have a plan."

Chapter Ten

Leena slid along the bench and gratefully sank against Taurin's solid chest as he wrapped his arm around her. Brother Aron's gaze fell to her exposed legs, making her uncomfortable, while Sister Bertrice gave her a disapproving frown.

To avoid looking at them, she closed her eyes, letting her body melt into Taurin's contours. She forced herself to focus her thoughts on their goals rather than on the jostling ride and the unpleasant couple sitting across from them.

After what seemed like an interminably long period of time, when dusk was falling and Leena despaired of ever reaching shelter for the night, they turned down a path heading west onto higher ground. Towering trees shaded the road. These appeared to belong to cultivated rows that stretched into the distance. Their large oval leaves were bright green and tapered.

Taurin straightened to gaze at the fruits dangling from the trees. Brown pods hung from the branches, ripe for harvesting.

A frown creased his brow. "This must be one of the Chocola Company's plantations. How did they get property rights when the Black Lands are prohibited territory?"

No one answered as they approached a two-story brick mansion. A bright glow from within welcomed them as the front door swung open and a dark-haired young man stepped outside.

"Ah, Ives. You've brought guests for tonight." The well-dressed fellow regarded their group with interest.

Ives introduced them, twisting his hands nervously. "I hope you don't mind our unexpected visit, Master Alber. But you always said to bring outsiders your way."

"Indeed I did, Ives. Indeed I did." Alber rummaged in his pocket and tossed a few coins to the older man. "You can get a meal in the common house. I'll take care of our guests."

He ushered the visitors inside. After snapping orders to his servants, Alber led them into a furnished library.

"Would you care for some wine?" he asked.

"I'd appreciate a glass," Taurin replied. He accepted a crystal goblet filled with a rich burgundy and took a sip. "It's very good, thank you. Tell me, I thought commerce was prohibited in these parts. How did your company acquire this land?"

"We have our resources. Our operation is known only to a few outsiders." Alber gave a grin that reminded Leena of a cat about to devour a mouse. "I trust you will not reveal our presence on this island to anyone else."

"But who authorized it?" Taurin persisted.

The missionaries could care less, Leena noted. They circled the room, perusing the texts lining the bookshelves. She accepted a glass of wine with a grateful nod. The tart liquid eased her parched throat. She surveyed the room, noting several carved stone statuettes and other pieces of art. None were of exceptional value, but at least Alber had an eye for aesthetics.

Alber's gaze chilled as he responded to Taurin's question. "How we got approval for this facility doesn't concern you. The Chocola Company is a major industry on Xan, and certain allowances have been made to increase productivity.

"But where do you get workers?" Leena inquired. When she saw the smirk on Alber's face, she understood. "You employ those who are exiled here."

Alber twirled the ruby liquid in his goblet. "I wouldn't say *employ* is the correct term. I offer people a trade. They provide me with their services, and I give them food and shelter. It's an amiable exchange. We create jobs for the inhabitants. I see it as using the richness of this land for a rewarding purpose."

"I'd call it slave labor," Taurin said half to himself.

Leena viewed the arrangement more as indentured servitude.

Either way, someone at a high level in government must have skirted regulations concerning the Black Lands. Authorization had to come from one of the ministers. She'd bet someone at the Palisades was lining his pockets with revenue from this place. Her brother should add this matter into his investigation.

"Do you have a line to the mainland?" she asked their host. "I'd like to notify my brother that we made our journey safely."

Alber gave her an expansive smile. "I'm afraid direct communications with the outside world are forbidden. We conduct business via a system of mail boats and freighters. It works well for us, madam. We wish to keep things that way."

Leena didn't like the warning note in his voice and neither did Taurin. Taurin's body tensed as he gave the man a dark scowl that would make a lesser man quiver in his shoes.

"We should discuss the rest of our journey." Taurin spoke gruffly, as though realizing that if Alber wanted to detain them, he had only to give word to his servants.

"We haven't considered the payment for your accommodations yet."

"Ives said nothing about us having to pay you."

"You travel in luxury, my friend. Surely you can share some of your bounty with those who are less fortunate."

Taurin glanced around, a sardonic look on his face. "Your place doesn't appear to be lacking in comfort."

"No, but you forget I have to maintain a work force. That costs money. Any extra contributions I can obtain aides the cause. Thus I take in visitors when they arrive."

"How many visitors do you get?" Leena observed him curiously. She'd had no idea people could come and go from this island. How were the dissenters kept in line?

"Representatives from my company come by on occasion, and sometimes other guests pass through." Alber didn't elaborate, while Leena's distrust grew by exponential leaps.

"How much did you have in mind?" Taurin put down his empty wine glass on a side table.

"Oh, I'd say a hundred chekels for each of you should do. And twenty-five more each for your meals. That's a total of five hundred chekels."

Sister Bertrice, who'd been listening to their conversation, snorted with derision. "We don't carry that kind of money, Brother."

"I'm sure your friends would consider sharing their wealth." Alber kept his gaze fixed on Taurin.

"And if I refuse?" Taurin's mouth thinned.

"We have other accommodations available in the common house. You can join the rabble there."

The man's meaning was clear. If Taurin didn't pay, they'd be imprisoned with the rest of the work force. In that case, their chances of leaving the island were almost nil.

"Very well." Taurin consented. He handed over the requested amount, none too happy about it from his dark expression.

They'd better stay on guard throughout the night, Leena thought, lest the rest of their funds be taken by force.

After a generous dinner, they were assigned suites on the second floor. The rest of the evening passed without incident. Following morning prayers early the next day—Alber apparently subscribed to Lothar's teachings—and a simple meal, the travelers started on their journey once again.

To their pleasant surprise, Alber supplied two riders for their convenience. These open-air vehicles had transparent shields in front to provide wind protection and huge tires to allow passage through difficult terrain. Each rider had seating for four plus storage space in the back. Ives and the missionaries took the lead in one vehicle, with Leena and Taurin following behind.

"Have a safe journey." Alber waved from his front stoop.

The missionaries raised their hands in farewell, but Taurin didn't give the man the courtesy. Leena surmised he didn't appreciate Alber's extortion last night nor the secrecy about the company's operations. She wished they'd been able to contact her brother. Hopefully, Bendyk had gained more answers than she and Taurin.

****

Bendyk and Swill were making slow progress. Swill had nearly completed her examination of the Treasury records but was dissatisfied with one of her findings. Each month, exactly on the thirty-fifth day, someone made a collections deposit into the Receipts account in varied monetary amounts. Sirvat claimed this was a miscellaneous category for income that didn't fit into any of the other classifications.

Feeling she was being misled, Swill had demanded a more detailed explanation and was told to consult Magar. His department was responsible for the revenue.

Meanwhile, Bendyk was looking into Sirvat's personal background by interviewing her acquaintances. He'd found out she lived a rather frugal life and kept a quiet residence in one of the larger towns where her family resided. Her penchant for travel had taken her to some of the more exotic locales on Xan. According to one chatty neighbor, she traveled alone but met friends along the way.

Bendyk wanted to tell Swill what he'd discovered and was waiting for her in their shared office one afternoon when Karayan and Zeroun stormed in.

"How is your research progressing?" Zeroun asked in a tone as sleek as oil.

"Well enough, thank you. Did you wish to see me for a particular reason?"

"Don't get your hackles up, my boy," Karayan responded. He examined one of his manicured fingernails. As usual, the Minister of Justice wore an impeccably tailored frock coat and a pair of matching trousers. "You know, you really should learn to control your temper. It isn't suitable for a missionary to be so turbulent."

Bendyk stifled a retort, knowing the man was right. He'd always struggled to keep his volatile emotions in check. Praying for serenity hadn't helped him. He feared it was a state he would never attain, unlike his sister.

He glanced toward the door. Where in tarnation was Swill? She was late for their appointment.

"Did you learn anything more about Rey Niris?" Karayan inquired, his piercing gaze boring into Bendyk.

"Perhaps." *So this is why they've come to see me.*

"His home is located in the same town as Magar's estate, is it not?" Zeroun demanded.

"Aye, and so what if it is?" Bendyk had meant to look into their relationship but hadn't had the time. After he was finished investigating Sirvat, he'd start with Magar.

Karayan had other ideas. "Did you see his place when you took Leena to him? What was the fellow like? Was he enthusiastic about helping us in our quest?"

Bendyk rose from the chair behind his desk. "I believe my sister and I are the ones in charge of this investigation, gentlemen."

"Yes, but we're concerned for Leena's safety. Zeroun and I plan to take a look around Rey Niris's property. If you want to come, you're welcome."

"How did you get the location?" Bendyk narrowed his gaze suspiciously. He didn't think Magar would share that information so readily.

"We have our sources," Zeroun replied in a haughty tone.

Pretending to adjust his shirt, Bendyk considered his options. Better to go along with them than have them snoop around on their own. "When are you leaving?" he asked.

"Right now," said Karayan. "Will you join us?"

"Very well." Bendyk scribbled a note for Swill, explaining the circumstances of his departure. Fingering the medallion hanging over his tan longshirt, he followed the ministers outside.

The drive into the countryside seemed fast as he sat in the rear passenger seat, lost in his thoughts. Before he knew it, they were turning down the private drive that led to Taurin's tidy house. Zeroun's white robe, cinched at the waist with a gold sash, fluttered in the breeze as they emerged from the rider. The weather had cooled, but rain had not yet come, and Taurin's fields lay fallow. After walking about the grounds, the trio climbed onto the porch that wrapped around the exterior.

"You know," Karayan mused, a thoughtful gleam in his eyes, "I believe this piece of land is considered part of Magar's territory. He showed me the boundaries once, and I could have sworn this plot was included." He looked over the fields that eventually ended in a forest, beyond which, Bendyk had learned, was Magar's family residence, a large mansion by most people's standards.

Zeroun peered into a window. "I'd be interested to learn where Magar met this Rey Niris fellow." His gaze fell on something in the interior that made him cry out. "What is that? Karayan, come here."

The two men huddled together, staring through the windowpane.

"Archeology texts," Karayan observed. "And look at those drawings."

"Magar said the man fights like a warrior," Zeroun mentioned. "Where do you suppose he comes from? No one around here has such skills."

"Magar is concealing his knowledge of this man," Karayan concluded. Turning his attention to Bendyk, he gave him an intense glare. "You'll have to learn what Rey Niris's purpose is here. Magar would be the best source of information."

"I'll question Magar when I'm ready," Bendyk stated. He didn't appreciate being told what to do.

"It can't be soon enough. If you won't interrogate him, then I will."

Bendyk raised his hand. "I said, I would handle it. Please don't interfere."

During the return drive to the Palisades, Zeroun sat stiffly in front. Karayan sped over the winding roads faster than Bendyk would have liked, but he said nothing, immersed in speculation. He wondered if he should pursue his investigation of Sirvat or interrupt it to question Magar. He'd like some answers from the man.

Feeling uncomfortable with his dearth of knowledge about Rey Niris, he didn't deem it wise to mention the bonding ceremony he'd performed between Leena and Taurin, though he'd duly registered the event in the village ledger.

Inside his office, he found Swill at her desk reviewing her notes. His mood brightened at the sight of her. She glanced up as he entered.

"I need to discuss my findings with you." She spoke in a low tone as though wary of being overheard.

"Sorry I'm so late. Did you get my note?"

"Yes, but I thought it odd that Zeroun and Karayan decided to check out Rey Niris's place. That should be our job."

"That's why I thought it best if I accompanied them. All they did was peek through his windows. Anyway, I need to tell you what I've learned about Sirvat. How about joining me for dinner?" he asked in a hopeful tone. Swill had not yet accepted an invitation from him, although he tried every day.

"Do you propose we eat in the dining commons?" she asked.

Bendyk's eyebrows shot up. She was actually considering his offer? "No, I thought we might try a new café that's opened in town. The chef specializes in roast game. It's a quiet place, and we can talk there undisturbed."

"That sounds lovely."

All thoughts of work fled Bendyk's mind when they sat in the restaurant at a small table with a white cloth and a glass-enclosed candle. He liked the provincial decor that gave a cozy ambiance to the place. A fire burned in a stone fireplace to ward off the night's chill.

Taking a sip from his glass of white wine, Bendyk let his eyes feast on Swill. She wasn't the sort to wear feminine frills. She preferred a simple style of dress that almost came across as rebellious. Bendyk was getting used to her ways and found her independent streak to be refreshing. She wore a burgundy blouse with a low scoop neckline and a long black skirt. A string of colored beads adorned her neck. It complemented her healthy tanned complexion. In the muted candlelight, her amber eyes shone like topaz gemstones.

"Let's talk about you," he suggested. "It's a far more interesting topic than the Treasury records or Sirvat's background."

****

"I don't have much to say," Swill replied, too stunned to think of a proper retort. She didn't care to talk about herself and hoped to continue their work discussion. But the atmosphere there was more intimate than she'd expected, and it made her uncomfortable. So did the man sitting across from her. Bendyk was very handsome when his righteous airs didn't pucker his face or tighten his mouth.

The way he looked at her now made a warm feeling settle in her stomach. He'd removed his cloak and sat facing her in a fawn-colored longshirt that went well with his blond hair. It did nothing to hide the wide set of his shoulders or his broad chest.

She wondered what he did to stay in shape. So many of the priests she'd known had grown flabby from years of indulgence. But Bendyk had his career ahead of him, and it struck her that he might be aiming for a position in the very Synod they were investigating.

She resented the way he'd recruited her, but after beginning the work, she had realized its importance. Bendyk and his sister had a weighty responsibility on their shoulders. She admired the way he bravely forged ahead, assuming a leadership role as though he were born to it.

"I'd rather learn more about you," she suggested, hiding her shyness by taking a hasty swig of wine.

He smiled, an even, white flash of teeth. "You don't like talking about yourself, do you? I've seen where you live. You've accomplished a lot with your life. Why did you take the job you did? Was it for the travel benefits, or do you just like helping the villeins during your tithing counts?"

She lifted her chin. "I try to help people who don't have the same advantages as others. But I also needed a change of scenery. You've met my parents. The atmosphere at home is stifling. The job seemed like a golden opportunity to get away. And besides, I've always been good with numbers."

"How long do you plan to keep the position?"

"I haven't thought that far ahead."

"Oh no? Surely you have some hopes for the future?"

"I want the family I never had," she blurted unexpectedly. "I'd like a small house in a quiet neighborhood with several children and a man who makes enough of a living to support us. That's all I've ever hoped for. It's not very modern, is it?"

Bendyk reached across the table to touch her hand. "Perhaps we share the same values."

She gaped at him. "What do you mean? I'd have thought you would be aiming to become a Docent or even a Candor like your father. Or maybe you have your eye on the Synod."

Bendyk quirked an eyebrow. "I always thought that was the route I'd take, at least after I entered the calling. Before that…" His words trailed off, and his face closed as though in painful memory.

"What is it?" she asked in a soft tone. His hand remained on hers, its warmth trailing up her arm.

"Before the accident that killed my mother, I wasn't sure what I wanted to do with my life. I'd been spoiled, never having to work hard for anything. If I hadn't been so reckless that night, I might not have driven so fast. It was winter, and snow covered the road. I should have been more careful, and when we hit that icy patch…" His voice faltered and stopped.

Swill realized that night must have changed his life. Perhaps that's when Lothar had called to him. Offering himself in service to the Lord would have brought comfort and a renewed sense of purpose.

Bendyk downed the rest of his wine without speaking further.

Swill changed the subject, aware she'd stumbled onto a painful topic. The realization that she wanted to help Bendyk struck her with a blast of irony. Bendyk, a missionary, had set his goal in life to help others. Yet he appeared to have a deep need within himself for solace.

Swill had never thought of herself as the nurturing type. She'd never allowed herself to become personally involved in village affairs, afraid that emotional entanglements might make her too vulnerable. She'd had enough pain throughout her childhood and meant to spare herself further anguish.

But seeing Bendyk's world-weary face made her want to comfort him. It was a new feeling for her, almost like a springtime bud growing on a bush until it burst into blossom. Did her new friend have this effect on everyone, or was she the only one? Either way, he truly did have the power to inspire and to change one's outlook. And such a personality was usually evident in men destined for greatness.

****

Leena settled back in her seat, enjoying the caress of a warm breeze on her skin. The rider jolted and bounced over the rocky road. A canopy of tree branches provided shade, cooling the air.

"I hope Bendyk is having more success than we are," Leena told Taurin as they headed inland. "Hopefully we can confer with him once we finish this part of our mission. How do you propose we reach Grotus's island?" Worry nagged at her over the prospect.

"I know a way. Trust me. I've brought along some of the supplies we'll need, and we can scrounge for the rest."

Their lead vehicle turned west toward higher ground, the route punctuated by tall, leafy trees, dense underbrush, and a profusion of wildflowers whose perfumed scent invaded the air. Splashes of pink, orange, and orchid blooms appeared by the roadside as they lumbered past. Taurin stared at them appreciatively. He'd bet there were some exotic specimens among the foliage that would flourish in his garden. Too bad he didn't have time to look around.

After a while, they stopped to get drinks from the cooler in the back of the missionaries' rider and snacks from provisions Alber had provided. Taurin wondered why the plantation owner had been so accommodating when he didn't want them to reveal the Chocola Company's investment in the Black Lands. Did he trust them not to reveal their knowledge, or did Alber plan to silence them through other means? Taurin was surprised the man hadn't offered a bribe, but that could be expensive for all four of them. He decided to be on the alert just in case.

His precautions proved wise when, two days later, his party found themselves abandoned on the trail. They were high in the mountains, and their guide, having stopped the journey to take a break, suddenly vanished. Since the road didn't appear to be well-traveled, Taurin deduced their route had been chosen for nefarious purposes. He said as much to his companions.

"Native tribes reside in the interior," he warned them. "It could be dangerous to encounter them. Likely we've been led astray on purpose."

Leena wrinkled her brow. "I did think we were headed too far west." The cooler air made her glad she'd worn her work shirt and breeches. She could use a wrap for warmth.

"Which road should we follow?" Sister Bertrice indicated a fork in the road ahead.

One branch led down the mountainside presumably toward the valley they'd been advised to follow. The left-hand trail veered upward in steep, winding curves. At least they'd filled their fuel tanks recently, but if they took a wrong turn, they'd risk running dry. Then they would have to proceed on foot.

Leena glanced at her two suitcases in the rear of their vehicle, realizing how ludicrous it was to have brought so much luggage. One of the bags held a backpack with her archeological supplies. If necessary, she could stuff a few outfits in there.

"We'll take the road going down." Taurin signaled the

others to board their vehicle. "If the river's there, we'll know we're on the right track."

"I'll send a prayer to Lothar so he may guide us," Brother Aron shouted.

Taurin rolled his eyes. "Do as you wish. Maybe it'll help."

Slowly they started down the decline, thick trees and gnarled vines on either side of the road obstructing their view. They were halfway along toward the base of the slope when the woods seemed to move straight into their path.

Taurin brought their vehicle to a screeching halt. The missionaries, in the lead, stopped as well and turned toward him with fearful expressions.

Scores of natives faced them. Their brown bodies were plastered by a covering of leaves. They wore headdresses with antler-like protrusions and colorful feathers. Streaks of paint adorned their cheeks and foreheads. They glowered at the unexpected visitors.

Or were they unexpected?

"Our guide knew we'd go down this road," Taurin said. "We've been led into a trap."

"He's obviously following Alber's orders," Leena surmised. "Do you think many visitors to his plantation disappear this way?" Glancing at the warriors whose primitive spears pointed in their direction, she gave an involuntary shudder.

A fierce-looking warrior stepped forward and nudged Taurin with his spear, indicating he should get out of the vehicle. He obeyed, realizing it was useless to resist when they were so outnumbered. He motioned for the others to copy his action.

Babbling amongst themselves, a group of natives began ransacking their supplies while Leena and the others were herded away at spear point.

Her heart hammering, she stumbled over tree roots and rocks underfoot as they trudged through the woods. The scent of rich, earthy humus mingled with a spicy aroma, but she was too scared to notice her surroundings. Could these savages speak

Xanese, the standard language? If not, how would they communicate? Their dialect was incomprehensible to her.

"Can you understand them?" she whispered to Taurin, who strode beside her. Whenever they had to cross a particularly difficult stretch of territory, he held her elbow to assist her. She was grateful for his presence and wondered if they'd have any chance for escape.

"I have no idea what they're saying," Taurin replied, his face grim.

They seemed to walk for hours. By the time they reached the native encampment, dusk had fallen. Leena felt ill from hunger, although they'd been given drinks of water along the way. Her muscles ached from hours of exertion.

Her mind numb, she obeyed without question when they were directed to enter a small round hut built of mud bricks with a thatched roof. There was one slatted window for ventilation, but it was high up and didn't provide much light when the door was shut and sealed. Enclosed by darkness, despair overwhelmed her. She sank to the ground, covering her face with her hands.

****

Taurin took out his cloth and quickly swathed it around his head so his eyes would be screened. His hearing picked up a conversation outside the thick walls of the hut, but he didn't understand the language and couldn't make out what was said. The tribesmen were probably deciding what to do with them. Their situation didn't look good.

If necessary, he'd use the blaster secreted on his person. Magar had forbidden him to bring along any weapons when he'd offered Taurin sanctuary, but Taurin had slipped it in unnoticed. He'd kept it locked in a cabinet at home, but this mission had necessitated its removal. As Leena's protector, he deemed it his job to give them every advantage, and Taurin admitted that it gave him a measure of comfort to feel the weapon strapped against his calf.

The air outside had cooled considerably by the time they'd reached the camp, but inside the hut, it remained warm. He noticed a grating in the far corner from which steam emanated.

He gestured to the others. "Look at that. Where do you suppose the heat originates?"

Leena raised her head. "There could be a hot spring nearby," she suggested. "If they've dug conduits to their village, it would mean they're more intelligent than we thought."

"We'll have to see what happens next before planning an escape," Taurin replied. He lowered himself to a spot beside her on the packed dirt floor.

The missionaries sat on her other side. "We must pray for deliverance," Brother Aron said. He folded his hands together and bowed his head.

"You can do it for us," Taurin told him. He wrapped an arm around Leena's shoulder and drew her near. She must have appreciated his gesture, because she snuggled closer, giving a soft sigh of pleasure. He tightened his arm around her, vowing to get them out of this one way or another. For now, they should rest until daylight.

The warmth from her body penetrated his skin and lulled him to sleep.

He jerked awake as the first rays of sunlight pierced the room. Chilly air made him shiver, and he realized the steam must have been turned off for the night. Leena was still asleep, leaning against his shoulder. Her golden tresses streamed over her bosom. Her sweet womanly scent made him wish they were alone, but the missionary couple snoozed nearby in the tiny hut.

Gently he roused her, unable to keep his lips from brushing hers in a tender good morning kiss. She smiled up at him, her eyes dewy. After a quick glance at the missionaries to make sure they were still in slumber, he pressed his mouth to Leena's with greater urgency. She responded eagerly, moving her body so that she molded into his angles. He held her closer, his need escalating, the desperation of their situation driving him to seek the oldest comfort known to mankind.

His mouth slanted over hers as he sought solace in her sweetness. When her hands roamed his broad back, he moaned with pleasure before thrusting his tongue into her mouth. She took it greedily, playing with him, her own need evident in the tautness of her nipples against his chest that he could feel through their clothing. By the stars, he'd like to take her right here and now, regardless of who was watching.

A loud throat clearing told him someone else was awake. He sprang back, releasing Leena. His gaze met Sister Bertrice's disapproving frown. The missionary's eyes widened in fright as footsteps approached from outside.

The door crashed open. A bright stream of sunlight poured inside the hut. Brother Aron awoke noisily, muttering a prayer. A native woman shuffled inside to leave a meal of gruel and water for the prisoners. She didn't look at their faces as she left just as quietly.

****

While they ate, Leena surreptitiously studied Taurin. He'd removed the cloth from his head and looked ruggedly handsome with his thick ebony hair and clear gray eyes. She'd awakened once during the night and had glanced at him. She thought she'd seen a faint glow coming from the front of his face, but because his head was swathed in cloth, she couldn't be sure.

Her mouth still burned from his kiss, and the memory brought a hot flush to her face. She'd been disappointed when he drew away, but they couldn't very well continue with Sister Bertrice looking on.

A tribesman came inside and indicated they should follow him. Flinching from the brightness outside, Leena obeyed as they were led to an outhouse. Then they were prodded at spear point to accompany a group of warriors clothed in furs and shell necklaces, their faces streaked with paint. Huts similar to theirs dotted the hillside.

Apparently, they'd come quite a distance the day before. The elevation made her breath come short, and her exhalations steamed from the cold. A wooded path took them to a shady grotto with crumbling stone pillars and other structures familiar to her.

"By the grace of Lothar, it's a ruin." She glanced excitedly at Taurin, whose face wore a look of nonchalance.

Her pulse racing at the prospect of exploration, Leena yearned to examine the structures. Instead, they were driven in front of a rectangular, flat stone, which had the ominous appearance of an altar. Here they were forced to their knees. Leena swallowed past a lump in her throat. A man faced them who wore an ornately feathered headdress. His fierce features proclaimed his leadership as he raised his staff above their heads and muttered incantations she couldn't understand. The warriors chanted and swayed, their voices rising into a shrill crescendo.

Behind the altar rose a stone pillar. Leena noticed a lazy stream behind it. Her ears picked up the sound of gurgling water along with a strange sucking noise.

When the rising sun reached the top of the column, a ray pierced forth with sparkling radiance, and she saw what hadn't been visible before—a round, faceted crystal embedded inside the stone column. In the direct light of a sunbeam, the crystal began to glow, and the sound of the stream changed from a happy bubbling to a hissing boil.

Leena pointed. "I'll bet that's the source of their heating system. The crystal appears to power the stream somehow."

Taurin grunted his acknowledgment of her theory. His expression appeared harsh in the dappled light from the grotto, the angles of his face gaunt. Dark stubble covered his jaw, and circles shadowed his eyes. Leena hadn't realized how burdened he must feel with the responsibility for their safety.

Brother Aron joined them. "Look, the stream divides over there. Part of it siphons off below."

The tribal leader barked an order, and a thrust of spears indicated they should be silent. Several of his followers advanced upon Sister Bertrice. They seized her by the arms and dragged her to the altar, where they forced her onto her back.

The chief withdrew a curved dagger from his belt and held it above the shrieking missionary while the tribesmen restrained her arms.

"Dear deity, they're going to sacrifice her." Leena clapped a hand to her mouth.

"Not if I can help it." Taurin went for his weapon, but just then a cloud drifted across the sun, dampening the light.

The tribal leader's eyes widened as he glanced at Taurin. The dagger dropped from his hand. Without a word, he turned on his heels and fled.

The tribesmen, following his example, dropped their spears and wheeled away as though pursued by demons.

The cloud broke, and as the sun brightened the sky, Leena frowned in puzzlement. "What just happened?"

Sister Bertrice sat up and rubbed her arms, a dazed look on her face. Leena hastened over to assist her off the sacrificial altar.

"Something must have frightened them away," Taurin said in a mild tone.

"They were looking at you," Leena remarked.

He shrugged as though unwilling to give an explanation. "We don't have time to analyze their actions. I suggest we get away from here."

Brother Aron, who'd been standing behind the rest of them, whipped out a blaster. He pointed it at Taurin. "You and your lovely lady friend aren't going anywhere. You'll be viewed as unfortunate sacrifices to the native savages. Sister Bertrice and I will be the only ones who make it to safety."

"Where did you get that firearm?" Taurin demanded.

"It doesn't matter. If you believe in a god, I suggest you pray to him now. And you, madam"—he nodded at Leena—"may request Lothar to receive you."

"Receive me! What do you mean?" Stunned, Leena watched Sister Bertrice move to Brother Aron's side. Surely the pair didn't mean to kill them and leave them there? "Why are you doing this?"

Brother Aron smirked. "I have friends in high places who don't want your quest to succeed. My instructions were to see that you met a fatal end. So be it." He raised his weapon.

Taurin's muscles tensed. "Who sent you? Surely you can tell us before we die."

"Wodeners don't betray their sources. Prepare to meet your maker."

As his finger twitched on the trigger, Taurin threw himself into a flying leap that landed him a kick at Brother Aron's knee. Knocked off balance, the missionary's shot went wild. A beam of red light sizzled through the air as he toppled backward. Taurin sprawled atop him, and the two rolled in the dirt, struggling for control.

From the corner of her eye, Leena noticed Sister Bertrice dashing by. She charged after the woman, skidding to a stop when the missionary whirled around brandishing a knife in her grasp.

Sister Bertrice pounced on Leena, grabbing her by the hair and thrusting the blade at her throat. The missionary's gaze swung to her companion who lay still on the ground. Beside him, Taurin staggered to his feet.

"Stay where you are, or I'll kill your woman," Sister Bertrice warned him.

Leena held herself immobile, afraid the dirk at her throat would pierce her flesh if she moved. Shouts from the village drew Sister Bertrice's attention enough for Taurin to grab a rock and hurtle it through the air. It struck the missionary right between the eyes. Her legs crumpled, and she sprawled next to her senseless companion on the packed earth.

"Come on! Let's get out of here." Taurin called to Leena, whose own knees wobbled from a delayed reaction.

"What about those two?" she asked, her voice hoarse.

"Leave them. I suspect they belong to the Truthsayer movement."

Leena didn't hesitate further. She followed him into the woods away from the village, or so she thought until Taurin called for a halt beside a thicket of tall shrubs.

"Wait here. I'll see if I can recover our gear."

Before she could protest, he disappeared behind a clump of leafy trees. Leena waited, biting her lip and reflecting on their close call with the missionaries—if they were, indeed, members of the clergy. Likely they'd assumed those disguises to put themselves above suspicion.

Taurin loped into view, carrying their sacks and a few unfamiliar items. Cautious to avoid attention from the tribesmen, they didn't speak as they descended the hill in search of their abandoned riders. When they did find them, Taurin was dismayed to see the lead vehicle had been completely dismantled by the curious natives. Fortunately, the one he and Leena had used was still intact.

A heap of parts on the ground attracted his attention. He threw several of the items into the backseat of their rider along with their salvaged goods.

"Get in," he ordered as he slid into the driver's seat.

Soon they were rattling downhill at a rapid pace, neither one daring to look behind to see if they were being pursued. Their only thought was to reach a reasonable level before darkness fell.

"We have to avoid Alber's men," Leena shouted over the engine noise.

"They won't be looking for us. Ives probably went back and told Alber we'd been conveniently lost."

They drove for hours, each immersed in their own thoughts. Eventually, Leena succumbed to exhaustion and fell asleep, awakening when they reached the valley below.

Taurin stopped for a break by the banks of a stream. Wild berries and fruit hanging from trees provided a meal. They happily picked their fill of nature's bounty and quenched their thirst with cool water from the stream.

"We need to find shelter for tonight," he said. "I'd like to hide our rider in a secure location. Let's move on for now."

Feeling grimy and bedraggled, Leena climbed back into the vehicle.

Taurin sped along a paved road that twisted in and out of various settlements. As they approached an offshoot around dusk, he chose to drive up the hillside to a plateau. Here he parked at the edge of a flower-strewn meadow.

"I'm amazed by the wildflowers," he said, stretching his arms outside in the fresh air. "How does Lothar's beneficence extend here, while he plagues our land with drought? The people who live on this island don't follow the Faith. They were banished here because they're dissenters. If you ask me, Lothar isn't playing fair."

Leena glared at him, hands on her hips. "I thought you didn't believe in Lothar."

"Maybe you're convincing me there's something to believe in." Taurin gave her a heated glance that made her skin flush. At one of their stops, she'd changed behind a clump of bushes into a ruby-red gown, the velvety fabric keeping her warm against the cooler temperatures that prevailed on this side of the island. Taurin's gaze darkened as he lazily surveyed her curves.

Fearing he might come closer, she turned away and strolled across the meadow. Her feet stumbled over a solid object poking from the ground.

She stooped to get a closer look, and her mouth dropped open. Dear deity! That piece of rock looked like it came from the same type of carved stone as the ruins she'd studied.

Chapter Eleven

"Taurin, look at this." Leena knelt and used a dried twig to scrape away the dirt until she'd dug the stone from the soil. "Can you get my supplies, please?"

Taurin brought her the sack with her archeological tools. She took a brush and gently swept away the surface grime. Years of wind and rain had taken its toll. She could barely discern the symbols.

"The Black Lands must be dotted with these ruins. Pieces could be scattered anywhere." She sat back on her haunches to gaze up at him.

He stood by patiently, the breeze ruffling his hair. She thought he'd never looked more magnificent than now, with the setting sun emitting a tangerine glow behind him. With his tall frame, broad shoulders, and menacing aura, one might fancy he came from the demon world—except that his expression was tender as he watched her, and it melted her heart.

She ignored the wave of warmth that seduced her senses under his scrutiny. "It's curious the Synod has never mentioned these finds."

"Outsiders are forbidden to come here," Taurin reminded her. "These ruins must not be important enough to be studied."

"What about the crystal used by those natives in the mountains, the ones who captured us? I wish we could have examined it. That crystal must have been the source of power for the steam heat."

"It's too late for that now. Let's make camp."

While she chose a likely spot, he strode to the rider and obtained a blanket he must have stolen from the villagers. After spreading the material on the ground among the wildflowers, he sat with Leena to watch the sun descend in a brilliant display of colors. As the sky darkened, a perfumed scent pervaded the air.

"This island is lovely," Leena commented, while every fiber of her being sprang into awareness at his proximity. "I don't understand why they call it the Black Lands."

"Perhaps it's related to the evil hearts of the men who are sent here. Or does it derive from the evil intentions of the people who banish them? I'm not sure who is right or wrong anymore."

Startled, she glanced at him. She hoped his fears were ungrounded, and the Synod wasn't guilty of treachery. Yet one member had stolen the horn, and in so doing, threatened their chances for survival.

The horn had to be restored to maintain the balance of society, especially in stabilizing the climate and providing the wellness lozenge.

Already they'd learned someone in the hierarchy had permitted the Chocola Company to harvest beans on this island. That person was profiting off the misery of the inhabitants. If only she could contact Bendyk, but it would have to wait. Tomorrow they'd make for Grotus's island, and who knew what discoveries awaited them there?

In the meantime, she had to spend the night with Taurin under a star-studded sky. It was growing cold, and she was aware of his attention focused on her. By all that was holy, how could she rid herself of this restless urge she had in his presence? It destroyed her peace of mind, knowing he was so near. Daring to look at him, she gasped to find his gaze locked on her mouth.

"We need to get an early start in the morning," he said in a gruff tone. "Get some sleep." He pulled out his familiar cloth and swathed it about his head before lying down and turning away from her.

Leena felt a wave of disappointment. For a brief moment,

she'd thought he meant to kiss her. Why did he so abruptly change his mind?

She put her head down on the rumpled shawl she'd fashioned into a pillow and squirmed with discomfort. Every inch of her was aware of him lying beside her. Piqued that he wouldn't remove the cloth that shadowed his face and share his reasons for wearing it, she tried to imagine what he might be hiding. She gave up the conjecture as a useless exercise.

As the air cooled, the warmth from his body seeped into hers, keeping her from getting too cold. Or was it the hot blood that coursed through her body at his nearness that made her feel so warm? How could she want him when he was unlike anyone she'd ever known? It should be Malcolm's image that sprang to mind when she closed her eyes, not this man's.

Malcolm represented security and stability—qualities she'd thought she wanted in a husband. Now she doubted Malcolm could ever arouse her passions in the same manner as Taurin. She was fond of him, but as a dear family friend. Being bonded to a man like Taurin would be infinitely more exciting.

I am wed to him, she reminded herself. *Lothar save me, but I'm beginning to wish he would treat me as his wife.*

As soon as the thought entered her head, she chastised herself. *Shame on you!* You're nearly pledged to Malcolm. Would you dishonor your family by taking such a man as this to bed? Their marriage was in name only. It would be annulled as soon as they completed their mission. And despite the freedoms allowed in their society, she knew Malcolm would expect her to be faithful.

Yet as Taurin shifted his position, his buttocks inadvertently bumping against hers, Leena couldn't help the small moan that escaped her lips. Every bone in her body stiffened, and she held herself rigid until he regained a position of comfort. His breathing sounded ragged, as though his rest was troubled, but she didn't dare move lest she betray her desire.

He must never know how much she craved his touch and yearned to feel the pressure of his mouth on hers.

****

Sometime during the night, Taurin awakened to find Leena's legs entwined with his, one arm thrown against his chest. Earlier, he'd struggled to fight his attraction to her. With the glow from the sky backlit against her hair, it seemed as though she were lit with an ethereal aura. Her pink lips were soft and full, tempting him to sweep her into his arms and lie with her upon the bed of flowers. But he didn't dare start something he couldn't finish. One kiss wouldn't be enough. Afraid he'd lose control if he touched her, he had swathed his head in his usual cloth and settled onto his side.

As he shifted his position, she murmured unintelligibly. He agonized with each contact between them and slept very little, savoring the silken feel of her hair against his arm and the luscious warmth of her body. Overhead, a myriad of stars glittered in the night sky as cool air swept across the meadow. Taurin wasn't cold. He desired Leena until the flames of lust consumed him, heating his blood to a raging torrent.

Stop this insanity. The woman is forbidden fruit.

He couldn't have her, and it broke his heart that while she was wed to him, she was almost promised to another. Perhaps Malcolm would reject her, and she'd seek him for solace.

No, that was absurd. Why should Leena ever come to him again? Once she was back at the Palisades, she'd resume her former life, and her position did not include associating with people like him.

Casting off his daydreams as a waste of time, Taurin tucked his elbow under his head and closed his eyes. It was his fate to live in isolation. He'd just have to isolate his emotions as well, in order to preserve his sanity.

****

Leena awoke to a fresh dawn, scented with the fragrance of wildflowers. With her eyes still closed, she reached out to touch

Taurin, seeking reassurance from his presence, but her fingers met empty air. Her eyelids snapped open, and she peered at the rumpled blanket beside her. He was gone.

Frightened, she bolted upright, giving a cry of relief when she spotted him across the meadow, bending beside their rider. She stood and shook out her stiff joints. Then she headed toward him.

He'd tucked his black shirt into a pair of matching trousers. His booted feet were a dark contrast to the brilliant flowers surrounding them. He appeared to be assembling a piece of machinery.

"What are you doing?" she asked as she approached.

His face brightened, and he gestured to his apparatus. "I'm building us a means of transport to Grotus's island. I took this fan motor from the other rider, and I'd had the foresight to bring a sail from the ship. Here, help me spread the canvas."

He'd attached various ropes to different edges of the sturdy fabric. He had also removed the seats from the other rider and secured ropes to the seating platform.

She helped him spread the canvas material over the dewy grass. "I don't understand. How does it work?"

"You'll see. The weather is perfect. It's cool, and there's a slight breeze. According to what I've read, morning is the best time for flying this contraption."

"What on Xan is it?" Curiosity sluiced through her.

"A hot air balloon. It's the only means I could think of to reach Grotus's island. We can't hire a boat to take us there, and the higher air currents are too turbulent for commercial flight. We should be able to make it if we remain at a low altitude."

"But we don't even know where his island is located. There could be thousands of them in the archipelago."

"Have faith, madam. Lothar will guide us." He gave her a sardonic grin.

Leena's lips tightened. "You mock me, sir."

His gaze softened as he regarded her. "I'm sorry. Perhaps

we should say morning prayers together. If there is any divine help available, we could use it."

What? Had she heard him correctly? Taking advantage of the moment, she bowed her head and began her litany.

"Praise be to Lothar for all our blessings—for life, for work and rest, for home and love and friendship. May we continue to be worthy of your generosity, dear lord. As this new day dawns, we awake renewed and refreshed, inspired by your love for us and by your graciousness. May our day be filled with beauty, goodness, and truth as we follow the path of your righteousness."

"Mahala," Taurin murmured. Getting back to the business at hand, he removed a couple of cans from his heavy burlap sack, rummaged around in the bag, and then cursed.

"What is it?" Leena asked. Her stomach growled, reminding her they hadn't eaten since yesterday. She pressed a hand to her middle without complaining.

"I forgot to bring something as simple as a can opener. I have tools in the back of the rider, but they won't do the job."

"There's got to be something you can use. Let me get my archeological equipment." She hastened back to the blanket where she'd left her gear.

A few minutes later, Taurin was foraging through her sack containing short-handled shovels, hoes, cutting shears, a small ax, a knife, string, trowels, tweezers, paint brushes, and assorted report forms. He chose a sharp-edged tool and hacked away at the top of the can until the space was big enough for him to pour out the granules inside.

"This isn't the way I'd normally mix these compounds," he explained. "When I combine them, they'll make a volatile substance that will serve our purpose."

After they'd gathered their belongings and grabbed some fruit for a quick meal, Taurin pronounced them ready to cast off. He fired up the makeshift burners to pump hot air into the fabric's expanding envelope.

"What if the sail catches fire?" Leena asked, her pulse accelerating.

"If direct heat touches it, the fabric might melt, but it won't burn. Go ahead and step inside. Don't be afraid."

She obeyed, clinging to the rim since the space was cramped. The fabric swelled upward. Taurin joined her on the platform and tossed off the tether lines.

Their makeshift balloon began to rise. As their height increased, the meadow below got smaller and smaller.

Leena dropped into her seat and clutched the sides as their platform swayed back and forth. Dear diety. What if the fabric got pierced somehow, and they plunged to their deaths?

"We'll head west," Taurin shouted over the roar of the burners. He yanked on the blast lever to send another shot of hot air up into the envelope.

Leena turned her face away from the searing heat of the blowers. Since talking was so difficult over the roaring noise, she concentrated on quelling her panic instead. Periodically Taurin used shots of the burners to lift the balloon or to maintain a steady altitude as the air cooled inside the envelope. By pulling on the lines connected to the vents high in the fabric, he could release air on either side of their craft. This rotated their direction so that their voyage became a feat of juggling between heating and venting.

As they rose toward the sky, Leena glanced around in amazement, forgetting her fear in the magnificence of the view. The volcanic origin of the Black Lands soon became evident. As they floated by the mountain ridge to the north, a white plume of smoke spewed from a still-active vent. Taurin steered clear of the higher range. Lush greenery covered most of the island except for the west coast, where lava flows had reduced the land to a black, rocky void.

"So that's why this place is called the Black Lands." She leaned forward for a better view. Her motion rocked the platform, and she jerked back with a cry of alarm.

"Don't move too fast," Taurin cautioned, pulling on one of the side vents to steady their course.

Beyond the blackened shoreline was a stretch of sea that

shimmered in reflection from the rising sun. Leena shaded her eyes as she peered toward the archipelago in the distance. She could barely make out the series of islands dotting the water, but they loomed larger as their craft approached. Terrified they'd fall into the water if a gust of wind caught them the wrong way, she sat rigidly in her seat.

Taurin appeared fully in control of the vessel, however, and he took a pair of viewfinder glasses from the sack at his feet. He clamped the strap around his head and gazed out to sea through the magnifying lenses.

It wasn't until they had passed over the first of the islands that he gestured and cried out. "Over there!"

Leena barely heard him over the intense roar of the blowers, but the animated expression on his face was self-explanatory. She rose carefully and glanced over the side. Taurin jiggled a finger, yelling something at her. Sure enough, she could make out a spot of color on one of the islands below. No doubt Taurin could see more clearly through his special glasses.

He waved at her, but she didn't understand what he was trying to say until he yanked on one of the cords and the platform shifted. She fell back into her seat and remained there, her knuckles white as she clutched the armrests.

They'd begun their descent, and her stomach lurched as Taurin vented hot air through the top of the balloon. Their rate of decline increased rapidly. If that was Grotus's hideaway, Taurin must be planning to put them down right smack in the middle of it.

She glanced at him questioningly, but his mouth was set in a grim line, and his shoulders were hunched as though he were deep in concentration.

The island below consisted of two mountainous humps. Nestled in the valley between them sat a palatial structure with manicured lawns and formal gardens. A natural forest, woven with streams and brooks, surrounded the estate. An approach road ran along the ravine.

They continued to lurch downward. Upon Taurin's signal, she slung her backpack over her shoulders. Before their launch, she'd stuffed her meager belongings inside, along with her most valued archeological supplies. Taurin had done the same with the items he wanted to keep.

As they veered in on their final approach, Leena surveyed the four-story mansion in more detail. It consisted of fitted lime stones decorated with intricately carved woodwork. Lush shrubs, cultivated beds of flowers, and tall maple trees bordered a series of gravel paths winding through the grounds.

Their imminent arrival had been detected, and armed guards rushed onto the lawn. As they briefly touched down, Taurin urged her to jump. She swallowed her fright and leaped over the edge. As she landed on a soft bed of grass, she heard Taurin's thud beside her. The balloon lifted and soared away into the sky.

She scrambled to her feet, trembling as a bevy of guards surrounded them, weapons drawn. They wore nondescript clothes, but the hard look in their eyes told her they knew their job. Their armaments were foreign-looking devices with long barrels.

"Who are you? Why have you come here?" snapped a man with a flat nose.

Leena jutted her chin. "I'm Leena Worthington-Jax representing the Synod. It is imperative we speak to Grotus. Our business is urgent… and private."

The leader of the guards surveyed Taurin. "What about you?"

"I'm her escort." His tone implied they'd be well advised to regard him with respect.

A heavy silence followed, then the man said, "Follow me."

Leena's apprehension vanished, replaced by a sense of triumph. Her heart beat rapidly. News of the horn could be forthcoming! Muttering a prayer that their talk with Grotus would be fruitful, she strode ahead, her chin uplifted with pride.

****

Bendyk and Swill finally found a moment to confer together in their office. They sat at separate desks but could easily see each other from their upholstered swivel chairs.

"One of Sirvat's neighbors said she likes to travel," Bendyk told Swill, proud of the information he'd gleaned. "Sirvat always returns in a jovial mood, wearing a new piece of jewelry. Apparently, the trinkets she brings back are unlike the usual gold pieces people wear."

"How so?" Swill asked with a tilt of her head.

"The neighbor said they're embedded with polished gemstones that must cost a fortune. Sirvat's predilection for fancy jewelry isn't generally known. She doesn't wear the pieces while on duty, but this neighbor told me she has quite a collection."

"Is it possible she meets a male admirer?"

"It's more than likely." Bendyk's gaze shifted to Swill's simple sheath dress. Its rust color brought out the golden sparkle of her eyes. He wondered how she would look with a gold choker around her neck and had a sudden urge to present her with a gift. "You said there was a miscellaneous entry being made into the Treasury records each month?" he inquired, attempting to steer his thoughts back to business.

Swill nodded, her expression thoughtful. "When I pressed her, Sirvat admitted Magar was responsible. She said his department receives the funds, so we should ask him about the source. She didn't know what the receipts meant."

"So basically what we have on Sirvat is that the Treasury records check out except for one entry that Magar might be able to explain."

"Correct. Sirvat's personal finances are in order, but this matter of her traveling and coming home with new jewelry bothers me. It's uncharacteristic of her, at least according to the image she presents at work."

Bendyk pressed his lips together. "We should assign a

couple of Caucus members to tail her. It wouldn't hurt to find out where she goes the next time she takes off on one of these trips."

"Good idea."

Swill smiled at him, and Bendyk's heart somersaulted. He didn't understand why earning her admiration was so important to him, but somewhere along the way she'd become more than a business partner. At least he wanted to regard her in a different fashion if she'd let him. The woman fascinated him, and he found he couldn't get enough of her company.

"What about Magar?" Swill asked.

"I have an interview scheduled with him next. Would you like to come?"

"Sure, if you don't think it would upset him to confront us both. By the way, would you care to join me for dinner afterward?"

Bendyk gaped at her, too astonished to speak. Since their last dinner together, their relationship had been fairly formal and their conversations confined to the topic at hand. Although he'd been hoping for more, he hadn't really thought Swill was interested.

"I'd love to," he told her. "Thanks for the invite."

He rose and donned a gold-lined cloak over his longshirt and trousers so that he would appear more impressive when they saw the Minister of State.

Magar was waiting for him in his spacious office. His eyes widened when he saw Swill at Bendyk's side, but the statesman quickly recovered his composure.

"Brother Bendyk and Sister Swill. Please, be seated. What can I do for you?"

Bendyk started with the matter uppermost in his mind. "You sent my sister off with Taurin Rey Niris. How do you know this man? Where is he from?"

Magar leaned back in his chair and folded his hands together. "I met him during a diplomatic exchange. He wanted to relocate, and I said I'd help him."

"Why?"

Magar shrugged. "He grew edible flowers, and we needed

farmers here. We don't have enough growers in this area. So I obtained permission from the Population Council for him to immigrate."

"How did he end up on a piece of your property?"

"The man didn't know anyone here, so I offered to sell him a plot of land."

"Did he pay you in cash, or is he paying you back year-by-year?"

"We made a trade." Magar's gaze skittered away as though the topic made him uncomfortable.

"A trade? What sort of trade?" Bendyk persisted.

"Let's say we each had something the other wanted."

"You told us the man was from Iman. I checked the census. There's no such person listed from Iman," Bendyk said.

Magar's complexion grew a shade paler. "Is that so? I'm only repeating what the man told me. I didn't delve into his background."

Bendyk raised his eyebrows. "Then how did you know he could protect Leena? Where did he gain his fighting skills?"

"He will take care of her. You have my assurance on that."

"Why is he so interested in archeological symbols?"

"It is an interest of his," Magar replied in a patient tone.

"You said you met him at a diplomatic exchange?" Swill said, hunching forward. "Who were the parties present?"

Magar simply stared at her, remaining silent.

"On another subject, we found a series of regular entries in the Treasury records," she went on. "Sirvat said your department was responsible for this revenue. Can you tell us the source?"

Magar gave them a small smile. "It's a catchall for funds that don't fall into any special category."

"Nonetheless, we'll want to examine your department's transactions for the last few years," Bendyk stated.

"I don't see why that's necessary," Magar snapped. He rose, pressing his hands against the polished wood desk. "And now I'm afraid I must call an end to this interview. You should be looking for the person who stole the horn instead of wasting time with me."

"And who do you suggest we investigate?" Swill asked sweetly.

"Try Karayan. He's too ambitious for his own good. I'd watch out for him if I were you."

Karayan? My father's friend is the last one I would suspect, Bendyk thought as he and Swill left Magar's office. *Magar is just trying to throw suspicion off himself.*

"I believe Magar is purposefully withholding information," he said to Swill as they walked back toward their office.

"Why don't we enlist some of the Caucus aides to look into his latest trade agreements?" she suggested. "Perhaps we'll find the source of revenue that way. We could also obtain a record of Magar's movements if we dig further."

Bendyk scowled. "I'd like to find out how he met Rey Niris. There's something odd going on between those two that Magar is unwilling to discuss."

Swill wound her arm through his. "Let's have dinner and forget about business for now, shall we?"

Her familiar gesture startled him. "Of course. Where would you like to go?"

"I'll fix something in my apartment."

His ears perked up. Her apartment! Briefly he considered refusing. He wasn't sure he could behave with the proper decorum in such an intimate setting. Swill was a temptation he was finding increasingly difficult to resist.

Wondering what she had in mind, his imagination soared with different possibilities, most of them erotic. A thrill of anticipation shot through him at the idea of spending the evening alone with her, regardless of the outcome.

Chapter Twelve

"Nice flowers," Taurin muttered as their captors took them between sculpted garden paths and up to the front portico of Grotus's mansion.

Leena rolled her eyes. Leave it to him to comment on the gardens. She was too concerned that they meet their goal to care. If Grotus knew anything about the horn, they'd soon find out. Trembling with excitement, she preceded Taurin into a huge reception hall, ornately decorated with gilded ceilings and cherubs painted on silk-lined walls. Expensive objets d'art were displayed in strategic locations meant to provide maximum viewing pleasure.

Leena wondered if Grotus ever brought guests here and, if so, what method of transportation they used. A number of other structures had been visible outside. Presumably, some of them were guard quarters, but she had no idea what the others represented. Grotus would have to keep his own gardeners and housekeepers. Did his staff live here permanently, or were they sworn to secrecy and allowed to return home for periodic visits? If the latter was the case, how did they get off the island?

She'd seen no visible means of transportation, such as aircraft or ships, in the vicinity. So how did Grotus and his people come and go? For that matter, how would she and Taurin leave when it was time to do so?

While one of the guards scurried off to alert Grotus to their arrival, she surveyed the hall. Her eyebrows lifted as she recognized a set of bronzes by Anton Luye, a famous sculptor.

She'd seen some of his pieces in Karayan's residence. Flanking the statuettes was a pair of candelabra made of sparkling silversheen.

Woven tapestries decorated the walls, but she preferred the ceiling tiles painted with scenes from ancient legends. A polished gold disk hung above a central archway. It was an artifact from the Kelleran Age, no doubt stolen by Grotus's ring of smugglers.

Unfortunately, many people were interested in buying artifacts for their private collections. Archeological looting had been recorded since the times of ancient kings, and it continued to this day. Many sites she'd explored had been ravaged by looters. Illegal marketing of artifacts from unsupervised excavations made for a lucrative business, one that the Ministry of Religion had been unsuccessfully trying to stop.

Grotus was a kingpin among the unscrupulous dealers. Taking him out of action would ensure that historical sites were preserved for professionals to excavate. But Grotus always covered his tracks. No one had ever relayed a description of him, so she wondered what he looked like. For that matter, where did he obtain his guards and the servants who waited on him?

She and Taurin were shown into a library paneled in rich koobi nut, with a magnificent woven carpet depicting the Apostles. On a mantle above a black marble fireplace stood jadestone figurines representing Vestia, goddess of water and Demeter, goddess of the earth. Hanging between the figures was a seventeenth-century Aurin tapestry.

A globe sat in one corner behind a comfortable seating arrangement that included plush furnishings upholstered in royal blue. Bookshelves filled the walls from floor to ceiling. Her gaze lit on two statuettes carved from backenstone heralding from the Triceras Age. They provided more evidence of looting from early tombs.

"Our host is quite a connoisseur of ancient artifacts." Leena withdrew her circlet from inside a deep pocket and placed it on her head of blond waves. Hopefully Grotus would respect her position.

"I would expect that's his main interest." Taurin studied each object in the room as though weighing its potential as a weapon.

A side door opened, and a tall man strode into the room. He looked to be in his late forties. He'd pulled his black hair into a severe ponytail and wore a multi-colored longshirt cinched at the waist by a wide leather belt. Leena recognized the jewel-encrusted buckle as a relic from the Moradean excavation site. His baggy black pants tucked into a pair of polished knee-high boots.

Her gaze riveted on his nose ring as he approached. Dear deity, it appeared to be constructed of the same creamy translucent material as the sacred horn!

"I am Grotus. I understand you wish to see me." His gravelly voice grated on Leena's ears. "Your unorthodox arrival has drawn my interest, otherwise I'd have you disposed of in the same manner as other trespassers. What brings you here?"

"I am Leena Worthington-Jax." She spoke in a strong, clear tone as though unaware of the guards hovering behind. "This is my husband, Taurin Rey Niris. We're on a quest authorized by the Synod." Leena caught the warning gleam in Taurin's eyes but decided she could handle Grotus on her own. "We need information."

Grotus eyed her attire with a lecherous gleam. "I have to attend to some business. Join me for dinner, and we'll discuss this matter that you deem so important. My head housekeeper will show you to a room. I'd be delighted to have you stay overnight as my guests."

"He didn't give us much of a choice," Taurin muttered in a low voice as they followed the stern-faced woman up a curved marble staircase. Leena gripped the wooden banister while wondering if they'd be allowed to roam the house. Art treasures teased her from every corner, and she longed to explore.

After showing them into a sumptuous bedchamber, the housekeeper indicated a cord by which to summon assistance.

It's still morning, Leena thought, and they had the whole day ahead of them. Why was Grotus making them wait? Did he really have pressing business, or did he want to check into their backgrounds before dinner?

"Would we be permitted to explore the house and grounds?" she asked the gray-haired woman.

"If you wish." The housekeeper wore a starched apron over a plum-colored dress. "I'll have a guide escort you, say in half an hour. Will that be satisfactory? We'll provide you with midday nourishment so you won't go hungry."

Leena forced a smile. "That will be fine. Thank you."

As soon as they were left alone, she turned to Taurin excitedly. "Grotus must have raided half the sites on Xan." She pointed to more stolen objects lying about the room. "None of this is authorized to pass into the private sector. It belongs to the Ministry of Religion."

"Grotus doesn't follow the rules."

"No, he doesn't."

Leena glanced at the large bed in the center of the bedroom. "We should have told the housekeeper we need separate rooms."

Taurin's gaze darkened. "May I remind you that we are wed, madam?"

Self-conscious under his scrutiny, Leena avoided looking into his smoky eyes. He took a step closer, tilting her chin to force her to meet his gaze. Before she realized his intent, he lowered his head and pressed his mouth to hers.

Shock rolled through her, caused less by his action and more by the eagerness of her own response. Instead of pushing him away, she wrapped her arms around him and gave in to the incredible sensations spiraling within her. Her pliant body leaned against his hard length.

As though sensing her willingness, he crushed her in his embrace, his kisses increasing in intensity.

"Taurin," she whispered, wanting something more but not understanding what it was. She longed for a goal beyond her grasp and intuitively knew Taurin could satisfy it. His virility outshone any other man she had known. Because he was so different, he appealed to her even more.

His hand caressed her face. He brushed his lips lightly over hers and murmured her name. When his hand trailed downward, over the front of her bodice, she didn't resist. They were alone, man and wife, and the wide bed beckoned them.

Taurin nudged her over, and she stretched out, sighing with pleasure as he settled beside her. His mouth never left hers. When he brought his hand to her chest, she moaned with pleasure.

"I shouldn't let you do this."

"You're my wife."

His hand wandered to her breast, and Leena clutched at his back. She had an irrational urge to tear his shirt off so she could feel his bare flesh beneath. His kisses aroused her to a wild frenzy. She parted her mouth, inviting his tongue to enter, and when it did, she met it with her own dance of exploration.

"Lothar save me, but I want you to touch me," she said in a voice so husky she barely recognized it as her own.

"If we go much farther, I won't be able to stop." Taurin's eyes glazed with lust.

"We should be thinking of a way out of here."

"We can think later. I want you now."

Leena cried out when his hand slid inside her bodice and found her naked breast. Dear deity, what he's doing to me, she thought as he rubbed her nipple, sending coils of delight to the junction between her thighs. Please, don't stop, she urged him silently. The muscular planes of his back rippled beneath her fingers as she held onto him as though letting go would dispel the magic.

He rolled atop her, pushing her legs apart. She closed her eyes, hearing his grunts of pleasure as he rocked his hips back and forth. His bulge jabbed at her through her gown, but she wouldn't go so far as to remove her clothes.

Taurin apparently had other ideas. Suddenly the front of her bodice fell away, and she realized that he'd unfastened her gown. He pushed her binding out of the way, allowing him full access to her breasts. Moaning as his hands touched her skin, she accepted his inflamed kisses with renewed ardor. His hips moved atop her with increasing urgency, and his breath came in panting gasps.

A starburst of pleasure sprang from their intimate contact, and she was unable to stop its crescendo. She cried out as an explosive release gripped her in a series of spasms.

Taurin shuddered above her, crying her name, and then he lay still, as though his passion were spent. Stunned by what had happened, Leena let his weight rest upon her.

She had never experienced such ecstasy before, and she couldn't wait until they did it again. She hated herself for being so weak, but Taurin overwhelmed her sense of reason. *He's a demon, seducing me until I have no willpower to refuse him.*

He slid off her and lay on his back, staring at the ceiling. "I'm sorry. I didn't mean for that to happen." Then he swung off the bed and strode into the lavatory.

Leena stared after him, puzzled by his gruff tone. Did he regret what they'd just done? Why did he speak so harshly when she'd have appreciated a few words of kindness and affection?

Tears welled in her eyes as she regretted her inexperience. Perhaps she'd disappointed him.

It would be wise to pretend they were a happy, loving couple before Grotus. But how would that be possible when she had earned Taurin's disapproval?

Indeed, he emerged from the lavatory with a scowl on his face. He seemed almost relieved when a knock sounded on their door and a female guide introduced herself as Blanchette. Her manner of dress matched the head housekeeper's attire. Only Blanchette was much younger—in her twenties perhaps—with a sleek figure, shiny black hair, and a pretty face.

Leena ran into the lavatory to freshen up. When she emerged, Blanchette's gaze pinpointed her. "Grotus tells me you're a member of the Caucus. Why have you come here?"

"Our business is private. We'll discuss it with Grotus at dinner," Leena retorted.

She sensed the girl disliked her and wondered why. Perhaps it was because they were intruders. Grotus's staff would have to be very loyal to be trusted, meaning she and Taurin should be on their guard at all times. She glanced at him for reassurance but winced inwardly at the dark glare he gave her.

What's wrong? Why are you angry with me? She couldn't ask in front of Blanchette.

Her heart sank, and a heavy drape of depression covered her. She followed Blanchette out of the room and tried to rouse some enthusiasm for the magnificent artworks displayed throughout the mansion. But she was too aware of Taurin's silent tread beside her and the closed look on his face to enjoy their tour.

They began on the second floor, one level down from the bedroom suites. Blanchette showed them into a billiard room. Sporting pictures and theater prints adorned the oak paneling covering the walls. Leena recognized the leather settees and chairs as styles made by the well-known Morant furniture company. She liked the bronze sculpture of a warrior astride an *enix*. She'd seen similar ones in the tomb of Antiok, a ruler from the third dynasty. Her expert eye told her this was the authentic article, as were most of the objects she'd noted in the place.

They entered a banquet hall boasting ceiling arches seventy feet above the huge expanse. Tapestries hung on the walls, interspersed with ornate wood carvings. The dining table itself was made of polished bennir wood. Seating for twenty indicated Grotus might often have guests. Perhaps he invited his fellow smugglers for dinner, she thought, again wondering how they would arrive on the island. She'd seen no visible means of transportation.

A music room nearby held a stand for lyrics and a magnificent grand piano. Seats were arranged as though for a concert, while tall vases of fresh flowers lined the perimeter.

"Does Grotus play the piano?" she asked Blanchette in surprise.

Blanchette gave her a smile that did not extend to her eyes. "He's an accomplished musician. I'm sure he'll play for you tonight."

"He appears to be a man of exquisitely fine taste."

"Yes, except for his clothes," Taurin murmured.

Leena shot him a reproachful glance, but luckily Blanchette hadn't heard, or else she chose to ignore his remark.

"He does have a wonderful eye for art," Leena remarked on their way to a salon filled with comfortable sofas and armchairs, bright lighting, and a stenciled ceiling with linenfold paneling on the side walls.

"He's a thief, and you'd do well to remember that fact."

Leena's eyebrows raised. Taurin almost sounded jealous of the man, but that certainly couldn't be. More likely the man was figuring a way out of there. She'd leave the logistics of their escape plan to him, while she learned more about Grotus's operation.

"You don't see the horn anywhere, do you?" Taurin muttered on their way back to the third floor.

"Not yet," she replied in a low tone, mindful of their guide's presence.

They glanced into a couple of unoccupied guest rooms, an upstairs sitting room which Blanchette said they were welcome to use, and a parlor filled with potted plants and wicker furniture. An air-filtering system cooled the sunny room and emitted a faint fragrance of orange blossoms.

Under other circumstances, Leena could easily have spent several days exploring the house. But finding the horn was her priority, so she kept her eyes open during the tour.

"What's on the fourth floor?" she asked Blanchette.

"The servants' quarters are upstairs."

"And below?"

"Kitchens and workrooms."

"Do all the staff who work here live on the island?"

"Yes, of course," Blanchette replied in an annoyed tone, as though Leena lacked common sense. A clock chimed in the background. "I believe it's time for midday nourishment, after which I can show you the grounds."

"That would be lovely," Leena said, aware they had no choice.

Blanchette led them back downstairs to an informal dining room. The oval table was set with a white tablecloth and gold-rimmed dinnerware.

A couple of ladies were already present. They wore brightly colored garments and vacuous expressions. A scruffy fellow occupied the head of the table, his unshaven face sullen as he waited for his food. The ladies claimed to be friends of Grotus, while the man said he was a business associate.

After Leena and Taurin took seats opposite the two women, the wait staff served their meals. She enjoyed the baked cloinder fish, mixed greens, and buttered tortas along with a glass of vintage wine. Her attempts to get the strangers to talk met with mono-syllabic responses. Soon she gave up the effort and ate her fill.

As soon as she and Taurin had finished the sweet pudding for dessert, Blanchette reappeared to continue their tour. They spent a pleasant but unproductive afternoon strolling through the gardens. Taurin's face became animated as he exclaimed over the cultivated flower beds. Neither of them learned a thing about Grotus's operation, nor how he came and went from the island. Leena wondered if he already knew of their mission, since he didn't seem to be in any hurry to find out their reasons for coming to see him.

She readied herself for dinner later with rising excitement, eager to learn what Grotus knew of the missing horn. Showered and dressed, she preened before the mirror in her topaz gown. She'd only had room for three ensembles in her bag. The rest of the space was taken by her archeological tools, work breeches, and the tunics Taurin had bought her.

Taurin emerged from the lavatory, his jaw freshly shaven and his ebony hair damp. His black shirt was half open at the chest and tucked into a pair of tight black trousers that tapered into a pair of polished boots.

Leena couldn't stand the tension between them any longer. "What's wrong? Why aren't you talking to me?" she asked, turning to regard him.

"Nothing is wrong." He stuffed his few toilet articles back into his bag in case they had to make a hasty exit. He'd advised Leena to do the same.

"You're displeased with me, aren't you?"

"Displeased with you?" He glanced at her then, studying her and no doubt noticing her tremulous lower lip. "Why do you say that?"

"I… I disappointed you earlier. You got up and left, and you've seemed angry ever since."

****

Taurin's heart squeezed at her pained expression. She looked a vision in her yellow gown, with her golden hair streaming over her shoulders. He dare not tell her how he really felt.

He despised himself for taking advantage of her innocence. Nothing could be more despicable, especially when he knew nothing could come from any relationship between them. She might be the most desirable woman he'd ever met, but once they finished this mission—assuming they escaped from Grotus's place—they'd go their separate ways.

Yet his silence dissipated in the face of her anguish. "I am not angry with you, Leena. On the contrary, I'm so mad for you that I have difficulty restraining myself. If I had my way, I'd keep you as my wife. But both of us know that can never happen. We wouldn't be allowed to stay together."

She pressed her lips tight and averted her gaze. Likely she believed that lust drove him and nothing more. Taurin yearned to tell her how she brightened his life, how her inner serenity provided a balm for his troubled spirit. But their union could come to naught, or else he'd have her brother's wrath to answer to and perhaps the Synod's as well.

Besides, he couldn't afford for anyone to look too closely into his background. Hopefully, Magar had been able to fend off any questions about him. Leena would be horrified if she knew his true nature. He didn't trust himself where she was concerned and strengthened his resolve to keep his distance.

"I may want you, but you deserve better than me," he said in a quiet voice. "You don't know anything about my history or origins."

She took a step toward him, as though sensing his longing. "Then why won't you tell me? I can help you settle your issues."

"I don't need your help, woman."

"Perhaps it was a poor choice of words. I mean… I know you're not happy."

He squared his shoulders. "I'm very happy. I have my farm and my flowers. They bring me peace and harmony. That's all I want from life."

"Is it?"

Her question went unanswered because Blanchette arrived just then to take them to dinner.

Chapter Thirteen

Leena hadn't decided what to say to Grotus as she and Taurin accompanied their guide toward the formal dining room. What if the smuggler decided to disrespect her authority and get rid of them, like other unwanted visitors to his island?

She wouldn't give him the chance and rehearsed what she might say to convince the man to cooperate.

Grotus sat at the head of the table. He wore a turquoise shirt encrusted with silver spangles that clinked whenever he moved, plus white linen pants pressed to perfection. Besides his nose ring, he wore two sets of earrings in both ears and a number of flashy rings on his fingers.

He smoked a rolled *mogur* root, and the pungent aroma stung Leena's throat. She coughed behind her hand as she took a seat. Taurin claimed the spot beside her.

"Where are your other guests?" Taurin said.

Grotus blew out a puff of smoke. "You'd indicated our conversation was meant to be private. Would you care for an aperitif?" He rattled off a list of exotic choices. Taurin chose a drink, but Leena declined.

"How are you familiar with Muer's brandy?" Grotus asked Taurin, narrowing his eyes. "It's not readily available in these parts."

Leena felt Taurin tense beside her. "It sounded as though it would have a rich flavor. I have discerning tastes," he replied.

"Ah." Grotus eyed him keenly. "What is your occupation, sir?"

"I raise edible flowers and sell them at market."

"So you're a farmer."

"That is correct."

Grotus glanced at Leena. "You're married to this man?"

Leena's cheeks heated. "Yes, we are wed."

"Isn't your father the illustrious Cranby Worthington-Jax?"

"Yes, he is," she replied, wondering how far the smuggler's intelligence network extended. He'd obviously checked up on them earlier.

"And you obtained his permission to marry a farmer?" Grotus scoffed.

"I believe our personal issues have nothing to do with our business here. We're searching for a missing artifact, one the Ministry of Religion values highly. We are wondering if you might have heard of its whereabouts."

Grotus signaled for the first course to be served. "What kind of artifact?"

To Leena's relief, he stubbed out his *mogur* in a tray placed beside his plate for that purpose. Her throat was dry, and she gulped down several swallows of water from a crystal goblet provided on the table.

"It's a ceremonial object," she explained. "You would know what I meant if you had seen it. The Synod is willing to pay a substantial sum for its return."

"Perhaps a more detailed description would aid my memory," Grotus said in a coaxing tone.

Taurin cut in. "If you don't have the item, maybe you know who does."

Grotus stared at him for a full moment of silence. "Would the same reward be offered for information leading to the return of this valued object?"

"A lesser payment to be sure," Leena said, "but still a generous one."

Grotus signaled for the entrée to be served. Attendants brought steaming plates heaped with juicy steaks, sautéed vegetables, and fragrant cronsom rice. Then the servants withdrew, leaving them alone.

"Your background is in archeology, is it not?" Grotus directed a hooded gaze at Leena.

"Yes, I have advanced degrees in the subject." Leena rattled off her credentials, pleased when Grotus appeared impressed.

A messenger scurried into the room. He handed Grotus a folded parchment sealed with wax.

"I'm sorry to interrupt, sir, but the sender said it's urgent. Shall I wait for a reply?"

"Not now. You can go."

As the fellow scampered from the room, Grotus opened the document. He frowned as he scanned the contents. Then a chuckle erupted from his throat. "A bit late, aren't you, my little magpie?" he murmured.

Leena caught sight of the seal and gasped. Why would Sirvat send Grotus a private message? Was the Minister of Finance warning him of their arrival? How much did she reveal of their mission? Moreover, how did she know where to contact Grotus when she'd claimed no prior knowledge of this island's location?

Clearly, Sirvat could no longer be trusted. She'd ask Bendyk to look into Sirvat's relationship with the smuggler at the earliest opportunity.

Grotus addressed her. "I may not have the exact information you need, but I can offer you something else in trade."

"What would that be?" Leena chewed and swallowed a tender piece of meat while considering that Grotus might know who possessed the horn. He could be manipulating them for his own purposes.

"I'll share a secret closely guarded by the Synod, but this knowledge comes at a price."

"Such as the ransom we planned to pay you for the missing holy artifact?" Taurin asked in a sardonic tone.

"Oh, no. You see the objects I collect. I'll bet you have something I might like."

Taurin's gaze lit with understanding. "I do have an item in my bag upstairs. With your permission?"

Grotus motioned for Taurin to go.

A moment later, Leena's companion returned holding a small book in his hand. From the looks of it, this wasn't an ordinary book. How did one open it? By the circular depression on the tooled leather cover?

Wait a minute. Wasn't that inscription on the front written in the same symbols she'd been studying? The same as the ones in Taurin's drawings as well?

"Where did you get that?" she demanded, annoyed that he hadn't shown her this book before now.

He ignored her question. "Grotus, would this satisfy you in return for your so-called secret?" He plopped the book down on the table in front of the smuggler.

Grotus's eyes rounded. "A bibliotome! I have a few of these in my collection. Have you learned how to access it?"

"Not yet. Have you?"

"No, I've not had any success."

Leena puzzled at their exchange. She had no idea what they were talking about or where this item originated. She'd never seen anything like it among the artifacts she'd recovered.

"What is it you have to tell us?" Taurin said, reminding the smuggler about his part of the deal.

Grotus scratched his jaw. "An ancient temple exists deep in the jungles of Morasia. The Ministry of Religion has obliterated any record of its existence. Rumors say death stalks any intruders, and even my men have failed to get past the entrance. Supposedly, this Temple of Light hides a great treasure." He pointed to the large crystal ring on one of his fingers. "I suspect it holds more of these brilliant stones. I would give anything to find them."

Taurin leaned closer. "That gemstone looks familiar." He turned to Leena. "Isn't it similar to that crystal stone fixed in the pillar at the Black Lands?"

"Why yes, I believe you're right. You say this Temple of Light might have more of them?" she asked Grotus.

The smuggler nodded. "The story goes that the Temple of Light guards the secrets of the Apostles. I assume these crystals have a power we don't yet understand."

Leena's pulse accelerated at the possibilities. "How do we get there?"

Taurin tapped her arm. "Are you out of your mind? We're supposed to be searching for the missing relic."

"But if we could find a storehouse of these crystals, they might unlock the secrets of the past."

"And when you return, I may have information on the item you seek," Grotus offered with a wily grin. "Come, let us retire to the library. We can have our kava and dessert in there."

Once in the library, the smuggler drew a map from a locked desk and handed it to Leena. "Study this diagram. The path to the temple is through the jungle."

Taurin held out his hand. "I'll take my bibliotome back now, if you please."

"I don't think so. You offered the book to me in trade, and I gave you this map in return." He glanced at Taurin consideringly. "Perhaps you'd like to engage me in a bout of ramagan? We could save dessert for later."

"Ramagan? What's that?" Leena glanced between the two of them in confusion.

"An ancient sport." Taurin's eyes never left Grotus's face. "It would be my pleasure."

"There's a gymnasium downstairs. Follow me."

The men turned, and Leena hurried after them. "Hold on. What does this game involve?"

It didn't take her long to find out. Ramagan was a combat sport in which opponents used long sticks to knock each other off balance. Both men stripped to the waist, and she saw that Grotus kept himself in trim shape, no doubt with the help of the exercise machinery in the far corner. He paused in his warm-up stretches, his gaze fixed on the strange band Taurin wore around his upper arm.

"What is that?" Leena approached for a closer look. She hadn't noticed this armband on him before. By Lothar, it appeared to be constructed from the same creamy material as the sacred horn. She'd seen him without his shirt, but he must have kept this hidden.

"Now, that must be worth a fortune." Grotus licked his lips appreciatively.

"It's not for sale or trade." Taurin's chilled tone left no doubt he meant what he said.

"Where did you get it?"

"That doesn't concern you. Let's get on with the match."

The sparring lasted a good thirty minutes. The two opponents were well suited. They sweated and fought and finally called it a draw. Neither one could best the other.

After drying himself with a towel, Taurin threw on his shirt.

"Let's retire to the salon," Grotus suggested. "I'd like to show you my porcelain Apostles."

Grotus showered his attention on Leena while Taurin stood by. He accepted a glass of honeyed ambrosia from the smuggler who proudly exhibited his figurines to Leena.

"I could use someone with your expertise on my staff," Grotus told Leena.

"I'm flattered." She cast a troubled look in Taurin's direction. He stood with his back toward them to admire a tapestry on the wall. She could tell by the hunch of his shoulders that he wasn't pleased by Grotus's focus on her.

"Where did your man get his arm bracelet?" Grotus asked, his gaze darkening.

"I really don't know." Discomfited by his proximity, Leena changed the topic. "If Taurin and I mean to explore the Temple of Light, we should leave soon."

Their host gave a short, raucous laugh. "Not yet, my lovely. We still have much to discuss." He touched her arm. "This gown makes your hair gleam like the sun."

She took a step back. "You're too kind. But it's getting late, and I should retire. Thank you for a delicious dinner."

"Here, have a drink before you go. The food tonight was highly salted. It must be making you thirsty."

She accepted a goblet of nectar and took a few sips of the sweet beverage.

"Think about my offer while you sleep," Grotus said.

"Your offer?" Leena felt a wave of drowsiness. Unable to suppress a yawn, she raised a hand to cover her mouth. Grotus's face loomed larger in front of her as he took her glass and put it down on a side table.

"Stay here with me. I can give you more than any farmer, and I'm not just talking about wealth." Grotus kept his voice low so Taurin wouldn't hear. His hand darted out and rubbed her crotch in a crude manner that left no mistake of his meaning.

She jerked away. "How dare you? Taurin!"

Her husband no longer stood upright. He'd slumped into a chair. His head lolled back, and his eyes were closed. Alarm surged through her fuzzy mind. What was wrong with him?

She moved in his direction, but dizziness overwhelmed her.

"Here, my dear. Allow me to assist you," Grotus said close to her ear.

The last thing she heard was his malicious laughter as she fell into a deep slumber. Her final chilling thought was that Grotus coveted her as another treasure to add to his collection. Wherever she went, he or his agents wouldn't be far behind.

****

"Demon's blood! Where in Xan are we?" Taurin sat and rubbed the back of his head. An unfamiliar shoreline met his groggy gaze. From the position of the sun, he determined it must be morning. A calm blue sea stretched to the horizon.

It appeared he and Leena had been deposited on a beach with their packs of belongings and a pile of containers he didn't recognize.

"How do you feel?" he asked Leena, who was beginning to rouse.

"I've been better." She struggled to a sitting position and brushed her face with her hand. "What happened?"

"We must have been drugged. I'll bet it was in that nectar drink Grotus gave us."

He peered inside one of the containers, where he discovered a supply of food. It would be enough to last them several days. His guess was confirmed by a note, signed by Grotus, telling them they'd been dropped off at Morasia. They had five days in which to find the Temple of Light, explore the site, and return to the beach. Return transportation would be provided on the morning of the fifth day.

Other than some tracks in the sand that led into the water, there was no other sign of habitation.

Leena's yellow gown stuck to her body in the warm, humid air. He couldn't keep his glance from raking her slender form. Memories of their other time on a beach flitted into his mind, and a surge of heat swelled his loins. He suppressed his response. This wasn't the time, nor the place, for personal desires.

"Do you suppose Grotus has a vessel that travels under the sea? That would explain why no one ever sees him going or coming from his island," Leena said.

"You may be right." Taurin narrowed his eyes. He knew submersibles existed on Yllon as war machines used to attack rival territories. But Grotus would have had to pay dearly to obtain one, unless he'd made a substantial trade instead. Had he dealt directly with Drufus Gong, the most notorious gang leader on Yllon? Taurin's blood chilled at the notion. The gangster had put a price on his head. Should he ever learn Taurin's whereabouts, his life wouldn't be worth the price of a *eulich*.

He'd been so preoccupied with his role as Leena's protector that he hadn't given a thought to his own safety. After seeing his bibliotome, Grotus might make the connection that he was from Yllon, especially if Captain Sterckle had sold him the volumes Taurin used to pay for his passage to Xan.

How many of his secrets did Grotus know? Earlier, the smuggler had mentioned Muer's brandy. Taurin had recognized the drink as a specialty liquor made on Yllon. Had Grotus been trying to provoke Taurin into a disclosure about his origins?

"Do you still have the map Grotus gave us?" he asked, focusing on their current situation.

Leena rummaged in her sack. "Here it is. He must have put it in there."

Taurin unfolded the document and identified their location on the beach. "Grotus wants us to find the legendary treasure for him."

She arched her brows. "It might be worth the effort if he finds the horn in our absence. By the way, Sirvat told him we were coming."

"What? How do you know that?"

"The message he received at dinner—I recognized its seal as Sirvat's personal stamp. What I don't understand is why the Minister of Finance didn't tell us she knew him."

"You can ask your brother to look into it. Investigating the Synod falls under his jurisdiction."

Leena pulled an outfit from her bag and rose. She brushed the sand from her dress.

"What are you doing?" Taurin leapt to his feet as she strode toward a strip of tropical vegetation lining the beach.

"I need to change my clothes. This gown is unsuitable for a trek through the jungle. I'll be back in a minute."

By the time she'd returned, he had packed Grotus's containers inside their bags. "Let's move out," he told her.

They were able to find the trail marked on the map easily enough, but it was mostly overgrown. Taurin hacked their way through with a machete, which Grotus had provided. They took care not to walk into any of the glistening cobwebs or insect mounds blocking their path.

After a while, the undergrowth thinned, and the trail began an upward climb. They passed through a stand of fragrant calyp trees and stopped beside a running stream to refill their canteens.

Leena scraped bits of leaves from her hair and regarded him with a weary expression. "I'm hungry. We need to eat."

He rummaged through their bags for a couple of snack packs. "Here, try this dried fruit and nuts. It'll give us energy."

Soon they headed off again. The trail seemed endless as they proceeded through the increasingly hilly terrain. He estimated they would reach their target tomorrow. Then they'd need another two days for the return trip. That meant they'd have one full day to explore the temple, assuming they could get inside.

He skirted a dead root in their path and glanced at the sky to read the weather. Fluffy white clouds gathered overhead. He hoped they wouldn't bring rain. The trail would turn into a river of mud, making their path treacherous. As it was, the trek was arduous enough.

Curiosity about the archeological site kept them going throughout the long day, the cool night, and the following morning. Taurin was solicitous of Leena's comfort, but he made no overtures toward her otherwise, even though he yearned to kiss her again.

It was Leena who turned the conversation personal during a rest period.

"I feel like we've been married for months," she announced after they'd cleared away the remnants of a light meal.

"How so?" He gave her a sharp perusal. He'd kept his head swathed during the night, so she hadn't seen his eyes. They had kept moving for a while after dark, and she'd questioned his keen vision. He had shrugged it off as a talent of his to read shapes in the night.

"I've seen you do your morning exercises every day now," she told him, sitting on a flat-topped rock and letting her fingers trail into a cool stream. "I'm beginning to learn what annoys you and what pleases you, but there's so much more that remains a mystery."

Taurin leaned against a thick tree trunk and scowled. "It's best if you don't know everything about me."

"Is it?" She got up and sauntered toward him. "We're alone in the jungle. We've slept side by side for several nights now. We are man and wife. Is there not more you wish to learn about me?"

Taurin averted his gaze before she saw the flare of passion in his eyes. "I dare not answer that question."

She continued to approach. Her golden hair streamed over her shoulders as her lithe figure moved toward him. He wasn't sure she understood her own allure, but he wasn't going to let her find out what she did to him.

"You won't like the man I am inside," he warned, his voice gruffer than intended. Prickly spines from the tree trunk bit through his shirt, but he didn't budge. The discomfort would help him maintain his focus. "My world is different from yours. You wouldn't understand the violence even if I explained it. I've had to kill people."

"What? You… you've killed people?"

Taurin flinched inwardly when she stopped in her tracks. It saddened him that he had to resort to the truth, but it was necessary to avoid further intimacy. Despite their formal bonding ceremony, she was nearly betrothed to Malcolm—at least she hadn't indicated otherwise to him. Upon their return, her brother would annul their marriage. She'd be free to pledge herself to her former suitor. So why start something he couldn't finish?

"How can you so casually say you've killed people? I don't understand."

He leveled his steady gaze on her. "I didn't expect you would. Our worlds are vastly apart, and not only in distance. You belong with your brother and his kind."

"Yes, I suppose you're right." She picked her sack off the ground, turned her back on him, and started along the trail.

****

He's confessed to being a murderer, Leena thought, struck speechless with horror. Such violence was unheard of among her people. Why hadn't he been banished to the Black Lands for such a vile deed? Instead, he lived on Magar's land with the minister's sanction.

There had to have been extenuating circumstances. She knew there was goodness in his heart and that he unknowingly ached for deliverance. Her heart was torn between wanting to show the depths of her caring and her abhorrence at what he had revealed.

And yet, his mystique surrounded her, enveloped her, until she wanted nothing more than to peel away his layers and see him for who he really was. The man could follow a path in the dark like he could see clearly, and he heard animal sounds before she knew any creatures were near. Then there was the weapon strapped to his leg—a type of armament she'd never seen before. The challenge to unravel his secrets tempted her despite his revelation.

Sharing nothing of her thoughts, she continued along until they'd reached the ruin. Crumbling stone walls, partially covered by vegetation, showed the ravages of time via myriad cracks and missing edgework. Tangled vines crept over headless sculptures coated by a coarse white mold.

"Look, the branches of life are missing." She pointed upward toward the pyramid-shaped tower that capped the temples in their land. Missing were the antler-like decorations that represented Lothar.

"The wind and rain must have weakened them," Taurin replied, standing by her side.

"It's a shame we couldn't have seen the place sooner. This site has been partially excavated. You can tell by those markers laid out in a grid. The Ministry of Religion must have authorized a dig, but then for some reason they terminated it. Why would they erase all records of this find?" Leena's pitch rose with her excitement.

"Good question. What do we do now?"

She lowered her sack to the ground. "I'll look for the datum point. That's the spot from which all measurements originate," she explained. "During an initial survey, a permanent marker is placed in the ground at a corner of the site. It gives future investigators a place to identify where the excavation began. This spot is used as the starting point for laying out the exploratory grid."

"So the grid pattern is a set of squares that covers the entire area?" Taurin asked, scratching his jaw.

"Yes, but with all this vegetation, we might not be able to locate the starting point."

"Who cares? You're not here to do an official survey."

She spied something gleaming in the grass and stooped for a closer view. It appeared to be a pottery shard. Grabbing a brush from her bag, she dusted it off, labeled it, and stuck it in a small container. She was writing notes on where she'd found it when Taurin snatched the notebook from her hand.

"Why are you wasting time scrabbling in the dirt? Let's go inside." He collected her tools and tossed them into her satchel.

Annoyed with herself for becoming distracted, Leena followed him toward a recess in the wall. Vines dangled from overhead like a curtain, as though warning trespassers to stay away.

Her breath hitched at the familiar sight of two stone helixcats, their faces partially eroded. They stood as sentinels on each side of the entrance.

"I'll go first," she said. "I'm familiar with these temples."

Her discerning glance observed a gap farther inside. She squeezed through the narrow opening into an interior passageway. The walls glowed with a strange luminescence that thankfully provided illumination. She watched her footing as she made her way along, with Taurin at her heels. As the walls closed in on them, a musty odor entered her nose.

She glanced at him over her shoulder. "Don't stray from the path. This temple might have hidden dangers."

"Now you tell me." His voice sounded loud in the confines of the tunnel.

"Maybe that's why the excavation stopped," she suggested. "The early explorers might not have been able to get past the obstacles. Grotus's men wouldn't have had much more success."

Halting as she came to a wide archway, Leena glanced at the floor of the room past the arch. It consisted of a patchwork of evenly-shaped stones. At the other end of the cavernous room was another open archway flanked by two huge stone statues. But what made her emit a soft cry was what she saw in between.

"What is it?" Taurin said, peering over her shoulder.

"Nothing good." Leena pointed to the bones littering the chamber ahead.

Chapter Fourteen

"This is the first challenge," Leena said. "If it's similar to ones I've seen before, there's a deadly ray that gets you if you don't step on the right stones. The trick is finding the correct combination. Get me one of my brushes." She placed her sack on the floor within his reach.

He gave her the requested tool and perused the environs while she patiently dusted away the symbols on the floor in front of her. She was careful to keep her feet firmly rooted in the passageway so her weight did not rest on any of the stones.

"These symbols correspond with the others I've been studying," she said, sitting back on her haunches. She caught sight of Taurin. "By the grace of Lothar!"

His eyes emitted a frightening greenish-yellow glow in the darkened corner where he stood. He stepped forward immediately, the illumination from the passage restoring his vision to normal.

"Don't be afraid. This is why I shade my face in the dark. Where I come from, children born with eyes like mine are viewed as demons. I learned at an early age to hide my features from others during periods of darkness."

"What demons are you talking about? I'm not familiar with any such mythology."

She could understand why he covered his head in that cloth. To see his eyes emit that strange glow was enough to frighten anyone. It almost made him seem… alien. The man had said he was from Iman, hadn't he?

"This curse is seen as a mark of evil," he explained, "and infants born this way are usually destroyed. I was lucky. Rather than murder me, my parents left me for a foundling."

"Murder you! I don't understand. Who… what are you?"

Taurin sank onto the floor across from her, resting his back against the wall. He rubbed a weary hand over his face as though considering how much to tell her.

"I'm not sure what I am," he replied at last. "These symbols are my only clue to my true origins." He rolled up his sleeve and showed her the bracelet fixed around his upper arm. She had noticed the unique material before, when he'd bared his chest to fight Grotus, but she had not observed the symbols etched into the band. Gathering her courage, she crawled closer and gingerly traced them with her finger.

"This bracelet was left with me as a child," he explained. "It is the only remnant of the past I have left, other than my books."

"This armband is constructed of the same material as the horn and the ring I found on my last excavation. How is that possible?"

"I don't know. I was hoping you could help me interpret these symbols."

"I've never been able to decipher them. Perhaps this temple holds the key."

"How do we get in there?" Taurin gestured toward the chamber.

Realizing she still had many questions, Leena crept over to the opening and peered at the stones covering the floor. "I've determined from my studies that there are seven symbols, presumably representing an alphabet of some kind. There's also an eighth, but it's actually a combination of two others. One particular string appears repetitively. It's the same string of symbols that is etched onto your bracelet and on the horn."

Using her fingers, she drew the symbols in the dust at Taurin's feet. "This is the sequence. If it's a message from the Apostles, no one has been able to decode it. There's another design I've found on occasion, too."

Drawing a diamond shape with an antler-like branch coming out of the left corner, she frowned. "This representation doesn't appear to be associated with the other string."

"Can you get us inside?" Taurin asked.

Examining the inscriptions on the chamber floor, Leena grimaced. "Each one of the squares has a different symbol on it. Perhaps if we follow the string, we'll be okay."

"Let's see what happens if you're wrong."

Before she could stop him, Taurin withdrew a tool from her pack and threw it onto one of the stones. Red light shot out from the eyes of the stone statues at the far end of the room. The cross-beam aimed at the stone Taurin had hit. With a crack and a sizzle, the beam died.

"Good thing we weren't standing there," he muttered. "You'd better get it right."

The floor was three squares wide. In the first row, Leena studied the symbols from left to right. The first one looked like a pair of mountain humps. The middle was an oval with a horizontal line dividing the center, and the one on the right looked like a backward crescent moon. Since the common string she'd found on most of the digs began with the backward crescent, she decided to put her guess on that one.

"Give me another tool," she instructed him.

He handed her a small hoe, and she tossed it onto the block to the right. The stone statues at the opposite end of the room remained lifeless.

"It's safe," she said. "I'll go first."

Before Taurin could object, she boldly stepped across the threshold and onto the first block, careful to avoid the bones gathered at the edges. Taurin grasped the sacks, flung them over his shoulder, and followed after her.

As soon as he crossed the threshold, a stone slab slid down from behind, cutting off their exit. Silent walls surrounded them. Now there was no way in and no way out unless Leena determined the correct sequence. She read the symbols in each row, taking her time to make sure she got it right.

Fifteen squares later, they had made their way to the opposite end, where the vee symbol with a dot in the center was the final choice. She'd made the correct selection, as evidenced by their safe passage through the open archway.

"You did it!" Taurin put his foot forward to rush ahead.

"Wait." Leena gripped his arm. "Each room has a prescribed way to get across. We have to get past the booby traps."

More bones littered the passageway into the next chamber, and she realized that the few souls who had made it through the first section hadn't survived the subsequent challenge.

She peered inside the next chamber. "I don't see anything on the floor except those odd piles of dust. The walls have carvings, though."

Taurin stared at the unusual mounds scattered throughout the room. "Strange, aren't they?"

Leena walked forward before he could stop her. Again, as soon as Taurin followed her inside, a slab lowered behind them. This time there was no visible opening at the other end. The luminescent glow in the room reflected the odd light in Taurin's eyes.

"Can you interpret these inscriptions?" he asked her.

She studied the carvings on one wall. "I don't see a familiar sequence anywhere. Look, this diamond shape has the branch sticking out, but it's in the wrong place. And here are more of the same."

Taurin moved beside her to peer at the symbols with the antler-like branch growing out of a corner. "They all look alike to me."

"Wait a minute. Look, this branch rises from the upper right corner. There, it's on the left. And down here, it's the other side. They are different." As Leena came to this realization, a jolt rocked the room.

"What was that?" Taurin's gaze darted about the musty chamber.

Leena traced the outline of a diamond shape with the antler

symbolizing Lothar's branch of life on its upper left corner. As she applied pressure, the stone pushed in. Her scalp prickled. The walls seemed to be encroaching upon them, or was it her imagination playing tricks?

"Something is moving, and it's not just that stone," Taurin noted. "It's the whole place."

"What?" Leena glanced around. Sure enough, the walls slowly scraped inward. Her glance dropped to the strange piles of dust on the floor. "Dear deity, now we know what caused those mounds. We've got to find a way out of here, or we'll be crushed." She splayed her hands on the walls. "The key has to be here somewhere."

"Maybe there's a pneumatic door. If we step on the right spot on the floor—"

"No, I don't think that's it. Help me look for the diamond shape, the one with the branch in the upper left corner. We need to activate all of them."

Taurin followed her instructions, and her theory proved correct. As the walls moved closer and closer, they scrabbled to find all the matching diamond shapes and push on them. The ceiling was low enough that they didn't have to reach above their height.

"We've done it, but the walls haven't stopped moving." Leena's voice contained a hint of panic.

"No, we must have missed one." Taurin crouched down, his body pressing against hers as the walls compacted further, narrowing their space. "Hurry. There's not much time."

Leena got on her knees to examine the bottom row of stones. "I don't see another symbol with the branch in the correct position."

Taurin could clearly see the carvings with his luminous vision. His sharp gaze zeroed in on a single diamond shape with a branch on its upper left corner.

"I've found it!" Quickly he pushed on the symbol, and as it gave way, so did the floor beneath them.

Leena shrieked as she tumbled into blackness, her body

slipping along some kind of slide. She squeezed her eyes shut against the steep decline as she bumped against the sides on her way down. Just when she despaired of reaching bottom, she landed with a huge *whump* onto a soft surface. Taurin followed with a grunt, almost landing on top of her.

For a moment she lay there, breathing hard. Hopefully, the place had enough air to sustain them since they were trapped inside. Her eyes adjusted to the luminescent glow from the walls.

"Are you all right?" Taurin asked her. "We seem to have landed on a bed of feathers."

"So I see." She giggled, a note of hysteria escaping her lips. Their cushion must have been made from a lot of plucked birds.

Taurin rolled over, his concerned gray eyes meeting hers. "We passed another challenge, thanks to you. This calls for a celebration." He planted his mouth on hers, his action removing her fear and refocusing her energy. When she didn't resist, Taurin deepened the kiss until she trembled in his arms.

"I'd like to continue, but we'd better move on," he said in a reluctant tone.

"I'll keep you to your word."

"What do you mean?"

"We'll continue this later." With a grin, Leena rose and strode past him to take the lead.

****

Taurin gathered their belongings and cautiously followed her through a curving corridor where they couldn't see around the next bend. A strange, acrid odor pierced his nostrils, and he wrinkled his nose. "What's that smell?"

Leena didn't bother to answer. Instead, she stopped abruptly. He bumped into her with a muttered curse.

His heart sank when he glimpsed the sight ahead. The floor dropped away to reveal a cavernous hall, the bottom of which was filled with a pool of liquid that sputtered ominously. A rickety suspension bridge reached across the room to a ledge at the opposite end. With its tattered ropes and broken rungs, the bridge looked as though no one had walked its slats for ages.

"Acid," Leena remarked, nodding at the pool below. To test her theory, she threw one of her tools into the pool. The liquid sizzled and boiled as the item disappeared beneath the surface. "How will we get across? Our journey can't end so soon. We have to learn the secrets hidden within the Temple of Light, and I don't mean the treasure Grotus wants us to find. These traps indicate something significant must be secreted here."

Taurin agreed. This place, with its immense proportions and devious traps, pointed to a greater importance. They hadn't come across any living quarters that might indicate dwelling space, nor had they seen remnants of an altar. If not a worship center or a residence for the Apostles, what purpose had this temple served? And why had the Synod suppressed all records of its existence? Had they deemed the temple too dangerous for anyone else to explore?

He considered the dilemma in front of them. "I saved some ropes from the *Predator*. We can use them here." From inside his bag, he withdrew a long cord. "This one might reach the other side. We'll use the second line to tie ourselves together in case one of us falls."

Leena gazed at him in horror. "You're not thinking of swinging across on a rope?"

"No, it'll be a safety line. We'll use the bridge as much as possible." He tilted his head. "Wait a minute. If this bridge were in perfect condition, what would stop anyone from walking across it? The acid pit is here for a reason."

Leena's eyes widened. "There's another hazard to knock people off the bridge."

Both of them peered intently around the room. Finally Taurin shrugged.

"We'll just have to make a go for it." He tied a knot at one end of the rope. "At least I learned a few things on the *Predator*," he told her, a smug expression on his face. "One of the sailors taught me how to tie knots."

"That's good and welfare, but can you toss a line to the other end?"

"We'll see."

He straightened, stretched back his arm, and tossed the rope across the chamber. The first time he missed his target. With a grunt of dismay, he yanked on the rope to retrieve the end before it dipped into the acid.

On his second try, he looped it over the pointed ear of a stone gargoyle guarding the entrance into the next passageway. After he gave it a firm tug and it held, he nodded his approval. He tied the other end to a promontory jutting from the wall just inside the chamber entrance. Then he used the other cord to tie himself and Leena together at their waists.

"Your weight is lighter," he told Leena. "You go first."

"Thanks," she said, her tone sarcastic. Poised at the rim, she glanced at the rickety swinging bridge. Below, the murky pool sputtered and spit as though awaiting its next victim.

With a brave thrust of her chin, she grasped the safety line and began the trek across. The bridge swayed underfoot with each step. She was careful to test each rung before putting her weight forward. Taurin's heart thumped as he followed close behind.

Once or twice the forward rung gave way, and they had to stretch their legs across to reach the next one over.

About halfway along, a grating noise sounded overhead. Taurin glanced up and saw a panel had opened in the ceiling.

"Hurry!" He gave her a light shove as spears began pelting down on them.

Leena covered her head with her hands. He tapped on her shoulder to indicate she should keep moving. She advanced along the swaying ladder, crying out when a spear glanced off her upper arm.

"Move!" They didn't dare to stop. Taurin ducked as another spear flashed past. His action rocked the bridge, flinging Leena onto her side. The frayed railing gave way against her weight, and she tumbled into empty space.

Taurin yelled her name. Just when he thought she'd be swallowed by acid, the line tying them together went taut.

"Hold on," Taurin called, peering over the edge. Her dragging weight made him grip the safety line to avoid being pulled after her. She dangled precipitously but hadn't touched the pool below.

****

Leena's blood ran cold, and her heart hammered so fast, she could barely breathe. Beneath her, the acid swirled and hissed.

"Pull me up," she cried. Why was he taking so long?

"I have to get my balance," he hollered back.

They managed to avoid the onslaught of spears as he hauled her to the safety of the bridge platform. Going at a speedy crawl, they finally made it to the other side.

Leena collapsed onto the ledge, her body shaking. The ceiling panel closed overhead, but fear still held her in its grip.

"You gave me a scare." Taurin knelt beside her, perusing her face. He stroked her cheek, his touch tender.

"Thanks for the save." Unable to help herself, she turned into his comforting embrace. His arms tightened around her, giving her a feeling of warmth and security.

She lifted her gaze. Taurin's eyes darkened as he lowered his mouth to hers. As he kissed her with hungry passion, her intuition told her what her rational mind had already accepted.

Malcolm wasn't the man for her. He'd never sweep her to the heights of desire as Taurin did with a simple kiss.

His tongue thrust inside her mouth, and he explored her with an intimacy that made her tremble from wanting more. All sense of reason fled her mind.

She pulled back to express her need. "Taurin, I don't care who you are or what you did in the past. I just want to be with you."

With a groan, he pulled her closer and plundered her mouth with renewed vigor. With one hand, he cradled the back of her head to lend support. His other hand roamed her body, inducing a rising heat that made her press herself against him.

Don't stop, she thought, the dangers they had recently shared making her yearn for a mindless escape.

But he didn't hear her silent plea. He released her, giving her a gentle smile.

"We should move on," he said, his voice thick. "Our time in here is limited, and we have to make the most of it. Otherwise, there could be dire consequences."

Chapter Fifteen

Leena took the lead along a dusty corridor, up a ramp to another level, and through a maze of passages, until they came to a halt. An empty space yawned in front of them. She peered over the rim. Blackness met her gaze except for the ever-present luminescent glow.

"Where do we go from here?" she asked. "I don't notice any way to get down."

He frowned at this latest puzzle. "Look, more symbols are carved into the walls around us. See if you can interpret them." While she studied the carvings, he surveyed the ground where it dipped under his toes. "Give me one of your brushes first."

She heard the urgency in his tone and hastened over with the requested item.

A moment later, he'd swept the dust away, revealing a circular depression. "Haven't we seen something like this at other entrances?"

Leena knelt beside him and traced the circle with her fingers. "I'm not sure."

"Could it be a pneumatic platform trigger?"

She straightened and stomped her foot around the circle. "Doesn't appear so."

"Then we've reached a dead end."

Leena eyed the solid wall opposite the gap, figuring a way to cross. "I think the next passage must be below. Do you see anything down there? We could use a rope to descend."

Taurin scrounged in her bag for a torchlight which he shone downward, but the beam didn't penetrate the distance.

"I suppose that's one option," he said in a morose tone.

Leena poked him. "Let's take a break. We may think more clearly after we rest."

She sat beside him, ate a fruit and nut bar, and took a long swallow of water from their canteen. Although her limbs trembled from exertion, she couldn't wait to explore further.

Taurin didn't seem in any hurry to rise. He removed the bracelet from his arm and twirled it on the floor, presumably as he'd done as a child. Leena was surprised at the musical tone emitted by the spinning gold band.

"That's delightful." The whimsical tune made her smile.

Taurin flashed her a wide grin. "Watch what happens when I separate the rings."

He took apart the interlocking bracelets and spun them one by one. Each emitted a distinctive melody, and all three were different than the one produced by the joined armband.

"I did this all the time when I was growing up and no one was watching. It brought me a measure of comfort."

Leena observed his brooding expression as he revisited his youthful memories. Was he wondering about his unknown heritage?

She considered the sequence of five symbols carved onto his armband. It was the same sequence she'd seen elsewhere. Maybe the middle symbol represented two letters combined. But what kind of alphabet had only seven letters? Could it be some kind of pictorial representation? Or a metaphoric language?

One of the rings he was twirling teetered into the circular depression and spun around, emitting its haunting melody. A vibration rocked the ground they sat on. Her heart lurched, and she glanced at Taurin.

"What's that?" He leapt to his feet, his gaze darting about the small enclosed space.

"If my eyes aren't fooling me, we're moving toward the opposite wall," Leena said in astonishment.

Sure enough, the ledge they were on extended toward the

farther end. When they reached it, a hidden door slid open, revealing a passage ahead.

They gathered their belongings before the ledge retracted. Taurin snapped his links together and thrust the armband up his sleeve. After slinging their sacks over his shoulder, he took the lead into the passageway.

The trek took them up and down several other levels, using a variation of ramps, narrow staircases, and slides. They were approaching what Leena assumed must be the bowels of the temple when they heard a strange scurrying noise ahead.

Taurin stopped abruptly in his tracks, holding an arm up to warn Leena.

"What is it?" she whispered.

"I'm not sure. But there's something around the next bend."

Her pulse raced. If they were nearing the treasure, the obstacles would become more threatening. But what could possibly be worse than what they'd already encountered?

"Wait here," Taurin said, his eyes glowing in the darkened corridor.

He gave her the torchlight to hold and advanced slowly, flattening his back against the wall as he rounded the bend.

Leena heard him cursing and hurried forward.

"Dear deity!" She halted at the sight of a large chamber covered with a giant web. "What kind of creature lives here?"

Taurin glared at her. "I don't know, and I don't want to find out."

"Do we have to cross through this room?"

"There's only one way to go, and it's forward."

An ominous rumbling sounded from back in the corridor. Leena pointed to a rounded depression on the floor.

"Try spinning your bracelet in there. Maybe it'll clear us a safe path."

Taurin was just reaching into his sleeve to obtain his armband when a whoosh of air roared through the passage from behind. The blast knocked them straight into the confines of the sticky web. Immediately the door shut behind them, trapping them inside. An ominous rustling noise sounded from a shadowed corner of the room.

"What is it? What's coming at us?" Leena's breath came short. She didn't need a sixth sense to know that whatever creature lived in this place was advancing on them. They were probably the tastiest meal to come along for a long time.

Her heart lurched when she saw the enormous eight-legged beast with bulging eyes and voracious teeth. Its spindly legs manipulated the web with ease, and it seemed to have a grin on its face, as though anticipating a treat.

Taurin cursed and fought, but the best he could do was to reach inside his pant leg and grab hold of his blaster. Leena hoped the arachnid would be susceptible to its charge.

"Fire at it," she yelled.

Beads of sweat covered Taurin's brow as he manipulated his arm into place to take aim. The sticky strands clutched at him as though they had a mind of their own.

Leena was closer to the creature and could see the hairs bristling on its legs. A cloudy fluid dripped from its feet, or whatever those pads were on the end of its legs.

It might be poison. If it smears that stuff on us, we'll be paralyzed. She squeezed her eyes shut and prayed to Lothar for deliverance.

Taurin fired. She snapped her eyes open in time to see red laser bolts sizzling through the room. They severed strands of the web that cut across their path and hit the creature.

With a roar of agony, the hideous being fell back into its own entanglement and lay there motionless.

Taurin cut them both free of the web using his blaster. They hurried toward a door on the opposite end. At their approach, the door swished open, and a blast of cool air refreshed them.

"We must be getting close to the temple's secrets," Leena said.

Across a short distance was a sturdy metal door without any

visible latches and with no circular depression at the entry. Two stone statues guarded the door on either side, fierce expressions on their animalistic faces.

Taurin studied the nearest statue for clues. "That's odd. This fellow has a different face on each side."

"So does this one." Leena examined the other stone guardian. As she touched it and applied pressure, the head rotated part way around. The door in front of them lifted half a foot and then stopped. "Holy waters, the door almost opened."

Taurin shifted the head of his statue to match hers, but nothing happened. "Try rotating yours again," he advised.

They shifted the heads around in various positions and in different orders, noting which combination produced a reaction in the door. Finally, when one statue had the feline face directed to the left and the other had it aimed toward the rear in a certain order of moves, the door slid fully open.

Another door immediately blocked their path.

"Look, this side has a slot in the wall." Sweat dribbled down the back of Leena's neck as she bent forward to get a closer look. She shined her torchlight inside the slit. "Wait a minute. I think there's a depression in here. Put your bracelet in and see what happens."

"All right." He took the armband off and inserted it into the slot. As soon as its weight settled in the depression, the rounded area began to spin. Musical notes sounded, and the next door slid open. A stale, musty odor entered her nose.

Taurin grabbed for his bracelet and snapped it on his arm as he sped through the archway. Leena made it to the other side just in time. The door behind them slammed shut.

They faced a cavernous hall, which contained pile upon pile of gleaming crystal rocks.

Taurin gazed around with an expression of awe. "Demon's blood! We've found it."

Leena couldn't believe her eyes. "This is incredible. The temple must be a repository for these crystals. And unlike most of the other holy places on Xan, the Apostles clearly didn't want our people to enter this one."

"Obviously, since they designed the place to be impregnable."

Leena turned to him. "Not impregnable. I'll bet anybody with one of those bracelets could enter. They act like a key."

Taurin nodded slowly. "It makes sense, in an odd sort of way. And if these spinning rings could affect entrance into this place, what else can they do?"

****

Taurin moved forward to examine the crystals while considering the implications. His parents had left him the armband, which likely had been passed down to them through the generations.

When he'd arrived on Xan, he had traded Magar some of the ancient bibliotomes he owned in exchange for a plot of land. Neither one of them knew how to open the books, but now into his mind's eye came the circular depressions on the cover of each heavy tome. If he spun his armband on the circles, would the books open to reveal their contents?

"I believe the crystals might act as a power source," Leena said, distracting him from his thoughts. "Remember how a crystal rock was used to heat the water in the native village at the Black Lands?"

She'd picked one up and turned it in her hand to examine the facets, her delicate features lit with awe. Her blond hair trailed over her shoulders like a golden mist, and Taurin thought she'd never looked lovelier despite the grime that covered them both. He suppressed his desire in order to focus on their mission.

"The stone wasn't solely responsible," he reminded her. "The crystal caught a ray of the sun, intensifying the beam of solar energy. And there may have been an underground heating source such as a hot spring."

"Maybe the crystals need energy from the sun to activate them." She pursed her lips. "Spin your bracelet and see if the musical tone does anything to them."

Taurin complied but nothing happened. "I wonder what use the crystals served if not as a power source."

"Maybe they had value merely for their aesthetics or even as a type of currency," Leena offered. "The different sizes of the stones lend credence to that theory."

"So why haven't archaeologists discovered crystals like these before? This place holds a huge stockpile of stones." He swept his arm in a broad gesture.

"People could have fought over them so much that the ancients decided to restrict access." Leena lifted the crystal in her hand to admire the play of multi-colored lights on its faceted surface.

"What's in the next room?" Taurin advanced, ducking under an arch to reach the adjacent chamber.

He stopped just inside the entrance. Great cosmos. Piles of books covered the floor. They were similar to the one he had shown Grotus. His jaw dropped as he walked further into the room. In another corner was a mound of rings made from the same material as his armband.

Leena entered with an exclamation as she took in the sight. "Those are similar to the ring I discovered on my last expedition. Zeroun confiscated it and ordered me not to tell anyone. I wonder if he knows that more exist."

Taurin twisted around to face her. "Look at the bibliotomes. They're similar to the ones I own."

"How many do you have?"

"Enough to have filled several trunks on my initial journey. I traded some to Magar in exchange for a piece of property. I believe he hopes to learn their secrets. So far none of us, including Grotus, has known how to open them."

Her eyes narrowed. "Where did you get your collection?"

"I came across the books in a library and managed to gain possession of them."

"A library? That makes sense." She paused. "I've always wondered if the temples in use today hold storerooms down below. The regional worship centers were built centuries ago. Only Candors or members of the Synod are permitted access to the lower levels. So even though I haven't come across these books on my digs—or any other rings, for that matter—it is possible they are stockpiled somewhere."

"We have to agree on a story to tell Grotus. Let's say we never made it past the first few challenges. If we tell him we got inside but the place was empty, he'll want to have a look for himself."

"We can bring him a few crystals for a consolation prize," Leena suggested. "If he asks, we'll say we found them in an outer chamber."

"Why don't you gather some of the rocks now? I want to remain here a bit longer."

Taurin watched her go before snatching up another bibliotome. He wanted to test his theory in the few moments to spare. Fitting his bracelet into the circular depression on the cover, he spun the entwined rings, producing the familiar musical tone.

Before his amazed eyes, a top section slid open, revealing a scrolling narration. He couldn't read the words, but their meaning became imprinted in his mind.

Quickly scanning several other volumes, he realized they recounted the history of the Apostles. The readings told about scourges of disease in their time, warfare and regional conflicts, dwindling resources and erratic weather patterns, and the people's lack of progress. The Apostles spoke as though they were superior and told of their plan to define a new order.

Taurin couldn't find any further reference to this new order, but he suspected it was the religion of Sabal, because the Apostles were the ones who had given the laws to the people. But if he'd hoped to find any truth behind the religious teachings, he was disappointed.

He figured the story continued in the bibliotomes he had brought from Yllon. He had never understood the link between their two societies, but now he had the means to unlock the mysteries of the past. These rings, in varying sizes, were the keys. He couldn't wait to get home to study the books in his collection.

The value of the crystals was still beyond his comprehension, but that knowledge might be in the books as well. If only he had more time to study these volumes.

Before he left the chamber, he selected a small ring from the pile in the corner and placed it in his pocket. They couldn't risk taking more, or Grotus would question their tale.

A tender smile tugged at his mouth when he found Leena sitting on the floor in the next room, surrounded by a pile of crystals. She held one in her hands and twisted it side-to-side, a look of rapt concentration on her face.

A world of longing hit him, but it wouldn't serve him well to dwell on impossibilities. When they returned home, Leena would regain her position in the Caucus, and he'd resume his role as a lowly farmer. Her family would annul their marriage and pledge her to Malcolm.

With a sense of regret, he pushed aside his personal desires as being a distraction he couldn't afford. He'd require all his mental faculties if they were to survive.

"It's time to move on," he said in a gruff tone.

"Did you learn how to read those books?" Leena demanded, her keen gaze assessing him.

He fumbled for an appropriate response. It wouldn't be wise to answer truthfully. The ancient words might refute her people's beliefs about their religion. He couldn't reveal what he knew until he learned more.

"Not quite," he lied, regarding his statement as a half-truth. After all, he was unable to read the lettering inside the books. The contents became known to him through some sort of mental transfer process. "I wish we could take some of them with us, but they'd be too heavy."

"Grotus would catch on to us, at any rate. I filled a sack with crystals to bring him."

"Good; that should make him happy." Taurin grabbed their belongings, prepared to depart.

"It's a shame we can't take more with us." Leena rose and gestured toward the archway. "What about those rings in the next room?"

He shook his head. "Grotus may have us searched. Now that we know the location of this place, we can always return. I don't think we should reveal what we've discovered here to anyone at this point, Dikran and the Synod included. Agreed?"

Leena gave a reluctant nod. "We still don't know why this excavation was closed and the records purged, but I intend to find out. In the meantime, I agree with you that we shouldn't say anything about it. Our knowledge of these items might come in handy later."

She followed him through the temple's maze toward the exit. At various doorways, Taurin placed his bracelet in the circular depression, and they passed unharmed through each challenge back to the surface. Stars twinkled in the night sky when they emerged from the temple.

"How many hours have we been in there?" Leena asked, a heavy weariness overtaking her.

"More than twelve. Let's make camp here for the night, and we'll head for the beach in the morning. We have plenty of time before Grotus's goons pick us up."

"I wish we could contact Bendyk. We need to tell him about the plantations in the Black Lands."

Taurin inflated the air-filled mattress Grotus had provided. "Let's hope your brother is proceeding at a faster pace with his inquiries than we are."

Chapter Sixteen

Leena watched Taurin work to set up their camp for the night. With his tall, muscled form, thick black hair, and glowing eyes, he appeared as she imagined Lothar to look, had he been merely mortal. A day's growth of beard covered her companion's face, giving him an even more dangerous air than he already possessed.

He'd referred to Xan with the phrase, *your world*, she recalled. Yet if he wasn't from here, who was he and where did he come from?

He spoke of demons in his past as though he feared his own heritage, but as she regarded his magnificence, she concluded that he must have descended from the gods.

Taurin caught her staring at him and smiled. His flash of white teeth lit his face with a devilish grin, but something very human sprang into his eyes. Suddenly she felt exposed in her short tunic.

"The temperature is cooler. I think I'll change into one of my warmer gowns."

She needed a moment of privacy, a few minutes away from him to still her rapidly-beating heart. Aware that Taurin's gaze followed her movements, she picked up her bag and meandered toward a clump of trees that would hide her from view.

The sound of trickling water brought her to a small stream. After washing the layers of dust from her exposed skin, she donned her ruby red gown. The long sleeves provided warmth for her arms, but the low-cut neckline exposed more of her cleavage than she would have liked. Aware of how attractive a figure

Taurin presented, she vowed to regard him in a cool, professional manner.

She needn't have worried. When she returned to their encampment, Taurin was already lying down on his side, facing away from her. His gentle snoring told her he'd wasted no time in falling asleep. She stomped her foot in frustration. At least he could have stayed awake to verify her safe return.

Too restless to fall asleep, she withdrew one of the crystals from her bag. Moonlight shimmered off its polished surface, reminding her of the time when she and Bendyk had played on the slippery stones in a brook near their home.

She wondered if her brother was all right and what he'd accomplished. Hopefully, they'd have the chance to exchange news soon.

****

Bendyk was enjoying another dinner in Swill's apartment. She'd invited him there several times recently, and he'd returned the favor by taking her out to restaurants on other evenings. They'd fallen into the easy habit of having dinner together every night, but Bendyk hadn't wanted to press his luck by pushing Swill any further. She seemed content to keep their relationship as an easy camaraderie, and he wasn't one to argue. His dreams of her were sinfully erotic, and as penance he forced himself to maintain a safe distance between them.

"I'm worried about Leena," he said between mouthfuls of baked cloinder fish with morels.

"Communication from your sister is overdue," Swill agreed, her amber eyes soft as she regarded him across the dining table.

Her cheeks held a faint flush that Bendyk attributed to maidenly virtue since she didn't wear makeup. He liked how her ebony hair, having grown longer, curled onto her neck. His glance dropped to her simple sheath dress. The gold choker he'd given her went well with the peach fabric. She hadn't wanted to accept his gift, but he'd insisted, saying it was a token of his appreciation for the help she'd given him.

Bendyk twirled the stem of his wine glass. "Perhaps we should send one of the Caucus members after my sister."

"I don't think so. We need them to help us conduct our investigation. Have you two always been close?"

"Not until after our mother died. Leena could have blamed me for her death, but she didn't. We needed each other too much."

"Do you want to talk about what happened?" Swill asked in a sympathetic tone.

He scraped his fingers through his hair as though to rake away the bad memories. Maybe Swill could help him expunge the guilt. "It was a snowy winter night. Our father had been called away for an unexpected meeting. I'd invited some friends over for dinner and needed to run out for supplies. Mother came along to do her shopping. Being in a rush, I insisted on driving. I took Father's rider because it was the heavier vehicle. The roads on our estate were steep and winding."

His voice lowered as he continued. "Despite the bad weather, I drove faster than I should have. There's a particularly treacherous stretch near our home. The brakes failed. I couldn't… I lost control of the steering. We crashed through a guard rail and fell into the ravine. My mother was killed on impact." He stopped as his throat tightened with sorrow.

The silence in the room stretched taut, like a rubber band about to snap. Finally he continued his story, feeling compelled to confess. "I was seriously injured, pinned in place. The rider was pretty badly damaged. My mother lay beside it, unmoving. I grew numb with grief and cold. Likely I'd freeze to death before anyone found us. Leena was visiting friends, so she didn't know we'd gone out. No one did. Maybe my friends, when they came to the house and nobody answered the door, would sound the alarm."

Bendyk shivered, reliving the horror in his memory. "My legs felt broken. My chest hurt when I breathed, and I had a gash on the side of my head that could hide a more serious injury. I prayed to Lothar to save me and begged his forgiveness for causing the crash. I dragged myself over to my mother's body, which still emitted a measure of warmth. I think that's what saved me from freezing to death. My prayers kept me awake. I knew if I fell asleep, it would be over."

He dropped his gaze. "Lothar heard me. Rescuers arrived hours later. I was airlifted to a trauma center, and the police had the unpleasant duty of notifying my father about the accident. That was the night I decided to devote myself to Lothar who'd responded to my pleas. I've dedicated my life to his service, but that doesn't mean I'll ever find redemption for my careless acts."

Swill reached across the table and squeezed his hand. "Didn't you say the brakes failed?"

"The roadway was slick. The tires couldn't hold the friction."

"What happened to your rider?"

"It was taken to a garage and sold for junk metal." Letting go of her hand, he took a large swallow of wine. "My father was devastated. This all happened just over five years ago. It was shortly after he'd been censured for his indiscretion."

Swill raised an eyebrow. "What did he do that was so terrible?"

"Father misinterpreted the Apostle's teachings that were written in a set of ancient scrolls. For his heresy, the Synod sentenced him to do a year of penance. He regarded my mother's death as an additional punishment sent by Lothar."

He rose abruptly, sniffing the air. "Do I smell something burning?"

Swill shot to her feet. "Cripes, I forgot about the bean fritters!" She rushed to the oven and muttered a blessing when she saw the food wasn't overcooked.

Following her into the kitchen, he watched as she withdrew the baking dish and set it on the counter. "I should praise Lothar for bringing you to me," he said, feeling lightened by her presence. He was grateful she hadn't judged him for his past misdeeds and felt a rush of desire for this woman who'd heard his deepest secrets.

Swill raised her face toward him. "Whatever do you mean, Bendyk Worthington-Jax?"

"Allow me to show you."

****

Swill didn't want to admit how much she'd grown to like Bendyk's company. He was totally the wrong man for the person she'd envisioned as her mate one day. While he still had his pompous moments, he'd given up on trying to convert her to his religious teachings. He attracted her more when he acted normal, especially now since he'd shared his history. She was warmed by his trust and unable to deny his appeal.

He wore none of his priestly robes this evening. His plaid flannel shirt stretched across his broad shoulders. He'd tucked it into a pair of navy trousers that molded to his slim hips. His shirt was modestly open at the neck, allowing her a tantalizing glimpse of his blond chest hairs.

Whenever he entered a room, sunlight seemed to accompany him even in the dark of night. Could it be the religious fervor that circled him like a halo? Or was it merely her response to his masculinity?

His face hovered nearby, inches away. As she held her breath, he brushed his lips against hers in a brief feathery touch.

"No," she murmured as his mouth descended once again.

He stepped closer so their bodies touched, but he kept his hands to himself as though waiting for her to make the next move. She swayed against him, savoring the lean, hard feel of his form.

Would he make love to me with the same passion he harbors for his god? she wondered. The other louts who'd chased after her were lowlife types who thought she'd be easy because she dressed plainly and came from a poor family.

Bendyk was too good for her, but she could enjoy him while their mission lasted. She might never have the opportunity to be with anyone like him again and wanted to ease his grief. Her fingers found their way to his shirt buttons.

"What are you doing?" Bendyk asked as she unfastened them.

"You'll see." With a seductive smile, she took his hand and tugged him toward the bedroom.

"Hold on," he said, halting.

"What's the matter? Don't you want me?"

"Of course I do, but this isn't right. It's not proper for us to…"

"What? Have sex?" Swill planted her hands on her hips. "Our society has no prohibition against relations among singles."

"That may be true, but you and I are not intending to bond. Sex is only condoned if it's part of a serious relationship."

"Is that so?" Swill slid close to him and rubbed her body meaningfully against his. "Why don't you set aside your lofty ideals for a change and experience your humanity?"

"If we do this, it will change things between us," he warned, his voice thick.

"No, it won't. We can each go our separate paths when we finish our job. Consider it a way to relax, to relieve the pressure upon us."

"I need relief from pressure, all right. If I stay away from you much longer, I'm going to explode." Bendyk nudged her toward the bed.

Her body charged with need, and she couldn't wait any longer. With a seductive smile, she unclothed herself before his hungry gaze.

****

Taurin awoke the next morning, noting with dismay that it was well past dawn. Leena appeared to be sound asleep on the mattress beside him, lying on her back, arms flung wide. A heavy layer of dew glistened on the grass, and the sound of trickling water reached his ears. So did the steady drone of insects and the occasional hoot of an owl or the howl of a wild animal. Exotic bird cries filled the perfume-scented air that was heavy with humidity.

Feeling Leena would be safe if he left her for a brief moment, he followed a trail through the jungle toward the sound of rushing water. The vegetation thinned, and he came upon a clear, cascading stream. He knelt by the bank and scooped cool water into his cupped hands, taking a fulfilling drink.

Reminding himself that they should refill their canteens before leaving, he proceeded to shave using the razor he'd brought along. After managing that feat without cutting himself, he washed as best he could, wishing the stream were wider and deep enough for a swim.

Keeping his shirt off, he trudged back to camp. The sun rose hot on his back, the start of what promised to be a sweltering day. They should get moving while it was still early, but he hadn't the heart to wake Leena. She appeared so peaceful in repose, and yesterday had been a strenuous experience. She needed her rest, and he wouldn't steal it from her.

After gathering their supplies and picking some fresh fruit off the trees for breakfast, he squatted on the mattress, contemplating Leena's lovely face. Her thick-lashed eyes were closed, but he could see the rapid movements that indicated dream sleep. A small smile played about her lush mouth, and he wondered what she was dreaming about.

Her blond hair spread out like a sheet of gold, gleaming in a shaft of sunlight. His gaze roamed her body. The ruby gown molded to her curves, and he imagined his hands roving where his mind dared to go.

If only she wasn't almost pledged to Malcolm. Had Cranby, her father, already arranged the match? A hard glint shone in his eyes as he imagined the Candor's reaction should he claim Leena for himself.

It wasn't his destiny to have her. And yet as he observed her chest rising and falling, he felt a yearning so intense that it became painful.

At that moment her eyelids fluttered open, and she caught him staring at her.

"I just had the most marvelous dream," she told him. "We'd just discovered the cache of crystals. You and I got caught up in the moment, and we…" Her voice trailed off when she noticed his intent expression, and her face flushed.

She'd been dreaming about him, he realized with a surge of desire. His loins tightened as his own erotic dreams surfaced to torment him. Demon's blood, how he'd like to make slow, passionate love to her. Her parted lips, dreamy expression, and soft form lulled him into a state of suspended reality. Here in the jungle, with the spires of a ruined temple rising behind them, nothing mattered but the most primal factors of existence.

Without conscious thought, Taurin stretched out beside her and leaned up on an elbow.

"Malcolm wouldn't approve of us being alone here together," Leena said, turning to face him.

"I don't care what Malcolm thinks." With his free hand, he traced a gentle line along her cheekbone. She drew in a tremulous breath that told him how much his touch affected her.

"He doesn't make my pulse race the way you do, or make me restless for something I can't define. Only you do that," she said in an innocent tone.

Taurin sucked in a breath, unable to draw his gaze from her face. He should get up now and move away from her before he acted in a manner they'd regret. But how could he feel remorse for bringing her the pleasure she didn't realize she craved?

"Have you ever lain with a man before?" he asked, knowing the answer, and yet needing to reassure himself that this was what she wanted.

"No." The word was a whisper on the wind. "But there's always a first time."

"Malcolm… your brother and father…"

"They've got their lives to lead, and I have mine. It's time I made my own decisions."

****

As soon as Leena said those words, she realized Malcolm had always been her father's choice for her. She'd gone along with the idea because it would have been an appropriate match and she liked Malcolm. But liking him, or even feeling a deep fondness for him, wasn't love; not in the sense of a woman and a man sharing a passionate need for each other.

In her heart, she sensed Taurin's longing for her, and it struck an answering chord within her soul. He still held many secrets, but he had an innate goodness that rang true. Perhaps he didn't realize it was there, but he'd shown her concern and consideration, and that meant more to her than any of his warnings about his violent past.

All of this flitted through her mind in a brief instant. Taurin hovered beside her, his gaze dark with desire, his hair tousled, his jaw clenched as he waited for her to answer the question in his eyes. Her glance lowered to his bare chest, and her blood stirred as she yearned to feel flesh against flesh, body against body.

"Make love to me," she told him in a soft voice. "Nothing else matters right now except the two of us."

"If you're sure… then my aim is to please you." His gaze deepened as he lowered his head to kiss her. It was a gentle touch, a mere brush of his lips against hers, but now that Leena knew what she wanted, her patience flew out the door.

She leaned up and pulled him over until he lay sprawled atop her.

"Gods, Leena," he said before his mouth claimed hers. His tongue thrust between her parted lips, making her gasp with heated pleasure. His deep kiss inflamed her senses.

She returned the favor, eager to progress and pleased to note how his breath quickened and the bulge prodding her thighs stiffened.

So this is what it's like to feel a woman's power, she thought with an inward smile.

Breaking free from his kiss, she sought to remove her gown, wishing to feel his hot skin next to hers.

"Let me help you." He edged the garment downward, over the swell of her breasts, past her waistline, and below the golden triangle of hair at the juncture of her thighs.

"You are beautiful, my *angella*," he rasped, his gaze devouring her.

Shyness wasn't a consideration. It was as though this was meant to be, and Taurin was the one she'd been waiting for all her life. Now she wanted to know him as only a woman could know a man—heart to heart, body to body, soul to soul.

Chapter Seventeen

"I'm not sure what I should do to please you," Leena said to Taurin as uncertainty overwhelmed her.

"Your beauty alone brings me pleasure." After a reluctant parting kiss, he sprang up and stripped off his pants and boots. In the next instant, he was beside her again, ravishing her with his hot gaze.

Her eyes widened at the evidence of his manhood. "How does it fit? I mean—"

"No worries. You're built to accommodate me. I promise I won't hurt you. Tell me now if you want to stop, because if we go further, there'll be no holding back."

She stroked his jaw. "I'm not afraid. Show me what to do."

In response, he lowered his head and melded his mouth to hers. The urgency of his kiss and the feel of her breasts pressed against his chest excited her to new heights. She raked her fingers through his hair while her nerves screamed for release from a tension she didn't understand. An ache began between her legs and spread through her like wildfire.

As though sensing her need, Taurin trailed his hand south even as his mouth plundered hers and his tongue claimed her for his own. Leena writhed under his searing touch as he stroked her nipples until they stood erect. Tingling sensations rushed through her, pooling between her legs.

She clutched at his back, arching beneath him, shifting her position so he lay fully atop her. His hard shaft prodded her inner thighs. She opened her legs, wanting to accept him, all rational thought evaporating from her mind as her focus centered on their bodies pressed together. An unbearable throbbing arose from her female parts.

"Now, Taurin," she pleaded.

He entered her gently and then stopped to access her reaction. "Are you all right?" His gaze, smoldering with passion, scanned her face.

"Yes. Please. Don't stop now."

With a groan, he initiated a rocking motion, each thrust bringing him deeper inside her while she relished the sensation of their union. Without warning he plunged to the depths, eliciting a cry from her throat at a sudden stinging pain. He waited a moment for it to subside before resuming his rhythmic motion that made a crescendo rise within her.

A wave swept from her core and blossomed into a cataclysmic eruption as spasms of delight shook her body. Taurin's climax followed, and they clung together, lost in a whirlwind of pleasure.

Sweaty and panting for breath, he rolled off her, collapsing onto his back.

"Are you hurting? Was I too rough?" he asked, his voice concerned.

Leena closed her eyes, too languorous to move. "I'm fine. You were perfect." She waited until her breathing calmed and her heart rate slowed. Then she leaned up on an elbow and regarded him with a sexy smile. "Taurin, I want to do it again."

"Cosmos, how can I resist you?" he said when she let her fingers play with his chest hair. "But if we don't start back to the beach soon, we may miss Grotus's rendezvous." He leapt to his feet, dressed quickly, and began to break camp.

Leena admired the play of muscles across his broad back and the tautness of his body. He was truly magnificent, and she ached with wanting him. He filled a need within her that she hadn't known existed, and now the desire for more consumed her.

I love him, she realized suddenly, gazing at the heavy arch of his eyebrows, the sleek line of his nose, and his finely chiseled mouth. *He's the only man I'll ever want.*

She'd lost interest in any liaison between her and Malcolm and would tell her former suitor at the first opportunity, being tactful so as to minimize any hurt feelings. In the meantime, she'd convince Taurin their match was meant to be. It didn't bother her that he kept secrets, because she'd learn them in good time. He treated her well, and that was more important.

She should tell him she meant to honor their marriage vows but grew hesitant. He hadn't admitted to having deep feelings for her. What if his affection was only skin deep and nothing more?

"Now I'm truly your wife," she said in a teasing tone to gauge his response.

He paused in his work, his expression shuttered as he regarded her. "Yes, you are. For today at least."

Her heart sank. Did he still mean to request an annulment when they returned? How could she bear to lose him when they were just beginning to truly know each other?

She rolled to her feet and grabbed her clothes. Time to move on and see what came next.

****

Taurin hadn't thought of the consequences of their lovemaking. Now that he'd awakened Leena's passion, she wouldn't be satisfied with one experience. This didn't mean their lack of a future together would change. She was exploring him the same way she might one of her temples—with an innocent excitement and an eagerness for discovery. Damned if he didn't want to explore along with her.

But once she learned the truth about his origins, she'd change her attitude. The affection he saw in her eyes would turn to loathing. His throat constricted as he imagined the pain of parting from her, knowing he'd caused her grief.

It would be better if he didn't let her get too close. Physical coupling was one thing. Emotional intimacy was something else entirely. He'd been good at separating them when seeking women for pleasure. Why was it so difficult now?

He turned away so he couldn't see her hurt expression and began preparing breakfast. They consumed their meal in tense silence.

Finally, they resumed their mission. When they'd progressed some distance through the jungle, he halted. He had to get her agreement on one important item.

"Leena, I want you to make me a promise. We don't know what's going to happen when we return to Grotus's hideout. Give me your word that you'll do as I command without protest."

She sat on a flat rock beside a stream, trailing her fingers in the cool water. "I will, if your request is reasonable. Do you feel our lives will be in danger once Grotus gets what he wants from us?"

"Possibly. It would be wise to be prepared."

She gave him a piercing glare. "What's the matter, Taurin? Why won't you speak about what happened last night? Are kind words so troublesome to your tongue, or do you not feel anything toward me now that your lust is satisfied?"

His heart squeezed, but he resolved not to reveal his true feelings. "It is for your own good that I keep my distance."

She rose to face him. "Why is that? Tell me what troubles you."

He glanced away. "I'm not someone who'd normally be on your family's approval list."

"Is this about Malcolm? Because if it is, I'm not interested in him. Taurin, you're the man I want for my life mate."

He rounded on her, his expression fierce. "You don't mean what you're saying."

"Yes, I do. I'm in love with you."

Her confession battered his emotional armor. "It's merely an infatuation. You'll get over me," he managed to say, his throat tight.

"Why do you refuse to believe I really care for you? Has your life been so grim that you regard yourself as unworthy? I'm offering you a part of myself I've never shared with any other man. Doesn't that mean something to you?"

"Of course it does, but you don't belong with a man like me. You can't know—"

"All I know is that we need each other. Can you deny that truth?"

"No, by the stars, I can't," he said in strained tone.

"Then let's make a deal. We'll consider this an actual trial marriage, like they have at Beltane. If by the end of our mission, you still insist on an annulment, I'll agree with no further opposition. Is that fair?"

He struggled to find a rationale that would work against her proposal, but failed. "All right, I can work with that."

She rose on her tiptoes to kiss him, while he hoped their dreams weren't about to be blown away by the winds of evil sweeping the land. If they didn't find the horn by the month of Fearn, peace and harmony would cease to exist on her world, and everyone's dreams would be shattered. Despite their personal issues, he mustn't lose sight of their goal.

****

"How much longer do we have to wait for our rendezvous?" Leena used her hand to shade her eyes from the bright sun. The tide had washed up on shore during the night, leaving a deposit of wet seaweed and shells on the sandy beach.

Taurin dropped their sacks onto the sand with a grunt. "Grotus's people should be here soon. Remember what we're going to tell him." He swiped droplets of sweat from his forehead. Their trek had been long and tiresome.

"We found a few crystals near the temple entrance," she repeated dutifully, "but we were unable to get past the third challenge."

"You can embellish on the bones we saw," he added, gazing out to sea.

They still needed to determine an escape plan should Grotus attempt to detain them, but as soon as he saw their means of transportation, he decided that would be their route.

On the water, an immense structure slid from the watery depths to the surface, its black hull gleaming against the deep-green sea. While he and Leena watched in amazement, a small craft was launched in their direction. As the motorboat approached the beach, they discerned a lone crewman aboard.

"Come," the fellow shouted. "Grotus is eager for news of your success."

Taurin assisted Leena into the craft and then seated himself beside her on a small bench. They veered out to sea, zipping across the waves toward the ominous black vessel. It was sleek and tapered at both ends, with a superstructure in the center. As they neared the submersible, another crew member helped them aboard.

He and Leena climbed down a hatch and found themselves in a control room filled with a confusing array of instruments and dials.

A young crew member dressed in a tan uniform was assigned to the visitors. "My name is Stoker," he told them. "Can I help you with your bags?"

"We'll manage, thank you," Taurin responded, signaling for Leena to stay close.

They followed their guide to a stateroom with twin bunks, a built-in set of drawers, and a small desk. Compared to their cabin on the *Predator*, this one was spacious.

"The toilet's at the end of the corridor," Stoker said as a shuddering vibration indicated they were underway.

"Any chance of our getting a tour?" Taurin inquired, raising his eyebrows. "I've never been on a vessel like this before and would like to see how things work."

"I guess I can show you around."

Taurin took advantage of the man's youthful gullibility by asking numerous questions, pretending he was merely curious but sharply observing the details. He coaxed Stoker into explaining the operating systems, communication network, and navigational computer, not that he understood everything. He'd become familiar with advanced technology on Yllon but lacked these particular skills.

Here on Xan, the Synod had repressed any development of advanced electronics, presumably so they could maintain control over the populace. Grotus's clout must reach far for him to smuggle in an item like this submersible. Or maybe he had friends in high places.

"How many crew members are aboard?" Leena asked after they'd seen the machine shop.

"Four of us can run the crew on a minimal shift. We don't need many for a sub this size. I didn't show you the cargo hold, but our main assignments are for shorter runs. The other vessels in the fleet are larger and capable of traveling a longer range. Those can hold a crew of twenty."

Taurin gaped at him. Grotus had a fleet? "Where does your employer get all these ships?"

Stoker shrugged. "Who knows? He pays well and gives us generous benefits. That's all I care about, so I don't ask questions."

"When do you estimate we'll reach his island?"

"The trip will take about twelve hours." Stoker led them back to their quarters. "If you're hungry, help yourself to chow in the galley. We fix our own food since we don't have a regular cook."

After he left, Taurin checked the cabin for surveillance bugs but didn't find any. "I can't believe Grotus keeps a fleet of these vessels," he told Leena. "I'll bet they're stationed around the world. This must be how he smuggles his contraband out of different territories."

"It makes sense," Leena agreed. "Hopefully, we can learn more from Grotus when we arrive."

Exhausted from their trek through the jungle, they collapsed onto their bunks and fell asleep until the submersible pulled into its berth. Stoker returned to lead them off the vessel to an underground complex. Bright lights lit the cavernous dock.

Now at least we know how Grotus's visitors come and go from the island, Taurin thought.

Stoker led them through the receiving chambers where Taurin spied cargo being unloaded. The sailor left them at a lift that would take them to the surface.

It was nighttime when they emerged into the outside air. The lateness of the hour prevented them from seeing their host until the next day. They were greeted by an attendant who provided them with a snack and then took them to their suite for the evening.

In the morning, the same fellow knocked on their door and served breakfast. He said Grotus would see them at noon. After their meal, Taurin and Leena lazed in bed where they enjoyed another episode of lovemaking.

"I could get used to this," Taurin said, flicking his tongue at Leena's earlobe. He held her naked body in his embrace, luxuriating in the warm, soft feel of her.

"Me, too. Kiss me," she demanded, while he wished this interlude would never end.

Their time together was like a dream. It would dissolve once they returned to the Palisades.

His mouth crushed down on hers as their bodies entwined. He entered her in a smooth thrust, his passage eased by her slick wetness. She brought her legs up to wrap around his, clutching at his back and riding him like a frenzied *enix*.

Taurin thought his heart would burst from joy and something else he felt deep inside and couldn't acknowledge. As his thrusts deepened, a low growl rolled from his throat, and all rational thought flew from his mind. He and Leena were one, and that was all that mattered.

Or was it? he asked himself later, when they rested side-by-side. Analyzing his emotions, he surprised himself by realizing his fears were for naught. He'd been afraid to unleash the violence coiled within his soul. Treating Leena with tenderness had come naturally to him. This response confirmed his notion that the supposed demonic influence was nothing more than a myth.

"What are you thinking?" Leena asked, cutting into his thoughts.

He glanced at her, smiling at the lovely portrait she made with her hair trailing across her bosom, her eyes still languid from their spent passion.

"I'm thinking how important you've become to me," he said truthfully.

She touched his arm, letting her hand linger on his skin. "I hope our marriage works out," she whispered.

"What are you going to tell people when we return home?"

Her expression clouded. "I'd like to speak to Malcolm and my father first. Would you mind if we delayed any announcement?"

He was more concerned for her safety. There were still things about him she didn't know, other reasons why he kept himself hidden away from public view.

"Not at all," he replied. "We should wait until the horn is recovered. That would be a more appropriate time for a celebration."

She might still despise him after certain factors came to light. If Grotus had news of the horn, it would speed their path.

At noon, they were ushered into the private dining room to greet their host.

"I was quite impressed with the mode of transportation that brought us here," Leena remarked once their meal—a curious mix of delicacies—had been served. She ate a bite of egg bread spread with fruit jam.

Grotus stuffed a leafy stalk of saltreed into his mouth. He'd changed his nose ring to one holding a topaz-colored gem that flashed with each movement of his jaw. He'd tied his ebony hair into a ponytail. As before, he wore a multi-colored longshirt over a pair of baggy trousers.

"No one has ever been able to determine what method of transport my agents use." Grotus's gaze raked Leena from the top of her loose, wavy hair down to the bodice of her ruby-colored gown. "Even if you inform the Synod, they'll not be able to track our movements. They haven't the equipment or the knowledge."

"Your operation is well organized." Leena's compliment drew a pleased look on the smuggler's face. "Do you keep the most valuable finds for yourself, or do you sell them to select buyers?"

Grotus didn't pass up the opportunity to impress her. "Many of my collectors don't care how the merchandise is obtained. They pay me well for the right goods. But I do keep some of the better treasures for myself. I'm sure a woman of your talents would appreciate them."

"Your taste in art is exquisite." Leena lowered her eyelids demurely, while Taurin grew restless beside her. What was she playing at with this thief?

"My puny possessions do not compare to your beauty," the smuggler stated.

Taurin coughed loudly. "Have you any news regarding our quest?" he asked, raising an inquisitive eyebrow.

Grotus's gaze swung to Taurin, and there was no friendliness in his cold black eyes. "We did agree to a trade, did we not? Were you able to access the Temple of Light?"

"The temple was booby-trapped. We couldn't get too far, but we did bring you back a bunch of these, which were near the entrance."

He withdrew one of the crystals from his pocket, handing it over to Grotus for examination. Figuring the smuggler needed further convincing that their tale was true, Taurin nudged Leena to support his claim.

"I'm familiar with many of the traps from other temples I've explored," she said, "so we were able to gain a further distance than anyone else, judging from the bones lying around. The third challenge was impassable, however. We barely escaped with our lives."

Grotus turned the crystal over in his hand to admire the facets. "How many of these did you obtain?"

"A whole bagful," Taurin replied with a hint of impatience. "I'm sure they're quite valuable. Now what have you learned about the horn?"

Leena gave him a startled glance. They hadn't told Grotus which relic had gone missing, only that it was important to the Synod.

Grotus didn't seem surprised by the news. He must have already known the horn was the object of their quest.

"Unfortunately, my agents were unable to pick up any sign of its whereabouts." Grotus placed the crystal on the table. "The sacred artifact has not been presented to me for sale, so I have little knowledge about who has stolen it."

"Do you have any theories?"

"Not at the moment. Meanwhile, rumors are spreading among the people about the recent natural disasters. They don't accept the story of a substitute trumpet being blown at Renewal. They're fearful of greater tragedies ahead if the horn isn't recovered." Grotus spread his hands, a wide smile on his face. "I'm just as eager as anyone to see the horn reinstated. My global empire is quite prosperous. Should a disaster occur because the horn isn't blown in time to reset the cycles, I would be most unhappy. If my agents learn anything new, I'll be sure to let you know."

"Taurin and I will need transportation back to the Palisades," Leena said, disappointment etched on her features.

"Don't be in such a rush, madam. I have much to show you."

Taurin gave him a suspicious glance, but Grotus ignored him, gesturing for one of his servers to clear their plates. Dessert followed while they discussed the varying weather patterns.

"Blanchette is waiting for you in the garden," Grotus told Leena when they had finished. "She'll take you to see a lake nearby that's quite pleasant. Your husband can join you shortly."

Taurin remained, sitting rigidly in his seat, wondering what Grotus wanted with him. He didn't have long to wait. As soon as Leena vacated the room, all traces of pleasantry vanished from Grotus's face, replaced by a snarl.

"When you find the horn," Grotus told Taurin, "I want it."

Taurin stared at him. "Why would I give it to you? You just said you want this world restored to order as much as we do."

"That relic is worth a lot of money. Dikran will pay highly for it. You will give it to me first, and I will ransom it back to the Synod."

"Go to the devil."

Taurin half-rose as though to leave, but Grotus stayed him with a gesture. "Who are you to speak of demons, Taurin Rey Niris? I know where you come from, and there they call you demon seed. Do you wish me to tell your enemies where to find you?"

Taurin sank slowly into his chair, too stunned to speak.

Grotus picked idly at his teeth with a lacquered fingernail. "After seeing your bibliotome, I had my suspicions. Captain Sterckle had sold me some bibliotomes that came from Yllon, so I made inquiries about you. It didn't take me long to learn you'd booked passage on his ship. I remembered your bracelet was constructed of the same material as the elusive horn. Are you still wearing it?"

Taurin nodded, not liking the way this conversation was headed.

"I'll pay you a good price if you sell it to me."

"No deal, Grotus. And you're not getting the horn if we find it first."

Grotus's shoulders hunched, and his brows drew together. "If you don't cooperate, I'll tell your friends where to find you. You're under a death sentence on Yllon. Your life won't be worth much if they come for you here."

A spearhead of panic shot through him, more out of fear for Leena's safety than his own. She was in danger merely by associating with him. His mind raced frantically as he sought a method of appeasement.

"We brought you the crystals. Didn't we fulfill our part of the deal?"

Grotus chuckled. "Whoever said I was an honest man? My agents will be watching you. Should they discover that you've recovered the horn and not given it to me, I will immediately contact your prior associates."

Taurin lowered his head as though defeated. "How can I get in touch with you?"

Grotus's smile broadened. "Sirvat knows how to reach me."

So Leena was right about the two of you. "What is your relationship to the Minister of Finance?"

"Sirvat would do anything to please me. She covets my attention and has provided me with certain tidbits of information in exchange for my favors. If you need to contact me, she'll be most happy to assist you." Grotus stood and tossed his napkin onto the table. "And now, you must excuse me. I wish to make your wife an offer." The way he emphasized the word *wife* showed that he didn't think much of their bonding.

Taurin shot out of his seat, his fists clenched by his sides. "What kind of offer do you mean?"

"It's a private matter that doesn't concern you." Grotus snapped his fingers, and a couple of guards arrived—armed guards, Taurin noticed. "You will escort our brother to his chamber," Grotus ordered.

Sensing it would be useless to argue, Taurin went willingly, his troubled mind imagining all sorts of threats Grotus would make to Leena. *They couldn't be as bad as the one he made me. If my identity is exposed...* He shuddered, blocking the violent images from his mind.

Chapter Eighteen

"Where is Taurin?" Leena asked, having been shown into the music room by Blanchette and left alone with Grotus. She'd had a pleasant stroll to the lake with her guide, but now she yearned for Taurin's company and wondered why he wasn't there to greet her.

"I wished to have a moment alone with you, my dear." Grotus's dark eyes gleamed with malice. "Come, please be seated. If you're thirsty, help yourself to a beverage from that carafe on the table."

Leena remembered the last time she and Taurin had taken a drink from Grotus and ignored his offer. Curious as to what he wanted from her, she sat in an upholstered armchair and waited. Grotus lowered himself onto a bench behind the magnificent keyboard instrument in the center of the room. In moments, his fingers flew over the keys, producing a beautiful melody that lifted her spirits and relaxed her mind.

"You play wonderfully," she remarked in astonishment.

"I've practiced for many years." As he played, his gaze roved over her, his expression leaving no doubt in her mind what he wanted.

Compressing her mouth, Leena glared at him meaningfully. "My husband would enjoy hearing you play. We should summon him."

"He complained of fatigue and is resting upstairs. Come, sit here on the bench with me, and I'll show you the music."

"I can hear quite well from this spot, thank you."

Grotus lit a candle of incense. "This is my favorite scent. I think you'll enjoy it. Come closer," he commanded, and this time she felt compelled to obey.

The spicy fragrance tickled her nostrils as she sat beside Grotus, modestly spreading her skirt about her legs.

"Have you ever played an instrument?" he asked her.

"No." Leena gave a small smile. "My brother Bendyk used to play the hironrod, but I was never musically inclined."

"Your artistic talents simply run in other directions." Grotus showed her how he placed his fingers on the keys. "There are seven basic notes to play, plus three tabs and notches. Once you learn the basic sets, the rest is easy."

Leena shook her head. "It could never be easy for me."

Grotus played a fast, catchy tune that caught her fancy, and she swayed in place, dreamily breathing in the tantalizing scent of the incense and enjoying the crescendo of music that thundered her senses.

"That was marvelous," she said after he had finished with a flourish. His nose ring seemed unusually large as she gazed into his face. He didn't seem quite as unappealing as he had before, and that strange gleam in his eyes held her transfixed.

"If you like my music, there are other things I can share with you." He took her hand as they stood and led her away from the bench and toward a doorway.

In the library, Grotus rotated a book high on a third shelf. A section of wall swung aside, revealing a passage beyond. "Go ahead," he urged. "I'll follow you."

Her mind in a state of numbed tranquility, Leena strode ahead. Facing her was a short corridor with a door ahead. Behind her Grotus laughed as he swung the hidden panel back into place. Recessed lights provided illumination as he sauntered next to her and pushed a touchpad beside the far door. It swung open, and Leena gasped at the sight within.

"This is the vault where you keep your collection." She rushed forward to study the ancient artifacts and other works of art he'd gathered there.

"I knew a woman of your fine taste would appreciate a private viewing. But these are nothing compared to my newest treasure. Follow me."

"What is it?" She moistened her lips as the smell of incense drifted her way again, lulling her into a calm serenity.

The next room appeared to be a bedchamber, with a large round bed on a central dais. Black and gold drapes decorated the space, which had mirrors covering the walls and ceiling. She heard the door latch shut behind her, but it didn't bother her. The cloud of incense thickened, clogging her nostrils until she could barely breathe.

She put a hand on her stomach. "I don't feel so good. We should find Taurin."

"You can rest here," Grotus said in a soothing tone, motioning to the bed. "Lie down, and I'll see that you're well attended."

Feeling dizzy, Leena did as she was told, but instead of leaving to seek her husband, Grotus sat beside her.

"I've never met a woman of your beauty who also has such excellent taste in art. It's an irresistible combination." He trailed his pudgy fingers down her arm.

Leena felt too weak to protest, or even to wonder why her head reeled. The soft bedding was comfortable, and she couldn't have moved her limbs had she tried because they felt so heavy. Grotus leaned over her, his face growing larger as her vision blurred.

"I'd like you to stay with me, Leena. Your man can find the horn. I need someone with your skills to appraise my acquisitions."

"Stay here? No, I can't." Leena began to rise, but Grotus pushed her down.

He studied her face, an expression of concern on his visage. "You look pale, my dear. I think perhaps your gown is too tight. I will help you unfasten it."

Before she could protest, he rolled her to the side and unzipped the fastening in the back. His fingers lightly caressed her flesh, and a shudder of revulsion coursed through her veins.

"Don't… don't do that."

He pushed her onto her back and gazed into her face, his teeth bared in an evil grin. "I'll show you the pleasures that will be yours should you decide to remain. You don't need to go away with that farmer. Stay here and reap the glories of my empire. Rey Niris will find the horn, and he'll bring it to me. He has no choice."

"I'll not be your hostage," Leena murmured, wishing she could gather her strength.

Grotus's hand groped inside her loose bodice, finding her breast. His other hand pushed her legs apart. "You're not a hostage. You will be the supreme addition to my collection. A treasure beyond comparison."

Leena couldn't understand why the incense didn't bother Grotus. Choking from the cloud that pervaded the room, she closed her eyes, barely aware of Grotus's hands roaming her body. Her mind wandered and replayed the tune he'd performed in the music room.

C-D-E-F. Leena rattled off the keyboard notes that Grotus had taught her, only those weren't all of them. Try again, she told herself, focusing her mind on her one rational thought. C-D-E-F-A-B. Was that right? She counted them all together. No, one was missing. It should be C-D-E-F-G-A-B.

That's it! There were seven notes, plus the other notches he'd pointed out to her that made for the different combinations. Seven. Why did that number ring a bell?

Leena moaned as Grotus's probing touch dipped between her thighs.

The smuggler chuckled. "I knew you would enjoy this, my dear. The perfumed incense is very hypnotic, is it not? I am immune to its power, but you are quite susceptible."

Seven notes, Leena thought in her hazy mind. Just like the seven letters that she couldn't decipher in the ancient symbols. If they were letters, that is. In her head, she replayed the tone of Taurin's spinning bracelet. What if the seven symbols inscribed there represented musical notes?

Stunned by the revelation, she sat upright and stared at Grotus. "Get off me. I must speak to Taurin."

"You're not going anywhere."

"Oh, yes I am." The fog dispelled from her mind, and she leapt off the bed. Her heart racing, she lunged for the door.

Grotus reached her in two quick strides and grabbed her by the arm. Leena whirled around, her anger bringing clarity.

"What would you do? Keep me hostage while sending Taurin off to locate the horn on his own? Is this how you hope to obtain it for your collection?"

Grotus glowered at her. "Rey Niris will bring me the horn, but you are not the bait. I want you here for my own reasons."

"May I remind you that without me, Taurin has no way to verify the authenticity of the horn?"

"You will authenticate it here."

"The Synod would not stand for you to hold me captive. My brother Bendyk is a partner in this investigation. He will see to it that you are hunted down."

Grotus snickered, his fingers digging into her arm. "No one can reach this island."

"We did." Leena thrust her jaw out stubbornly. "I'll not work for you, no matter what you do to me. Release me at once."

Grotus appeared to consider his options. No doubt the man was uncertain that she and Taurin were telling the truth about their findings at the Temple of Light. He must suspect they'd penetrated farther than indicated, but he had no way of knowing for sure without forcing the truth from them. He couldn't harm them, because retrieving the horn was more important to his luxurious way of life. Leena and Taurin together had the best chance of finding it.

Abruptly Grotus released her. "Very well. I will make arrangements for your return to the Palisades."

****

Grotus escorted Leena to the main hallway and summoned an attendant to take her to her chamber. After they left, he hastened into the library, closed the door, and put through a private call to Sirvat's private suite at the government center.

"Sirvat," he said when he heard her voice on the line. "I am sending our two little birds back home. They have failed in their quest thus far, but I would appreciate it if you'd keep me informed of their progress." His voice lowered seductively. "I should be most grateful."

"Of course, Grotus." He could almost hear her purring on the line. "I miss you. When am I going to see you again? It's been too long since our last rendezvous." Her voice was edged with the desperation of a woman who knew that her man was not nearly as attracted to her as she was to him.

"Soon, my dear. Have you any news to report?"

"Karayan and Zeroun have expressed doubts about Magar's loyalty. They'd like to know more about his relationship to Rey Niris."

Grotus knew very well what their relationship was, but he didn't share this information with Sirvat. "Be cautious. Leena and Taurin are aware of our liaison. Call me if anything else develops."

He terminated communications, realizing he had no more clues to the horn's location than before. He'd impress upon his agents the urgency of the matter and see that they passed on any information gained to Leena and her husband, without tipping them off as to the source.

A rage of helplessness shook him. Not only did the Synod have to rely upon the couple to find the horn, but so did he, and Grotus didn't like having to depend on anyone.

****

Immediately upon their arrival at the Palisades, Leena and Taurin were summoned to a conference with Dikran. The Arch Nome greeted them in his private reception chamber. Seated in his large, throne-like chair, he seemed dwarfed by the furnishings around him. His gaunt face and slumped shoulders indicated a weariness that went beyond his years.

At least his keenness of mind hadn't faded, Leena noted with relief. His sharp gaze focused on her and Taurin as the Caucus member who'd escorted them into the room departed. The three of them faced each other alone.

"Well," Dikran said in a tremulous voice, "have you brought me the sacred horn?"

Leena hid her failure by lifting her head proudly. "No, Your Grace. We have not recovered the holy relic, but we've made other significant discoveries."

A look of anguish crossed Dikran's face. "You've not found the horn! Then what are we to do? The Truthsayers are making loud noises about rebellion, and Zeroun's enforcers are hard-pressed to quell the people's fears."

"We will continue our search. We're not yet done. I wish to consult my brother before we proceed any further." Leena smoothed her emerald-green velvet gown. The crispness of autumn had finally arrived in the area, and she'd wisely chosen a heavier fabric.

After a moment of tense silence, Dikran addressed Taurin. "I don't believe we've met. Who are you and why are you qualified to act as Leena's escort?"

Taurin appeared startled by the directness of the questions. "I own a farm, sir, in Lexington Page. I possess certain skills that have come in handy on our quest."

Dikran nodded. "Karayan told me your property abuts Magar's estate. How do you two know each other?"

"Magar and I met during a trade exchange between our two lands," he explained. "I expressed interest in immigrating, and he agreed to help me. I raise edible flowers, which is rare in your territory."

Dikran folded his gnarled hands together in his lap, his gold robe reaching to his feet. He'd forsaken his headdress, and without it, he appeared merely as he was—an old man who kept his dignity but had lost his strength. His powers of observation had not lessened, though, and Taurin must be feeling the intensity of the Arch Nome's gaze boring into him.

"The trade records have been examined. There is no report of a meeting between you."

Taurin shrugged. "Magar probably deemed it insignificant to record. My background is not the issue here. We didn't find the horn, but we did come across some important finds."

Leena pitched in and told the Arch Nome about their excursion to the Black Lands, including the attempts on their lives and the illegal transactions of the Chocola Company on the island. Dikran's brow furrowed at the last, and he promised to look into the matter.

She continued on, describing their encounter with Grotus but omitting any mention of the Temple of Light. She and Taurin weren't sure what they should do with that knowledge and had decided to keep quiet about it for now.

"If Grotus could tell you nothing," Dikran commented, "then where do we go from here?"

Taurin wagged his finger. "I have an idea. Brother Aron, the missionary who tried to murder us, mentioned that Wodeners don't betray their friends. I gather he was from the Woden district. Leena and I could travel there incognito to see what we can learn about the Truthsayers."

Dikran raised an eyebrow. "It is possible Grotus may still hear news of the horn, but we cannot rely on him. I will make arrangements for your journey to Woden."

"Just give us a rider," Taurin said, making an impatient gesture. "We'll do this our way."

Leena glanced at him in surprise. His tone of voice denoted no disrespect, but it sounded as though he were ordering Dikran, not the other way around.

Dikran pursed his lips, studying the younger man. "Less than two months remain before Lothar is due to reset the cycles. If the horn is not blown at the Grand Altar by then, disaster will ensue. The people may not wait that long before they revolt. The Truthsayers are using this situation as a weapon against the Synod. They must be stopped." He leaned forward in his chair. "You and Bendyk are our only hope. You have to locate the horn."

Leena bowed her head, too choked with emotion to speak. It was a heavy burden, and she didn't feel worthy of it, especially after their lack of progress thus far. She promised to report as soon as they had news and accompanied Taurin from the chamber.

"Your brother said he would wait for us in his office." Taurin put his hand lightly on her shoulder. Her body drooped with discouragement. She hoped her brother had achieved greater success than she and Taurin.

"Sister, how good it is to see you!" Bendyk's handsome face burst into a grin when she and Taurin appeared in the doorway of his office.

"Bendyk! Oh, I'm so glad to be here." She rushed into her brother's arms, crushing him to her.

"I must bless your return," Bendyk said after they broke their embrace. He gave Taurin a solemn nod of greeting.

Swill rose from her desk, giving Leena a friendly smile. They fell silent as Bendyk raised his arms and intoned, "We give thanks to thee, O Lothar, for delivering these children back unto us in safety. You are our lord, the source of life and all its blessings. The harmony and grandeur of nature represent your majesty. We owe you our eternal gratitude for sanctifying life and granting us peace. Mahala."

"Mahala," Leena murmured, surprised to hear Swill and Taurin mutter in unison after them.

Bendyk's gold medallion flashed against his white shirt as he motioned for Taurin to close the door so they could talk in private. They moved their chairs into a circle.

"Swill, how are you?" Leena asked the tall, slender girl.

"I'm fine, thank you." Swill cast a fond glance in Bendyk's direction, making Leena raise her eyebrows. She would have expected a snappy retort and wondered what had occurred between the two of them in her absence.

"Did you find the horn?" Bendyk asked without preamble.

"I'm afraid not." Leena related to him everything they had told Dikran.

"Your plan to visit Woden makes sense," her brother said. "How can we help?"

"I want to go home first and visit Father."

"What? You'll waste valuable time. Why not leave at once to continue your mission?"

"I wish to show Taurin our estate and Father's temple," she added, emphasizing the last word.

Taurin caught the gleam in her eye. "Of course. I would be most honored."

"Father doesn't know about your vows," Bendyk reminded her. "I could annul the marriage now if you wish. It has served its purpose."

Leena cleared her throat. "We've decided to consider this a trial marriage, like the ones performed at Beltane. Taurin and I have reached an understanding, and we want to stay together." She was gratified to see the pride in Taurin's eyes as he returned her gaze.

Bendyk stared at her, clearly taken aback by her announcement. "What about you and Malcolm?"

"I'm no longer interested in Malcolm. I'll tell him so when I get the opportunity, but I'm eager to introduce Taurin to our father."

Hopefully he'd recognize that Taurin was a man of character, whereas Malcolm was accustomed to the easy life. Her former suitor enjoyed the accoutrements of wealth through his inheritance and lacked ambition to further his intellect.

In contrast, Taurin had come to this land with nothing but his name and had developed his farm into a thriving business. She was better suited to a man who met challenges head on and could protect her in times of adversity.

Perhaps Bendyk was concerned about Taurin's irreverent attitude toward Lothar, but he had to understand that everybody had the right to their own beliefs. It no longer seemed important to convert those who doubted their faith. Bendyk's calling should be more in the line of helping people, as Swill tried to do.

"Well then, I must extend to you both my congratulations," Bendyk said. "I offer my blessings and my counsel should you require it for any reason."

Taurin gave him a nod. "I promise to look after your sister."

"We'll pretend to be new settlers when we go to Woden," Leena explained. "Dikran is arranging for the proper document-ation. Now tell me, have you and Swill made any progress?"

Swill answered, tugging at the long sleeves of her burgundy blouse. She'd tucked it into a black skirt that hugged her hips. "Magar makes regular entries in his receipt book. These deposits have no mention of the source. Sirvat transfers the money into the Treasury account. Her financial records are impeccable, but she takes trips every so often, returning with a new piece of jewelry each time. It's odd, because normally she's not one to adorn herself."

"I'll bet I know where she gets those pieces." Leena related what they'd learned about Sirvat's relationship to Grotus.

Bendyk shook his head. "She seems so strait-laced. It's hard to believe she'd fall for a rogue like him."

"Perhaps Sirvat hides a passionate nature. Now that I think about it, some of the items I saw in Grotus's mansion are similar to pieces in Karayan's house. The minister has quite an extensive art collection."

"Are you implying he buys goods from Grotus?" Bendyk asked with a horrified expression.

"Not necessarily. They may simply share the same tastes, although Karayan is a much better dresser."

Taurin snorted. "We're not here to discuss anyone's preference in art or clothes. Did you investigate Zeroun? As Minister of Religion, his department is responsible for administering the Black Lands. Someone there has granted illegal rights to the Chocola Company."

"We'll check into it," Swill assured him. "We've cleared most of the other Synod members but weren't sure about Sirvat's trips or Magar's secretive dealings in his trade commissions. I still feel he's withholding information from us."

"I'm more willing to trust Magar," Taurin said. "It's Zeroun who needs further investigation."

"By the way, Karayan wants to see you while you're here," Bendyk told his sister. "He's been concerned about your safety."

"Of course," Leena said, pleased her father's friend would take such an interest in her well-being. "I'll stop by and say hello before we leave. Why don't the two of you come home with us to see Father?"

"Swill and I made plans to go the Festival of Hathalat tomorrow. All the offices will be closed."

Leena's eyes widened. "But the Festival of Hathalat is where young maidens are…"

She stopped when she saw the amused expression in Bendyk's eyes. How was it that he and Swill were socializing together? Could it be that their relationship had progressed beyond a professional one? They certainly seemed to share an easy camaraderie. Swill showed little of the rebelliousness she'd first demonstrated, and Bendyk wasn't at all his usual pompous, preachy self. Her heart warmed to the young lady who might have mellowed her brother.

Rising, she turned to Taurin and linked her arm with his when he stood. "Let's keep in touch, Brother. Dikran said the people are getting restless. We must conclude this business quickly."

Karayan was not in his office, so Leena and Taurin proceeded outside to the sleek rider that had been lent to them. Taurin started the engine, then glanced at Leena. "Why did you not tell Bendyk and Swill of your discovery regarding the seven symbols?"

"We still have no idea what they signify." She'd determined

the symbols represented musical notes and the common string correlated with Cadega, the constellation.

"It means the Apostles might have come from there," Taurin said, pointing heavenward.

Leena gaped at him from the passenger seat. "Are you saying they originated from another planet?"

"Why not? Didn't you tell me the horn was constructed from a material unlike any other found on Xan?"

"Well, yes."

"Doesn't that mean the substance could have come from another world? It would explain why the Apostles were so much more advanced than the native population."

His words fired her imagination, confirming a theory she'd held but hadn't dared to acknowledge. "Wherever the Apostles came from, they brought us Lothar's teachings," she reminded him.

Taurin shook his head. "I believe they established the religion of Lothar because they knew it would appeal to the primitive intellect of the inhabitants. The Apostles wrote the laws as guidelines for an orderly society. There was no supernatural entity involved."

"You speak heresy. Are you saying there is no Lothar?"

Taurin shrugged, as though unwilling to commit himself to a direct response. Leena fell silent, lost in her own musings about Lothar, the Apostles, and the history of her world.

Chapter Nineteen

At the Palisades, Bendyk was having second thoughts about taking Swill to the festival. Ever since that first night when they'd made love in her apartment, he had been visiting her a couple of times a week. Neither one of them had said any words of commitment. Swill made it quite clear that physical satisfaction was her main motivation, and Bendyk wasn't ready to admit to any stronger emotions as far as she was concerned.

The purpose of the festival was to induce young maidens to succumb to their suitors' charms, and the notion weighted him with guilt. A bonding ceremony remained the ultimate goal for most young people, and his continuing to enjoy Swill without any plans in that direction preyed on his conscience. He was using Swill as she was using him, and such selfishness was unworthy of Lothar's blessing.

His steps took him once again to Swill's suite. Aware she was not expecting him, he was nonetheless surprised when she opened her door wearing nothing but an overshirt with a scooped neckline. His gaze swept from her damp hair to her bare legs, and he surmised she'd just come from the shower.

"Please come in," she said, her face coloring to a maidenly shade of crimson. She led him into her living area.

"I don't think we should go to the festival tomorrow," he stated. "Let's go visit Father instead. I'd like to show you around our estate."

Swill's mouth dropped open. "You want to take me home?"

Bendyk interpreted her hesitation as being due to her desire to continue their work at the Palisades. Accordingly, he paced the room, hands folded behind his back, as he addressed a topic he wouldn't have spoken of otherwise.

"Before the accident that killed my mother, Father had spoken out against the teachings of the Synod. Studying ancient scrolls had always been his avocation, and the ones he'd been examining were a recent find from the caves of Halea. His interpretation was grossly misguided. Charged with heresy, he was threatened with banishment to the Black Lands unless he rescinded his words."

Bendyk paused, fingering a pottery vase displayed on Swill's bookshelf. "Zeroun was responsible for assigning him penance. Father was allowed to keep his position, but the censure destroyed his faith in himself."

He fell silent, and when he said nothing more, she asked, "Why are you telling me this?"

His gaze locked on hers. "I told you the brakes failed on our rider the night of the accident. I didn't see the mechanic's report, but my father told me it showed nothing irregular. Now that we are investigating the Synod, I am wondering…"

He let his voice trail off, confusion and doubt assailing him. He'd had his suspicions, but they'd been suppressed in the aftermath of the tragedy. Until now, he'd had no reason to bring forth the matter again. He wasn't sure he even wanted to dig any deeper at this point in time, but then, he didn't have to be the one to pursue the subject. Swill could do it for him.

"I'd be happy to look into it," she said when he'd explained his request.

He left Swill so she could prepare for their excursion. What if his suspicions were true, and the brake failure hadn't been an accident? Did he dare mention the matter to his father? It would throw the government into a further state of chaos if someone at a high level was involved.

His shoulders hunched as he headed to his own suite. His father might know what really happened that night. Bendyk resolved to discuss the matter with him to clarify the issue once and for all.

Satisfied with his reasoning, he never once considered why he needed an excuse to bring Swill home.

****

Taurin was impressed by the richness of Leena's familial estate as she conducted him on a tour. He'd met Cranby earlier and endured an interrogation worthy of an Inquisitor from Yllon. Cranby must have been satisfied with Taurin's responses, because he'd offered his congratulations and dismissed them both, shuffling off to his library to pursue his studies. Leena had excused herself to make a private call to Malcolm.

"This is too easy," Taurin muttered to himself, gratified that Cranby had accepted him so readily. Apparently the older man was happy to see his daughter wed, as long as her mate was honorable and offered the proper respect.

"How'd it go?" he asked when Leena strode into the foyer where he awaited her.

"I'd hoped to see him in person, but Malcolm has a business appointment later. I told him the news over the messager. He was outraged and deeply hurt." Her eyes reflected her pain. "Once he thinks it over, I'm sure he'll realize this way is best. I just hope he doesn't complicate matters by speaking against us. His comments were not very complimentary."

"His pride is wounded, but he's a good catch. Someone else will snare him before long. If he's a gentleman, and you've indicated that he is one, I doubt he would malign you to others."

Leena advanced toward him and kissed him soundly on the mouth. "You make me feel so much better. I'm glad you're mine."

He embraced her, sensing her need for comfort. After planting a light kiss on her forehead, he stepped away. "How about completing our tour?" he suggested.

They were nearly finished when Bendyk and Swill arrived.

Leena greeted her brother inside the gilded foyer. "What are you doing here?"

"We decided not to go to the festival today," Bendyk said. "I'd rather show Swill around, especially since you're here. We're just in time for lunch, are we not?"

"You would remember it is mealtime," she replied with a cynical curve of her lips.

Her father retained several servants, so providing for an extra pair of visitors was an easy task. The guests sat around a table laden with gold-rimmed dishes and gleaming silver flatware.

"Is Father not joining us?" Bendyk's brow furrowed with dismay.

"He's engrossed in the library. You know how he doesn't like to be disturbed," Leena reminded him.

Bendyk rolled his eyes before helping himself to a biscuit and butter. Leena engaged him in conversation while Taurin consumed his food in brooding silence. Swill ate quietly, casting nervous glances at Bendyk each time a new course was served.

"What are you two planning to do this afternoon?" Bendyk asked, finishing his meal with a slice of juicy porcheberry pie.

"I'm planning to show Taurin around Father's temple. What about you?"

"I'll introduce Swill to Father. Then she'll be heading into town to make some inquiries."

"What sort of inquiries?" Taurin asked in a mild tone.

"I've asked her to check into the report of brake failure from the night of the accident that killed our mother."

Leena gaped at him. "Why would you want to do that?"

Bendyk shifted in his seat. "I was never fully satisfied with Father's explanation of the mechanic's report."

"You mean, you don't believe the brakes failed? How would you account for the accident otherwise? Or do you blame it on your reckless driving?"

"Don't open old wounds," Bendyk snapped. "I'm seeking a better explanation for what happened."

"But why now? Why not five years ago?"

"I knew Father believed the accident was a punishment sent by Lothar for his blasphemy. The way things have been going around here lately, I'm not so sure we should let the matter go so readily."

"What did your father do that caused censure?" Taurin asked.

"He interpreted an ancient scroll that said Lothar existed in men's minds and was created in the spirit of love," Leena replied. "His judgment was erroneous. We should serve Lothar with love, and he will bring peace to our land. If we don't maintain harmony, Lothar will become angry. You've seen the results with the weather disasters."

Taurin raised an eyebrow. "You mean your father actually implied Lothar is not a supernatural entity, as the rest of you believe?"

Little did she know that her father had discerned the truth, Taurin thought. He had always suspected that the Apostles, revered on Xan, had also come to Yllon. There they'd been regarded as demons rather than disciples of a god. What had happened to make the difference he had yet to discover, but he hoped to find out while on Xan. He was a direct descendant of those ancients, and learning more about them would help him understand himself and his purpose in life.

****

Unaware of the reason for Taurin's sudden silence, Leena attempted to explain. "Father admitted he was wrong. He apologized for his misinterpretation and paid the penance. One of the reasons why I joined the Caucus was to find a way to clear his name. It hurts me to see him act so subdued around the Synod members. His scholarly efforts have always been valid. I can't help wondering if there is any truth to his findings, although it goes against everything we've been taught."

Bendyk compressed his lips, as though he didn't give credence to the idea. "I intend to have a talk with Father. I'd like to hear his opinion about the cause of the accident."

The four of them rose, and an awkward silence ensued.

"Swill, do you know the way into town?" Leena asked, feeling sorry for the girl, who'd mostly been left out of the conversation.

Swill lifted her chin. "I'll find the way."

"Let me walk outside with you." Once they were alone, she turned to Swill. "How do you feel about my brother?"

"He's the most unusual man I've ever met." The young woman cast her gaze upon the circular brick driveway.

"He cares for you."

"We're working together. It's a business relationship."

"No, it's more than that. He's never brought a woman home before."

"I'm not his girlfriend. And even if I wanted to be, I'd never fit into your family."

Understanding dawned. "Do you mean to tell me you don't think you're good enough for Bendyk?" Leena laughed aloud, astonished by the revelation. "By all that is holy, he needs someone like you."

Swill shuffled her feet. "I don't come from a background anything like yours."

Leena's face sobered. "Listen to me. Bendyk didn't plan to be a missionary. He took on the calling after the accident. Before that, he was spoiled and aimless. Religion has given him a purpose in life, but it's not enough for him. He yearns for something more. I think your liaison has been good for him. He's looking happier than he has in a long time."

"What of you?" Swill asked softly. "You're married to a farmer."

"I love Taurin. He may be a flower grower but there's much more inside of him than that, just as there is in you, Swill. You have to believe in yourself. Give yourself the respect you want others to feel for you, and the rest will follow."

Swill's expression clouded but not before Leena saw the longing in her face. "I have to be going. Bendyk asked me to interview the mechanic who inspected the wrecked rider after the accident."

Leena grasped her shoulder. "Tell me what you find out, will you? And Swill, I do appreciate the help you're giving Bendyk."

"He's lucky to have a sister like you."

On an impulse, Leena embraced her. "Be careful. You could be stirring the proverbial hornet's nest."

****

Hours later, Leena and Taurin were exploring her father's temple. The regional worship center consisted of a complex of buildings located in the center of town. The characteristic antlers—the branches of life representing Lothar—could be spotted from miles away, sticking up from the various spires and the central pyramid point of the temple itself.

They'd viewed the cathedral, side chapels, and offices, but now as they entered the Candor's private robing chamber, Leena hesitated.

"I suspect the entrance to the lower chambers is hidden in here, although Father has never spoken of it. What's down there is a secret known only to the Candors, given to them by the Synod when they take office."

"Is this where your father does his private worship?" Taurin asked, standing before an altar at the far end.

"No," Leena replied. "You see that receptacle?" Beneath the statue of a naked male cherub was a wide dish fashioned entirely of gold. "Lothar's lozenge pops out of the loins of the statue each month of Mistic."

"You mean the lozenge comes out of the…" Taurin pointed to the very masculine appendage on the cherub.

"Not just one tablet, but hundreds of them. They overflow the basin. And yet Lothar always seems to know how many people to provide for. The count is nearly accurate, with only a small variation."

"Your father keeps a census tabulation, does he not? He can tell Lothar how many lozenges to provide."

Taurin's mouth twisted wryly. He had no concept of how the lozenge was created. This prevention of sickness was one of the wonders of Xan, and it made him almost want to believe in their god. With a derisive snort, he surveyed the rest of the room.

"Where do you suppose the hidden entrance is located?"

Leena shrugged. "I've not been in here that often. Your guess is as good as mine."

"Another puzzle," Taurin murmured. He moved briskly through the room, poking and prodding various objects while hoping to push a secret lever. "Did you check your father's desk? Perhaps a clue can be found there. Look for a key."

Leena's face flushed. "I don't know if I should. It feels like an invasion of privacy."

"Demon's blood, woman. We're already trespassing."

Leena was rummaging in her father's desk when voices sounded outside the room. Her eyes widened in panic.

"Go see who it is," he said in a low tone. "Let me know if your father is coming."

"He said he had a meeting with the town council this afternoon." She closed the desk drawer and hastened toward the exit.

"Shut the door behind you," Taurin ordered. He continued to search the office until she returned a few minutes later.

"It was just some villeins seeking solace in the chapel."

"Perhaps it would be best if you stood guard outside."

Leena appeared to weigh his words. "All right," she agreed finally. "Call me if you find anything significant."

Once she'd left, Taurin paused before the cherub at the altar to study the exaggerated features, including the enormous organ that brought forth Lothar's lozenge. The figure certainly didn't impress one with its divine origins, despite the halo.

His gaze fixed on the circular object positioned atop the

cherub's head. Wait a minute! Wasn't that made from the same creamy, translucent substance as his bracelet?

He grasped the halo, and it snapped off in his hand. Held thus, it looked similar to the rings they'd found in the Temple of Light. Unsure of what response his action would produce, Taurin spun the ring in the gold basin beneath the cherub.

A light, musical tone reverberated throughout the room, followed by a low, grating noise coming from behind. Taurin whipped around in time to see a partition opening as a large painting swung aside. A dark hole gaped from the wall.

"That's it!" he exclaimed. Without considering the consequences, he dashed over and plunged into the darkness.

Inside a narrow passageway, he groped for a light switch. Finding none, he had to rely on his night vision. The path led to a stairwell ahead. He descended the steps carefully, perplexed when he faced four blank walls at the bottom level.

His blood chilled. Hopefully, this place wasn't full of traps like the Temple of Light.

Feeling around, he smirked in the dark when his hands outlined a familiar depression in the floor. He removed his bracelet, hoping the ring from the cherub wasn't required and that his own armband would suffice.

He needn't have worried. As he spun his bracelet, the musical tone produced had the desired effect. A wall swung open, revealing a series of chambers opening one into the other.

As he entered each room, it illuminated automatically. He passed quickly through the first few, which stored old scrolls and stacks of more recent files. The air smelled dank, like an old library and a crypt combined. He didn't stop to search through the documents. When he came to a fourth chamber, he halted to stare in awe.

The immense hall must take up an entire square block beneath the temple, he guessed. Its bright overhead lighting revealed a matrix of glowing crystals inside. They pulsated with a hum of energy.

I'll be damned, he thought. *The crystals are some kind of power source, after all. But how do they work?*

Some of the crystals lying around appeared dark and lifeless. Why didn't they glow like the others?

He pushed aside his questions to stride forward into the next chamber. Here a mesh of wires ascended to the ceiling. A display on the wall showed their attachment to the antler-like decorations on the temple's edifice.

Taurin's jaw dropped. "Cosmos, those things aren't just decorations. They're an antenna system."

He examined the diagram, his technical knowledge enabling him to interpret the data. This matrix, whatever it represented, sent signals back and forth to weather satellites orbiting the globe. There must be thousands of setups like this one originating from temples around the world.

So that's how Lothar controls the weather patterns.

There had to be a central monitoring station, most likely located at the Palisades. Did the Synod know how to manipulate the controls, or had they lost the knowledge through the years? This might be why the system was failing. Computers had never developed on Xan, but they were commonplace on Yllon. Could this be the legacy left behind by the ancients?

Everyone who extolled the Faith, except perhaps for the Synod and Candors, believed Lothar controlled the weather, including Leena. How could he disillusion her by revealing their climate was manipulated by a crystalline energy source linked to weather satellites, rather than by their god?

Stroking his jaw, he contemplated the function of the sacred horn. Was blowing the thing merely for show, or did it actually serve to reset the central computer?

Supposedly the horn had to be blown at the Grand Altar in the Palisades, meaning there had to be a link between the sound of the horn's frequency and the main weather controls. Since the Synod was so frantic to find the relic, he assumed they needed it to reset "Lothar".

Curious to see what he'd discover next, he strode ahead. The huge hall beyond contained a power grid large enough to supply the entire city and its surrounding region with electricity. Taurin followed a line of cables back to the room with the glowing crystals and realized they were the power source for this as well.

How were the crystals activated? When he and Leena had seen them in the Temple of Light, they were as lifeless and dark as those trapped here in the matrix. Did they die out with age, or was there a way to get them to function that was beyond the comprehension of the Synod?

Perhaps the mechanism for delivering their power was faulty, and the Synod lacked the technical expertise to initiate repairs. Most likely, the dying crystals were responsible for the weather disasters.

Another thought struck him, and he sucked in a sharp breath. Upon entering Xan's air space in Captain Sterckle's cargo transport, they'd waited for a window to open in the planet's protective energy shield. How was this defense maintained, and who operated it? Could the shield be powered by these same crystals, some of which were failing?

Other scenarios filtered into his mind. What if the horn had to be blown to reenergize the crystal lattices each year? If that were so, then the horn had to be blown to fortify Xan's defense net. That made it even more imperative to recover the holy artifact.

His heart sinking, he debated what to tell Leena as he trudged up the stairs back to the Candor's private office. A partial truth might be better than the whole, he decided, not wishing to be the one to tell her that a machine was responsible for the weather cycles on Xan. In any event, he had to confirm his theories.

When Leena appeared, she found Taurin lounging in a chair behind her father's desk.

"Did you find the entranceway below?" she asked him.

Taurin averted his gaze so she wouldn't see how it pained him to evade the truth. "Sorry, I couldn't locate it. Let's return to your father's house. We need to prepare for our trip to Woden."

Leena agreed, but her eyes narrowed as he continued to avoid her gaze. "Are you sure you're telling me everything?"

Taurin rose and hastened to her side to allay her suspicions. "Don't you trust me?" He bent his head to lightly kiss her mouth. He hated himself for deceiving her, yet she'd despise him even more for exposing the truth. Like the bearers of bad news to kings in days of old, he didn't care to be the one responsible for destroying the illusions of her faith.

He cupped the back of her head with his hand, intending to seduce her to distraction. But when she swayed against him, he moaned her name aloud. As she kissed him back, he nearly lost his sense of reason. It took a strong effort to exert his self-control and step away.

"Not here and not now," he said in a terse tone.

"We'll finish this later." A smile of promise played enticingly on her lips before she spun around, prepared to depart.

"Bendyk," she cried, as they spotted her brother inside the cathedral. "What are you doing here?" Her face flushed, as though they'd been caught red-handed doing some vile deed.

"I thought I'd stop by to say hello before meeting Swill." He glanced at Taurin, a scowl on his face. "What were you doing in Father's private chamber?"

"Greetings, Brother," Taurin drawled. "We were searching for the entrance to the secret rooms below. When you return to the Palisades, look for a hidden entry there as well."

"What are you talking about?"

Leena touched her brother's arm. "Each major worship center has a lower level. We haven't been successful in finding the entrance here. It would be useful if you could find the access point at the Palisades."

"But why? Only the Synod and Candors are privy to the secrets of the temples. Why were you looking in Father's place of worship?"

"We'll explain another time," Taurin inserted.

For a brief moment of insanity, he considered telling them

what he'd learned and showing them the wonders below, but would they truly believe a machine was responsible for the weather cycles? It would still seem logical to them that their god provided for the people. After all, who had programmed the main computer?

"I don't see any reason to delay our journey until morning," he announced to Leena. "We can get in a few hours of driving before dark."

Leena looked crestfallen. "I'd hoped to spend time with Bendyk and Swill later."

"You should go," Bendyk agreed. "There's no sense in waiting. Just be careful. Woden is a den of Truthsayers. If they learn you're a member of the Caucus, your life will be worthless."

"We'll be travelling incognito," Taurin reassured him. "We'll stay just long enough to learn whether or not they have the horn."

Bendyk muttered a brief prayer of blessing, and Taurin followed Leena's example by bowing his head.

How can I destroy their faith when it occupies such a significant part of their lives? And yet if I don't, someone else might expose their planet's frailties first.

Already the people were clamoring for explanations about the missing horn. If it wasn't returned soon, the Synod would lose credibility, and anarchy would result.

He'd never let that happen. This world was his home now, and peace had to be maintained. If his identity was exposed as a result, perhaps it meant Lothar's will was at work after all.

Chapter Twenty

Woden was one of the larger towns in the province of Prefectus. Since they were unfamiliar with the territory, Leena suggested they stop at the worship center and introduce themselves to the local priest. The official might offer suggestions as to where they could find housing.

"What about a Realtor's office?" Taurin countered, keeping his focus ahead as he drove down a tree-lined thoroughfare in a business sector. Storefronts hosted banners welcoming members of the International Merchants Association.

"The priest would know more about the people. If this place is the center of Truthsayer activity, he should be aware of the dissension."

"But if we're seen in his company, it'll link us with the Sabal order." Taurin shook his head, his mouth set in a determined line. "I think we should steer clear of any connection to the priesthood."

He glanced approvingly at Leena's attire. Gone were the elegant gowns and the telltale circlet. Instead, she wore a simple day dress with a fitted bodice and flounced skirt in a pastel floral print. He'd chosen to forego his usual black clothing in order to appear less noticeable. His outfit consisted of a blue longshirt belted at the waist, navy pants, and scuffed black work shoes.

They should both blend in well with the inhabitants, he thought, noticing how the business people scurrying about their afternoon rush were similarly dressed.

Leena accepted his advice, and after finding a parking space, they entered a real estate office.

"Good and welfare, citizens," said an attractive brunette who stood at their arrival. "How can we help you?"

Taurin chose his wording carefully. "We're looking for a place to rent, but we'd like to be among people with more progressive ideas. We've just been married and have received permission to relocate." He drew the appropriate document from his pocket and handed it over.

"I see." The woman gestured toward two chairs facing her desk. "Please have a seat. Why did you choose Woden to settle in?"

"We've heard the folks here aren't stuck in the old ways like our parents."

"You might prefer Brantome, then. It's a restored area in the eastern part of town over by the river. The locals have a strong sense of community."

"Sounds good to me. How about you, *angella*?"

The endearment brought an instant image to his mind of the first time he'd seen Leena framed in the doorway of the tavern, her golden hair backlit like a halo about her lovely face. She'd brightened the depths of his soul and showed him how faith could offer courage and hope.

Leena turned to him and smiled. "Darling, that would be perfect." The tender look in her eyes along with her soft voice made him want to sweep her into his arms.

Anxious to be alone with her, Taurin completed the rental agreement. He turned down the offer to check out the place first, trusting the agent's description.

"It's a good thing you're not looking for a hotel," said the woman as she organized the papers he'd signed. "There's a convention in town, and all the rooms are booked."

"The International Merchants Association?" Taurin guessed.

"The group started in Woden, you know. Stephan Tom is the president. I believe he has a home in Brantome, so you might run into him there. Now he's a progressive character. In fact, some of his views are downright heretical."

"Really? What do you mean?" Leena asked, an eager look on her face.

The real estate agent glanced at her co-workers before lowering her voice. "If you're interested, check out the White Enix Pub. It's a reconstructed mill by the water."

Taurin thanked her and concluded their business. He and Leena left the office, the keys to their new home in hand.

****

Outside, Leena quoted from a guidebook the agent had given them along with copies of their rental papers. "Woden began as an early settlement alongside the Organdy River. Originally, the town consisted of a cluster of stone houses, a school, a small worship center, and a mill. As the town expanded, this area became known as Brantome, named after one of its founders. The broader region is called Prefectus. This forested district is noted as much for its flower-strewn meadows and rolling hillsides as for its classic cuisine and wild-growing *rushtees*, a type of fungus that is valued as an edible delicacy."

"I wonder if that's something I could grow at my farm," Taurin replied. "We should look for a farmer's market while we're here. That would be a good place to pick up local gossip."

He followed a road that led toward the river, passing slowly by the old stone building that had housed the former mill. A waterwheel churned in the swiftly-moving current. Weeping willows and red-leafed syca trees lined the riverbanks.

Veering away from the peaceful scene, they entered a residential sector and drove through narrow streets graced by buildings with fluted chimneys spouting pungent wood smoke. Blooming flowers kept company on window sills along with collections of colored glass bottles.

"What a charming neighborhood," Leena commented, peering out her side window.

At the designated address, Taurin parked their rider. "I believe this place is ours."

They emerged in front of a modest two-story structure with a stone façade. Its red-tiled roof was marred only by the antenna of a modern messager system. Taurin grunted as he withdrew their luggage from the trunk. They'd bought new suitcases and had filled them with wardrobes suitable to their current mission. He hoped they appeared to be a normal young couple as they proceeded into the house.

"Oh, I love it." Leena rushed from the living area to the kitchen to the bedroom level upstairs.

Taurin climbed after her. A spacious master bedroom faced the street, while two smaller rooms took up the rear. In the master suite, he set both suitcases onto the carpeted floor. Then he straightened and gave Leena a lazy grin.

"We're home, *angella*." His arms stretched out for her, and she ran into his embrace, lifting her chin so he could kiss her.

"We'll have to buy food and cleaning supplies," she said once they'd broken apart. Her eyes gleamed with excitement as though they'd truly moved in together.

"Remember, we're only here temporarily," Taurin reminded her.

"We still have to eat, husband."

"That's true. I'll go downstairs and see what's in the kitchen while you unpack. Or should we even bother with the suitcases? I'm hoping we won't be here that long."

Her face fell at his words. "Sorry, I keep forgetting why we're here, because I want so badly for this to be real."

Before he could respond, a loud knock sounded from below. They exchanged surprised glances and then both rushed downstairs.

"Who's there?" Leena called out.

"My name is Lilot," a singsong female voice replied. "I'm your neighbor from across the street."

Leena flung open the door, while Taurin stood beside her. She smiled at the young woman standing on the doorstep.

"Good and welfare, neighbors." The woman's reddish-blond hair reached her shoulders. She wore a rose-colored tunic top covered by an overblouse, along with leggings and sturdy black shoes.

"I saw you pull in right before I took my *criche* out of the oven," she said, offering Leena an aromatic casserole dish. "I thought you might like to have it, since you've just arrived. I grow all of my own vegetables, so you don't have to worry about contaminants. After the festival, I'll bake you a loaf of my bundan bread."

"Thank you," Leena said, accepting the dish. "My name is Leena, and this is Taurin."

"I hope we'll get to know each other better, but if you'll excuse me, I must hurry to complete my preparations."

"Which festival did you mean?" Taurin asked.

"Why, tonight starts Tu Imbol." Lilot gazed at him as though he came from another planet.

Little do you know, he thought, suppressing a grimace.

"By Lothar's grace, I'd forgotten all about the holiday." Leena's gaze swung to Taurin. "That means the restaurants will be closed. We won't be able to dine out."

"You'd best get to market if you want to do any shopping," Lilot told them. "It'll be closing by four today."

"Where is it held?" Taurin asked.

Lilot gave them directions. "Let me know if you need anything else. I've got to take my qiana fritters out of the oven." She turned away and headed down the drive.

Leena shut the door in her wake.

"We'll have to wait to visit the White Enix Pub," she said, disappointment lacing her tone.

Taurin glowered at her. "We'd better do what Lilot said and visit the market before it closes." He took a set of keys from his pants pocket and jangled them. "Are you ready?"

Leena nodded. "I'd like to attend services tonight. Tu Imbol is an important holiday. The grove festival—"

"No!" Taurin regarded her, his voice hard as steel. "We don't go near the worship center."

"Of course, you're right," she said, averting her gaze. "We can't afford to be identified with the religious order. I'm sorry, Taurin."

"You can say your prayers at home in private, if that is your wish."

****

Leena grabbed her handbag while hiding her true feelings. Taurin's reconciliatory tone didn't mitigate her dismay at his earlier admonishment. Clearly, he didn't regard religious services as anything of import, making her wonder how their differences would ever be overcome. While on this mission, they were working together, but what would happen if she ever moved in with him on a permanent basis? Would he expect her to give up her position and worship of Lothar?

Slinging her bag's strap over one shoulder, she stepped outside into the bright afternoon sunshine. This region should have been colder by now, with the beginnings of frost. Instead it felt like early autumn, with a fresh pine scent in the air. She took the abnormal climate as another sign of disruption in the weather cycles and mentioned her observation to Taurin.

"Perhaps we'll gain some useful information at the town market." Taking her by the elbow, he led her toward their parked rider.

As they'd suspected, the market turned out to be the heart and soul of the town. Its colorful sights and tantalizing smells converged to give it a sense of community that Leena found highly appealing. She counted more than fifty local farmers who tempted consumers with an array of fruits, vegetables, natural fiber clothing, and homemade products such as honey, cheese, wine, baked goods, and jams.

A flower seller attracted Taurin's attention, while Leena surveyed the varieties of mushrooms for sale. She'd never seen so many different choices.

"Who's cooking tonight?" Taurin asked after he'd rejoined her.

She gave him a quizzical glance. "I assumed it would be my role."

"Wild mushroom tart is one of my specialties. I can't resist when they're so plentiful here. I'll make dinner." He procured a wicker basket and began negotiating with various vendors as she trailed after him.

"I didn't know you could cook," she said, surprised by this domestic side of him.

His lopsided grin took her breath away. "I've got to do something during those lonely hours I spend by myself."

"I thought you studied archeological texts and worked on your drawings."

"They don't put food in a man's stomach." He patted his belly, while Leena smiled in response.

They passed stalls offering garlic, leeks, carrots, and an assortment of unfamiliar leafy vegetables. Clothing merchants, fishmongers, butchers, and cheese sellers hawked their wares. Live chickens, geese, and ducks strutted inside fenced enclosures, their squawking adding to the general din. Bundles of produce spilled into the aisles, crowded with buyers. Citrus fragrance spiced the air, along with the aroma of ripened fruit heating in the sun.

Taurin stopped at a baker's stall to obtain the flour and other supplies he would need to make his mushroom tart.

"I'm lucky I got me bakery," said the stout fellow wearing a flat-topped cap on his balding head. "Those produce farmers, they's real worried about the weather. If it don't get cool soon, their crops'll be ruined for next season."

A young man with an unshaven face and baggy pants overheard the remark. He gave up inspecting the squash at the next stall and sauntered over. "It's a ruse by the Synod to get us to tighten our belts. If you ask me, they're causing these weather disasters. They know when things are righted again, we'll be so grateful that we won't mind an extra tribute to Lothar." With a disgusted grunt, he spat on the ground.

Taurin took up the slack. "I'm in full agreement with you, Brother." He handed a sack of flour to the baker, who weighed it and pronounced the price. "Things have gotten out of hand. It's beyond me what can be done about it, though."

The stranger narrowed his gaze. "You must be new to these parts. Are you here for the merchant convention?"

"No, sir." Taurin put an arm around Leena's waist and smiled down at her. "We just got married and have permission to settle here. I have some experience in growing crops and was hoping to get a job at one of the farms."

"The farms won't have any jobs if the soil dries up." The man lowered his voice to a conspiratorial whisper. "We're fixing to do something about that real soon."

Pretending to examine a squash at the next stall, Leena leaned closer so as not to miss any of their conversation.

"What do you mean?" Taurin's mild tone belied the intensity that sprang into his eyes.

"You'll find out if you stick around long enough." The stranger winked and then sauntered off down the lane.

They completed their shopping, while Leena sensed an undercurrent of tension permeating the marketplace. Obviously something was in the works, but despite their subtle inquiries, they failed to learn what was going on.

When the vendors began packing away their goods, Leena and Taurin gave up trying to coax information from the reluctant merchants and headed for home. True to his word, Taurin prepared a savory mushroom tart, which he put into the oven to bake. Meanwhile, he assembled a chocolate salad for dessert. Leena peered over his shoulder to observe his technique.

"When we're ready," he told her, his hands moving deftly, "I'll combine these berries with the chocolate and orange sorbets we bought. Normally I'd include some of my edible flowers, such as pansies and violets, but there weren't any for sale at the market.

I'll have to talk to my distributor about supplying this region." Finished with his creation, he put the bowl of rinsed berries into the cooler unit.

Although Leena was hungry, she had another appetite in mind while admiring Taurin in the kitchen. Ashamed of her wayward thoughts, she turned to more spiritual matters to cleanse her soul.

"The sun is setting," she announced. "We should commence our prayers."

Taurin understood this holiday was important to her even if he wasn't familiar with the rituals. Following her instructions, he set the table for their repast.

"You can uncork the wine," she said. "We'll need both bottles opened, but pour the white one first."

When they were seated, Leena raised her glass. "Our initial cup of wine is entirely white, reminding us of winter, when nature sleeps and the land to the north is covered with snow. Let us give thanks that we are together to celebrate this holy occasion."

After she had uttered a prayer, she and Taurin sipped from their glasses. "Observe the fruits on the table," she said, pointing. "Each type of fruit represents a season. First we partake of varieties with a peel or shell that cannot be eaten."

She selected for herself a thick rinded citrus, a furry *kemeris*, and a nut with a hard shell. Taurin reached for a large round plum and began peeling off the thick skin.

"If I'm going to have to endure your rituals, the least I can do is make them more fun." Taurin tore off a section of fruit and offered it to Leena.

At first she was shocked by his sacrilege, but when she thought about it, she agreed there was no harm in making the traditions more enjoyable. With a smile, she leaned forward, taking a bite of the juicy fruit. The tangy flavor was tart on her tongue, but she licked her lips, eager for more of a taste—of Taurin rather than the fruit.

"Pour a bit of the red wine into your glass of white," she

ordered. "This symbolizes springtime, when the sun's rays thaw the frozen land. The earth changes color as the snow melts and the pink blooms of the cyclamen plant appear in the mountains. Before we drink, we hold up our glasses and recite the prayer."

This time Taurin humored her by repeating the prayer in unison with her.

"You may choose fruits with pits or seeds that cannot be eaten." Their eyes locked, and Leena watched as Taurin popped a few cherries into his mouth and spit out the inedible parts. She took a cherry for herself and bit daintily around the pit, but when Taurin reached for a date, her hand stilled his.

"Allow me." With her knife, she cut out the pit for him. Then she held the date toward his mouth and fed him. He plucked another plum from the dish and returned the favor. Leena didn't even notice the flavor. She was too engrossed in looking into his mesmerizing eyes.

"Don't forget the blessing over the fruit." Taurin's lip curled in a half-smile.

She uttered the prayer, the words automatic on her tongue. "We need to refill our glasses," she said, already feeling the effects from the first round of wine. She felt as if she were floating on air, or was that because Taurin's attention centered on her?

"Which color?" he asked.

"Fill them with red wine and just a dash of white. The mixture symbolizes summer, when flowers blossom and the ground softens."

"The time of plowing and sowing," Taurin said, nodding. "I assume we eat from the third category of fruits, the ones that are edible both inside and out." He didn't need any prompting to say the blessing over the fruit. The words spilled from his mouth before Leena even thought about them. Then they were feeding each other red seedless grapes and plump blueberries.

"I don't know if I can drink another cup," she said with a moan.

"We have to complete the ceremony." Taurin filled their

glasses to the top with red wine. "Summer ends, and the crops grow tall as autumn approaches. The harvest season. This is why you bought these packages of seeds, isn't it?"

"Tomorrow we are supposed to plant them, but we don't have a garden."

"We'll find a spot. Drink your wine," he urged, uttering the prayer for her. After she'd complied, he rose to get his wild mushroom tart from the oven. "I don't know about you, but the fruit just whetted my appetite. I'm ready for the main course."

A flavorful aroma reached her nose as Taurin placed the dish on the table, along with their neighbor's casserole. Despite her inebriated state, Leena's stomach growled in anticipation of a solid meal.

She jabbed her fork into a soft slice of mushroom pie and raised the morsel to her mouth. The blend of flavors made her roll her eyes in delight.

"This is heavenly." She delved into her second piece. "What are your other specialties?"

"I cook mostly vegetarian dishes. Don't worry; I have no intention of usurping your role in the kitchen."

She glanced up and noticed his eyes dancing with mirth. Nonetheless, this topic had to be addressed.

"We should talk about household chores. My term in the Caucus lasts for two years. During that time, I'll commute from Lexington Page. I'll be off on weekends. After that, I might return to my job at the museum."

She'd already told him about her former position as Director of Archeological Studies for the Javis Museum of Natural History. It would be a half-hour drive from where he lived.

"I thought you were undecided about your plans." His expression had turned serious, as though he knew this was a subject that concerned her.

"After exploring the Temple of Light, I realized that archeology is my passion... aside from you," she teased. "If I succeed in my goals, I won't seek a higher office or further training within the religious order. I only joined the Caucus to learn the secrets of the Synod."

Taurin's mouth compressed. "Isn't there a museum at the Palisades?"

"Yes, and they've offered me a position as curator. I refused, because it would mean I'd have to give up field work, which I love to do."

"So that means half the time, you'll be off on some archeological dig, and the rest you'll be commuting to the museum every day."

"Don't worry; you'll see enough of me. Now, shall we clear the table?" To mellow his mood, she fluttered her eyelashes at him. "I'll offer you my brand of dessert before we taste yours."

Upstairs, Taurin was more than happy to loosen her gown. "I've never dared dream about having a family," he said as her garment slid to the floor.

She smiled at the wistful expression on his face. "That's another thing we need to discuss."

"What is?"

"Starting a family."

He glanced at her, startled. "You needn't worry on that score. I am up to date on my birth inhibitors."

She laughed. "It really doesn't matter."

"Yes, it does. It's too early to start talking about children."

She faced him and trailed a finger along his bristled jaw. "Is it? Why do I get the impression you believe something is going to come between us?"

"Because I love you too much, and I'm afraid of losing you."

Her mouth gaped as she lowered her arm. "What did you say?"

"I love you, Leena." He grasped her by the shoulders and pulled her close, burying his face in her hair and clutching at her as though he'd never let go.

She sensed his desperation and wondered what made him

feel so insecure. Obviously, he didn't have much faith in her love for him. What could possibly happen to destroy their feelings for each other? Did he know something that made him afraid she'd leave him?

If anything, she should be annoyed that he didn't trust her. She knew he'd read the bibliotomes in the Temple of Light. Did he withhold his knowledge because he was afraid of her reaction should she learn the truth about the Apostles? And how would these truths, if that were the case, affect their relationship with each other?

"I want to be with you. You're not getting rid of me so easily." She tightened her arms around him, wishing she could slow time while they were together.

Her breasts pressed flat against his massive chest, and she leaned her head on his shoulder. They'd resolve their differences later. Right now all that mattered was this interval alone.

She lifted her face for his kiss and felt a swell of joy when his mouth covered hers. Her body ignited as he gyrated his hips against her belly, and rationale thought fled her mind as she gave in to passion.

"You're so beautiful. I want to savor every inch of you," he said in a husky tone.

After removing his clothes, he stretched out beside her on the bed. He trailed a line of kisses across her throat and down to her bared breast.

Leena closed her eyes and cried out with pleasure. "You're killing me with ecstasy."

"Then I will die with you." He moved to her other breast, his tongue rhythmically stroking her nipple until she moaned in heated frustration.

He shifted his position, crouching at the juncture between her thighs.

"Dear deity," she cried when his tongue found her sensitive parts. Opening her legs so he could have better access, she let her head loll back, concentrating on the building tension within her.

Taurin's finger sought her port of entry, and she groaned with need. He lifted atop her and thrust inside, making her beg for release.

"You are mine, *angella*," he said, his lips finding hers.

They melded together, flesh against flesh, a primal need consuming them as they spiraled toward greater heights. Taurin's explosive release stimulated her own climax. Shuddering spasms shook her body until she lay spent beneath the weight of his taut, muscled form.

"Maybe we should stay here and never go home," Taurin suggested as he rolled onto his back.

Too content to move, Leena slid him a sideways glance. "Why are you so afraid things are going to change?" When he didn't respond, she feared he was taking his role of protector too seriously. He withheld knowledge which he assumed would be distressing to her, and she resented his patronizing attitude.

"I'm not afraid to learn the truth," she told him quietly. "If you would share what you read in those bibliotomes—"

"Let's go have dessert," he said abruptly, rising.

"Taurin, I don't like how you're treating me. Trust has to be at the foundation of a marriage." Dismayed, she watched as he threw on his clothes without a single glance in her direction.

Fully dressed, he stood before her and his expression softened. "I'll share what I know when I learn the whole story. There's no need for you to be upset at this point, when we have to concentrate on finding the horn."

She sat up, pulling the sheet to her waist. "I can make my own decisions about what I need to know. You're not my keeper."

"Oh yes, I am." And his closed face told her he'd accept no further arguments.

Chapter Twenty-One

The next morning, Taurin received a rude shock. He peered outside the living room window after opening the drapes and noticed a man hovering beside a blue rider. His blood pressure rocketed when he realized it was the same fellow who'd spoken to him at the market about the adverse weather conditions.

Was it a coincidence, or had the man been posted there to keep an eye on them? In which case, for whom did he work? The Truthsayers? Or was he one of Grotus's agents, sent to keep tabs on their movements?

He didn't mention his concerns to Leena when he suggested over breakfast that they pack a picnic for the day.

"We'll find a spot of dirt to plant our seeds. It'll give us a good excuse to explore the area. And bring that wicker basket. We can always say we're hunting for wild mushrooms if anybody stops us."

"Are you going to cook again tonight?" she asked.

"We're going to the White Enix Pub later, remember?"

"Oh yes, how could I forget?"

Her sarcastic remark acted as a sharp reprimand. He hadn't said much after they'd returned to their room last night following dessert. His chocolate salad had been a success, and Leena had raved over it. But he'd kept his distance as they prepared for the night, wary of having her raise expectations about their future together.

She grabbed a shawl and pronounced herself ready to go out. "Shall we head toward the river?" she asked, tugging down the long sleeves of her wool dress that she'd donned for the cool morning air.

"That's as good a place as any to begin exploring." Taurin stood on the front stoop, picnic carrier in hand, glancing around with a frown. The stranger he'd seen earlier had disappeared.

"What's wrong?" She shifted the empty wicker basket to her other hand.

"Nothing." With a shrug, he started down the steps. The street was quiet, theirs being the only rider parked by the curb. Maybe he'd imagined someone keeping watch on them.

They began their expedition by a cluster of old stone houses along the riverbank, enjoying the overhanging trica branches, whose fallen crimson leaves floated on the water's surface. Ducks swam past, searching for their morning meal. Next to a clump of palmelo reeds, a wooden bridge led across the water to the ruins of an old abbey, now converted into a museum. Since it was a holiday, the place was closed, much to Leena's disappointment.

They passed the ancient mill that had been turned into the White Enix Pub, then followed a medieval road circling a wooded hillside. The dirt was packed firm, indicating the trail was well-used. He enjoyed the scent of fresh autumn leaves.

They hiked for some distance before coming to a meadow near an overlook where they could view the entire town and twisting river.

"This is the perfect spot for a picnic," Leena said with a lilt in her voice.

Taurin spread a blanket on the grass. They'd just settled down when a rumble shook the earth.

"What's that?" Leena pointed to a cloud of dust at the edge of the woods across the meadow.

"Let's go see." Taurin leapt up and dragged her after him.

"Shouldn't we fold the blanket and bring our things with us?" She shook out her shawl, which had become a receptacle for fallen leaves.

"That might be wise." He helped her to repack the items and then shouldered the burden.

"These are truck marks," he said when they came to the site of the dust cloud.

Leena's brow furrowed. "What would a truck be doing here? And why today when it's a holiday?"

"We should follow the tracks and see where they go."

The tire marks ended at a clearing. Taurin peered at the empty site straight ahead. "The truck has vanished. According to the tracks, it must have entered the forest, but I don't see anything."

He advanced to investigate, but no sooner did he go a few feet than he crashed into an invisible barrier. Pain exploded in his forehead, and he stumbled backward.

Leena rushed forward. "What happened? Are you hurt?"

"Something stopped me. There's some sort of barrier." Splaying his hands against the obstacle, he followed its outline for a short distance.

Chilling clarity breeched his mind. This could only mean one thing. The barrier was an energy shield, meant to keep out intruders. Xan did not possess this technology. It could only have come from one place—his homeworld, Yllon, a place fraught with violence.

Demon's blood! Now their doom was sealed. He couldn't conceive of how his fellow Ylloners were involved here, but he was determined to find out. Rather than attempting to penetrate the barrier, he suggested they return to the village.

"Tonight at the pub, we'll learn what's going on. I suspect the Truthsayers are mixed up in this, but they must be getting help from somewhere else." He turned away, wondering what her reaction would be when she learned that other place was another planet.

****

The White Enix Pub bustled with activity when they entered after dark. The rustic interior of the old mill was rife with the smells of sawdust and ripening barrels of wine.

A din of noise hit Taurin's sensitive ears, and he grimaced as he scanned the bar area that took up the entire first floor. He'd been told there was a restaurant upstairs and had called ahead to make reservations. After giving his name to a host, he allowed Leena to precede him up the staircase.

The dining room was intimate with yellow and white checked tablecloths, votive candles, and rural paintings decorating the walls. Wood beams and hanging plants contributed to the coziness of the décor. The tables were set far enough apart, and he was gratified that they might talk without danger of being overheard.

Leena ordered an appetizer of mushrooms sautéed with herbs and wine, tender fillets of kalmagn fish, crisp corn fritters, and a frozen chocolate soufflé with salisberry sauce. Taurin chose a simple salad of mixed greens, a pollentine with fig preserves, and nougat ice cream made from a local wildflower honey.

Despite his penchant for practicing the culinary arts, his everyday tastes were simple. On his home planet, scrabbling for a day's food was a major occupation and the cause of many conflicts. He'd learned to eat frugally and accept whatever fare was available. Spare plots of land, which were few in the urbanized centers on Yllon, were often converted to gardens. Heavily fenced in, they provided fresh produce for the lucky owners.

Taurin's gang leader had let him tend a small piece of land, which gave him his first taste of farming. It wasn't surprising that he'd chosen to pursue agriculture as an occupation when he'd moved to Xan. Blessed as it was with rich earth and plentiful rains, Xan offered vast expanses of fertile soil to its fortunate inhabitants.

Toiling in his fields, feeling the sun on his back and the sweat dripping from his brow, Taurin had tried to erase the days of hunger from his memories and the fear that there wouldn't be enough food. He'd spent hours raking his fingers through the dirt, reveling in its richness and his blessing at being able to reap the fruits of his labor. Growing edible flowers paid off the debt he felt he owed Baker Mylock.

A warm log of satisfaction settled into his stomach, lulling him into a tranquil state. Leena, seated across from him, looked especially lovely in the glow from the candlelight. The periwinkle blue of her gown highlighted her eyes, making them seem deeper and larger.

"Tell me about your youth," he said encouragingly. He reached across the table to grasp her small hand. As she recounted tales of her childhood, he traced small circles in her palm.

"Stop that," she said with a becoming blush.

His gaze fell upon her slightly parted lips. Her mouth tempted him with its sensual pink outlines. She reminded him of the tulip blossoms he grew in his fields. Like a honeybee drawn to a brightly colored flower, he craved a taste of her nectar.

"Don't you like it?" He widened the pattern of his circles.

Leena withdrew her hand. "Yes, but you're making me lose my appetite… at least for the food. We'll forget our purpose in being here."

"You're right. We should focus on our mission, although it's difficult when you drive me to distraction."

As soon as they finished their meal, they headed downstairs to check out the bar scene. The noise assaulted Taurin's ears as he descended the stairs. An argument about mushroom hunting prevailed among the patrons.

"You've got to leave enough stem for the fungi to grow again," said one red-faced fellow. "And don't use plastic bags. A wicker basket allows the spores to drop through and regenerate, which they'll do in four or five days given the right conditions."

"I pulled in fifteen hundred chekels yesterday," bragged a bearded fellow in a work shirt and cap.

"You've gotta keep a steady pace," the first speaker agreed. "We're lucky we had the rains in this district, or it would have been a bad season. Still, if it doesn't turn colder soon, we'll be headin' for trouble."

Someone else chimed in. "Other territories have it worse. There's no reliability to the weather anymore. At least Lothar hasn't forsaken our region yet."

Snickers of laughter greeted that announcement. One man stood up from the bar and whirled around. His eyes blazing, he addressed the crowd.

"Lothar has nothing to do with our climate changes. The Synod is responsible. They're forcing us to bend our knee to their laws. I say we've had enough of their oppression. It's time we stood up for ourselves and exposed them for what they are—a group of power-hungry old men, who rule the populace with fear."

Leena stared at him in shock. How dare he utter such blasphemy? Yet no one else seemed surprised by his rhetoric. People nodded in agreement around the room.

"Our numbers are growing," the man went on, his tone quiet. A hush fell over the crowd as everyone listened. All eyes turned in his direction. The man was tall and lean. Intelligence sparkled behind his eyes. His business suit indicated he was a person of position, more educated perhaps than the majority in the lounge.

"Who is that?" Taurin whispered to a well-dressed woman behind him.

"Why, he's Stephan Tom, our president."

"President?"

"Of the International Merchants Association. Aren't you a member?" The woman looked at him with disdain, as though anyone who was not a member of their organization was unworthy of respect.

"I'm new to the group," Taurin replied.

"Stephan, what will happen if the horn is found?" someone called out.

"It'll never be recovered," the leader retorted. "And everyone will see the power of the Synod is an illusion created to subdue the populace. If Lothar were a true god, he wouldn't be making people suffer. Religion should have no part in government. It's time we established an order where the people come first. We need elected officials, not an elite religious hierarchy, to govern our land."

"Hear, hear!" someone cried, and a cheer went up.

"We must spread the word through our organization," Stephan Tom continued, his voice ringing with zeal. "Our businesses cannot flourish unless we have the ability to expand. It's not right that we have to ask permission of an impersonal board to develop branches in other towns. Population growth cannot proceed naturally at this pace. I say the time for change has come. Luckily, we have friends in our struggle for freedom."

The man standing next to Stephan Tom, facing the bar with his back toward the crowd, turned around. Beside her, Leena heard Taurin suck in a sharp breath.

"Demon's blood! What is *he* doing here?" Grabbing Leena's elbow, he steered her toward a dark corner. "Come on, let's get out of the light."

"What's the matter?" She jostled into people as they threaded their way through the throng.

Taurin needed to get a better view of the fellow beside Stephan Tom without being seen. From his pocket, he withdrew his familiar cloth and swathed it about his head so his face would be shaded.

"That person standing next to Tom—I know him," he said to Leena, his voice low so they wouldn't be overheard.

"Who is he?" Leena asked.

Taurin shook his head. He couldn't tell her the man was one of his gang members from Yllon. What was the fellow doing here? Terror struck his heart as he heard Stephan Tom tell how, with his friends' support, their organization would march forward.

"Which organization is he referring to?" Leena whispered. "The International Merchants Association, or the Truthsayers?"

"I believe the two organizations are one and the same."

Taurin leaned against a wall where he could watch the crowd without being noticed. "It makes perfect sense. That's how the Truthsayers are able to spread their heresy—through the Merchants Association. The business sector would have the most to gain from a laxity in the rules, and it appears they have outside help."

His thoughts swirled in panic. Leena was in danger merely by associating with him. If that Ylloner, whose name was Testi, spotted Taurin, he was in deep trouble.

Taurin had left Yllon with a death sentence on his head. Exposure now would mean an end to his role. He had to know what the Ylloner was doing here, and how he'd received permission to travel.

Normally, no one from Yllon was allowed free run of the planet. The two worlds had a restricted trade agreement. Yllon's existence was known only to the Synod and a few trusted individuals on Xan. Aliens were not permitted beyond the spaceport.

So who had let Testi in, and why was he here? Was Stephan Tom aware that his friend was an offworlder? Someone in a knowledgeable position had to be involved in this, and Taurin wondered if it was the same traitor who'd stolen the horn.

Weighing his choices, he decided his best course of action would be to follow Testi. The Ylloner might be involved in an attempt to overthrow the government along with the Truthsayers, but there was more here than met the eye.

"I want to hang around for a while," he told Leena. "If you're tired, I'll find someone to escort you home."

"I'm not leaving just when this is getting interesting. Besides, you haven't told me who that man is." She indicated the fellow standing next to Stephan Tom.

"His presence concerns me, because it means outside interests are involved. I can't let him see my face, or he'll recognize me."

"So what?" She gazed at him in puzzlement.

Taurin's mouth tightened stubbornly, and Leena narrowed her eyes as she stared at him in the dim light.

"It's time you told me what you know, Taurin Rey Niris… if that's your real name."

Their gazes locked and held, hers demanding answers, his evasive and wary.

"He's leaving," Taurin said suddenly. Testi was heading out the door with Stephan Tom and several others among the crowd.

He and Leena trailed them, keeping back from the group so as not to be noticed. Outside, the scent of evergreens in the cool air refreshed the night.

They followed the crowd, blending in with a couple of stragglers and pretending to be part of the group. Gravel crunched underfoot, and overhead a myriad of stars shone in the darkened sky. The rush of water filled their ears as they passed by the huge waterwheel churning in the river, a remnant of the old mill that had been converted into a pub.

"Time to go to work on putting up the new village, eh, pal?" slurred a drunken fellow next to Taurin.

They followed a familiar trail into the woods, climbed a hill, and crossed the same meadow where they'd attempted to picnic earlier. Ahead of them, brightly illuminated by hidden spotlights, was the building site they'd observed. The energy field had apparently been deactivated because noises of construction rang heavily in the night air and villeins in all manners of dress worked at the site. Testi strode over to one of the men calling out orders and engaged him in private conversation.

"Get to work," Stephan Tom exhorted his followers. "Once this place is completed, our friends will bring in the weapons we need to empower our liberation from the Synod."

Leena gasped. "They're building an armory," she whispered to Taurin. "We've got to warn Dikran."

Careful to avoid detection, Taurin examined the foundations and assessed the layout. This was no armory. That huge slab of dormite was reminiscent of a launch pad, and the other structures had the marks of hangars and maintenance sheds. These people weren't building an armory. They were building a landing site.

He stopped in his tracks, stunned by the implications. This could mean only one thing. Yllon was planning an invasion.

Now he understood with perfect clarity why the horn had been stolen. It wasn't for money. That's why the relic hadn't passed through Grotus's hands.

If his theory held credence that the annual blowing of the horn reenergized the crystal lattice structures, and the crystals powered the defensive perimeter around the planet, then the horn had to be blown by the month of Fearn in order to fortify the defense shield. Otherwise the perimeter might crumple, and Yllon's ships would be clear to enter the atmosphere.

Whoever had stolen the horn had to be in league with Yllon in planning an invasion. Taurin thought his former associate, gang leader Drufus Gong, must be involved. But which Synod member was a traitor, and why? What did he or she hope to gain?

"What is it?" Leena asked, her eyes bright with concern as she touched his arm.

"We have to get away from here," he said, suddenly conscious that Testi was patrolling the site, talking to each of the workers. At any moment, the Ylloner might spot him.

Taking her hand in his own, he hastened her away, avoiding explanations until they were safely home.

Or were they safe? Rushing into the living room, he pulled aside a drape and looked outside. A strange rider had just pulled up to the curb. Someone was still keeping tabs on them, but who was it? Someone working for the traitor in the Synod, the Truthsayers, or Grotus's men?

He didn't think the Truthsayers suspected their identity, considering the lack of interest shown them at the pub. That left the other two possibilities, neither of which pleased him.

"Pack your things," he told Leena abruptly. "We're leaving."

"No, we aren't going anywhere until you tell me what's happening. It's time you trusted me enough to tell me the truth."

"You don't want to know the truth. It will hurt you, and you'll blame me for destroying your beliefs."

Her expression firmed. "Why don't you let me be the judge of what I can or cannot accept? Trust me, Taurin. I love you. Nothing will ever change the way I feel about you."

Unable to resist any longer, he swept her into his arms and kissed her. She was his haven, his safety amongst the swarm of hornets that threatened to sting him. She had no concept of the danger that threatened them now. It was far worse than he could have imagined.

He stepped away, pondering the implications of Drufus Gong's involvement. His blood chilled at what the future portended.

Leena remained silent, as still as one of the stone statues in the Temple of Light. At a loss for words, he swept his hand across his forehead in a gesture of helplessness. How was he to tell her she'd married an alien? That there was indeed life on other planets and his homeworld was preparing a hostile invasion? Would she laugh at him for creating wild fantasies, scream in rage, or recoil in terror?

He'd feared this moment ever since he had begun to care for her. And now, when he needed her so desperately, he couldn't bear to see her love turn into revulsion.

Chapter Twenty-Two

Taurin stood with his back to Leena. He faced a painting on the wall depicting a lakeside scene. The artist had frozen a duck in still life, its black feathers ruffled and its white neck erect, its orange beak jutting in the air as the creature glided on the water. Alone, it pursued its hunt for food, heedless of its loneliness on the vast body of the lake.

He'd felt adrift on a sea in the fabric of the universe, alone until Leena had entered his life. She had brightened his slate gray depths to a sunny blue. How could he tell her the truth?

"Do you believe life exists on other planets?" he began, unable to look her in the eye.

"I'm open to the possibilities," she replied, her tone cautious.

"The rings and the horn… the Apostles themselves… may have come from another planet. A system in the Cadega constellation, perhaps."

"So? We've had this discussion before."

"What if I told you that Xan isn't the only world in our star system to support life? Seven planets rotate our sun, and two of them have human populations—Xan and Yllon."

"You mean the Apostles came from this other world?"

"No, the Apostles visited Yllon just as they did Xan, and it's likely they seeded both our civilizations."

Leena frowned. "What do you mean, *both* our civilizations? What does this have to do with you?"

"How do you think I know about so much about Yllon?" He whipped around, his expression fierce to match his mood. "I'm from that planet, Leena. I traveled here in a spaceship."

Leena took a step backward. "What?"

He repeated his confession, hating what this would do to her, to *them*.

"But you said you're from Iman. What kind of joke is this?"

He shook his head, wondering how he could convince her of the truth. "It is no joke. I had to say I was from Iman to protect my true identity. It's a remote region, so I figured no one would question me about my origins."

"B-but you can't be from another world. You look just like us." She stared at him, horrified.

"Look closely at me, Leena. Does anyone else you know have eyes that glow in the dark?" He stepped into the shadows so she could see the luminosity. "Can anyone on Xan fight like I do? Go ahead, say what you're thinking. I can see it in your face. You want to be rid of me."

She didn't respond.

"I knew you'd be repulsed," he muttered.

"I just don't know what to believe anymore." She sank into an armchair and dashed a shaky hand through her hair. "Tell me more. I want to know everything, Taurin."

He took a seat opposite her, his posture tense. "Yllon is a violent world rife with gang warfare. Rauch's gang is the biggest group, led by Drufus Gong. He's the one who found me when I was abandoned by my parents. He took me under his wing and raised me as he would any young child of a gang member."

Leena frowned in puzzlement. "Who were your parents? Why did they desert you?"

He pointed to his eyes. "I had the sign of the curse. According to our legends, many eons ago demons came to Yllon, causing men to go mad and instigate killing sprees that destroyed our civilization. Pogroms wiped out most of these demons, but their bad seeds had already been planted. Every few generations, a child is born that shows the demon's sign. A child thus afflicted usually meets a quick, unexplained death. My parents decided to give me a chance to live, but not under their care."

"How generous of them," she said with a cynical note.

"Drufus Gong had ambitions of his own," Taurin continued. "He noticed my special gift and decided to take advantage of it. I could see in the dark, an ability he would use to conquer his enemies. Together we hid my special visionary power from others. People feared they'd go mad in the presence of a demonic offspring, but I could never tell if this were true because everyone on Yllon was hostile. Killings, beatings, and rampages were the norm."

"That's horrible," she remarked with a visible shudder. "I can't imagine what it must have been like growing up in a society so violent."

"See this armband?" He yanked up his sleeve to show her. "It's the only clue to my true heritage. I told you how I was able to separate the bracelets and spin them. I'd always thought it was a child's toy until I noticed the symbols carved on the sides."

"If the Apostles visited both our worlds as you believe, why didn't they establish the reign of Lothar on Yllon? It might have brought unity and peace."

Taurin shrugged. "That's one of the answers I'd hoped to discover here. The Apostles established an orderly society on Xan, whereas on Yllon, their presence led to warfare."

"Could it be some quality in the environment that made the difference?"

"I don't know." Other than Magar, Leena was the first person on Xan to learn his history, and he was relieved to be sharing it with someone else. His gaze roamed her lush golden hair, lovely features, and graceful body. Gods, how badly he wanted her to stay with him.

"I was sixteen when my gang went on a rampage and destroyed a bakery we thought belonged to a rival group. I was leaving the demolished interior when I heard someone sobbing. It was the baker hiding in a closet. Baker Mylock said he'd been forced to pay this other gang protection money. They hadn't lifted a finger to help him when we attacked."

"So he wasn't a gang member?" Leena asked.

"That's right. We'd destroyed his livelihood, and he had a family to support. I felt terrible and offered to help him rebuild the shop in secret. He introduced me to his wife and children, and soon they became the family I'd never had. Drufus Gong hadn't been much of a father figure to me. He'd been demanding and ruthless, aiming to make me into a warrior. In contrast, Baker Mylock treated me kindly and taught me how to read."

****

Leena remained silent, grateful Taurin was at last confiding in her. A marriage couldn't succeed if there were secrets between partners, and she hoped he would tell her everything, no matter how traumatic the revelations.

But was he for real? Did he truly come from another world, and not just from a faraway region of Xan? His admission coincided with her theories about the Apostles. She'd dared to believe they might be visitors from another planet, and now his story confirmed this heretic belief.

Taurin rose to pace the room. "A year or so later, my gang attacked a weapons storage facility. I was the scout man. When I broke inside, I discovered not weapons but a treasury of books. I tricked my mates into giving me responsibility for blowing up the place, which they thought belonged to another gang. Instead, with the help of some local hired hands, I secretly transferred the books to an abandoned warehouse."

"Books? You mean, like the ones in Grotus's collection?"

Taurin nodded. "These bibliotomes were ancient texts with symbols engraved on the covers. I realized the markings matched the ones on my bracelet. I had to know what they meant. In order to learn more, I contacted the rival gang leader, hoping he could tell me how to open the sealed books. I offered to return them if I could have use of the library."

A veil of pain descended over his face. "Drufus Gong discovered I had betrayed him. The price for treachery on my world was death. Then the rival gang leader marked me for stealing his property. Pursued by both groups, I was forced to flee my world. I had met Captain Sterckle, who traded with Xan, and I offered him some of the bibliotomes in exchange for passage on his ship. My only recourse was to seek asylum on Xan. Captain Sterckle introduced me to Magar, who directed off-world relations for your planetary government."

Leena straightened her spine. "Magar is in charge of affairs of state."

"Yes, and that includes trade relations between our worlds. Yllon provides technology in exchange for Xan's food surplus. Population overcrowding and constant warfare have depleted our resources, and food is a valuable commodity. Normally, no one from Yllon is allowed to leave the spaceport here, and the labor force is sworn to secrecy. The Synod and the spaceport crews are the only ones who know of Yllon's existence."

"So Magar offered you a piece of land on his property?"

"That's correct. He probably figured he could keep an eye on me if I was close at hand."

Leena was unable to fully comprehend all he was telling her. It was too much information to assimilate at once, and she still couldn't believe he was an alien.

Excitement swelled within her as she considered the ramifications. Space travel was an actuality, at least within their star system. The Apostles might have come from a world located in the Cadega constellation. But then, how did they establish the rule of Lothar on her planet? Was Lothar truly a god? If so, why did he rely on the Apostles to spread the word about his benevolence? Couldn't he show himself to the people? Obviously not, if he needed the priesthood to articulate his gospel.

"Why did you decide to run a flower farm?" she asked Taurin, curious about his interests.

He flashed her a boyish grin, and her heart warmed toward him. His confession made their relationship seem more intimate.

"Baker Mylock likes to embellish his sweet breads with

candied flowers. I decided to pay him back for his kindness by growing edible blooms and sending him a shipment once a month. Magar makes sure the containers reach him."

"Why has Magar been so good to you? Why would he let you, and no one else, settle on Xan?"

Taurin's gaze narrowed. "I offered him some bibliotomes in exchange for permission to immigrate. He recognized their worth and accepted the deal immediately. Although neither of us knew how to open them, their value was obvious. I had to swear I would never reveal my identity to anyone. Meanwhile, I chose to keep apart from others in case the curse was true. I might drive men mad by my mere presence."

"Surely you don't believe that absurdity after all these years?"

His expression softened. "You've shown me I have nothing to fear from my violent nature—at least not when I'm with you. I keep it leashed, like a wild animal, yet it's there should I need it. Unfortunately, I may require my skills rather soon. That man we followed from the pub? His name is Testi. He's one of Drufus Gong's lieutenants. His arrival on Xan alarms me."

"Testi must be supplying the weapons Stephan Tom mentioned," Leena said. "But how would Yllon benefit if the Truthsayers gained power?"

Taurin's face sobered. "The Truthsayers may believe they're constructing an armory, but I recognized the structure. It's a landing site."

"Meaning what?"

"Drufus Gong is planning an invasion."

Leena leapt up, her heart thumping in alarm. "First you tell me you're an alien. Now you're saying we can expect a hostile invasion from outer space?"

Taurin sent her a grim nod of acknowledgement. "This planet has a protective energy shield, and when the trade ships come through, a window is opened to allow their passage. Just how the system works is unknown to me, but I suspect Lothar is involved."

"Lothar? What does the Holy One have to do with this?"

"Lothar provides the main source of energy for your planet. He regulates the climatic cycles, supplies the lozenge against sickness, and likely he is also responsible for the protective barrier. That means if the horn is not blown by the month of Fearn to awaken Lothar, the shield will fail. Your world will be open to invasion."

Leena covered her mouth with her hand. "Holy waters, do you think that's why the horn was stolen?"

He nodded. "It wasn't taken for money, or it would have passed through Grotus's hands by now. The Truthsayers didn't take it to discredit the Synod. You heard them say in the pub that they hope it's never found. That means they don't have it."

"So where is it? Do you think whoever stole the horn still has it?"

"That's a plausible assumption. And if a Synod member took it to lower the energy shield, then they're in league with Drufus Gong."

"But how could anyone have been in contact with Drufus Gong when relations between our worlds are severely restricted?"

"Magar is in contact with them."

"Karayan and Zeroun suspect Magar because of his relationship with you."

Taurin grimaced. "They may be right. It's time we had a talk with Magar ourselves."

Leena noticed the taut lines around his mouth and wondered if he was feeling betrayed by Magar, whom he must have regarded as a friend. "Shouldn't we get proof to show the Synod? Photos of the landing site or something equally impressive? Otherwise it will be your word against Magar's."

Taurin frowned. "I don't know that proof is necessary. Our other option is to stay here and follow Testi."

"We could also talk to Stephan Tom," Leena suggested.

"To what end?"

"The Truthsayers believe they're building armories and will

receive weapons. Testi didn't just show up at the site. He must have been introduced by someone else—someone who is secretly supporting the Truthsayers."

"You mean, taking advantage of the Truthsayers for their own purposes. The Truthsayers are merely pawns in a high-stakes game of interstellar politics. I don't think we should talk to them just yet. Let's seek out Magar first. If he's guilty, he'll confess to using them for his own aims."

"What if Magar doesn't confess to anything? How will we prove our case against him?" Leena's eyes lit up. "The construction equipment at the landing site! We could trace its origins. Maybe there's a link."

"I didn't notice any markings on the crates, did you?"

She shook her head, crestfallen.

"We'll have to make a return trip to the site," Taurin determined. Changing the subject, he said, "Grotus knows who I am. He tried to blackmail me into giving him the horn when we found it, in exchange for keeping quiet about my identity. He's aware there is a death sentence on my head."

"Same goes for that fellow Testi. You can't run the risk of him discovering your presence. It would be too dangerous for you. I'll go to the construction site myself."

"No way. You're in danger just by associating with me. You should return to the Palisades now, while you have the chance to get safely away from here."

"I'm not leaving you."

They stared into each other's eyes, each one determined not to yield.

"Very well," Taurin said tersely. "We'll wait for morning. Hunting for mushrooms is a major occupation here. We can pretend we're stalking the woods for valuable fungi. As soon as we get the necessary information, we'll head straight for the Palisades. Hopefully, the crates or other equipment will have notations that are traceable."

"What if the barrier is in place?"

"Let's worry about that later. We'd better get some sleep."

His voice shook with weariness, and Leena realized his confession had been an ordeal for him. She was overwhelmed by all they'd discussed and readily agreed to his suggestion. It didn't take her long to prepare for bed. As she snuggled beneath the covers, Taurin's lean, hard body beside her, she felt a deepening sense of dread that chilled her bones.

"Come here," Taurin said, spreading his arms.

She folded into his embrace, grateful for the warm security he provided. She hoped he realized she would never desert him, no matter who or what he was. But… an alien? His body was nothing foreign, she told herself. He was quite human, with manly urges and the delightful ability to gratify her desires. And he had human feelings as well. He'd been afraid she would reject him once she learned the truth.

Feeling a compelling urge to offer reassurance, she said, "Taurin, you're still my husband. Just because you're from somewhere else doesn't mean we can't stay together. I love you."

Tightening his arms around her, Taurin buried his face in her loose waves of hair. "What did I ever do to deserve you? You belong with Malcolm and his kind, not the likes of me."

"That's not true. You're the perfect mate for me." She knew him as a gentle, caring man, and that was what mattered now.

Murmuring his name, she let her hot breath caress his ear. She flicked out her tongue, tickling his earlobe, until he moaned with rising passion.

He flipped her onto her back and gazed into her eyes. Noting her desire reflected there, he gave a whoop of joy and brought mouth down on hers. His tongue thrust forth as though thirsty for intimacy. She met his movements with eager ones of her own. She wanted him, regardless of any dangers encroaching on them from the outside world. *Their* world was all that counted.

She reached for him, letting him know what she had in mind. A gratifying gasp came from his lips as she found her mark. He expanded under her bold touch, showing her how much she aroused him. A swell of pure feminine power filled her with exaltation as she craned her neck so he could kiss her throat.

He pushed her hand away and leisurely explored her body with his sensuous touch. Finally, his large palms came to rest on her breasts. He held them as though he was starving and they were a source of sustenance. When he lifted her nightgown and massaged her naked flesh, a gasp of pure pleasure escaped her lips.

It took him but a moment to shed his underclothes, and then he was atop her once more, his powerful thighs opening her legs. He plunged inside her, letting loose an animalistic howl that threw her into a frenzy.

Panting, sweating, she rocked her hips to match his rhythm, clutching at his back. Liquid heat arose from the well of her being, sapping her will, rendering her helpless against the onslaught to her senses.

"Taurin!" she screamed when her body exploded into a cataclysm of delight. He moved against her, and she felt his spasms as he joined her at the pinnacle of pleasure.

Eventually, he rolled to his side, his strength spent. Listening to his steady breathing, Leena relaxed and drifted toward sleep. Her final thought was that he hadn't told her what he'd read in the bibliotomes.

Chapter Twenty-Three

Before they left the house the next morning, Taurin revealed the presence of the watchdog on the front street by briefly pulling back the drape in the living room.

"The Truthsayers would have exposed our presence here by now," Leena said, cautiously peering out. "That fellow has to be Grotus's man. It's not only the horn he's after. Grotus hopes to add me to his collection."

"What do you mean?"

Leena related what had transpired during their last visit to the smuggler's haven.

"Curse the man! I'll kill him for that."

"No, you won't." She put a soothing hand on his arm as he allowed the drape to fall back into place. "We've too many other important things to do. By the way, you forgot to mention what you read in those bibliotomes in the Temple of Light."

He stepped away. "We don't have time to talk now. Let's go before that hound realizes we've moved our rider to the rear of the house." Lifting their bags, he headed toward the kitchen.

Leena followed as he opened the back door to glance outside.

"All clear." He signaled for her to move out.

A crisp, cool morning breeze ruffled the hairs on her skin as she watched him load their bags into the trunk of their vehicle. He made a dashing figure, his black garb snugly outlining the muscled contours of his body. She wished their interlude here had lasted longer but was eager to continue their mission.

A winding rural road took them in the direction of the construction site. Along the way, Taurin explained how they would proceed. He found a secluded spot behind a clump of bushes in the surrounding woods and parked the rider.

After trudging a short distance across the meadow, he halted abruptly. Leena stopped directly behind him, waiting while he tested the space ahead. Sniffing the pine-scented air, she enjoyed the sensation of sunshine warming her neck. The material of her day dress was fairly thin, and standing in the shade by the rider had chilled her.

"Demon's blood! That damn barrier is in place again." Taurin hesitated, considering a course of action. "I'll use my blaster," he decided. "The villeins don't expect anyone to have weapons of this caliber. I can probably short-circuit the thing, but the discharge might set off an alarm in town. At the very least, I would expect Testi to be alerted that something is amiss. We'll have to act fast."

"Just do it." Leena stood back as he pulled his weapon.

Zing. Red laser fire cut through the air, impacting the energy shield with an eruption of sparks. For an instant, the entire defensive perimeter lit up like a neon sign. In the next moment, it went dead.

"Let's go," Taurin yelled, holstering his armament.

They dashed toward a truck that stood empty by the roadside. Searching for a vehicle tag, they were disappointed to find none.

"You check out the construction equipment. I'm going to look at those crates over there," Taurin ordered.

A few minutes later they regrouped.

"Got it," Leena said. She showed him the name she had written in her notebook.

Taurin nodded. "Westner Alliance Corporation. We'll enlist those members of the Caucus who are not busy helping your brother. They can trace this company to find the owners."

"Right." Leena nodded, anxious to be off. "Too bad we don't have a camera."

"Someone's coming." Taurin pointed to an approaching cloud of dust from the road to the village. "Let's move."

But as they turned to go, the protective shield flickered into life, and they were trapped inside. Taurin pulled his blaster and fired, but the level of the shield must have been strengthened because this time he didn't make a dent. With a cry of alarm, he drew Leena to his side as a four-wheel vehicle thundered into view.

****

"Who are you and why were you snooping around?" a thin-faced fellow with a sallow complexion asked Taurin.

They'd been taken prisoner and were now being held in a cellar beneath the White Enix Pub. Taurin gathered the pub served as headquarters for the Truthsayers. Stephan Tom was definitely their leader. He spread his gospel through the International Merchants Association.

Most of the small business people wanted the rules relaxed so they could expand according to their own wishes. They didn't condone the restrictions placed upon them by the Synod. Taurin had a lot of questions to ask about their goals, but right now he was the one being interrogated.

He glared back at the man. "I told you, we were hunting mushrooms."

"Aye, but your wicker basket was empty, and you were found within our defense perimeter. Where did you obtain this weapon?" The fellow held up Taurin's blaster.

"It was given to me as a gift. We're simple town folk. We were merely looking for some prime specimens of mushrooms. I thought I'd spotted a ring of *pieds de moutons*." He pointed at Leena. "My wife was after a bed of golden chanterelles. You know they're hard to find."

Their captor regarded them with disbelief. "Are you spies for the Synod? Is that why you're here?" His rough manner of dress indicated he wasn't one of the businessmen involved in governing the Truthsayers. He might be more prone to violence than his counterparts. They'd been left alone with him, the heavy wooden door shut behind them and guards posted outside.

Taurin and Leena stood side by side, holding hands. He felt her tense at the man's question.

"Of course not. We're newlyweds, and we've just settled into the region. Actually, we'd heard about your group and were interested in joining."

The man lifted the blaster and aimed it at Taurin's chest. "You're lying."

Taurin compressed his mouth, unwilling to say anything further that might incriminate them. The cellar held a wine storage vault, and the fruity aroma of wine-soaked oak permeated the air. A musty odor tickled his nose, making him want to sneeze. He suppressed the urge, holding tightly onto Leena's hand.

"I have orders not to hurt you. You'll be tried at a hearing. That's not the way I would do it, but I'm not the one in charge."

"A hearing?" Leena said, her voice squeaky. "Under whose authority?"

"Ours, madam," the man snarled.

He stuck Taurin's blaster into his belt, pivoted and strode toward the exit. A loud knock on the door brought a response from the guard on the other side. The man stalked out, and the door slammed shut after him, a heavy bolt latching into place.

Leena's rueful gaze lifted to meet Taurin's. "Got any bright ideas?"

Taurin shook his head. "Not at the moment. Let's look around and see if there's anything we can use to defend ourselves."

"You don't think they would hurt us, do you?"

"That depends on who's giving the orders. If it's Testi, we're in big trouble."

"Maybe they already know who we are. If we were betrayed by someone in the Synod—"

"I don't think that's the case. We got caught because we tripped an alarm." He strode down an aisle bordered by huge oak barrels on one side and filled wine racks on the other. "At least there's plenty to drink in here."

"This is no time for jokes. How are we going to escape?"

"We could try reasoning with Stephan Tom."

"By telling him the truth?"

He stopped and glared at her. "That's one alternative. Can you think of another?"

"We could insist we're just an innocent couple hunting mushrooms, and we were in the wrong place at the wrong time."

Taurin's mouth twisted into a wry grin. "Sure. And every ordinary citizen goes around with a blaster strapped to his leg."

Leena grimaced. "I forgot about that."

"If Testi sees it, I'm a dead man."

Leena stared wide-eyed at him. "Don't say that. I couldn't bear it if anything happened to you."

He walked over, swept her into his arms, and brushed his lips across her hair. "My sweet *angella*. I'm supposed to be protecting you from harm. I haven't done very well."

"We've made it this far," she said with an encouraging smile. She tilted her face upward as though inviting him to kiss her.

Time passed swiftly as they consoled each other with physical pleasures. Several hours later, a guard entered with a tray of food.

"I must talk to your leader," Taurin said to the man, a swarthy individual wearing a longshirt, dark pants, and muddy boots. A wicked-looking knife stuck out of his belt.

"You'll get your chance this evening. They's all at the meeting now." The guard put the provisions on the floor and then backed away.

"What meeting? The Merchants Association?"

"Aye, the boss man is issuing his orders."

"Stephan Tom will see us later?" Taurin persisted, hoping that Testi wouldn't be the one to question them.

A sly look came over the man's face. "You'll see for yerself." He snickered before leaving them alone once again.

They ate the meal, then stood around restlessly. It was getting cold, and Leena shivered in her day dress. Taurin tried to warm her by putting his arms around her, but she quaked in his embrace. There was no window in the cellar, but he assumed it was past the dinner hour. Surely someone would come for them soon.

Without knowing what odds they would face, he couldn't plan an escape. Taking out the guards was always an option, but Taurin would prefer to speak to Stephan Tom if they got the chance.

Unfortunately, they weren't going to be allowed a private conversation. Just when they were giving up hope that anyone would come to get them, the latch clicked, and the door pushed open. Four armed guards strode into the room. They bound the captives' wrists behind their backs.

"Outside," ordered one of the thugs.

"Where are you taking us?" Leena asked as they were marched along a hallway, up a flight of stairs, and out into the cool night air.

"Back to the place where youse was caught. The boss said we can't spare no time from our work."

Taurin went along without resistance, wondering who would be waiting for them at their destination.

****

Taurin's heart sank when he saw who stood ready to greet them at the building site. Testi was in a heated argument with Stephan Tom, but they halted their conversation when Taurin's group approached.

"Here's the couple we caught snooping around the place," said one of the guards, shoving them forward with a light push on their shoulders.

Testi's face blanched as he caught sight of Taurin. "You! What are you doing here?" His small, beady eyes regarded the newcomers over a hooked nose and thin lips. He wore a rust-colored tunic, tight trousers, and scruffy boots.

"A pleasure to see you again," Taurin said, tipping his head at Testi.

"Do you know this man?" Stephan Tom asked. Tall and broad-shouldered, he was the antithesis of the other man in his charcoal business suit. A thatch of muddy brown hair settled carelessly on his head, crowning a narrow forehead that creased into a suspicious frown.

"He's someone I knew in the old country," Testi said to Stephan. "This man is a criminal wanted for theft and willful destruction of property. He was convicted, but he escaped before his sentence could be carried out. You see that he has the light of madness in his eyes."

With his hands secured behind him, Taurin had been unable to swathe his head in the protective cloth, and Stephan recoiled at the sight of his glowing night vision.

"You don't have to bother with him," Testi continued. "I'll handle this matter."

"Not yet. I'd like some answers first. What are you doing here?" Stephan demanded of Taurin.

"My wife and I were hunting for mushrooms. We got lost in the woods."

"Don't take me for a fool. You're spies. Who do you work for?"

When the pair remained silent, Testi turned toward the Truthsayer leader. "Let me take them aside and question them. I know ways to get a man to talk."

"Will you tell me why you're here, or do I let this man have his way?" Stephan asked them.

"If you leave us with him, he'll kill me," Taurin replied. "Just how much do you know about *his* origins? Where did he say he was from, and why is he helping you?"

"Don't let his lies distract you. Why don't we just kill them both? We don't want them alive to tell tales," Testi suggested, an evil snarl on his face. He reached for the rod clipped to his belt.

Stephan compressed his lips. "Obviously, neither one of them is going to talk without persuasion, but you know I'm opposed to killing. Unbind them," he ordered one of the guards.

"What do you think we intend to do against the government?" Testi said to his colleague while Taurin rubbed his chafed wrists. "If you mean to be liberated, you have to fight for your beliefs. Throughout history, spies have been executed. Let me take care of them now."

Testi drew the rod, pointing it at Taurin, whose heart hammered in his chest. He'd been at the wrong end of one of those punishment sticks before.

"Wait," Leena cried. "I'll tell you what you want to know."

Testi swung his narrowed gaze in her direction. "Don't listen to her, Stephan. This demon has probably mesmerized her with his evil stare. Look at how his eyes glow."

"Leena, don't say anything," Taurin warned, his muscles tensing for a well-aimed kick if Testi threatened her.

"Why not?" she countered. Her chin lifted, trails of golden hair wafting about her face in the wind. "You said you wanted to talk to Stephan Tom. Now's your chance. Tell him what's going on here. Let him learn the truth about how he and his followers have been duped."

"I would hear this," said Stephan, directing a meaningful glare at the Yllon agent. "You said you would tell us the truth, Sister. Speak now, or I will see to it that your tongues are cut out so you may speak of this to no one and your fingers mutilated so you cannot write. I will not have you killed, but you will wish you were dead."

Leena stared at him as though struck speechless by his threats. "You talk like you're from his world," she said, pointing to Testi. "Has he so poisoned your mind that you're willing to commit acts of brutality against your own people? How can you say you're opposed to killing and condone such horrors? If you must know, we're here to search for the missing horn that was stolen from the sacred closet in the Palisades. We thought your group might have it."

"We stumbled onto this site accidentally," Taurin added. "You've been deluded into thinking you're building an armory, but it's a landing site for spacecraft. A neighboring planet called Yllon is planning an invasion. Testi is one of their agents. He has tricked you all."

"How do you know this?" Stephan demanded, his expression showing neither disbelief nor acceptance.

"I come from Yllon, where vision like mine is regarded as a curse. I was forced to flee my homeworld. I'd settled here, where I had hoped to live in peace. On Yllon, gang warfare is prevalent. The uncontrolled population rate and advanced technology have depleted their resources. Xan must be trading food surpluses to Yllon in exchange for technical advantages like farm machinery. But if Yllon has the chance to conquer this world, they'll jump at it. Someone is handing them that opportunity by stealing the horn."

"In other words," Leena added, "you're being used, Stephan Tom. You think you're leading a revolt against the government, but you're actually paving the way for an invasion."

"Ha! You expect me to believe these lies? That's the most absurd tale I've ever heard in my life." The Truthsayer leader turned to Testi. "See if you can force the truth from them before you cut out their tongues. But remember my sentence. They are not to be killed. I will not have their blood on my hands."

As he swung away, Taurin shouted desperately, "Listen to me! This is a landing site for spacecraft. Can't you see that slab is a launch pad?"

Stephan turned back, his laughter a harsh echo in the night. "That's the foundation for our weapons storehouse, and Testi is my friend. I don't think he likes having aspersions cast on his character."

"Where do you think the weapons are coming from? Who is

supposed to supply them?" Taurin's words dissipated in the air, and he received no answer.

Clenching his jaw, he realized a fight was inevitable. Testi motioned for a troop to surround them. He shuddered to think what would happen if they were left to Testi's control.

Leena gasped as one of the guards shoved her forward. She stumbled, her face pale and terror in her eyes.

A low growl burst from Taurin's throat as he erupted into action. At nearly the same time, an explosion on the opposite side of the field drew everyone's attention. Taurin used the moment to his advantage, shoving aside the nearest guard and flipping another one over his hip.

Leena screamed a warning as Testi raised his rod. Suddenly an armed troop burst from the woods, their clothing camouflaged by leaves. A skirmish began. One of the men moved in Leena's direction, making her shriek in alarm.

"Hush, Sister, we're here to rescue you."

Taurin would have thrown himself into the fray, but their savior yanked him aside. "Come with me. You have to get out of here."

He didn't need any further persuasion. Grabbing Leena's hand, Taurin charged after the fellow through the woods. "Who are you? Why are you helping us?"

The man stopped, and Taurin got a good look at him. By the gods, it was the same fellow who'd been their watchdog these past few days, taking up a post outside their house.

"I work for Grotus, and my name is Jette. You haven't found the horn yet, and Grotus's orders are to keep you safe until you do. I've moved your rider. You can leave this place, but we'll be keeping an eye on you. Here is your weapon."

He handed Taurin his blaster and showed him where he'd moved their vehicle. "Remember, my employer expects you to contact him as soon as the horn is in your possession."

"Like hell I will." Taurin eased into the driver's seat while Leena slid in beside him.

Jette's brows drew together in a scowl. "No one lives who plays games with Grotus."

Taurin nodded at the construction site. "My presence is known here now, so Grotus's threats bear no weight with me."

"Heed my words, Rey Niris, or Grotus will exact vengeance on you and your loved ones."

Taurin started the engine and backed away in a squeal of tires, disallowing any further warnings.

"At least we know Grotus hasn't any news of the horn," Leena remarked once they were safely on their way out of town.

Taurin took a circuitous route to make sure they weren't followed. "That doesn't help us. We still have no clue as to who has the artifact."

Leena fell into a thoughtful silence until they reached a reasonable distance from Woden. They'd send someone to pick up their belongings in town later.

"Let's head straight for the Palisades," she said. "We can take turns driving through the night."

"Aren't you too tired?" He glanced at her, concerned for her welfare.

"I'll be fine. When it's daylight, I can call ahead and alert the Caucus to check out that equipment company. Hopefully by the time we arrive, they'll have some answers."

Taurin grimaced. "I wish we'd had the chance to convince Stephan Tom of the truth."

"You may have planted seeds of doubt in his mind, which could be more important." She shifted her position with a wince of discomfort. They'd been driving for a while. "Whoever stole the horn must still have it, don't you agree?"

Taurin kept his eyes on the winding country road. "I'd like to believe the horn remains at the Palisades. I wonder if your brother has had any success with his inquiries."

With a tired sigh, Leena leaned her head back against the headrest. "Wait until he hears that a member of the Synod stole the horn to lower the defense perimeter around Xan, and that an alien invasion is planned. What I don't understand is why a member of the Synod would want to be involved in such a plot. It doesn't make sense."

"Money or power could provide a motive."

"But the Synod already wields full authority."

"Dikran remains at the head of the government. He might stand in the way of whoever wants to be in charge."

"Dikran is an old man. Why not simply wait until he dies?"

"There may be unknown factors involved." Taurin gave her a somber glance. "When you speak to Bendyk, warn him about this new threat from Yllon's agents. Somehow I doubt Testi is the only operative. Others might have infiltrated the Palisades."

"I don't see how that's possible. Whoever works in the holy center undergoes the most stringent scrutiny."

"Nonetheless, we must be extra cautious upon our return."

Testi would alert any other agents on Xan to hunt him down. Stephan Tom's organization was international, and that meant there could be many different cells around the globe—a notion that chilled Taurin. How many other landing sites were already completed? And how much of the defensive perimeter had failed simply because the crystals providing the energy source had lost power?

In his mind's eye, he saw the crystal lattice structure beneath the temple presided over by Leena's father. Likely a similar grid existed at the Palisades. That crystalline network must power the defense shield. It was imperative to find the entrance to the lower levels at the Holy Temple. A central control station had to be located there, and he needed to assess the damage.

"Grotus will know we're heading home to report to Dikran," Leena said, cutting into his thoughts. "I wish we could find a way to stop him. We've been trying to catch him for years but never had anything concrete to pin on him. If only we could devise a way to put the man out of action. Otherwise, we'll always have to watch our backs."

"Hasn't anyone ever tried to set up a sting?"

"Of course, but he's too smart. It's never worked."

"Maybe the right bait wasn't used."

Leena gave him a suspicious glance. "Your tone of voice tells me you have something in mind. You're not thinking of using *me* as bait, are you?"

That remark elicited a low chuckle from his throat. "I wouldn't think of putting you at such risk, *angella*. Grotus wants the horn more than he wants you. Ransoming it back to the Synod will make him rich, not that he needs more wealth. I know that's what he intends to do, because Grotus needs the horn blown as much as we do. If the weather cycles continue their erratic pattern, his smuggling operations will be disrupted."

Leena's forehead creased. "I'll bet Grotus doesn't know anything about this plot from Yllon. He has his connections at the spaceport, but he must be in the dark as far as what's really going on. I don't think he'd condone a takeover. He's too content with the way things are run now. If I were in charge of regulations, I'd disallow him access to the ruins."

"Are you saying someone is being lax on purpose?"

"Before all this started, I never would have thought a member of the Synod would take a bribe, but now I'd believe anything."

"Sirvat could be involved," Taurin pointed out.

"Yes, that's an avenue worth exploring, although I believe the excavations come under the auspices of the Ministry of Religion. Bendyk was investigating Zeroun. Perhaps he's uncovered something important."

Taurin tightened his grip on the steering wheel. A series of sharp curves loomed ahead. Luckily the road was well-lit by bright lamp posts. He could almost feel the lines of fatigue etching his face, just as he could feel the lead weight in his stomach. They were still no closer to finding the horn than they had been when they started on this quest.

Grotus's smuggling operations were minor compared to what faced them now. He wondered what Grotus might do if Taurin mentioned the threat from Yllon.

"I have an idea, but we'll talk about it after we see Dikran," he told Leena. "We may need to enlist Grotus's aid."

Leena glanced at him curiously. "Bendyk's discoveries might set us in a new direction. I'll call him as soon as it's daylight."

She settled back into her seat, her eyelids lowering. Taurin didn't disturb her, aware she'd need all her strength for the confrontations ahead.

Chapter Twenty-Four

Bendyk wasn't in his office when Leena called in the morning from a public messager at a recharging station along the road, but she did manage to connect with Dikran via his private, confidential line. She related what they'd learned and asked him to set the Caucus on the trail of the equipment supplier.

The Arch Nome was stunned by her words. "It has to be Magar. He's in charge of offworld relations. He's the only one who has regular dealings with the representatives from Yllon."

"Wait until we get there. Taurin will know what to say to him." Leena paused. "Has Bendyk reported any news? I tried to reach my brother, but he wasn't in his apartment or his office."

"You'd best speak to him yourself. Nothing is as it seems anymore. I don't know what will become of us."

"Your Grace?"

"Never mind. Just get here as soon as you can, child. And see to your safety."

Back in the rider, Leena related her conversation to Taurin while she took a turn driving.

"We'll find out what Bendyk learned soon enough," Taurin commented, closing his eyes.

Noting the weary look on his face, she fell silent, biting her lip with anxiety. They had too much to worry about during the long drive to the Palisades. Why not think of something pleasant instead? This interlude provided time for her and Taurin to be alone together. Soon enough, they would be forced to face the treachery of the various Synod members. And if they succeeded in recovering the horn, what then?

Her stomach churned. She was unable to discard a nagging sense of anxiety. Instead of appreciating Taurin's company, she wondered what would happen to their relationship once the horn was blown and stability was restored. He'd brought up some valid points to be considered, such as their differences in religious beliefs. These past few days had been woefully inadequate as an example of married life. All she knew was that she wanted to be with him.

Glancing at his profile, vulnerable in repose, she let an affectionate smile play upon her lips. In many ways he still seemed like a stranger to her, yet she knew, deep down inside, that they were compatible and needed each other. Her faith complemented his skepticism. His strength of presence erased her fears. Together they would face whatever obstacles lay ahead of them. Wasn't that what marriage was all about, meeting life's challenges together?

Her grip on the steering wheel relaxed as her mind emptied of worries. They'd get through this and settle into a routine that suited them both. Lothar would guide them.

Praised be the Holy One whose beneficence provides for our people.

****

Taurin awoke to hear Leena mutter a prayer aloud. A vise squeezed his heart. Whatever discoveries awaited them at the Palisades might set her against him. She'd blame him for withholding his knowledge of Lothar, but it was the Synod's fault for deceiving the populace. It wasn't his place to reveal the truth. Doing so would break the oath he'd made to Magar not to interfere in their world's affairs.

Magar. Was the man a traitor? Did he support the Truthsayers, urging them to armed rebellion while secretly plotting an invasion with the Ylloners?

Forcing those troublesome thoughts aside, he refocused on

Leena. Maybe they could work things out satisfactorily between them when this was over, but so many problems remained. Darkness seemed to loom ahead, no matter which direction they chose. If only he shared Leena's faith, it would brighten his outlook.

But was it his faith in Lothar or his faith in her that was lacking? Walls were tumbling down around him, Magar's potential treachery being the most painful. Leena's love was the guiding light that uplifted him and drew him from the darkness of despair. She was his savior, his *angella*. And he prayed—for the first time in his life—that he'd be able to keep her by his side.

****

Magar was not in his offices when they returned to the Palisades. A cold front had passed through the area, and the air in the complex was chilly despite the central heating system. Shafts of sunlight penetrated through the beveled glass windows, providing a measure of warmth. Leena wore a topaz brocade gown and a gold-sashed blue robe that signified her status. Her golden hair floated about her head like a mist by a waterfall.

Taurin had on one of his usual black outfits. They stood in the corridor outside the Minister of State's suite of offices, discussing their next course of action. Upon their arrival, he'd presented his bride with a wedding gift—the ring he'd slipped into his pocket at the Temple of Light. It was small enough to fit on her slender finger.

"This signifies our bonding," he'd said to her, his tone solemn, as they'd prepared in her apartment for their audience with Dikran. "I want everyone to know you are my wife."

She'd raised herself on tiptoe to kiss him. "I shall be proud to make the announcement."

But Dikran wasn't there when they went to see him.

"We've waited too long," Leena said with a pout. They'd arrived by four in the afternoon but had decided to freshen up before making an appearance.

"Try locating Bendyk, but use a public messager in the lobby. The communication system in your apartment might be bugged."

She acquiesced to his command. but neither Bendyk nor Swill was available. "Where is everyone?" she asked with a puzzled frown. Then her face lit with comprehension. "Oh, I totally forgot. Today is the Festival of Lanterns."

"What does that mean?" Taurin wondered how anyone could get their work done when there were so many religious holidays.

"People go home early to light lanterns and say a prayer for the dead. As though in mourning, one is to pursue no forms of entertainment, including answering the messager system. It would be a sacrilege to disturb anyone during this solemn time. We'll go back to my apartment. I have some lanterns there we can light."

"No, we'll go to my place."

She shot him a quizzical glance. "You won't need your apartment here any longer."

"I mean, we should go to my farm at Lexington Page."

Leena stared at him, aghast. "But why? We've just been on the road for days."

"We can still be here in the morning to speak to Dikran. In the meantime, I have chores to do at home. The recent frost might have killed my crops, since I wasn't there to tend them."

"If that's the case, we'll ask Dikran to compensate you."

****

Checking on his crops seemed to be the farthest thing from Taurin's mind when they arrived at his home several hours later. They'd found a food market along the way that was still open and had stocked up on a few supplies. Leena had bought lanterns there as well. As she set about preparing their meal and lighting the lanterns around the house, Taurin closeted himself in his bedroom.

"Won't you join me in prayer?" she called after completing her tasks. She stood outside his closed door.

"I'll be out in a minute."

She turned away, hurt that he would exclude her. What was he doing in there that required privacy? Disturbed by his behavior, she retreated to the kitchen and set the table for two. The aroma of spiced vegetable soup wafted into the air. Warmed by the hot stove and the efficient heating system, she'd removed her cloak and donned an apron. In another pot, thick noodles simmered in an orange-flavored tomato sauce, peppered with bits of dried *rasenbret*.

"Something smells good," Taurin said, his voice deep.

Leena whirled around, smiling at the sight of him in the archway. His tall figure and fiercely handsome features raised her temperature. He sauntered into the kitchen, a seductive grin on his face, but behind his eyes were traces of anxiety.

"The food is just about ready," she told him. "Let's say our prayers while we're waiting."

The smile on his face vanished. "Must you follow all the traditions so diligently?"

"Does it bother you if I do?"

"Not as long as you don't expect my compliance."

Leena wiped her hands on a dry towel. "I wish you believed in Lothar. It would make these traditions meaningful to you. I get the feeling you're humoring me by participating in the rituals."

His expression softened. "I aim to please you, *angella*. Go ahead with the prayers, and I won't interrupt."

They ate their hearty repast while engaging in light conversation. While scrubbing the dishes after they'd finished, Leena wondered how they would ever reconcile their differences. She didn't care for the notion that Taurin's prayers were hollow and he pretended tolerance to pacify her. Ideally, a marriage should be based on common values. That he thought so little of Lothar distressed her and boded ill for their future together.

Or perhaps she was the one being intolerant. She'd been

raised from birth to believe everyone worshiped Lothar. Why shouldn't others be entitled to different beliefs?

Taurin placed a hand on her shoulder. "Why don't you leave the rest of the dishes for later?" He nuzzled her neck, eliciting a purr of pleasure from her throat.

She turned off the sink and dried her hands before moving into his arms. His mouth came down on hers as she folded her body into his embrace.

"My bed is large enough for two. It's about time I had a wife to warm it for me."

His arm around her, Taurin led her to the bedroom, muttering a curse when she noticed the bibliotomes scattered on the coverlet. Hastily he scooped them up and piled them on a table in a corner of the room.

Leena narrowed her gaze. Had he been reading them?

His next action stole her attention. He stripped off his clothes and stood before her naked.

"You're next, my love. I wish to see you in all your glory." He gave her an encouraging grin.

Needing no further prompting, Leena slid out of her gown and undergarments.

Her husband studied her from head to toe. "Beautiful," he murmured, surveying her.

"You're embarrassing me."

"Nonsense. Looking at you brings me pleasure. See what it does?" He pointed to his erect appendage.

Leena's blood sizzled as a responding heat arose within her. The bed looked inviting with its covers thrown back, the white sheets crisp and clean. She felt the barest breeze against her exposed skin, a warm draft from the heating system that hummed in the background.

Taurin flipped off the light switch, leaving the room in the soft glow of lantern light. Every room in the house was lit with lanterns, remembrances for those long past.

We're here to celebrate life, she remembered, opening her

arms as Taurin approached. And celebrate life they did, joining together as one, murmuring words of passion into each other's ears. They melded together in a frenzied declaration of their love.

"I need you so much," Taurin whispered, locked in her arms after they'd satisfied each other's driving lust.

She kissed him on the mouth. "I need you, too. You make my life complete." Her hands splayed across his broad back, kneading his taut muscles. The manliness of him drove her wild. Entwining her legs around his, she reveled in the feel of his rock solid body against her softness. She'd never felt so feminine as when she was with him, and it was a joy to experience such a wonderful part of life.

"My wife," he uttered in a hoarse cry, and in it was an echo of the desperate longing in his heart.

The way he held on to her convinced Leena that he was troubled. "What bothers you, my darling?" she asked, staring into his glowing eyes.

He gazed back at her with such love and affection, she thought she would melt. "I'm afraid," he said, searching her face.

"Afraid of what?"

"That you'll leave me, because you won't want me after… after we finish this."

She realized he was talking about finding the missing horn. "We have to recover the horn and blow it so Lothar may awaken."

"*Lothar*. Always *Lothar*." Taurin flopped onto his back.

****

If only he could come home to his wife every night, Taurin would be a happy man for the rest of his life. She was his haven, the peace he'd been seeking, not the farm on this tiny bit of land.

He realized now that this was what he'd always wanted—a family of his own. He'd admired the bonds between Baker Mylock and his brood but hadn't realized it was something he sought for himself. He wouldn't let Leena leave him, no matter what happened.

She'd mentioned the horn, but that wasn't the issue here. It was more about Lothar. The Truthsayers may have been right when they accused the Synod of securing power for themselves to the disadvantage of the people.

He'd learned many revealing facts in his examination of the bibliotomes, but gaps remained in the information. Grotus had some of the books, obtained from Captain Sterckle, and Magar had others. The things he had learned were piecemeal, like segments of a puzzle that had yet to fit together.

The books in the Temple of Light were a valuable resource, but there must be another repository located in the Palisades. He'd asked Bendyk to search for the hidden lower level and wondered if he'd been successful.

Other than the bibliotomes, the symbols carved into the walls of the ancient temples were the only other clues relating to the Apostles. Leena could interpret them, but he wouldn't ask for her help unless it became necessary. He was able to read the bibliotomes only because the knowledge contained therein was transmitted to him via some sort of telepathic imprint. Taurin didn't understand how the method worked, but at least he wasn't required to read the symbols. Hopefully, a new source of bibliotomes would reveal the knowledge required to repair the crystals.

The secrets of Lothar had to be contained within the Palisades. Tomorrow, Taurin would force Dikran to disclose everything.

Chapter Twenty-Five

The next day, Leena and Taurin met briefly with the Arch Nome. "I directed the Caucus to check into the name of the equipment company you'd mentioned. They traced it to a larger corporation called Amiaus. We're checking into the details now," Dikran said, appearing more frail than when they'd seen him last.

A vein in his forehead throbbed conspicuously as he regarded them with a defeated expression. He sat, dwarfed by his throne-like chair, while they stood in front of him like sergeants being summoned before a superior officer.

"What about the defense shield around the planet? Is it weakening?" Taurin asked.

Dikran nodded. "I should have seen this coming, but I was convinced someone stole the horn for ransom. It began when Lothar started to malfunction."

"What are you talking about? The weather disasters?" Leena said.

Dikran gave her a startled look. "Huh? Oh, that's right. Lothar is displeased because of the Truthsayer movement."

When Leena appeared about to question him further, he rushed on. "You say Stephan Tom, the president of the International Merchants Association, is the leader behind this group? That means their influence extends to a wider audience than we imagined. The organization began as a grass-roots movement promoting greater freedom of choice. It's grown in popularity over the years. People chafe against the restrictions imposed on them."

"Why doesn't the Synod open talks with the Truthsayers?" Leena suggested. "I haven't thought about their viewpoint before, but in some respects they're right. Why can't people settle where they please? Why does one have to obtain permission to change residences?"

Taurin responded to the topic. "For society to grow, change has to take place. If that means progressing from towns to cities, with all their inherent problems, then it's going to happen. Perhaps it's time for the Synod to meet the people's needs in a new and different way."

"You forget," Dikran said, wagging a crooked finger, "Lothar set the rules. We follow his laws."

"And who wrote them?" Taurin asked in an even tone.

"The Apostles wrote the laws as Lothar dictated them."

"Really?" Taurin's gaze met Dikran's, and for a moment he saw a flicker of uncertainty in the Arch Nome's expression.

Dikran scrutinized his face, then turned to Leena. "Leave us for a moment, child. I wish to speak to this man in private."

"Now, wait a minute," Leena said, as though insulted by the dismissal.

"Go find your brother," Taurin urged. "I'll join you shortly."

"Very well." She spun around and stormed from the room.

Taurin turned back to face Dikran. "I know about the power grids. They relay information to the weather satellites orbiting the planet. The central control station has to be here."

Dikran compressed his lips, saying nothing, so Taurin continued. "Lothar isn't displeased with the people. Your power source is failing. I've seen the crystals." He noted with gratification the look of surprise in Dikran's eyes. "Not all of the crystals are functioning properly, are they? They're deteriorating, and that's what is wreaking havoc with the weather. What's happening, Dikran? Are the crystals wearing out? Were they a legacy from the Apostles that no one understands?"

Dikran's posture slumped. "You know too much, son. Does *she* know?"

"Leena? No, she hasn't a clue. She believes faithfully in Lothar. We are married, your eminence, and I love her dearly."

He gave a wry smile at the Arch Nome's astonished look. "I cannot be the one who disillusions her with the truth."

"She's an intelligent young woman. She must realize you are withholding information."

"Then the sooner we resolve things, the better. May I suggest you and I make a deal? I'll share what I know if you lay all your cards on the table. I give my solemn vow that what you reveal will not go beyond this room."

"Why should I trust you?"

"Because I'm from Yllon."

"What?"

Taurin explained his background. "I know what kind of terror my countrymen are capable of bringing to your people. The defensive shield has to be strengthened if you want to repel the coming invasion. Maybe I can fix the malfunction if I learn what's causing it."

Dikran spread his hands helplessly. "But the horn has to be blown to reawaken Lothar."

"Lothar be damned! You know there's no god as well as I do. I figure the horn has to be blown to reset the weather cycles, but what role does it play regarding the crystals?"

"Blowing the horn has no effect on them. We don't know what is causing them to fade." Dikran's face sagged. "Sounding the horn resets the climactic patterns, as you surmised, but it also provides a temporary energy boost that can fortify the defense perimeter, at least for a short time. It won't solve the problem in the long run. If the crystals continue to deteriorate, eventually all power will be drained."

With a swish of his robe, Dikran rose, his movements majestic despite his dejection. "Follow me," he said, heading for a doorway at the rear of the chamber.

"Are you taking me to the lower level?"

"The entrance is from my private robing chamber, behind the Grand Altar in the Holy Temple."

"Of course it is." Taurin followed him through the suite of

offices and into the maze of corridors that wound through the Palisades complex.

They strode past administrative wings, small chapels, and open courtyards before reaching the Arch Nome's private entrance to the Holy Temple. Along the way, Taurin filled Dikran in on the details he and Leena had learned—their discoveries in the Temple of Light, Taurin's relationship to Magar, and his encounter with Testi. The only thing he didn't reveal was the use of his armband. It might come in handy as a playing piece later on, and he didn't want to give away the game so early.

"We closed the Temple of Light for excavations because it was deemed too dangerous to explore," Dikran admitted after Taurin questioned him. "We had no idea what might be found there except that it must be highly valuable. I'll have to discuss this with the Synod. They may want to reopen the site now that you know how to bypass the traps."

"Be sure to include Leena in any professional excavation," Taurin advised. "She'd be deeply upset if you excluded her after her skills gained us entrance."

In the robing salon, Dikran shuffled up to a statue of a cherub, similar to the one in Cranby's office.

"How is Lothar's lozenge created?" Taurin asked.

Dikran detached the halo and spun it on the golden disk. "It's a gift from Lothar. The lozenges appear during the month of Mistic, and the count is always accurate. We have been unable to conceive how they are produced."

Taurin's admiration of the Apostles grew. Certainly they were an advanced civilization, but why had they left and where had they gone? And what relation were they to him? Some of the answers he'd gleaned from reading his bibliotomes, but the rest might be here, through that secret passageway that had just opened in the far wall.

A flight of steps led downward to a level filled with huge chambers, featuring vaulted stone ceilings, recessed lighting, and an air-filtering system that kept the temperature on an even keel.

The first room held an array of equipment that surprised Taurin in its complexity. Row after row of control consoles flashed with different buttons and dials. Peering closely, he noticed display monitors linking the houses of worship run by the Candors. A liquid crystal map grid made up an entire wall, showing the global weather system. This level of technology was beyond anything he'd seen before, even in the spacecraft that had brought him to this world.

"It's amazing," he said, staring about the room in awe. "You and the Synod are the only ones aware of this place?"

Dikran nodded, his expression sad. "We know so little. None of us understands what any of this means, nor did our predecessors. Magar said he would consult with his contacts on Yllon about repairs."

Taurin pointed to a pulsating brightness ahead. "That's a crystal lattice structure in the next room, isn't it?"

Dikran stopped in front of a receptacle before the adjacent archway and withdrew two pairs of dark glasses. "Here, put these on. The intensity can harm your vision."

Taurin donned the glasses and proceeded into the next chamber. Most of the crystals in the honeycomb structure glowed brilliantly, but a few flickered, and others appeared dead.

"Why haven't there been any power failures? Don't these grids supply electricity as well as power the satellite system?"

"They do in part," Dikran acknowledged, "but we have solar generators as backups. They've been able to function adequately. If more of the crystals fail, however, I don't see how the generators can be maintained. We'll have a planetwide power outage."

Taurin strode into the next room. Inside was a repository of inactive crystals, heaped in piles like so many inanimate rocks. Again he wondered how to activate them and puzzled over what was causing their demise. Perhaps another chamber held some answers.

The next room held an immense library of bibliotomes.

Stacks and stacks of books rose toward the ceiling. In the center of the room, on a raised pedestal and under a glass cover, was the largest bibliotome he'd ever seen. As he studied it, Taurin noted a familiar sequence of symbols on the cream-colored cover.

"What does this volume signify?" he asked the Arch Nome.

"It is our sacred Book of Laws and the bible for our society. The Apostles—"

Taurin pivoted. "The Apostles set up their own laws and established the rule of Lothar to suit their needs. They were aliens, possibly from a star system in the Cadega constellation."

"Whatever their origins, they brought peace and order to our society," Dikran countered, his voice firm. "They stabilized our weather system, provided rain for our crops, and gave us the lozenge to prevent sickness. Is there not the hand of a god in all this?" Dikran swept his arm to encompass the room. "Who gave the Apostles these gifts? Who were *their* progenitors?"

He stepped closer, his gaze piercing Taurin's. "I truly believe there is a higher order of intelligence, a superior being who is responsible for the patterns of life. This entity's name may not be Lothar, but he—or it—is the holy one I worship."

"Why don't you reveal the truth to the people? Are you afraid they will revolt against the authority of the Synod?"

"Of course I am afraid. But I see that progress is inevitable. The winds of change are blowing, and there is nothing I can do to stop them."

"Not unless you get the horn back and figure out what's wrong with the crystals."

"Can you assist us?" Dikran asked. "The other Ylloners said this technology was beyond their scope of knowledge."

"What other Ylloners?" Taurin demanded with a frown.

"Why, the ones Magar consulted, of course. No, wait a minute. I think it was Karayan who suggested we bring in technicians from Yllon to fix the malfunction."

"You actually had people from Yllon down here? How do you know they didn't sabotage the system?"

"It was already failing!" Dikran shouted, raising his arms in the air. "The technicians said they had to examine the regional worship centers in the outlying districts. They felt the fault might be there."

"So you actually gave approval for agents from Yllon to tour the countryside? Then that's how they were brought in. And you say it was Karayan who suggested consulting these experts?"

The older man's eyes crinkled in thought. "I believe so."

Taurin's mouth compressed. "I'd like some time alone in here to figure this out. Do you think you could notify Leena that I'll be late? I'll meet her back at our apartment."

Dikran gazed at him consideringly. "Why did you not make your marriage public?"

"We thought it best not to do so during our mission. Leena's life is governed by her religious traditions. I can't tell her about any of this."

"There is no need to disillusion her," Dikran agreed. "We'll tell her only what is necessary. See what her brother has learned and what you can piece together in this place. Then we'll meet again to determine a course of action."

"I tried to tell Stephan Tom the truth, but he wouldn't listen."

"He's blinded by his own ambitions. We'll put the Truthsayers in their place once the horn is recovered."

"Whoever stole it planned on the defense shield failing by Fearn. Yllon's agents are now planted around the globe. This plot must have been in the works for some time."

"Magar and Karayan are the most likely candidates," said Dikran, his voice grim. A wisp of white hair fell into his face, and he tossed it back with the air of a man determined to fight his foes despite his advanced age. At least he'd thrown off the mantle of dejection he'd worn earlier. "We need evidence in order to bring a charge against one of them, or perhaps both, if they're in this together. I'll look into the matter while you're occupied here. Contact me when you are ready for another meeting."

"It may not be safe to talk in your office," Taurin cautioned him. "The traitor, with the aid of his Yllon friends, may have placed listening devices inside the Palisades. We know Sirvat leaks information to Grotus, who could have spies here as well. I have an idea as to how we can use Grotus to aid us, but we'll talk more about it later." The smuggler would remain a threat to him and Leena until the matter of the horn was resolved.

As Dikran's footsteps faded into the distance, Taurin slid his armband off and disengaged the bracelets. The three large rings created a musical harmony when he spun them in unison. The soothing tone brought memories of his childhood, when he'd simply stared at the spinning rings, enjoying their music.

The rings were the keys to this library. He only hoped the books didn't contain a complete account of the Apostles' culture, because then it would take months for him to find the answers he needed. They didn't have that kind of time with Fearn less than two weeks away. This was his last chance to learn how the crystals functioned and how the horn served to reset Lothar.

****

Leena paced in Bendyk's office while her brother and Swill awaited her reaction in silence.

"You're telling me the brake line was cut the night of the accident?" she cried, glaring at Swill.

The young woman bobbed her head of short black hair. "The mechanic had been paid to say it was an accident."

"Paid by whom?" Leena brushed a shaky hand through her golden locks of hair. How could Bendyk have suspected this before and never confided in her?

"A representative from the Ministry of Religion was responsible," Bendyk answered. He sat at his desk, his manner composed. His medallion gleamed brilliantly against his royal blue longshirt. "Father had a meeting that night and would have taken his rider but arranged instead to be picked up by a friend. Mother and I got in the rider intended for Father."

"But he'd apologized for his transgression. You're saying someone still considered him a threat?"

"That's correct." The corners of Bendyk's mouth turned down. "The mechanic will testify, and the representative from the Ministry of Religion has agreed to act as a witness. He received his orders directly from Zeroun."

Leena's throat tightened at the implication. "But that means Zeroun ordered our father to be murdered."

Bendyk nodded, his expression grim. "Others who have defied the faith have vanished under mysterious circumstances. If you remember, Karayan came to Father's defense, citing his exemplary record as a factor to be considered in his sentencing. Zeroun must have realized that if his verdict was too harsh, he would be censured, and so he took matters into his own hands. He's zealous about his faith, quick to punish anyone who deviates from the norm."

"You mean anyone who threatens his power structure," Swill cut in. "He wouldn't have taken the horn. It's too important to him to maintain Lothar's stability."

"But he's a murderer," Leena said in protest.

Bendyk held up a hand to pacify her. "That is a matter to be dealt with separately."

"How can you sit there so calmly? He was responsible for the accident that killed Mother and injured you. We must tell Dikran immediately." And then she remembered that Taurin was closeted in a secret meeting with Dikran that didn't include her.

Swill gazed at Leena with sympathy. "We learned something else. Those plantations in the Black Lands—the ones that grow beans for the Chocola Company—the land rights were granted to the Amiaus Company, of which Karayan is a large shareholder. We've received reports from Caucus members that Karayan made some bad investments in the past few years. He would be in dire financial straits if it weren't for this additional income. Illicit income, I might add."

Leena shook her head in disbelief. "Is there no end to the corruption?"

Her father's closest friend was guilty of illegal business transactions. Zeroun was responsible for murder, and Sirvat was prey to Grotus's whims. But which one of them had taken the horn? They'd eliminated nearly everyone else.

"Wait a minute. What about Magar? He's responsible for contact with offworlders," she reminded her brother. She'd told him and Swill about their sojourn to Woden and their discoveries. "He could be in league with Drufus Gong from Yllon."

"All of our probes have come up negative on him. He appears to be clean."

"I'll bet Taurin knows more about Magar."

"Then we'll have to wait and see what he says, won't we?"

The messager rang. It was Dikran's aide, telling them Taurin would be delayed and would meet Leena back at their apartment.

"Damn the man," she muttered. What wasn't Taurin sharing with her? Why was he shutting her out?

Bendyk gave her a sharp gaze. "How are you two getting along, Sister?"

"We're managing fine except that he doesn't trust me." She broke down and told him about their discoveries in the Temple of Light. "I believe he's figured out how to read those books, but he won't talk about it."

"Interesting," Bendyk mused with a keen light in his eyes. "I'll have to corner him for a talk myself. We've too many questions that need answering at this point, and if he has some of them figured out... Taurin will tell us what he knows, or else."

"Or else what?" Leena couldn't imagine her brother physically defying Taurin. Taurin's strength and skill would outweigh him by far, even though her brother was no slouch.

Bendyk stood and squared his shoulders. "I still have the power to annul your marriage. If I must invoke my authority, I shall do so."

"But I don't want an annulment."

"If he loves you, he won't risk losing you. He'll tell us what we want to know."

Leena was disturbed by the prospect of forcing Taurin to reveal his knowledge. He should trust her enough to confide in her himself. Her hurt went deep, and she carried it along to her apartment. It began as a sinking feeling in her gut and rose to a throbbing ache in her heart when he didn't return.

Too weary to wait for him, Leena went to bed, depressed as she crawled under the sheets, cold and empty without her soulmate.

He must have a reason for his behavior, she rationalized. Maybe he felt he was protecting her, but protecting her from what? The truth? What truths would she fear to hear?

She considered her question and the various options it presented but was unable to reach a conclusion. Too fatigued to think on it further, she let herself drift into slumber.

****

Bendyk sank onto the sofa in Swill's living area, having been to her apartment in the Palisades enough times to feel at home. After their visit to his family estate, he'd noticed her reticent behavior toward him and meant to address it, especially after hearing Leena's doubts about Taurin. Lack of communication plagued both of them, and it was about time he and Swill had a frank discussion on where their relationship was headed.

He had proposed discussing the new developments as an excuse to accompany her home, although both of them knew that wasn't what was on his mind. Swill had gone into her bedroom to change into something more comfortable—presumably, one of the seductive nightgowns he'd purchased for her. Heat warmed his face as he recalled his embarrassment in the clothing shop, but he had wanted to give her a gift of finery, and what better choice than a couple of silk shifts to wear against her soft skin?

Fire spread through his veins, spinning him into a sensual coil as the image of her naked body came to mind. *Stop it,* he chastised himself. He hadn't come here for that purpose.

"Bendyk, you look uncomfortable in a longshirt," Swill's low voice crooned as she entered the room. The burgundy lingerie revealed a tantalizing glimpse of her cleavage and bare legs.

Bendyk gave her an appreciative glance. "Let's talk first," he suggested, making room for her on the couch.

As soon as she sat, nudging her hip against his, a wave of desire rocketed through him. He suppressed his reaction.

"I was troubled to hear of Leena's difficulty with Taurin," he began. "For a married couple to get along, they have to share their secrets. Mutual trust must be at the foundation of a relationship."

Swill observed him warily. "I agree."

"I get the feeling you're not being entirely honest with me. Ever since we visited my father, you seem more reserved. What's bothering you?"

An emotion he couldn't identify flickered behind her eyes. "Why does it matter?"

He'd asked himself the same question. "It just does, that's all. I care about what you think."

"If you must know, I felt uncomfortable in your home, as though I didn't fit in. You saw how I was raised. I'd never belong in your social circles."

He reached out to tickle the soft skin on the underside of her arm. "When order is restored to our land, I'd hate to see you waste your talents on the tithing counts. You have a keen mind and an admirable grasp of finances. Have you considered applying for a higher position?"

A look of disappointment crossed her face, as though she'd expected him to say something different. "Not really," she replied. "I haven't thought that far ahead."

"I should like to see you, and if you were to live nearby—" He shook his head. "No, that's not what I mean to say. You've made me realize there's more to life than preaching the words of Lothar. Thanks to your insights, I've cast off the guilt over my mother's death. You've given me a new lease on life, and I need you with me. Say you'll be my bonded mate."

Swill stared at him in astonishment. "You really want me?" she asked in a small voice. "I hadn't dared hope… I mean, I dreamed about this, but I never… Bendyk, do you love me?"

He planted a fervent kiss on her lips. "Yes, I love you, and I'll cherish you as my wife. Being with you is all that matters."

"But will your friends accept me? I don't come from the same elevated background as you and your sister. My origins are more humble. You've seen where I grew up."

"That doesn't matter. Once you are mine, people will respect you. Heck, they already do."

She threw her arms around his neck. "Then I accept. You've made my dreams come true. I promise to be a good wife, even if I have to bring you down from your pedestal now and then."

Bendyk laughed with joy. "I'll look forward to that, my sweet."

As he led her into the bedroom, he felt gratified to think that on this night, rest would be a long time in coming.

Chapter Twenty-Six

At some point in the night, a low clicking noise startled Leena into wakefulness. Her groggy mind wondered if it was Taurin returning. She stretched out her hand and encountered a warm, lifelike presence. He was here, lying by her side.

Glancing in his direction, she noticed his eyes were open, glowing luminously. He appeared to be listening. When he realized she was awake, he tapped her arm indicating she should be quiet.

"Someone is attempting to break in," he whispered, obtaining his blaster from the nightstand. "Perhaps we should allow our intruder to kill his mark."

"What do you mean?"

Taurin described his plan. A few minutes later, Leena stood concealed by the side of a tall wooden wardrobe. She waited with a pounding heart and icy fingers as footsteps sounded from the living room. Taurin had taken a post behind the door, his weapon ready. They'd propped pillows on the bed to make them look like bodies—an old trick, but she hoped it would work. And if it didn't, no one would hear her screams for help in this unpopulated wing of the residential complex.

She held her breath as the intruder approached the partially open bedroom door. Leena spied a tall, lean shape framed in the doorway. The man pointed a rod-shaped object at the bed. Before he could discharge his weapon, Taurin smashed the door into his shadowy figure.

The impact slammed the intruder against the wall, where he accidentally hit the light switch. It flicked on to a dim setting.

"You!" Taurin aimed his blaster at Testi.

"Demon!" said the agent from Yllon. He'd dropped his rod and clutched his lower back where the door had hit him. "What they say about you is true."

Taurin's glowing eyes never wavered. "Stand up straight. I want some answers from you."

"Fat chance." Testi drew a hidden blaster and fired at Taurin.

Taurin's weapon crashed to the floor as he stumbled back with a surprised cry. Testi raised his blaster to fire again, but Taurin dodged the sizzling gust, throwing himself into a somersault that landed him at Testi's feet. He yanked his opponent off balance, and the two grappled on the floor. With a howl of rage, Taurin reached for Testi's throat.

"Tell me who the traitor is on this world. Is it Magar, Karayan, or both of them? Talk!"

Testi's face darkened. Hovering behind them, Leena feared the man would choke before uttering a word.

"Taurin, let him speak," she urged.

Taurin's jaw worked as he fought to gain control of his temper.

"You're under a death sentence," the agent croaked. "It is my duty to carry it out."

"You're the one who's going to die," Taurin said, tightening his hands.

"No, Taurin, stop!" Leena tried to push him aside.

As though he were swatting a fly, Taurin shoved her away. "Keep out of this!"

But his motion cost him the advantage. Testi thrust his fingers at Taurin's eyes. Taurin howled at the attack and fell back.

"Drufus Gong will reward me for carrying out his sentence," Testi said. He pounced on Taurin, fastening his wrists and ankles with restraints he'd brought along. When Taurin was sufficiently trussed, Testi sat back on his haunches, satisfied by his work.

Taurin glared at him. "Why bother tying me up? You might as well kill me and be done with it."

“Not yet,” Testi sneered, approaching Leena. “I think I’ll have some fun with your woman first.”

Leena shrieked and tried to run past him, but he grabbed her by the hair and tossed her onto the bed. “Now you can show me what he sees in you.”

Leena scrambled to crawl off the bed, but he seized her arm and forced her onto her back. She stared into the sadistic gleam of his dark, beady eyes.

“Get off me,” she shouted, rage giving her courage.

A glow came from the darkened corner where Taurin struggled against his bonds. “Curse you,” he cried. “I’ll kill you if you hurt her.”

“Go ahead and try.” Testi moved his hands to her shoulders, where he found her nerve centers and pinched hard.

An agony of pain shot through her. She squeezed her eyes shut, biting her lower lip to keep from screaming. He was tormenting Taurin by hurting her. She tried to steel her body against the pain, but Testi’s onslaught was relentless. A cry of anguish escaped her lips. Weakened by the pain shooting down her arms, she didn’t resist when he kneaded her breasts.

Suddenly his weight on her shifted. As her eyes flew open, she glanced at him in astonishment. He sat upright, clutching his temples, his face a mottled shade of red.

“Stop it,” Testi croaked. “The pain… it’s killing me.” He began to drool, and then his eyes rolled up in his head and he toppled over.

Leena sat up and stared at Taurin, whose face had gone white. In another instant she was by his side, unlocking the restraints with a key she’d recovered from their assailant’s pocket.

“I’ve killed him,” Taurin said, his voice filled with self-loathing as he got up to examine Testi’s body. “He’s dead.”

“You? How is that possible? He must have suffered a stroke.” Leena sank onto the bed, her knees wobbly. She trembled with fear and relief and would have sought comfort in her husband’s arms, but the look on his face forbade her.

"I thought of strangling him, and then he died." He gazed at her in horror. "It's true, the curse. I have the power to—"

"To do what? Drive men mad? He was already insane with wanting to kill us. You didn't cause him to feel that way."

"No, I've merely murdered him." Taurin retrieved his blaster from the floor and changed the setting. "This has four levels," he explained in an impassive voice. "Levels one and two are light and heavy stun. They affect the nervous system. Level three is kill mode. And level four… well, see for yourself."

He aimed and fired. As Leena gasped in dismay, Testi's body vaporized into the air.

"Good riddance," Taurin mumbled. He yanked on a robe and stumbled from the room.

Leena stared after him, too stunned to move. But after a moment, she decided his need for support was greater than her shock at his casual disposal of their attacker. Rushing into the living area, she found him seated on a couch, his head held in his hands. A surge of tender emotion overwhelmed her, and she sank down beside him.

"Don't be so harsh on yourself," she said in a soothing tone, putting her arm about his shoulders. "You've shown me nothing but kindness. Perhaps this curse, if it actually exists, pertains only to people who are already aggressive in nature."

Taurin glanced at her, and she winced at the look of despair on his face. "The entire populace on my world was affected by this curse. When the Apostles came, they inspired madness. It is their genes that I carry."

"But I don't understand. How could they have done so much good on my world and then traveled to yours and committed evil?"

Taurin compressed his lips. "Perhaps we should ask Bendyk to perform an annulment in the morning. It would be best if you were rid of me as soon as we recover the horn."

She stroked his cheek. "I won't hear you talk that way. We belong together."

Taurin said nothing. She didn't like the brooding look on his face and hoped he wouldn't take any action on his own that they'd both regret.

Realizing it was useless to comfort him, she returned to bed, shivering despite the warmth of the blankets. The memory of Testi's hands on her body made her flesh crawl, but wishing for Taurin to soothe away her memories was a waste of time. Instead, she turned on her side and considered how to get Taurin to share his secrets.

****

"Did Taurin tell you anything last night?" Bendyk asked Leena while they awaited an audience with Dikran. In the anteroom, he'd taken his sister aside for a private conversation. He and Swill had revealed their betrothal earlier. She and Taurin had offered the couple their heartfelt congratulations.

She shook her head. "He's still hiding something."

"That's not good. It doesn't bode well for a marriage if a man withholds confidences from his wife. I will speak to him."

Before Leena could reply, the doors to the reception chamber opened, and an attendant ushered them in for a private audience with Dikran.

Their leader sat in regal glory on his throne, dwarfed by his voluminous golden robes. A resplendent headdress crowned his thin white hair. It gave him height and dignity, affirming the intelligence in his eyes and commanding respect.

"Report," Dikran ordered without preamble.

Bendyk revealed what he'd learned about Zeroun's role in his mother's death and Karayan's financial status. "As for the plantations in the Black Lands, we discovered the property rights were granted to a corporation called the Amiaus Company."

"The Amiaus Company?" Taurin jabbed a finger in the air. "Isn't that the same group that's supplying construction equipment to the Wodeners?"

Dikran nodded, meeting his gaze with a penetrating one of his own. "Aye, so it is."

"Karayan is a major shareholder in this company," Bendyk added. "That's the link we've needed. It means he might be the one involved with the Ylloners."

"What about Magar?" Leena queried. "I thought he was in charge of offworld relations." She still found it hard to believe her father's friend could be involved in such a devious plot. Karayan had always been so supportive.

"I've been unable to speak to Magar," Taurin cut in. "He's away at a district meeting, but he should be back later. It doesn't matter. I have a plan to coax the thief into the open so we can recover the horn."

"Oh, it's a trap." Swill clapped her hands as though entertained by the idea.

"I may not have given you enough credit," Bendyk told his girlfriend. "It's possible the Synod does wield too much power. Perhaps the people's protests aren't so about much rabble-rousing as a push for human rights."

"Now you're getting it," Swill replied with an approving glance.

"Call a meeting of the Synod for tonight," Taurin told Dikran. "I'll announce that Leena and I have found the horn. We'll say we paid ransom money to get it back from an antiquities collector. Sirvat stole it months ago to please Grotus. She gave it to him in exchange for a fake reproduction. As Renewal approached, Sirvat got nervous and stole the substitute horn in order to avoid detection. Meanwhile, Grotus sold the genuine article to the collector, who in turn ransomed it back to us. Leena has verified the horn is authentic."

Leena snorted. "So the thief will believe he has a fake, and he'll want to exchange it for the real thing. However, Sirvat will be at this meeting. She'll refute your story."

Taurin raised an eyebrow. "She may deny that she stole the horn, but then she'll have to admit her liaison with Grotus.

Leaking information at such a high level of government is a punishable offense." He directed a quizzical gaze at the others. "How do you get rid of unworthy Synod members? Zeroun has overstepped the bounds by collusion in murder, and Karayan is engaged in illegal financial transactions. Both of them should be removed from office."

"I appointed the Synod," Dikran said in a haughty tone. "I have the power to dismiss them from their posts."

"How will you support the claim that we have the sacred horn?" Leena asked Taurin.

"We'll set a new Renewal ceremony to be held four days hence. I'll say I'm going to blow the horn to reset Lothar. As far as I understand, there is no formal training required. Normally the honor is bestowed on the horn blower as a form of special recognition. The ceremony must occur at the Grand Altar for Lothar to respond. I would expect the guilty party to show up before the appointed time. Now, regarding security arrangements, can anyone show me a layout of the Palisades?"

"I can." Dikran withdrew a document from a pocket in his robe. "I thought you might need this."

Taurin spread the diagram across the surface of an ornamental table while the others hovered nearby, including Dikran.

"Here's the Holy Temple." Taurin indicated the pyramid-shaped structure that dominated the complex. "And that's the residential wing. What are these other buildings?"

"This entire structure contains over one thousand rooms," Leena explained. "Most are connected via internal corridors, or walkways through landscaped gardens. This sector here belongs to the Arch Nome. These other areas contain the reception halls, dining commons, chapels and museums."

"Museums?"

"The Palisades Museum contains a priceless collection of statuary, valuable antiquities, and modern religious art. The Archives, which you see over there," she said, pointing, "hold religious documents. And the Library has one of the world's largest collections of early manuscripts."

"How do you prevent thieves from stealing these valuable works?"

"We have our own internal security force," Leena replied. "The Elite Guard is unarmed but well trained in surveillance techniques and self-defense tactics. We've been fortunate not to have had too many incidents."

Taurin's gaze narrowed. "If the traitor in our midst makes his move alone, we'll have little trouble. But if he calls for backup from his Yllon friends, we'll need people who can fight. There's only one place where we can find that level of aid."

"The Caucus?" Bendyk asked. Standing at Swill's side, he had a bewildered look on his face.

"No. There's a singular force on this planet adequately trained to defend against an armed attack."

"You can't mean the Truthsayers," Leena said. "They're planning their own insurgence. Then again, if we could make Stephan Tom realize the truth, he might persuade his followers to join us in fighting the invasion."

Taurin shook his head. "Stephan Tom's people are playing at being soldiers. I meant Grotus's ring of smugglers. He can get here fast using his submersible fleet, plus his men are armed."

"But why would Grotus agree to help us when he wants the horn for himself?"

"The smuggler intends to ransom the horn back to the Synod. He needs the weather restored to normal conditions, same as everyone else. Otherwise his smuggling operations will be jeopardized. Ditto for an invasion force from Yllon. Grotus favors the current power structure because his transgressions are overlooked. But if someone else takes control, that leniency may change."

"Fearn is rapidly approaching," Leena reminded him. "If the horn isn't blown by then, the defensive shield will crumple. Will Grotus get here in time?"

"I believe so, but we must act fast."

"How will you get in touch with him?" Dikran queried. He'd been silent up until then, absorbing their discussion with a rapt look on his lined face.

"We'll tell Sirvat the truth," Leena suggested with a lift of her eyebrows. "Perhaps her sentence can be lightened if she cooperates."

"Agreed," the Arch Nome said, "but let's wait until after we announce the new date for the Renewal ceremony to the Synod. Her response to our accusations will be more credible if she believes herself to be wrongly accused of stealing the horn."

"What excuse do we use in the meantime for the delay?" Leena asked. "Why not just blow the horn at the meeting? Wait, I know! We'll say that I need to restore the horn to its pristine condition as it was damaged during its sojourn."

"Good idea," Taurin said, his warm smile heating her blood.

Distracted by the lights of desire dancing in his eyes, she forced her attention back to their tactical discussion.

"Will the traitor allow me to complete the restoration? This person won't interfere if he wants the weather cycles stabilized, but not if he's working with the offworlders."

Taurin grimaced. "We won't allow you to be alone. Either myself or Bendyk will be with you at all times. We'll post Elite Guards around the grounds, but they won't be an adequate force if the Ylloners attack before Grotus arrives. There has to be something else we can do to tighten security."

"Your Grace," Leena addressed Dikran. "Are there any booby traps inside the Holy Temple, like the ones I've found on other excavations?"

Dikran gave her a startled glance. "I'm afraid not. This temple has been in continuous use since the days of the Apostles."

"Not the entire temple," Leena countered. "Just the central, older portion, right?" At Dikran's nod, she went on. "There's a high probability that traps were laid, but they were never activated. I'd like to take a look around. Now that I know how to read the carvings, perhaps they'll provide a clue to our defenses."

Taurin touched her elbow, providing a flood of warmth up her arm, while his eyes shone with the thrill of the hunt. "We'll set you up in one of the workrooms in the museum. That's where you'll do your supposed restoration, but during quieter hours, you can study the carvings in the Holy Temple."

Since Taurin was utilizing her expertise, maybe now he'd be more willing to include her in his secret talks with Dikran. She smiled at him, acknowledging his regard.

"I can talk to Sirvat," Swill offered, "while you get established in the museum."

"You'll need to emphasize the gravity of our situation to her," Taurin instructed.

"What if Grotus demands a reward in return for his services?" the young woman asked.

"Tell him we found more crystals. That should be enough of an enticement."

And so, they set their plan into motion. Leena prayed that all would turn out as expected.

Chapter Twenty-Seven

At a special meeting convened for the Synod, Taurin revealed that he and Leena had recovered the horn and would be blowing it at a Renewal ceremony four days later.

"Praise be to Lothar!" Zeroun shouted, raising his arms in the air. "We are saved."

"Where is the horn?" Magar piped in, his narrowed blue eyes regarding them. The silver-haired gentleman wore his priestly robes with dignified grace despite his portly figure.

"After its sojourn, the horn truly does need a cleaning," Leena said. "I'm going to work on it over at the museum. There's some minor damage that needs fixing as well."

"Where did you find it?" Zeroun asked.

Taurin set his play into motion. When the accusation about Sirvat's role in the theft was made, the woman turned pale with outrage.

"I didn't steal it," said the red-haired Minister of Finance. "I had nothing to do with the theft."

"You don't deny your liaison with Grotus, do you?" Leena said. "When you speak to him next, express our gratitude for his aid in recovering the horn."

"I'll do no such thing. That lying bastard! He told me he knew nothing about the horn's whereabouts."

Leena smiled inwardly. Sirvat had just admitted her guilt in leaking information to the smuggler. She'd have to cooperate with their plan now.

Swill stayed behind to talk to Sirvat, while Taurin and Leena set off for the museum. Bendyk departed to locate the Elite Guard.

Leena selected an appropriate workroom, which Taurin approved after inspecting the premises. Their preliminary job done, they headed back toward the residential wing. They were passing through the Holy Temple when Taurin stopped.

"I need to consult Dikran about something," he said, his gaze averted. "You go on ahead. I'll catch up to you later."

"Oh no, you don't. I'm coming with you."

Taurin's gaze met hers, his expression unreadable. "You need to concentrate on deciphering those carvings." His sweeping gesture encompassed the nave's ornate interior. "If there are booby traps around here, we need to activate them. Your role is important."

Leena wavered, considering what she should do. Logic told her to start looking for an alternate means of bolstering their security arrangements.

"I'll meet you at our apartment," Taurin said before stalking off in the opposite direction.

Making a hasty decision, Leena followed him at a discreet distance. She ran into Bendyk and Swill, who were rounding a corner ahead of her.

"Where are you going, Sister?" Bendyk gave her an indulgent smile. He held an arm draped around Swill's shoulder.

Leena considered how her brother had mellowed under Swill's influence. His open attitude would make him more approachable to his flock.

"Taurin has headed off by himself again, supposedly to confer with Dikran. I'm following him. I won't let him exclude me anymore."

"We'll join you," Bendyk offered.

The trail led to the Arch Nome's private robing salon. Leena knocked softly on the partially open door. When no one responded, she stepped inside and was surprised to see nobody there. Across the room, an empty gap yawned in a far wall. As she approached, she heard muffled voices from beyond.

"I don't understand why you refuse to tell her," Dikran said in an admonishing tone.

"Leena's religious traditions are very important to her," Taurin explained. "It will destroy all she's ever believed in if she learns the truth. Those rituals give her life meaning. What would she have left if she discovers Lothar is nothing more than a mere machine?"

Leena's breath hitched at his words. She peered down a long staircase. The voices seemed to come from farther below. She leaned forward, listening more acutely.

"Lothar is more than a computer that controls the weather cycles and provides our lozenge against sickness," Dikran replied. "Believing in Lothar is a sign of faith, my son. Maybe Lothar doesn't exist as the image people hold in their minds, but don't you believe a higher intelligence exists somewhere out there?"

Leena could almost picture Dikran gesturing toward the heavens. Lothar, a machine? What were they talking about?

She glanced at Bendyk and Swill, both of whom eavesdropped as shamelessly as she did. They both wore expressions of disbelief mixed with fascination.

"I've read our history in these bibliotomes," Taurin went on. "The Apostles came here from another world because their sun was dying. They hoped to live in peaceful coexistence with the indigenous population on Xan, until they discovered their presence caused problems. Coming from an advanced race, they communicated telepathically. They didn't realize their intense mental energy would adversely affect humanity. The minds of primitive men could not accept the powerful neural stimulation. Continued exposure caused a disruption in the cross-communication of brain hemispheres, producing headaches and mental aberrations in the native inhabitants."

"But the Apostles brought order and civilization to our world," Dikran reminded him.

"True, but they didn't give us an interpretation of Lothar's laws. They created the laws, and that's what is related in the bible next door. When they saw how their influence, although beneficial, physically pained the humans, they decided to leave. Some of them did not wish to travel to the stars. Instead, they journeyed to the next habitable planet, Yllon. There they set up a society with a non-interference rule. They thought perhaps if they did not influence human affairs, as they had done on Xan, the Ylloners would not be similarly afflicted."

"Something must have gone wrong," Dikran surmised.

"Yes, the effect of their presence on Yllon was even worse. The Ylloners, who already possessed a high degree of aggressiveness, went berserk. Eventually they killed off the newcomers, but not before the Apostles had seeded the population to ensure the continuation of their species. They didn't know if their mother ship would make it to the next star system."

Leena glanced at her brother, aghast at what she'd heard. If Taurin was correct, then Lothar was no god. He was simply an invention of the Apostles, an entity created to appeal to the primitive natives. Mechanical devices were responsible for the weather cycles and the lozenges.

She'd begun to suspect something wasn't right when the climactic disasters started, and now her suspicions were confirmed. But then, why was the horn still needed to awaken Lothar? Couldn't the computer be reset in another manner? What was causing the disruption in weather?

Dammit, why hadn't Taurin confided in her?

She marched down the stairs, her fists clenched at her sides. Her brother's heavy breathing from behind told her he was just as outraged. Swill murmured something, no doubt attempting to soothe him.

Down below, an array of strange flashing equipment met her gaze. She'd never seen anything like it, not in all her experience.

"So it is true," she accused Dikran, catching him and Taurin off-guard. "The Synod does control everything. You've been perpetuating the myth about Lothar in order to retain power."

Dikran shuffled forward. "I tried to convince your man that you would accept the truth, child."

Her angry gaze slammed into Taurin's. "You have no faith in me, do you?"

"I didn't want to disillusion you." He spoke soothingly, as if she were a young girl rather than a grown woman whose intelligence deserved respect.

"What does all this mean?" she demanded, glancing around the room. Bendyk and Swill moved to either side of her as though to lend their support.

"It means the Truthsayers are right," Bendyk said. "Lothar only exists in men's minds. Is that correct?" He directed his question to Dikran.

The Arch Nome thrust out his chin. "The concept of Lothar was created to give hope to the people. Believing in a higher intelligence gives them strength to carry on. They need something to believe in."

"But you're not letting us progress," Swill cried. "Don't you see what this falsehood has done? You've stunted our intellectual growth. Do you truly believe this was the Apostles' intent?"

"The Apostles gave our people their laws and helped our civilization to blossom. They tamed the weather and gave us the lozenge to prevent sickness. People should be content to live under Lothar's beneficence."

Taurin spoke, an earnest look on his face. "It might have been their goal to enrich humanity with their seed and thus accelerate the time frame in which we'd reach the stars. Likely, we're all descendants of an earlier progenitor race. In that respect, we may be part of a unity that's greater than all of us combined. A higher form of life, if you follow me. Besides, Lothar is more than a machine. Come with me, and I'll show you what I mean."

He led them into a room with mounds of crystals. Even wearing a set of protective eyeglasses, Leena could detect the brilliance of the pulsating matrix.

"I was able to read the bibliotomes," Taurin said. "I didn't need to decipher the symbols. Once I'd opened the books, the contents were revealed to me through a scrolling telepathic imprint. The Apostles must have been able to activate the crystals with a mere thought. Lothar, if you want to keep the name, is a biomechanical construct that functions through the feedback of positive emotions. Rising discontent on Xan with the ruling Synod is the most likely reason the crystals have been failing."

"My father was right," Leena said, in awe of her parent's perception. "He claimed our duty was to serve Lothar with harmony and love, and now you're saying that Lothar—or this machine—can't function unless there is peaceful coexistence."

Taurin nodded. "Stephan Tom's inclusion in our plans is essential, since the Truthsayers' dissension is the main cause of the malfunction."

"Assuming the horn blowing is still needed to reset Lothar—I mean, the central computer—what happens if our plan fails and we don't recover the real artifact in time?"

"Let me handle that problem. Regardless of how we accomplish the Renewal ceremony, the Synod will have to make concessions. Dikran may accept the need for change, but others will have to be convinced." His gaze hardened. "First, we have to repel the threat from Yllon. If Stephan Tom and the Synod can air their differences, the resultant cooperation may please Lothar. The malfunctioning crystals might reactivate under these circumstances. It's essential to strengthen the defense shield and to stabilize the weather cycles."

Dikran adjusted his robe, which hung loosely over his thin frame. "I fear these matters are far beyond the ken of an old man. Perhaps the time has come for me to pass the torch."

"Please don't say that, Your Grace," Leena protested. "Your knowledge and wisdom are needed now more than ever."

"After we get rid of the vipers in our midst, a new government will have to be formed," Dikran mused. He glanced at each one of them in turn. "I have in mind certain replacements. It's time for some fresh, young blood in the upper echelons. If I do retain my position, I'll need trustworthy advisors. Your father will be one of them," he promised Leena.

"Father will be gratified to have your redemption," she told him in a humble tone, feeling grateful that her goals in joining the Caucus were finally being met. It made her continuation in the aide corps almost an afterthought.

She supposed she'd have to serve her time, something she'd totally forgotten about in her involvement with the missing horn. Her museum job was waiting for her. She'd regarded her appointment to the Caucus merely as a sabbatical. She realized now for certain that her true calling was in archaeology.

As the others conversed, her thoughts drifted to their earlier discussion. It seemed inconceivable that the god she'd believed in all her life was nothing more than a collection of... what? Machinery?

Her people had no knowledge of such technology. Apparently it was even beyond the advanced Ylloners' capabilities. If the Apostles had left them a legacy through bibliotomes, truly their peoples had much to learn now that Taurin knew how to access the ancient writings.

"How did you unseal the holy books?" she asked him.

He gave her a wry grin. "I spun my rings in the depression on each cover."

"Those rings have a lot of uses." She warmed to his responsive grin. Nonetheless, she wouldn't forgive him so easily. Many issues still separated them, but she'd deal with it later.

Dikran addressed Bendyk. "You'd better prepare your evidence against the guilty members of the Synod."

"You mean Zeroun and Sirvat," Leena's brother replied.

"Don't forget Karayan," she said. "He's involved in illegal business transactions. And we still don't know Magar's part in all of this."

"We should wait and see who shows up at Leena's workroom," Taurin suggested.

They stayed to discuss the security protocols and then split up in different directions.

The trap was laid. Now they only had to bide their time until someone fell into it.

****

Back at their apartment, Leena prepared for bed. As she brushed out her long waves of blond hair in front of the dressing table mirror, she searched her soul for her feelings regarding Taurin. Even though she'd finally learned his secrets, she felt betrayed by his lack of trust in her.

Maybe Lothar wasn't a supernatural being, but the traditions of her people still had meaning. The rituals served an agricultural society, with celebrations of the harvest and other significant events. As for her prayers, she would pray now to a higher intelligence. Lothar might be a tool supplied by the Apostles, but the natural beauty of her world could only have been created by an entity beyond their range of understanding.

Now that she knew life existed beyond the stars, a greater joy enveloped her, and her faith swelled with gratitude to this Creator.

Her philosophical musings carried her through the rest of her nightly preparations. She was applying a lotion to her hands when Taurin's footfalls sounded from behind.

"I can do that for you," he said in a seductive tone.

Seated at her dressing table, Leena glanced back at him, unable to contain her joy at his presence. She tried to calm her rapidly beating heart, telling herself she should be angry with him. It was impossible when he took the tube of cream and began smoothing a palmful across her bared neck.

She closed her eyes, enjoying his gentle massage, until a rising coil of desire made her spring from her seat.

Turning, she wrapped her arms around his neck, drawing his head down for a kiss. "I love you, Taurin," she murmured against his mouth.

Despite his lack of faith in her, she couldn't help her surge of affection toward him. She knew he regarded himself as her protector, but did that mean guarding her from life's disappointments as well as its physical foes? He didn't give her enough credit, although at the moment she felt the total satisfaction of a woman being cherished by her man.

Letting her hands roam the broad planes of his back, she gave herself in to the deep yearning she felt for intimacy. Evil forces may stalk her world, but this man could protect her people.

Taurin was the keeper of the rings. His bracelets were the keys to the storehouses of knowledge contained within the bibliotomes.

But none of that mattered now. The outside world disappeared as she yielded to his tender touch. Everywhere his fingertips met her flesh, her skin seared with heat. As his mouth claimed hers, she writhed against him, wanting to join with him, to be united as husband and wife.

"You're mine," he said in a husky voice, showering her face with kisses.

He led her to the bed and watched as she removed her flimsy nightdress, his gaze devouring her. With a cry of impatience, he tugged off his briefs. Then they lay naked, side by side facing each other. He caressed her skin, searching for her secret places until she clutched at him, moaning for him to complete her satisfaction.

Moving atop her, his passion surged. With a mighty thrust he slid inside her, filling her so completely that she cried out with pleasure. If only they could stay like this, attached to each other, with all the cares of the world gone from their minds. Rational thought escaped her as Taurin tempted her to match his rhythmic movements.

When his hands found her breasts, she whispered his name. A sheen of sweat covered her body as she arched under him, tension spiraling through her body. She soared to the heights of ecstasy and shuddered against him. His explosive response spilled within her and caused her to gasp with joy.

Life could never be more complete than this.

****

On the last day before the reinstated Renewal ceremony, a knock sounded at the door to the museum workroom. Leena sat reading a text while Taurin paced restlessly. He'd been hoping someone would show up to claim the horn, and his heart quickened as he responded to the summons.

"Who is it?" he called, aware the Elite Guards had not yet deployed their defenses.

"It's Magar. I've come for a chat."

Taurin's heart sank as he threw open the portal. Magar's visit was a strong indicator he was the thief who had stolen the horn. No doubt he'd come to get a look at the supposedly authentic artifact that Leena was restoring.

The Minister of State ambled inside. His friendly smile was like a knife twisting in Taurin's gut. Like Baker Mylock, Magar had been a role model whom Taurin could admire and respect. Now he tasted the bitter taint of betrayal.

"I regret not having seen you more often lately," Magar said, his voice tremulous as he glanced around the utilitarian work space.

"I suppose you have come to view the horn," Taurin remarked, folding his arms and leaning against a counter.

Magar appeared surprised by his suggestion. "Why, the idea hadn't crossed my mind. I'll admit I was looking forward to hearing it blown at Renewal, but I understand Leena is repairing the relic." The minister glanced at her. She sat frowning at the book in her lap. Obviously, she wasn't at work restoring an artifact.

"If you're not here for the horn, then why did you come?" Taurin demanded. Maybe he'd been wrong about Magar's aims.

Magar plucked at his robe. "I could tell from the way you looked at me during our last meeting that you knew. Did you inform Dikran?"

Taurin stared at him. "What are you talking about?"

"Why, my problem, of course." Magar's troubled gaze met his protégé's eyes.

"I have no idea what you mean, sir. What problem?" For the first time, Taurin noted Magar's strange pallor and fine tremors. What was wrong with him?

"I have the Agus," Magar confessed, in a tone so low Taurin had to strain to hear him.

"What? The Agus!" The genetic disease had no cure. In one's later years, it produced tremors, progressive debilitation, and eventually, death. Was this the reason Magar had been avoiding him? "Have you been to a clinic for a solid diagnosis?"

Magar nodded mutely, and Taurin read fear in his eyes.

Striding forward, he grasped Magar by the arms. "I will help you. Whatever I can do."

"There is nothing. I thought you already knew, but now I see I was mistaken. You realize what this means when word gets out, don't you?"

"Medications can help. It doesn't mean you'll have to resign your post." *Especially not now, when there are so few people we can trust.*

Shame swept him like a tidal wave. To think he'd suspected Magar of complicity in the horn's theft. How could he have been so faithless?

"We could use your advice," Leena said. She rose from her seat to face the older man. "Drufus Gong must know Taurin is here by now. He could be in danger from Yllon's agents. There's a death sentence on his head."

She recapped their adventures for Magar's benefit. During her recital, the Minister of State gazed at her with a shocked expression.

"I will aid you in any way I can to catch those felons," Magar said in a firm tone. His eyes gleamed with renewed strength as he squared his shoulders like the proud man Taurin remembered. "Your security arrangements should be put into effect immediately. I'll keep my ears open. Count on my warning if I see any Ylloners around."

"It's best if you pretend ignorance around the other Synod

members," Taurin cautioned him. "Karayan hasn't come forward yet. He's the most logical culprit, but he may be too smart to fall for our ruse."

Leena shook her head. "I still can't believe he could be so deceitful, and yet it all fits—his extensive art collection, his ornate mansion, his ambitious nature. Didn't Dikran say it had been Karayan's idea to summon agents from Yllon to deal with Lothar's malfunction?"

"We should make an announcement that your work is complete," Taurin replied. "That might draw him out."

"He may be waiting for reinforcements from his Yllon friends. You'll be their main target," she told him, anxiety reflected in her tone.

"I'm more concerned about your safety," he retorted.

Putting her hands on her hips, Leena glared at him. "First you wouldn't tell me anything because you didn't trust me, and now you think I can't protect myself. When are you going to realize I'm not one of your delicate flowers?"

"You're accustomed to a peaceful way of life. You have no concept of the violence these people are capable of enacting."

"Yes, I do. That's why I'm worried about you. If you'd stop treating me as though I have a brain the size of a *tupa*, then you'd realize I've dealt pretty well with our situation so far. I resent your patronizing attitude."

"My job is to keep you from harm, or did you forget why you came to see me at Magar's bequest?"

At the mention of his name, the Minister of State gave an embarrassed cough. "Children, this isn't the time to—"

Leena ignored him and continued her tirade. "You've tried to protect me from everything, including challenges to my faith. You thought I couldn't handle even the slightest test of my beliefs. Let me tell you that your findings have not only confirmed my faith in Lothar, but now I know he's more than a god who maintains our planet. So what if a machine is responsible for controlling the weather cycles and producing the lozenge? Somewhere out there"—she gestured toward the heavens—"the Great Creator exists. That is Lothar's true nature."

Taurin wasn't in the mood for a philosophical discussion, but deep down inside, he agreed with her. It wasn't Lothar she believed in now as much as the concept of a higher intelligence.

As a woman, she wanted to be admired and appreciated for her skills. Instead, he'd put her on a pedestal as a symbol of purity. Perhaps it was time to respect her as an equal. But first, a show of trust was called for in order to demonstrate his good intentions.

"I should check on Bendyk's progress with the Elite Guards. Come on, Magar, I'll escort you back to the administrative wing. Will you be all right by yourself?" he asked Leena, fully intending to be within calling distance once he'd finished talking privately with his mentor.

"Don't worry. I'll be fine," she announced, stepping toward the workbench.

Taurin hoped he wasn't making a mistake by leaving Leena to her own resources, but it was the only way to win back her regard.

Chapter Twenty-Eight

Leena decided to focus her attention on the carvings in the Holy Temple. She'd located a couple of booby traps, but there had to be more.

She'd gathered a few tools to take with her when a commotion sounded outside the door. Thinking it must be Taurin returning, she didn't pay any attention when the door crashed open.

Glancing up, Leena gasped. Karayan's tall figure stood in the doorway. There was no sign of the Elite Guards or anyone else outside the room.

The Minister of Justice was groomed impeccably as usual, from his styled brown hair to his tailored navy frock coat and matching trousers. He strode into the room with an easy smile on his face.

"Leena, my dear, how go the repairs?"

"Very well," she said with a bravado she didn't feel.

Karayan sauntered closer, his grin widening. "May I see the horn? Have you finished restoring it to its prime condition?"

"Oh, yes." She eyed the leather briefcase he carried. It bulged strangely, as though there were an object inside with an irregular shape. "What have you in there?" she asked, keeping her tone neutral.

Karayan stopped in front of her. "I'll show you after I see the horn." His gaze swept from the empty work counter to her book on the chair. "I don't see the artifact. Where is it?" His tone had lost any hint of friendliness. His cold gray eyes assessed her.

If that briefcase held the real horn, she had to get it from him. "You've brought the counterfeit one, haven't you?"

Karayan withdrew a cloth-covered object from his satchel. He removed the cover, exposing the sacred horn. Leena's heart leapt with joy, but she erased all emotion from her face.

"Why did you do it, Karayan?"

He put the horn back in the sack, tightened the loop, and slung the bag over his shoulder. "This government is run by a bunch of old fools who are out of touch with the world. They're letting the insurgents get the upper hand. We need a strong leader who can rule with an iron fist."

"Like you, I suppose." She edged closer to the workbench to grab a tool in case she needed one for self-defense.

Karayan's eyes glittered. "With the Ylloners by my side, I'll face little defiance. Our friends can offer us technology beyond our dreams. We have the agricultural resources that they need. An open exchange of trade between our worlds would benefit us both. I merely intend to lead our people into a new age of enlightenment."

"So you stole the horn, knowing our defensive shield would fail by Fearn?" If she could keep him talking, Taurin might return. Leena backed up against the counter and held her position. The minister stood between her and the door.

"Once the takeover is complete, and I'm declared the new Arch Nome, I will blow the horn to restore Lothar to his former status. This will take place only after I am put in power."

"But you're already a member of the Synod."

"That's not enough. Our civilization must be brought back on the right track. Technology has to advance. The Synod is too smug. I am the catalyst for change!"

"You're using the Truthsayers. Do you intend to squash them once you've achieved your goals, or do they share the same ideals as you?"

"They're a bunch of idiots who will follow anyone with charisma. Once my order is established, they'll obey my dictates or perish."

"You've profited from the status quo," she pointed out. "You get money from the Chocola Company for their rights to the plantations in the Black Lands."

He gave her a sardonic grin. "Once I'm in power, I won't have to worry about income anymore."

Leena bit her lower lip. She couldn't keep him talking forever. Wasn't anyone going to show up to help her? Why hadn't Taurin returned by now?

Karayan read the expression on her face and smiled. "You've stalled long enough, Leena. Where are you hiding the horn?"

She stiffened, remaining silent.

Karayan withdrew a wicked-looking blade from an inner pocket of his frock coat. "Don't force me to use this," he said, approaching her. "Your face is too pretty to ruin. Tell me what I want to know."

"It's not here. I'll take you to it," she offered, hoping to elude him along the way. The only problem was getting hold of the horn in that sack.

"If you're lying to me, I will kill you. Now move." Karayan gestured toward the door.

Outside the small workroom, she searched for Taurin, but he was nowhere in sight. Praying that she'd meet someone along the way to whom she could appeal for aid, she led Karayan through the maze of museum corridors and outside to the cloister with vaulted archways and stately columns.

They crossed a courtyard and passed through the western entrance to the Holy Temple. Unlike other times when she'd enjoyed the beauty of the Chapel of Pyr on her right, she ignored the stained glass windows and woven tapestries.

Beyond a chantry adorned with fifteenth century sculptures, they climbed a set of steps to the next level where they walked among other chapels and vaults. The eerie silence made her tiny hairs stand on end.

What if Karayan's allies from Yllon were already here?

They could have subdued the guards throughout the Palisades complex. That would explain the absence of any security forces. She had to warn the others, but how?

Karayan caught her arm. "Don't make a sound." The point of his blade pinched her back as he emphasized his warning.

The Holy Temple was devoid of worshippers. He'd chosen a good time of day to make his move. It was evenlight, when most people were home preparing supper and making plans for the day ahead. The populace would have cleared out by now, and the administrative offices were closed.

She was alone, with only her own wits to save her.

****

Staying in the shadows, Taurin glided silently after Leena and Karayan. He'd purposefully kept away from her workroom, intending to give the thief who had stolen the horn an opportunity to confront her. It had worked, but now he had to devise a way to get her to safety.

She appeared to be winding in circles in the Holy Temple, and it wouldn't take long for Karayan to figure this out. Then Taurin would have to make his move without any backup. Karayan wouldn't be a problem, but Taurin puzzled over what had happened to the guards. He feared Karayan's forces had arrived before Grotus's people.

Dikran was unavailable, being closeted with Stephan Tom, who'd arrived earlier that day. If the Truthsayer leader would listen to reason, maybe they could yet convince him this plot was real. Unfortunately, he couldn't count on Stephan Tom's supporters for assistance in the immediate future.

The silence of the Holy Temple unnerved him, like the calm before a storm. He followed his quarry with stealthy movements, biding his time until it was safe to act. Leena appeared to know what she was doing. He'd let her play her hand unless Karayan became too threatening.

A surge of rage filled his veins as he watched her being forced ahead at knifepoint. Her crimson gown made a splash of color against the gold-painted cherubs and religious ornaments adorning the temple. Her hair, hanging free down her back, cascaded like a thick curtain of golden silk. The thought of Karayan harming her made his throat constrict. His mind reached out to touch the thieving bastard... *No, stop!*

With a jolt of awareness, Taurin realized what he had almost done. After what happened to Testi, and from what he'd recently read in the bibliotomes, he understood that he must possess some of the Apostles' telepathic powers. This was the true demon's curse if he attempted to use it for evil. And if he committed another bad deed, wouldn't he be as drenched in sin as his fellow Ylloners? Wouldn't it tempt him into using his power again, until he couldn't distinguish right from wrong?

He must not abuse his heritage in this manner. The Apostles had inadvertently caused pain through their use of telepathy. For him to purposefully do so would be a grievous wrong. He must forbid himself to ever use his ability again.

Squelching any thoughts of mentally assaulting Karayan, he focused his attention on Leena. What plan did she have in mind?

****

In the Inner Sanctum, Leena approached the Grand Altar with trepidation. The awesome splendor of the hall challenged her to defile its sanctity. Karayan followed on her heels, his blade pricking her spine as he urged her forward.

Dim rays from the waning afternoon sunlight penetrated through the stained glass windows. Down a side aisle, a shadowy movement caught her attention. She glanced over there but saw no one.

Her heart thumping, she strode ahead and climbed to the dais, where the initiates had been honored during their acceptance into the Caucus.

The Caucus! Where were her fellow aides? They were supposed to be helping catch the thief, and yet she hadn't spied any of them. Her skin crawled as she observed the silence around her.

Fortifying herself with a deep breath, she faced the colorful frieze above the altar that represented scenes from the Apostles' lives. She stood on an engraved pavement made of porphyry and marble. Across the rear wall, statues of the Apostles lined up in a row, divided by the holy closet itself.

"I've put the horn back inside its resting place," she said, pointing to the closed wooden doors embellished with intricate carvings.

"Open it," Karayan ordered, pressing his knife a bit deeper.

Leena approached the sacred doors, feeling as though she were committing a sacrilege just by stepping near the holy closet. To open the hallowed doors without it being the appointed time of year was a horrendous sin. The Apostles had known this, and one of the traps was located here.

When she'd been making her rounds, inspecting the carvings, she had dared come to this holy place and peruse the carvings on the wooden doors. She'd noted a depression in a recess by the wall and had spun in it one of the rings Taurin had given her. This motion had activated the booby trap. Now the trick was to get Karayan to open the doors.

"I will not commit such a sinful act. You will have to take the lead," she told him, raising her chin defiantly.

"Hold this."

Karayan thrust the sack at her, apparently unconcerned that she might take off with the fake horn inside. As far as he knew, the authentic relic was inside the holy closet.

His eyes gleaming with the lust for power, he approached the carved wooden doors. Leena carefully backed away. She had no idea of the nature of the trap. It was enough for her to discern its existence.

Just as Karayan reached out to open the doors, he hesitated.

Narrowing his eyes, he glanced at her with suspicion. "Come here. You should do it."

"No, I won't."

Karayan took a menacing step in her direction.

"Run, Leena!" Taurin's voice sounded from behind. "I'll take care of him."

"Wait," she called, spinning around. "You don't understand."

But it was too late. Karayan tossed his blade through the air in Taurin's direction. Taurin dodged the missile and stumbled while Karayan lunged at Leena.

"Bitch! You tricked me."

She cried out as Karayan caught hold of her arm and jerked her backward. The sack she held in her hand fell to the floor. Both she and Karayan flung themselves after it.

"Now," Karayan screamed. "Get them now!"

A troop of men burst from the recesses. They were armed with blasters and rod-shaped objects similar to the one Testi had been carrying. They all wore black, as though that were the uniform of Yllon.

Karayan grabbed the sack containing the horn while Leena slowly straightened. Taurin hastened to her side, his shoulders hunched as Karayan's allies surrounded them.

"Damn you, Taurin," Leena said to him in an undertone. "I nearly had him. The holy closet houses a trap."

He cast her a startled look but didn't respond. Karayan, who had been issuing orders to his men, turned his attention to them. Triumphantly he held up his prize.

"Now I understand what you two were trying to pull off. I had the authentic horn after all. Good try, Leena. You'll both be confined with the others."

"What others?" Her voice came out as a dry croak.

"Dikran and your brother. The Caucus and Synod members. The Elite Guard. They're all being held in the crypt. You'll join them."

"What do you intend to do?" Taurin demanded, his posture tense.

"The invasion will happen in a few days. The takeover should be swift, once Yllon's ships arrive. After I'm proclaimed Arch Nome, I'll decide your fate. Perhaps I will banish you to the Black Lands." Karayan threw back his head and chortled like a madman.

Leena stared at him, wondering how she had ever considered him a friend. The man was crazed with the lust for power.

"It won't work," Taurin told her as an armed escort led them away. "If he blows the horn after the takeover, the crystals will continue to fail. He won't be able to restore the weather patterns to normalcy."

"So what?" Leena said as they passed the choir stalls. "Once Yllon invades, everything will be lost."

At the north transept, they were forced down a narrow spiral staircase toward the crypt below. Leena and Taurin were dismayed to find there the other members of the Synod, the Caucus, and most of the palace guards.

"Bendyk!" Leena rushed into his embrace. "Where's Swill?"

"With Sirvat. They went to meet Grotus."

"Karayan has the horn," she said bitterly as Dikran and Stephan Tom approached.

The Truthsayer looked her in the eye. "I'm sorry I didn't listen to you earlier. Your story was true. This fine gentleman is your brother, is he not?" He put an arm around Bendyk's shoulder in a brotherly fashion. "He and I have been having quite an interesting discussion."

Bendyk's face broadened into a grin. "It appears we have a lot to learn from each other."

She glanced at Dikran, hovering in the background. The Arch Nome didn't appear to be distressed by recent events.

"Aren't any of you worried about what's going to happen to us?" she asked, puzzled by their calm demeanor. They couldn't rely on Grotus. Karayan's men might intercept him.

Bendyk grinned. "We're not really trapped down here, Sister. There's an entrance to the lower level."

"Where is it?" Taurin asked with a glance at the armed Ylloners retreating up the spiral staircase. The captives were to be locked in from above.

Bendyk leaned inward. "Let's keep this amongst ourselves. If Sirvat and Swill are meeting Grotus, we've got to warn them that Karayan's allies have taken the Palisades. Dikran made an announcement that the complex would be closed to the public until after Renewal. We don't have to worry about innocent citizens being hurt until things are straightened out."

"We'd better hurry," Taurin advised. "Karayan might decide to do away with us all."

Leena tugged on his arm and steered him aside. "What about you? Even if the rest of us are spared, you're under a death sentence from Yllon."

His jaw tightened. "Don't worry about me. Let's go."

"Where are you heading?" a familiar voice called from behind.

Taurin spun to regard Magar. The silver-haired Minister of State held out his hands in the customary greeting. Taurin grasped them firmly, an affectionate look on his face.

"There's a way out of here. We're going to get help. You stay with the others and reassure them that a rescue plan is in the works."

"I'll do my best, son. May Lothar guide you." Magar released his grip and stepped back.

Taurin signaled to Leena. "Come on. I see your brother has already left." Bendyk had disappeared from sight along with Stephan Tom and Dikran.

As they passed through the interconnecting chambers of the lower level, Leena was dismayed to note how many more of the crystals appeared lifeless. At this rate, they'd all blink out by Fearn if harmony wasn't restored to her world.

When this was over, assuming they defeated Karayan and

returned the horn to its proper place, should the Synod restore the people's faith in Lothar? That path would certainly cause less disruption than telling the truth, as proposed by Stephan Tom. She didn't envy Dikran having to make the choice.

If it were her decision, what would she do? Was it better for everyone to believe that Lothar's beneficence provided for them? Or should they know their fate was subject to a network of circuitry and their own peace of mind?

A weight of sadness settled over her as she recalled the traditions that had made her life meaningful. Whom would everyone worship if Lothar was revealed to be a mere machine?

The answer sprang into her mind. The carvings she'd been studying didn't apply to Lothar, a false creation of the Apostles. Initially, the Apostles believed they would be remaining on Xan. The inscriptions spoke of their own faith, a belief in a higher intelligence, an ideology she shared.

Enlightenment brightened her mind in a brilliant flash. Dear deity, the answers had been right in front of her all this time. She'd just never understood them until now.

She glanced at Taurin, who'd caught up to her brother and was speaking to him in low tones. Somehow she knew he'd share this new faith. He hadn't realized his destiny was in the stars, as well as inside his own heart.

Overlapping the vast reaches of space and the inner depths of the human soul, the threads of life encompassed all living beings. The changes about to occur could even be part of a divine plan that mapped their evolution as a race.

As they approached the exit that led upstairs to Dikran's robing salon, the Arch Nome announced his intention to remain behind.

"I need to ponder upon our future," he said. "I'll leave the heroics to you young people."

"Where is Swill meeting Grotus?" Leena asked Bendyk, her voice hoarse. They'd reentered the main level and didn't see any Ylloners in sight.

"By the east gate of the Palisades."

"Then we need to go this way." Having spent several weeks in training for the Caucus, she was more familiar with the grounds than her brother or Taurin. "Follow me."

Leena's heavy velvet gown kept her warm as they exited the building complex and entered the cloisters. Dusk had fallen, and the evening air had chilled. She turned down a garden path crossing the north entrance to the archives. The pungent smell of wood smoke permeated the air.

They approached the east gate, a massive wrought-iron structure set into the wall that surrounded the Palisades. Voices sounded up ahead, and she saw a blur of movement.

Swill stepped out of the shadows.

"My love." Bendyk swept her into his arms and pressed his mouth to hers in a frantic kiss.

"Save it for later," Leena said, relieved that Swill was safe. "Has Grotus arrived with his people?"

"I'm right here, my dear." The smuggler's loud voice made her jump.

Pivoting, she stared into the gleaming eyes of her former adversary. He'd toned down his manner of dress. Instead of his usual flamboyant longshirt, he wore a military-style belted jacket and pants with enough armaments hanging off his belt to take out a squadron of opponents.

Taurin strode up to him, holding out his hands in greeting. After a moment's hesitation, Grotus returned the gesture.

"Thank you for coming," Taurin said with a slight bow.

Grotus inclined his head in acknowledgement. "In this case, your fight is my fight." He turned to his men, who regrouped behind him. "Prepare for assault. Who is the traitor?" he asked Taurin.

"It's Karayan. He's sequestered the members of the Synod and other personnel in a crypt beneath the complex. Karayan has the horn, and he also has the following of Yllon's agents."

"The rest of my troops are taking positions at the other gates.

At my signal, we'll rush the complex, but I need to know where Karayan is stationed."

Leena spoke up. "I would guess he's moving up his timetable. That means he'll need to use the control panel to lower the defense perimeter."

"Magar will know where it's located," Taurin said. "Demon's blood! He can operate the controls. Karayan will force him to turn off the shield."

He turned and ran off into the night before anyone could stop him. Terror pounded in Leena's heart. She gestured for Grotus to follow. "Hurry! If we lose the protective barrier, we're doomed. The invasion will follow."

Grotus mobilized his men, and they all charged down the floodlit path after Taurin.

Chapter Twenty-Nine

Grotus's men engaged the Yllon agents almost immediately. The Ylloners were guarding the various entrances to the Palisades structures. Taurin had veered toward the east ambulatory, presumably because that route would take him into the Chapel of the Benedines, where he could easily access the Arch Nome's robing salon and the lower level.

But if Karayan had gone after Magar, he would have headed through the crypt. Hoping to cut him off, Leena entered the Holy Temple through a different entrance.

As she passed a stone effigy of Avus, the third Arch Nome, loud voices reached her from the Inner Sanctum. She crossed the nave, hurried past the choir stalls, and halted by the screen shielding access to the organ loft.

"You'll lower the defense perimeter *now*," Karayan shouted. A loud slap resounded, the sound of a hand hitting flesh.

"I will do nothing," Magar's tremulous voice cried. "Kill me. I refuse to leave our world defenseless."

"Foolish old man. I know it has something to do with playing this organ. What is the correct sequence of notes?"

Collapsing against a wall, Leena gasped. Seven notes, seven symbols. Could the secret Karayan sought be the same repetitive string she'd encountered elsewhere?

"Why don't you try blowing the horn?" Magar sneered. "See if that opens the defense shield for you."

"Do you take me for an idiot? The horn must be blown at the Grand Altar, or it doesn't work. Besides, blowing the horn would strengthen the shield. You're trying to trick me."

Leena heard Magar give a low chuckle. "Maybe you don't really have the true horn in your possession."

"Of course, I do." A rustling noise sounded, as though Karayan withdrew the relic from its sack. "See? Here it is."

"Give it to me."

A scuffle ensued, followed by thuds and grunts. Holy waters, the two men were fighting. Magar was no match for Karayan.

Leena rushed upstairs. The horn lay on the ground. She dove for it, slithering along the cold marble floor until her outstretched hand grasped the sacred object. With a cry of triumph, she leapt to her feet, but she was too late to save Magar. Karayan hovered over the older man's limp form.

"You!" Karayan said upon spotting her. He lunged in her direction.

With a shriek, she ran and tripped over a protuberance on the floor. As she tottered off balance, the horn slid from her grasp.

Karayan halted, a look of indecision on his face, as if he didn't know whether to attack her or retrieve the horn. With an angry snarl, he pounced on her, grabbing her by the sleeve and hauling her to within a hairsbreadth of his fierce face.

"You know how to lower the defense shield, don't you?" Karayan said with a snarl.

"I have no idea."

"You understand the symbols. Make it work." He shook her violently until her teeth rattled, then shoved her at the organ keys. She crashed against the instrument's hard edge. Her hip flared with pain.

"She doesn't know how to play the instrument as well as I do," a gruff male voice said from the entranceway.

Grotus sauntered into the room, stooping to retrieve the dropped horn. "It's mine at last," he said, his eyes gleaming with avarice.

"Give me that," Karayan ordered.

Grotus's complexion darkened. "You've done enough

damage. It's time you reaped the consequences. Leena, move aside."

As Grotus advanced, she scurried over to Magar to feel for a pulse. Relief swamped her. His beat was rapid and thready, but he'd live. As she straightened, she noted that her escape route had been cut off. What could she do to help Grotus?

The smuggler clutched the horn, unwilling to let it go even in the midst of a deadly struggle against his opponent. The smell of sweat filled the air as the two men battled each other amid a flurry of punches and kicks.

"Leena," Taurin called from far away.

"I'm here," she hollered. "In the organ loft."

Her gaze centered on the enormous musical instrument. What would happen if she played the sequence of seven notes? Would it reset Lothar, or might the action open another window in the defense shield? If only she knew, she'd be able to influence the course of events in their favor. Hesitating, she watched the frenzied fight.

As physical opponents, Grotus and Karayan were about evenly matched. Karayan might be older, but madness gave him energy. Grotus's propensity for fine foods acted against him, even though his physique was more muscular. Perspiration trickled down his wide forehead, his nose ring quivering as he combated Karayan's determined assault.

"Leena, take the horn." Grotus threw it in her direction.

She caught the sacred artifact before it hit the floor. Standing in a corner, she inspected it for damage. The creamy translucent surface was thankfully unmarred.

"Aargh!" Grotus's face turned an ugly shade of purple as his opponent's knife found its mark. His expression registered shock at the blade lodged in his chest. As Leena watched in horror, the smuggler slid to the floor.

"No!" she cried as Karayan turned in her direction, an evil grin on his face.

"Hand over the horn, Leena, and I'll spare you."

"You'll have to take it from me."

He pulled a blaster from a holster inside his frock coat and aimed it at her. "I won't hesitate to use this. Do as I say."

"Fine. Catch it." She tossed the horn at him.

Startled, Karayan let loose a wild shot. It sizzled through the air in a bolt of red laser fire. One instant the horn was airborne. In the next, it had been vaporized, caught in the stream of fire.

"Dear deity! The horn. You've destroyed it." Leena stared at the empty air in disbelief.

Karayan approached her with a murderous look, his blaster aimed at her chest. "You made me lose it. You'll pay for your interference."

Behind them, footsteps thundered up the stairs. Taurin threw himself at Karayan's legs, jerking them out from beneath him.

Karayan dropped his weapon and tumbled to the floor. Recovering quickly, he rolled to his side and leapt to his feet. He hesitated while a mixture of emotions crossed his face.

He must have realized Taurin was an adversary who could prove a challenge, because he threw Leena a regretful glance before charging down the stairs toward the north transept.

Taurin dashed after him.

"Wait!" Leena yelled, but he failed to hear her.

They had more important things to do. The horn had been destroyed. How would they reset Lothar in time for Fearn? Now they had nothing to stop the Ylloners from their attack.

Since Taurin had vanished in Karayan's wake, she turned to Magar, who was stirring on the ground. She assisted him to a sitting position. The sounds of battle reached her ears. It was a sacrilege to fight in the Holy Temple. But then again, who cared? Lothar didn't exist. This place was holy to no one except the Apostles who had established it.

Their purpose came to mind, and faith filled her with renewed hope. Her own faith wasn't lost. It had just been misguided, and so it would be with her people.

Her gaze fell upon a familiar symbol carved into a column

beside her. It was the diamond shape with an antler rising out of its upper left corner. Of course, why had she never realized what it meant before? Now she finally understood.

A ruckus from below caught her attention. Someone stumbled up the stairs, and her heart leapt with joy when she saw it was Taurin, disheveled and weary. With a cry of relief, she rushed into his arms. He held onto her tightly, as if she were his haven of peace.

"Karayan escaped, along with the agents from Yllon," Taurin said, releasing her.

"That's too bad. I suppose he'll seek refuge among them until their invasion force arrives. At least he won't pose a direct threat to us here any longer."

"You're right, and neither will anyone else when I tell you what I've figured out."

****

Leena learned what he meant when Dikran convened an emergency council meeting two days later, after the remaining men in Grotus's party finished the cleanup. They'd left by now, and Dikran presided over the assembly held in the Inner Sanctum.

All of the Candors were present, along with the Caucus, certain members of the Synod, and Stephan Tom. They sat facing the Grand Altar, where Leena stood to address them.

She wore her hair loose, aware that the dark blue of her veil contrasted sharply with her golden hair. The circlet crowning her was a source of pride. Her marriage had been formally announced, and she'd happily accepted her friends' congratulations. Now she only needed to fulfill certain obligations before she and Taurin could be alone. She smiled at him, where he lounged casually in the front row.

"The diamond sign represents the Cadega constellation," she said to the assembly. "That branch in the upper left-hand corner depicts a star system, and I believe its offshoot indicates the second habitable planet orbiting the sun. According to the inscriptions left to us by the Apostles, I believe this is where they headed when they departed Xan." Her voice shook with fervor. "If we ever achieve the means to travel beyond our star system, we could visit their descendants."

Dikran gave a tired shrug. "What good does this knowledge do us now, child? The horn has been destroyed. We have no means of resetting Lothar."

He'd revealed the truth to the Candors, and they had agreed to call the computer device Lothar. It would be more acceptable to the people that way. Besides, there was a higher faith to worship now, since Leena had shared her beliefs.

Silence fell heavily in the great hall. No one wanted to acknowledge their defeat, but Fearn was nearly upon them and there was no horn to blow.

"Do not despair," Taurin said. He rose and lumbered toward Leena. "I should let you do the honors, *angella*. It was your faith in me that got me through all this." He slipped his armband off his muscled limb.

Leena stared into the amused light in his eyes. "What are you talking about?"

"That receptacle in the recess beside the holy closet… it doesn't set a trap. You must have misinterpreted the symbols. I suspect the horn, when it was blown, contained inside it a set of rings similar to these, but smaller."

He took apart his bracelet, showing the viewers what he meant. "The air sent the rings spinning inside the horn where they rubbed against protruding nubs. This action produced a musical tone. Watch this!"

He climbed onto the dais and headed for the depression in the wall beside the holy closet. Into the depression he set his rings, where he spun them one by one.

"Your single ring didn't have much effect, just like these," he told Leena, "but observe the response when I spin my set together."

The musical notes blended into one melody. With the specialized acoustics, the tone produced by his spinning rings reverberated throughout the holy place. The lights, which had been dim, suddenly brightened.

"Behold the Renewal ceremony!" Taurin shouted triumphantly.

Dikran, who'd been sitting on his throne-like chair during Leena's explanation, shot to his feet. "You have reset the computers?"

Taurin nodded. "Consider it a done deal. The rings are the keys. They can unlock the secrets of Lothar and the Apostles. The horn is no longer required. Spinning the rings will serve the same purpose at Renewal, but it must be done in this receptacle." He snapped his bracelets together and shoved the armband back in place. "Dikran, I expect you to keep your promise," he added, tilting his head at the dignified leader.

Dikran clasped his gnarled hands together, his golden robe swishing at his feet. "We have several vacancies to fill among the Synod. First, I have created a new Ministry of Internal Affairs, of which Stephan Tom will be minister."

Applause sounded, and the Truthsayer leader beamed happily. He seemed pleased by the concessions made in his favor as Dikran elaborated on his duties.

"Sirvat has resigned as Treasurer," the Arch Nome continued. "Swill, I hereby appoint you as Minister of Finance. You have proven your worth. Even though you are not of the religious faith, I think it is time we had representatives from the laity on our council. We need to broaden our viewpoint. Bendyk, you will replace Zeroun as Minister of Religion. I believe your directives will be more sympathetic to the people."

Bendyk jumped up, enthusiasm lighting his face. "I have learned my lesson well, Your Grace. We exist to serve the people's needs, not to impose religious doctrine upon them. Hopefully they will come to seek our counsel and respect us for our wisdom, rather than fearing reprisals for misconduct."

"Hear, hear," the other council members agreed.

"Father," Bendyk said, turning to Cranby, who sat among the Candors, "I seek your permission to marry Swill. Thanks to her, my eyes have been opened." The blond young man beamed at his intended bride, who sat in the second row beside his father.

"You have my blessing, son," said Cranby.

Dikran turned his attention to the Candor. "You were censured for your honesty, sir. Your study of ancient religious texts has been forthright and accurate, and it is known that your work as a judge is widely respected. I hereby appoint you as Minister of Justice in Karayan's stead."

"What of Karayan?" someone shouted. "Has he been found yet?"

Taurin descended from the dais, glowering at the assemblage. "He escaped with the Ylloners. We tried to close the window but failed to do so in time. The agents escaped, and Karayan went with them. We shall have to bolster our defenses against the Ylloners, in case they find a way to pierce the shield in the future. Now that we've found peace among us, the crystals have been reenergized. But we shouldn't become complacent again."

Dikran's gaze focused on Taurin. "I would ask you to head a new Defense Ministry. You shall be known as Keeper of the Rings, since you understand their function. Will you accept this office?"

Taurin stood before Dikran and bowed. "I would be honored, Your Grace. At last I have found my destiny among your people. I shall ensure that no further threat from Yllon remains."

"Good. Then that leaves you, Leena," the Arch Nome said, smiling broadly at her.

Leena glanced at him, startled. She had supposed she would go back to work at the museum once her term in the Caucus was over.

"It has come to my attention," said Dikran, "that the regulations concerning archeological sites need to be updated. I propose creating an Office of Antiquities, with you as Director. It will be your responsibility to coordinate the work at our various excavations around the globe. This will no longer come under the auspices of the Ministry of Religion."

Leena's expression brightened. "*I* get to set the rules?" Her mind reeled with the possibilities. She wouldn't have to give up her field work. On the contrary, her new role would necessitate on-site inspections, and she'd ensure that professional archeologists led the digs.

Grotus's smuggling ring had been put out of operation by their leader's death, but other unscrupulous individuals were eager to gain possession of valued artifacts, either for their own collections or to offer them for sale. She'd like nothing better than to halt their illegal acts.

"If you wish, I'll release you from your pledge to the Caucus so you can assume this position immediately," the Arch Nome offered, his eyes twinkling.

"I accept," she announced with pride.

After the shouts of congratulation had died down, the party split up. Leena said goodbye to her brother, Swill, and Cranby. She and Taurin were returning to his farmhouse for a much needed rest before assuming their new duties.

"I can't believe you reset those computers with your bracelets," she told Taurin, when they were finally home and relaxing in the living room. She'd lit candles around the place, and the flames flickered, casting shadows into the far corners.

"Do you mean to say your faith in me has been restored?" he teased.

She turned toward him on the sofa and lifted her face. "I've always believed in you, Taurin, and I always will, now and forever."

"And wherever your faith takes you, I shall remain by your side. Your loves sustains me and transcends this mortal life."

She stared into his glowing eyes. "You're the one I'm going to worship from now on."

"No, you won't. We'll pray to the god of the Apostles and give thanks for being brought together. For I truly believe it was divine will that sent you to me."

He lowered his head and brushed his mouth across hers. "I love you, my *angella*."

As she melted into his embrace, they joined the music of the heavens as the gods spun them a song of love.

THE END

Author's Note

Keeper of the Rings is the book that taught me how to write a murder mystery. It was the fourth novel I wrote for Dorchester in my early days as a romance writer. How did this book inspire me to write a whodunit?

At the heart of the story is a mystery. As an archeologist, Leena is assigned the perilous mission to retrieve a stolen sacred artifact. Her brother takes on the task of investigating the theft. Who had access to the relic? Only the twelve members of the ruling council, the Synod, had the opportunity. That meant each one was a suspect.

These could easily be the characters in a murder mystery. With a limited number of suspects, most of whom know each other, an amateur sleuth, and a confined setting, it's the prescription for a cozy mystery. I've combined this element with a "quest" theme in the search for the missing artifact.

What was my favorite part to write? I loved planning the booby traps in the ancient temple and figuring out what was hidden there. As a fan of Indiana Jones, I couldn't help conjuring a tale of mystery, fantasy and romance all rolled into one grand adventure.

****

Thank you for taking the time to read my book. If you enjoyed the story, please consider writing a review at your favorite online bookstore. Reader recommendations are critically important in helping new readers find my work.

Please join my reader list for updates on new releases, giveaways, special offers, and events at https://nancyjcohen.com/newsletter. Free Book Sampler for new subscribers.

Glossary

Apostles – The ancients who established the religion of Sabal on Xan

Arch Nome – The religious leader of Xan

Backenstone – A substance similar to obsidian

Bundan Bread – A savory egg bread like challah

Calyp Trees – Trees with fragrant leaves like eucalyptus

Candor – A title of authority in the priesthood

Caucus – A group of trained aides to the Synod

Chekels – A form of monetary exchange

Criche – Casserole dish

Cloinder fish – A succulent white fish

Datum Point – The datum point is the spot from which all measurements originate at archaeological digs

Demeter – Goddess of the earth

Elgar – An animal with horns

Enix – Strong, proud beasts of burden easy to domesticate

Eulich – A coin of small denomination on Yllon

Helixcat – A sphinx-like creature

Hironrod – A musical instrument

Kalmagn – A firm white fish

Kemeris – A fruit like a kiwi

Koobi Nut – Used as a decorative material in wood paneling

Langmuir – A wild feline creature

Lothar – The god responsible for Xan's beneficial climate and for the wellness lozenge

Mogur Root – A plant that can be rolled and smoked

Palisades – Palace where the Synod rules over Xan
Pollentine – A terrine made of poultry
Porcheberry Pie – A fruit pie
Qiana Fritter – A sweet corn fritter
Rider – A motorized ground vehicle
Rushtees – A type of fungus valued as an edible delicacy
Sabal – A religion based on worship of the god, Lothar.
Salisberry Sauce – Similar to raspberry sauce
Saltreed – A celery-type vegetable
Silversheen – A silver material used for decorative arts
Synod – Twelve-member ruling body of priests
Tortas – A root vegetable
Tu Imbol – A religious festival
Vestia – Goddess of water
Xan – Leena's planet

World of Xan

The prehistoric peoples on Xan lived by hunting, fishing, and gathering. Eventually agriculture developed, and settlements grew into small cities. Contact between cultures expanded and population increased. The dawn of recorded history began about six thousand years ago. Great civilizations flourished and floundered. These included the mighty Credes whose powerful armies subdued neighboring kingdoms; the Ulellos whose engineering skills created systems of aqueducts and sewage; and the advanced Simerans who were skilled artisans.

Then a Great Conflict tore the world apart, causing chaos in its wake. It ended with the Awakening by the Apostles who came less than two thousand years ago. They were an advanced race of people who said they came from a distant land. Political strife distressed their peaceful nature and compelled them to unify the various factions under their leadership.

The Apostles stressed the importance of moral standards, set a code of behavior, and established Lothar as the God of the faithful. As proof of their teachings, the land blossomed with fertility. The skies blessed the soil with rain and life-giving sunshine. The terrible winds that had ravished the earth subsided. The Apostles were regarded with awe for the miracles they worked. Major illnesses were eliminated in those who accepted the sacred lozenge at Renewal. The teachings of the Apostles became the law.

Then came a wave of mysterious symptoms including headaches and strange mental visions. As suddenly as they'd arrived, the Apostles vanished. The weird illness departed with them. They left behind a structure of government ruled by priests and led by faith in Lothar. Lothar continued to provide for the people, and they worshiped him with fervor. The priests produced the lozenges at the prescribed ritual every year and enforced the dictates of their faith.

The priests didn't know where the Apostles had originated, but one theory was that they came from outer space. These notions were kept secret from the people. Doubts about Lothar's existence could lead to skepticism, or worse, to anarchy.

System of Government

Arch Nome – Dikran lives at the Palisades and rules over the Synod.

Synod – The twelve-member body of high priests that advises the Arch Nome and determines government policy under his direction. They live at the Palisades and maintain the Holy Temple.

Minister of State – Magar supervises relations among the different districts. His office is responsible for entertaining visiting dignitaries.

Minister of Agriculture – Jirair monitors farm production and regulates crop allowances.

Minister of Commerce – Voshkie regulates trade between the different provinces.

Minister of Transportation – Anoush oversees public transportation.

Minister of Housing – Gayane approves new settlements.

Minister of Education – Hagop sets the curriculum in schools.

Minister of Religion – Zeroun is responsible for enforcing religious law. His office administers the Black Lands.

Minister of Energy – Nishan supervises the global network of solar panels that power the electrical grids and supplement the energy produced by the crystals.

Minister of Health – Kolb supervises training of healers for trauma centers.

Minister of Justice – Karayan is the ultimate supreme judge.

Minister of Finance – Sirvat is responsible for government finance and for funding any government-sponsored programs. Her office sets the taxes.

Minister of Labor – Eznik deals with tradesmen and regulates work conditions.

Candors are provincial leaders. Provinces include the Black Lands, North Prefectus, South Prefectus, Celia (home of the Palisades), Perusia, and Iman.

Docents are regional leaders who run the higher courts.

Village Councils are town administrators who split duties among Religion, Schools, Health, Trades, and Agriculture.

About the Author

Nancy J. Cohen writes the Bad Hair Day Mysteries featuring South Florida hairstylist Marla Vail. Titles in this series have been named Best Cozy Mystery by *Suspense Magazine*, won the Readers' Favorite Book Awards and the RONE Award, placed first in the Chanticleer International Book Awards and third in the Arizona Literary Awards.

Her nonfiction titles, *Writing the Cozy Mystery* and *A Bad Hair Day Cookbook*, have also garnered numerous awards. These include gold medals in the FAPA President's Book Awards and the Royal Palm Literary Awards, First Place in the IAN Book of the Year Awards and the *Topshelf Magazine* Book Awards. *Writing the Cozy Mystery* was an Agatha Award Finalist.

Nancy's imaginative romances have proven popular with fans as well. These books have won the HOLT Medallion and Best Book in Romantic SciFi/Fantasy at *The Romance Reviews*.

A featured speaker at libraries, conferences, and community events, Nancy is listed in *Contemporary Authors, Poets & Writers*, and *Who's Who in U.S. Writers, Editors, & Poets*. She is a past president of Florida Romance Writers and the Florida Chapter of Mystery Writers of America. When not busy writing, she enjoys reading, fine dining, cruising, and visiting Disney World.

Follow Nancy Online

Website – https://nancyjcohen.com
Blog – https://nancyjcohen.com/blog
Twitter – https://www.twitter.com/nancyjcohen
Facebook – https://www.facebook.com/NancyJCohenAuthor
LinkedIn – https://www.linkedin.com/in/nancyjcohen
Goodreads – https://www.goodreads.com/nancyjcohen
Pinterest – https://pinterest.com/njcohen/
Instagram – https://instagram.com/nancyjcohen
BookBub – https://www.bookbub.com/authors/nancy-j-cohen

Books by Nancy J. Cohen

Bad Hair Day Mysteries
Permed to Death
Hair Raiser
Murder by Manicure
Body Wave
Highlights to Heaven
Died Blonde
Dead Roots
Perish by Pedicure
Killer Knots
Shear Murder
Hanging by a Hair
Peril by Ponytail
Haunted Hair Nights (Novella)
Facials Can Be Fatal
Hair Brained
Hairball Hijinks (Short Story)
Trimmed to Death
Easter Hair Hunt
Styled for Murder
Star Tangled Murder

Anthology
"Three Men and a Body" in Wicked Women Whodunit

Nancy J. Cohen

The Drift Lords Series
Warrior Prince
Warrior Rogue
Warrior Lord

Science Fiction Romances
Keeper of the Rings
Silver Serenade

The Light-Years Series
Circle of Light
Moonlight Rhapsody
Starlight Child

Nonfiction
Writing the Cozy Mystery
A Bad Hair Day Cookbook

Order Now: https://nancyjcohen.com/books/